HEART OF ANNIHILATION

HEART OF ANNIHILATION

C. R. Asay

WiDō Publishing

Salt Lake City • Houston

WiDō Publishing
Salt Lake City, Utah
widopublishing.com

Cover design by Steven Novak
Book design by Marny K. Parkin

Print ISBN: 978-1-937178-57-4
Library of Congress Control Number: 2014946925

Printed in the United States of America

For
Dad who pioneered the way
and
Brett who proved to me the way was possible

PROLOGUE

The space between dimensions compressed Caz's lungs, her brain—even the beating of her heart. She clenched the warm, silver orb to her chest as the nothingness around her threatened to steal it away. It wasn't so much pain she felt as the sensation that she was going to implode. With a fiery burst of energy, her heart resumed beating with an irregular thump, thump, thump.

The momentum of the portal jump threw her onto her knees. Something spiny bristled through the legs of her pants. A hot breeze prickled her brow with sweat. The sun scorched her neck, uninhibited by clouds. Her lungs finally expanded, filling with thick, rich oxygen saturated by the wild, pungent scents only found in the envirophylums on Retha. She inhaled again and again, certain she'd drown in the overwhelming atmosphere of this foreign dimension.

The blue, zapping electrical light from the portal brightened the ground around her. Her hand slipped through the blood on the silver orb, and she cradled it close to her chest.

Blood.

The blood glistened crimson in the over-bright sunlight. This wasn't just anyone's blood. This was Vin's blood.

Caz staggered to her feet.

A collection of alien buildings rose to her right. Caz bore left. She didn't know where she was going, but it wouldn't be there.

Her legs shushed through the dry plants. Grass, it was called. Dry grass. What dimensions had grass? Ehtar? Uninhabitable. Treah? Earth?

Earth. She recognized it now. The scents were the same ones that permeated her munitions lab at home. Earth. Why Earth?

The ground leveled under her feet. The coarseness of dirt became something more substantial. Hard and smooth. Almost like a road but, strangely, not made of metal.

One foot in front of the other. She followed the road because it took her away from the buildings and because it made each step easier than walking in the grass.

Someone was sure to follow her here. Somewhere, dimensions away, Zell would put things together and track her. They would find her and there was only one punishment for what she'd done.

The road became softer. Dust clogged her throat. How did they live here, these Earth children? How could they stand the complete and total inability to communicate with the almost nonexistent electrical fields?

It was torture of the worst kind. But she couldn't think about that now. She needed to focus. They would expect her to go far afield, place after place, confuse them. *What wouldn't they expect?*

Caz stopped her mindless tread. A building stood before her, long and squat with arches trailing to the left. The entrance had three larger archways topped by a matching number of bell towers. A cross was mounted above the center bell, another one behind on the higher roof.

Ancient, wrinkled skin surrounded brown eyes of the man standing before her. Human. His clothing was coarse and earthy. Dirt smudged his hands and face. A large wooden beam lay at his feet. The hammer in his hand dropped onto a small pile of tools with a clunk.

"*Hola.*" He stood there motionless.

What did he see when he looked at her? Blood covered her in delicate spatters, and was streaked and drying on her hands. The red contrasted the silvery-white of her clothing. She held the warm, glowing sphere to her chest, while her other hand clutched the equally bloody knife.

So, either she was a threat or someone in need of help. She saw something in his eyes. Something devout. Not many Rethans believed in any deity beyond their sciences, but the ones that did could always be counted on for one thing: compassion.

Caz fell to her knees.

"Please," she whispered.

He held his ground. "Are you injured, *Señorita?*"

Caz clutched her precious Heart of Annihilation tight to her chest. Her fingers clenched on the knife. With a painful release she placed the sphere on the ground.

"Please," she repeated. "Please hide this for me."

He shook his head very slowly.

"Please." Her voice elevated to desperate pleading. It was all she could do not to raise her weapon and force him to comply. Caz rolled it toward him but kept her fingertips on it. "It must be hidden. Here. Where no one will find it. No one but me."

The man took a step back, hesitated, and then approached. He dropped to his knees.

"Who are you?"

"Take it." Caz pressed the sphere toward him.

"Is it dangerous?"

"No." The lie came easily.

He placed his hands on it. Caz's fingers locked onto the sphere. Their eyes met. This had to happen. The marshals would take her, convict her, and send her through the RAGE portal. The only way she would ever keep the device from them—the only way she would ever be able to retrieve it again was right here.

"I will save it for you, *Señorita*. Right here." He gestured toward his tools where a hole had been dug in the ground.

She needed to give it to this stranger, this simple man. There were no calculations that could help her this time. No science, no math to give her a controlled outcome. All she could do was commit this place to memory and use Ben Attikin's key to jump across dimensions. Run through the different worlds. Confuse them. Lose them.

"It's warm," the man said.

"Hide it." Caz retracted her hand and clenched her fist. Her fingers were cold. Her cheeks were wet. A scream caught in her throat and hung suspended in an agonizing lump. She charged the silver coin in her hand, using the remaining voltage in her body, and tossed it out to the side. Lightning exploded from the core, drenching her surroundings and the man in a cacophony of dancing blue light.

The man scrambled backward, pulling the sphere with him.

Caz took one last agonized look at the Heart of Annihilation . . . her Heart, and stepped through the portal.

CHAPTER 1

21 years later
Rose

My knuckles cut across Lieutenant Justet's teeth in a breaking cascade of pain. Electric, blue light burst across my vision and the bulb above my head exploded in a shower of sparks. I stumbled and ducked in surprise.

My hand throbbed, going numb. The gash across my knuckles welled up with blood and I gripped my wrist, mouthing "ow." I staggered to my feet, chest heaving. The coin tumbled from my hand and clattered next to Justet's boot.

The hallway was much darker now, even with the flashing echoes of light blistering across my retinas. Lieutenant Justet lay sprawled across the tile floor like a pile of trailer trash, shock showing in his crossed eyes. Blood smeared his peach-fuzz mustache. I swear he must've had a mullet at some point and an engine hanging from a tree behind his doublewide.

The noise of the NCO club resurfaced. A baseball game shouted from a TV above the bar, joining its racket to the heavy beat of a metal remix. Chairs scraped and a chorus of "ohs" mingled with the chaos. A crowd of soldiers collected at my back, gawking down at the officer I'd just floored. An ache pounded deep in my skull above my left ear, and I flinched shut the accompanying eye.

I looked from Justet to the coin and back, my heart hammering. He followed my gaze and jolted up onto one elbow. His hand closed over the coin before I could make a grab for it.

"You hit me," Justet said, sounding surprised and winded. I felt the same. "You never . . . I can't believe you dared . . ." Our eyes locked and his lips pulled back, revealing bloody teeth. He tightened his hand around the coin. "Why'd you take it, Kris?"

Kris? I took an angry step, my fists clenched. Nobody called me by my first name anymore. Specialist Rose or simply Rose was proper military etiquette. Rose itself doubled equally as well for a first name. Kris was . . . well, someone I hadn't been for years.

Yeah, I'd taken the coin from his desk in an impulsive moment of larceny. But it wasn't his. That much I knew. If only he'd told me where he'd gotten it when I'd asked him tonight instead of offering a lot of toothy innuendo, I wouldn't have had to clock him in his slimy, puckering kisser. I swallowed back my desire to interrogate him some more with my fists.

This is exactly why I don't wear civilian clothes to a club, I wanted to point out to Justet and the gawkers. A uniform stated that I was a co-worker, a comrade, rather than a female available for trawling. It was simple, really. Not that someone like Justet could understand such a concept. He tried to get to his feet but fell back on his elbow.

Frayed strands of my waist-length, braided hair floated around my head and tickled my cheek. I combed it back with trembling fingers as a couple of privates rushed forward to help Justet. They gave me and my bloody hand a wide berth. Justet jerked away from their attempts to help him up.

"Do you want me to get the MPs, sir?" one private asked.

"No!" Justet and I said together.

We exchanged startled looks. The last thing I needed was the MPs nosing around in my personal business—and my wall locker. Every tidbit of information I had about Dad was stashed in there, including some documents stamped classified, I was ashamed to admit. I eyed Justet. I would've thought he'd want to have me court-martialed on the spot. What was he hiding that he didn't want the MPs involved?

"It's fine. He's fine." I said, turning to the crowd. My voice sounded way too loud. There were shrugs and some covert snickers. I could hear them thinking that it was only Justet and he'd probably deserved it. Which he had. The shoulder-to-shoulder crowd thinned as they went back to their drinks and dates.

The lieutenant crawled to his feet, his ruddy face flushed.

"Fine? You think I'm fine? You hit me." His voice squeaked like a prepubescent boy. Sweat dripped from his carroty head.

"Sir?" The private who'd offered to get the MPs raised his eyebrows in question. Justet looked torn for a moment, but he clearly didn't want the MPs any more than I did. With an irritated flick of his hand, Justet waved the private off and the kid left us alone, relatively speaking. The club crowd pressed a noisy, camouflage wall of support at my back.

Justet absently walked the coin between his fingers. I followed the flash of silver with my eyes. I knew every detail of the thing from the ridged edges, the impossibly smooth surface, the symbol of lightning on one side and five capitalized letters raised across the other. RETHA.

That coin was the best clue I'd found concerning Dad's disappearance, and it was back in the hands of none other than Lieutenant Justet.

Justet saw my eyes on the coin and quickly shoved it into his pocket. I watched it disappear with a sense of loss and found myself rubbing my dog tags hidden under my shirt. I wished I hadn't dropped the stupid thing.

"Nice hook, Rose!" Corporal Devon Thurmond, a.k.a. the Thurmonator, broke through the wall of camouflage.

I half turned. Thurmond stood behind me, fists clenched. He looked strange in jeans and a plain white t-shirt when I was used to only seeing him in uniform, but his thick neck and high and tight hair cut could have belonged to any of the dozens of soldiers in the noisy bar.

"The offer still stands." Justet's expression was earnest, his persistence almost admirable.

"Screw you, sir," I said.

"Damn, Rose," Thurmond breathed. "It's like a whole new you."

"You don't know what you're messing with, Kris." Justet's eye twitched.

"Do you?" I put my face in his, one heartbeat away from taking the coin by force.

Thurmond grabbed my arm and dragged me away before we started brawling again. It was only with the greatest restraint that I let him. Another second of looking at Justet's stupid face or smelling the sour tobacco on his breath, I would have done something I'd really regret.

Realization of my actions came full circle as we skirted tables and chairs and wove between hot bodies, packed together like M-16 rounds in a full mag. I ran a trembling hand down my face.

I'd just struck an officer.

Thurmond pushed his way through the crowds to the bar. For a moment I thought he was going to get me a drink, but he just grabbed a small, white towel proffered by the bartender. Blood flowed freely from the open skin on my knuckle. I took the towel and applied gentle pressure. The coarse fabric sent a sharp sting up my arm. Why hadn't anyone ever mentioned that punching someone hurts you as much as it does them?

"You know, earlier today when I said you should work on your right hook, I didn't mean on an actual human." Thurmond shouted over the music and the ball game. "Even a creep officer like Justet."

The spot pounded above my left ear. I acknowledged it by squeezing shut the accompanying eye. We pushed our way through the crowd.

"What was I supposed to do? The 'No sirs' didn't work."

"The . . . Wait, did he come on to you again?"

I mimed gagging and cut him a look.

"Fine. I'll just go finish the bastard off, then." He back-stepped in the direction of Justet.

I snagged his sleeve. "Thanks, but I'm already in enough trouble."

"Yup." He let me pull him toward the door. "Don't worry. I'll tell everyone he was drunk and acting in a way ill fitting a man of his rank. He does that a lot, right?"

I coughed out a humorless laugh. "Yeah. That'll fly. I'll save you a seat at my court martial."

I avoided eye contact with other members of our 19th Special Forces group as we waded through the masses of soldiers packed into the small space. Music hammered against my queasy stomach. Colored lights flashed to the beat.

"Rose!" A nasally voice shouted in my ear.

I jumped. A young private blocked my way. What was his name again? Luigi? Loogie?

"Hey, yeah, can I buy you a drink?" He said it very fast as though to get it all out before I could hand out my rejection. His eager grin showed me a half-rotted front tooth that made it appear as though his teeth were gapped. I recoiled, not sure how to respond.

"Luginbeel. Really? Your timing sucks, man," Thurmond said and elbowed him out of the way. "Come on, Rose, I'll walk you back to the barracks."

"Thanks." I rubbed my eyes with two fingers. "Did I really just hit Justet?"

"Yep. Floored him. You could hear it all the way across the room." Thurmond brushed his hand across my back. A shiver of energy ran the length of my spine. "You sure you didn't tase him too?"

I looked at my hand and remembered the flash of blue light as I'd struck him. There'd been a surge of power as well, and the bulb above us had exploded. What had really happened?

I reached for the door handle. The door flung open into my face. I stumbled back to avoid being bludgeoned and stumbled on Thurmond's foot. He caught me under the arms and hoisted me back to my feet. I mumbled thanks to Thurmond and presented the assailant a scowl from the darkest depths of my tired soul.

Major Jaimie Kuntz, the commander, held the door open with her foot. Her stern cut hair swung across her face and caught on her lip. She brushed it away and softly touched the thick scar on her face that went from hairline to cheek.

The ache exploded above my left ear. I groaned and kneaded the spot with my knuckle.

Yep, I was in trouble.

CHAPTER 2

The commander might as well have invaded the men's shower. Someone acknowledged the gold oak leaf on her uniform by yelling, "At ease!"

Chairs screeched, some toppled. Every soldier in the room clambered to parade rest. The music shut off leaving the club in abrupt silence. The civilians remained where they were but hushed.

It hadn't taken long for the members of the unit to nickname her 'The Hornet.' Her waspish features and a razor tongue kept everyone in line with the subtlety of a handful of grenades.

Major Jamie Kuntz stayed in the doorway, her eyes on me. Unreadable, blue ice. A shiver traveled up my spine.

"What's going on here?" The commander's lips thinned against her teeth. "Lieutenant?"

Soldiers parted to let Justet through. A towel matching mine was pressed against his mouth. His eyelid twitched.

"She hit me," Justet said, his voice muted by the towel.

I narrowed my eyes, willing him to shut up.

"Is this true, Specialist?"

"Ma'am," Thurmond broke in, "this isn't just—"

"Quiet, Corporal!" the commander snapped. "Specialist Rose?"

"Yes, I hit him." I shot Justet a sour look. "But, in my defense—"

"That's enough." The commander straightened. "I'll speak with you both outside. The rest of you, carry on."

The chatter and music resumed, chairs scraped. Everyone watched us as we exited the club. Pieces of the story would be told, retold and put into a thrilling tale of military disobedience and action-packed drama. By tomorrow I'd either be a pariah or a hero. I was looking forward to seeing which way rumor swayed.

I followed the commander outside, pulling my cap from my pocket and straightening it on my head. Laughter and music stalked after Justet as he joined us. The door clacked shut muting the noise.

The base sagged in silence, the hot air and the late hour having driven everyone indoors. Prickles of sweat stood out on my forehead. The commander halted out on the road and turned on us. I snapped to parade rest. Justet lifted the towel from his mouth, revealing a cut splitting his upper and lower lip in a straight line. The skin was already puffing around the injury. He wiggled a tooth with his tongue and covered his mouth with a clean corner of the towel.

"Ma'am—" I said.

"Lieutenant." The commander touched Justet's shoulder, her eyebrows high. "I believe there's something you need to be doing right now."

Justet jerked his arm up to check his watch. He flicked a smug look in my direction, smiled at the commander, and quick-stepped down the road toward the barracks.

I followed him with my eyes, my mouth hanging open. What was so important that the commander didn't want to hash this out right here and right now? Either I was in trouble or he was. And since I was the last one standing here, I guess it was me. I rubbed my tags beneath my shirt, wishing Justet a staph infection and an early medical discharge.

When I turned back, the commander was watching me from under her scarred brow. The streetlamp cast an orange glow on the top of her head making her eyes black holes of shadow. She laced her fingers behind her back and planted her feet apart in parade rest.

"Ma'am, I swear—" I started.

"That's enough." Her tone was cold. Whatever kindness she had toward Justet clearly didn't extend to me.

"But he was completely out of line. It wasn't just tonight either. This has been going on for—"

"I said enough, Specialist."

The rest of my defense evaporated in an angry exhalation. I wanted to pound my forehead and shout at her to listen, as a human being, to my very reasonable explanation. She took a single step closer. I retreated, wary.

"Do you think I don't see what you're doing?" Her voice was a soft rattle. "That I don't see you hiding there with your passive face and quiet words. That I don't know what's deep inside you?"

Sweat trickled down my neck. "Ma'am?"

"But you outed yourself tonight, didn't you?" The commander's smile didn't come close to reaching her eyes. A shiver traveled up my arms like a warning shot across the bow. "I knew you couldn't hide forever. You're good, but you always show your hand in the end. I caught you early this time. How'd it feel? No, don't answer that." She chuckled.

I blinked my bewilderment, wishing I was on a fifty mile ruck march with a thirty-plus pound pack rather then standing under this streetlamp with my commander wondering if my next meal would be in a military prison.

Did she know I'd stolen Justet's coin? Or was she accusing me of something else. Like something to do with what was hidden in my wall locker.

I had a sudden desperate need to hightail it back to the barracks and relocate the stash of information I'd collected about Dad.

"Ma'am, if there's nothing else, could I just—?" I jabbed my thumb in the general direction of the barracks.

"No."

The door to the NCO club opened, spilling light and sound across the road. Two sergeants wandered out, gave the commander a tipsy salute with a mumbled, "Good evening, ma'am," and stumbled down the road toward the barracks. She watched them go and then turned, beckoning me to follow. I heaved a sigh and obeyed.

Her long legs took us at a brisk pace past the officer's quarters, the darkened Post Exchange, and several unmarked structures, before coming to a stop in front of a redbrick building across from the parade field. It was the Special Forces Armory—my home base.

The commander placed her hands behind her back and turned on me. I snapped to attention, my gut wrenching.

"Did Justet talk to you about the security briefing I need you to give tomorrow?"

"The . . . what?" My mind did a massive shift from the drama of the club and the fear that my military career was over, all the way back to the meeting I'd had with Justet earlier that evening. Come to think of it, he had mentioned something about a security briefing. I'd been too preoccupied at the time, what with discovering the RETHA coin just lying on his desk. Why on earth did he have that coin?

The commander raised her eyebrows. I nodded, pretending I wasn't playing catch-up. "Right, yes. Of course, ma'am."

"You are our resident counterintelligence Agent, aren't you?"

I sighed. Yeah. The one and only. Also known as Agent Rose, Spook, or oh-crap-here-she-comes-where's-the-shredder. Usually, my job meant going through top-secret message traffic in the SCIF—secure compartmented information facility—pestering other members of the company to be careful with what they said and threw away, the whole digging-through-garbage-cans thing while looking for discarded personal and classified information, prisoner interrogations, and of course, the occasional security briefing.

So far I'd been lucky enough to avoid the briefing part. The senior CI agent had always taken the job but within the last month the first sergeant over me transferred out leaving me the temporary senior agent. It hadn't been a problem until now. In fact it was great. I'd found more time to work on my personal Dad project.

"Yes, ma'am. Uh, tomorrow, you said?" I put a bend in my knees to aid circulation in my tired lower limbs. "I mean, I have to put together the briefing and find evidence that—"

"Yes. Tomorrow." She folded her arms and leaned toward me. "I'm sorry, do you have something better to do? Drinks with friends? A little hanky-panky? Maybe bust the lip of another of my officers?"

"No, ma'am." My face flushed hot. "Of course not. That was . . . just an accident, sort of."

"No, it wasn't."

I dropped my eyes.

"Tomorrow, oh-six-thirty." She put her hand in her pocket.

"Oh-six—!" I cut myself off before becoming truly belligerent. I couldn't keep the surliness out of my voice. "Yes, ma'am."

"You do this, and I'll talk to Lieutenant Justet about letting the incident slide." The commander released a huff of animosity. She pressed her lips tight, narrowed her eyes, and studied me.

"At ease, Specialist Rose."

I widened my feet and clasped my hands behind my back. My shoulders slumped.

She retrieved a small notebook from her pocket and flipped through several pages before jerking out a page and handing it to me. I reached for it. Our pinkies touched. A tiny shock of electricity jumped between.

The flash of blue light back in the club. The bulb exploding over my head. I jerked my hand away.

"There're a few names of our worst offenders when it comes to information leakage," the commander said as though nothing had happened. "As you can see, they're officers and some of our older noncommissioned officers. Now, I understand why calling them on the carpet might be uncomfortable for you, but I think with the right kind of evidence your security briefing will set fire to this company." The commander jabbed her finger at the armory. "Get in, dig through a few garbage cans, and get out. I think it's time to bring a few of our troops out of hiding." She tossed me two keys on a ring, which I fumbled and then caught. "Don't worry about Lieutenant Justet, Specialist Rose. I'll take care of him." She brushed past me. "Lock up when you're done and bring me the keys. I'm in room one-twenty-three in the officer's quarters."

Without a backward glance, she marched briskly away. A lonesome truck rumbled across the parade field and quietly muttered out of sight around a corner.

I squeezed my hand, sending pain shooting through my knuckles. I looked down, surprised to find the towel still clenched in my fist. I relaxed my fingers and looked under the towel. The cut didn't look as bad as I'd thought. Not worth bothering a medic about.

I absently toyed with the keys. Six names graced the commander's list, but there were eight offices. Of course the commander wouldn't be on the list, and the other missing name was none other than Lieutenant Justet—who until very recently had a coin in his office with the word RETHA printed on it.

I trotted up the stairs to the armory doors, a single thought on my mind.

What else was Justet hiding in his office?

CHAPTER 3

The armory door emitted a tortured squeal as I opened it, startling me out of thought. I inhaled the stale coffee, gunpowder, weapons lubricant, and the hint of stagnant sweat that still hadn't crept from the building. All the comforting scents of home. I pulled off my cap, folded it, and placed it in my pocket along with the keys. I didn't bother with the lights, taking instead a red-lens penlight from my cargo pocket.

I wadded up the list the commander had given me and chucked it in the nearest can.

The CTA's stillness made everything surreal. The hollow, echoing room usually sounded of squeaking boots, shouted commands, and the ordered mayhem of a functioning company.

High ceilings and cinderblock walls resonated my lonely steps as I crossed to the second office on the right of a narrow hallway on the far side. Staff Sergeant Wichman's name had been the first on the trashed list. With his nearly bald head, bushy mustache, and fatherly vibe, I confided in him a lot more than I probably should. My fingers brushed across his door but I kept walking.

I finally stopped at the next to last office. My flashlight highlighted the nameplate on the door: Justet's lair. Was it really just a couple of hours ago that I'd taken the coin from his desk? Funny how everything looked so different in the dark.

I rattled the doorknob, expecting it to be locked. It turned. I released the trapped air from my cheeks and glanced back at the hallway. Empty. It was almost too easy. My towel-wrapped hand ached on the doorknob. I really needed to go patch the gash and probably take that security briefing a little more seriously. But when else would I get an opportunity like this?

I hesitated for another second and shoved the door open.

I don't know what I'd been expecting. A file marked "The Kidnapping Conspiracy of Officer Benjamin Rose"? Or perhaps a secret map pointing to Dad's location? I still couldn't help the drop of disappointment at the stark, whitewashed, cinderblock room.

I tried the handles of the filing cabinet, finding the bottom one unlocked but filled only with office supplies. I rattled the other drawers for good measure before turning my attention to the trash.

A person should only have to go through a garbage can like this once in their life. Candy wrappers, banana peels, coffee grounds, no idea. *Ick.* I wiped the sticky residue onto my cargo pocket and pulled a handful of papers from the bottom. I held my penlight between my teeth and unfolded the first paper from the crinkly wad. A memo about the forthcoming Independence Day parade, then junk mail, junk mail, junk mail, and a coupon for half off an entrée at some restaurant in Arizona. Weird, but not interesting or incriminating.

Although, now that I thought about it, there were those two disappearances around Fort Huachuca in Arizona . . .

Among the information hidden in my wall locker there was a list of message traffic printed from an old dot matrix printer. This particular paper had only been relevant to me.

The DLA has identified RETHA activity on the outskirts of Fort Huachuca, Arizona. Advise military personnel to avoid the north-western ranges for the following dates:

The dates listed had been twelve random days during the summer months one year ago. But now on the same day, in the same office, I'd found the RETHA coin and a coupon for half off an entrée in an Arizona restaurant.

I rolled my neck and rubbed at the ache in my head. I'd been to Fort Huachuca several times now, and could picture the small, pink diner belonging to the coupon. It was just north of the base, and famous for its home-cooked meals. Was there a connection?

It was a bit of a stretch. I swallowed back my frustration.

The penlight bobbed in my mouth. The red glow flashed across the walls and floors—and several dozen ammo cans stacked behind the door.

They weren't here earlier. Empty, no doubt. They had to be empty, or filled with ear plugs, or baseball cards, or chewing gum, or . . . ammo.

The flashlight fell from my mouth and buried itself in the trash, plunging me into darkness. I sat back on my heels and stared unseeing in the direction of the door, my heart hammering. This was far from what I'd expected. In fact, it would hinder any momentum I'd already gained.

I felt through the revolting contents of the trash to find the penlight, muttering under my breath about Justet and his biohazard-of-a-garbage-can. When I found it, I aimed the red light back at the stack of cans.

Silence stretched before me. The cans sat in all their solid glory, taunting me to do something about them.

My hands were numb and I kept clenching them in an attempt to return feeling. I could scarcely snap open the can on top. The mystery guck from the garbage made me fumble with the lid and the whole container capsized with a thundering crash.

A strike of energy scorched across my nerves, returning feeling to my fingers. I shook out my hands while staring at the contents of the can. Small brown boxes, no larger than a deck of cards, spilled from the open mouth and littered the floor at my feet.

I picked up a box, pulled out a line of M-16 rounds, and plucked one from the clip. Even in the red light, I could see the tip was painted— orange if I were to guess—making it a tracer round.

I shouldn't have been surprised at the contents. How many of these boxes had I held in my military career? Hundreds? Thousands? They were about as common as a sandwich. However, unlike sandwiches, they were usually in a heavily secured, armored room; or taken from a strongbox directly to the firing range or ammo dump site. They were never stacked behind a door in an unlocked office of a young lieutenant.

I counted twenty-four, twenty-five, twenty-six other cans.

What was Justet doing with twenty-seven cans full of live ammunition?

The main armory door opened with a paralyzing squeal, slightly muffled considering the distance. An electrical charge jolted down my spine. I crammed the line of rounds back into the box with shaking fingers and then tried to shove the whole thing into my pocket. My fingers refused to work right. The box fell onto the spilled ammo can with a loud thunk.

I pressed the crook of my arm to my mouth and held my breath. The single pilfered round bit into my palm. After another brief, nerve-rending second, I stuffed the round into my pocket and moved.

Behind the desk? I took a step in that direction. No. I needed to get out of this office. I took a deep breath. *Calm down,* I told myself, willing the panic to fade.

If only Justet's name was on the commander's list, I would at least have an excuse to be here. But it wasn't, and here I was in his office, with a bunch of stolen ammunition, in the middle of the night. Authorization or no, what would happen if the thief found out I'd discovered his little—okay, whopping—secret? Especially since I'd just popped him in the mouth in front of a room full of soldiers.

I tripped over one of the boxes of ammunition on my way to the door. Rounds rattled across the floor.

"Who's there?"

The voice bounced against the walls in the hall, trying to flush me out. It worked.

In two steps I was in the hall. Light from the streetlamp backlit a figure facing me. I couldn't take another step. He'd already seen me, what was the point of trying to hide? Perhaps it was just another soldier from the company with a lame-o mission like me—

"Luginbeel, is that you? Lewis? Did you get that ammo back to the Deuce?"

—or not.

I didn't speak or move. The moment I moved, the moment I opened my mouth, we would stop being strangers staring at each other in the dark.

"Sanderford?"

Now I recognized the voice. The spot above my ear throbbed so badly blue spots popped across my vision. I pressed two fingers to my head.

Lieutenant Justet took a step. "What the hell?"

He reached toward the light switch at the end of the hall. A current of energy raised the hair on my arms. I braced myself for the hallway to be flooded with light. Instead he seemed to change his mind, because his arms disappeared behind his back.

If the cans of ammunition in Justet's office didn't imply guilt, the sound of him racking the slide of a pistol screamed it. Adrenaline flooded my veins. I turned and raced down the hall in the opposite direction, my boots squeaking on the polished floor.

"Stop right there!"

There was another door that exited into the side parking lot near the mess hall. I skidded, catching the corner of the door with my hand to keep my balance. The green exit sign glowed above the door.

Something struck me from behind, slamming me into the opposite wall. The side of my head smacked into corkboard. Papers and thumb-tacks rained down. A heavy body held me in place, his forearm jammed against my throat.

"Who are you?" This was a different voice than Justet's. An angrier, heavier voice to match the thick arm. "What are you doing here?"

"Get off me!" I slammed my elbow into his ribs, and brought my knee up into his groin.

Jackpot. The arm jerked away. I shoved him and the man fell against the opposite wall, groaning and cursing between breaths. A couple more steps took me to the door. A boot smashed into my lower back, throwing me against the glass pane of the door.

I caught the push-bar, throwing the door open against the brick exterior with a violent clatter. My thigh hit the edge of a step. Hip, elbow, and shoulder struck concrete before I came to rest on my face, unable to breathe.

CHAPTER 4

I gasped like a landed fish. A desperate roll put me on my back. I coughed, gasped, and coughed again before managing to catch my breath.

The abrasions on my hip, arms, and hands stung with astonishing pain. My head pounded.

Shadowy figures eased into my line of sight. I couldn't seem to formulate a thought or a plan. I knew lying on the ground wasn't a good idea. If I could only move. A boot pressed onto my collarbone, holding me in place. I grabbed the man's ankle and tried to wrestle his foot off my shoulder.

"Specialist Rose," said Justet with a grin. A hushed rattle of laughter echoed from the surrounding figures. "Are you following me?"

A shiver stole across my nerves like there was voltage racing through them. My muscles tensed.

"N-no. Of course n-not." I shuddered out a breath. "Sir."

I blinked and found myself staring down the barrel of an Army issue, 9mm handgun. It looked as beefy as a 50 caliber machine gun under the circumstances. Justet's finger hovered near the trigger.

"Then what were you doing in my office?" His voice was sharp and loud enough to carry to the men behind him.

"I wasn't in your . . ." I let the lie die on my lips.

A brief lilt of music echoed from the distant NCO club. A chatter of voices and smattering laughter rolled after the sound. Lieutenant Justet glanced behind him. Nothing said foul play quite like threatening a US Army soldier, on a US Army base, with a US Army-issued weapon. He hid the pistol in his belt, straightened his fatigues over it, and brushed casually at his sleeves.

"Talk, Rose."

"Let me up first, sir." I raised myself onto one elbow, expecting at least that much respect.

Justet leaned over me, resting his forearm on his thigh. His weight forced my elbow to skid painfully out from under me.

"Just answer the question," Justet said.

The voices from the direction of the NCO club increased in volume. Several of Justet's men shifted uncomfortably. I was surprised that I recognized most of them. A couple stood too far in the shadows for me to identify.

There were a couple of privates, including Private Luginbeel; an overweight staff sergeant from another company and, unfortunately, Sergeant Sanderford. Sanderford was a former drill sergeant, and there couldn't be a worse person glaring down at me. He stood in a partial hunch, and I realized who I'd kneed back in the hall.

"What the hell were you doing in the armory?" Sanderford tore the wad of papers from Justet's garbage can out of my hands. I hadn't realized I still had them. He smoothed them out, studied the words with a rapid flit of his eyes, and then tossed them on the ground. "Who sent you?"

Sanderford grabbed for my lapel. Justet put an arm across his chest and heaved him back.

I opened my mouth to reply that the commander sent me—yes, that's right, the Hornet herself. For a moment I enjoyed the thought of her sharp face and razor tongue coming down on Justet. And Sanderford. And every last one of them.

Or she'd just pat them on the head and give them a gold star.

Lieutenant Justet ground my shoulder into the asphalt. I wheezed, grasping his boot with one hand.

"What makes you think I didn't have permission to be in there?" I barely got the words out.

"Did you?"

Our eyes locked. I pressed my lips together, breathing shallowly through my nose. The energy surging through my body was incredible.

He ground his heel into the soft spot between my shoulder and chest. I groaned to keep from crying out and dug my fingers into the laces of his boot.

"Get off," I gasped, my teeth clenched.

"Just tell me who sent you."

"Get off. Get off!" The energized tension spread throughout my body, threatening to tear me apart if Justet didn't comply. I slammed my fist into his calf. The raw wound on my knuckle split my hand with pain. Justet grunted and then laughed.

"Get off me!" I shouted.

A metallic taste filled my mouth. Voltage-charged fire raced through my hand. I struck him again. A fierce electrical surge rushed from the open skin in my knuckle, into Justet's scrawny leg.

A flash of jagged blue light and a violent popping sound severed the air. The back of my hand smacked into the ground, driving agony through my knuckles.

I barely noticed Justet's foot releasing me from the ground or the long string of cuss words he was yelling. I rolled onto my side and stumbled to my feet, cradling my damaged hand.

Justet groped for the gun tucked in his belt.

My mind rode a maelstrom of conflicting emotions. I couldn't decide what to do. Should I run? Fight? Justet's pistol whipped around. Fear ate into any residual composure I might've had. I ran for it.

A hand grabbed my braid before I'd taken two steps and yanked me back. Several chunks of hair parted ways with my scalp. I stumbled, barely managing to keep my feet. Cold, heavy metal pressed against my neck. I dropped to my knees and stared up at the stars. Justet's face hovered over me, his fist tangled in my hair. Moisture glistened at the corners of his mouth.

"Let's get her inside," Sanderford said.

I kept my eyes on the man with the gun at my neck. I watched in silent fascination as a drip of blood leaked from Justet's nose and spread across his fuzzy mustache. Justet's hand jerked to his nose, the gun still tight in his grip. He brushed his nose with the back of his hand and then stared at the blood there.

"Sir," Sanderford repeated.

Justet hauled me to my feet by my hair. Several other soldiers moved in, grabbing my arms and shoulders. I couldn't seem to catch my breath, and barely struggled as they wrestled me back into the armory. They dragged me down the darkened hallway, the sound of their boots and harsh breathing thunderous, before shoving me to the floor in one corner of the company training area. I scrambled to my feet and stood at a half crouch, my hands partially raised. Blood pounded in my ears.

"Luginbeel, Lewis." The staff sergeant's voice made Justet jump. "Let's get that ammo to the truck, shall we?"

The privates melted away into the darkness of the CTA, followed by the staff sergeant and the two unknown figures. Justet and Sanderford were all that remained.

"What the hell happened out there?" Justet said, wiping his hand on his pants.

Well, there was the gun. Boy, did I remember the gun. There was the shock of electricity powering into Justet's leg—no, I couldn't think about that.

Voltage, volted, volting, whispered a voice.

I looked up and around. The voice sounded familiar. But the only people nearby were Justet and Sanderford, black ghosts against the whitewashed walls. I inhaled and stood up straight. My dog tags clinked together. I reached for them, discovering that my jacket had torn sometime during the melee. My tags hung outside my shirt. I rubbed the pendant I kept on my tags that my dad had given me hours before he'd disappeared. Numbness bled through my extremities.

Voltage, volted, volting.

Justet fumbled in his pocket and a second later a bright light flared inches from my face.

"Rose?"

Voltage, volted, volting. Voltage, volted, volting.

Blue lights popped in my vision, courtesy of my blistering head.

"Rose!"

The mantra silenced, and I dragged my jacket protectively across my shirt.

"Sir," I finally acknowledged Justet.

"At ease, Specialist," Justet said calmly, as though he and his freak squad hadn't just assaulted the crap out of me.

I mentally searched for an escape route or weapon of some kind. The door to the female latrine was several paces to the right, complete with a deadbolt and, if luck was with me, a toilet plunger I'd used a couple of days ago. I did the deer-in-the-headlights thing a moment more and then forced myself to move a single step to the right.

"What do you want from me?" I let the aggression smolder.

"Sanderford, could you give us a minute?" Justet lowered the light out of my eyes.

"I'll check on the ammo and be right back. Take care of this." Sanderford jabbed a finger at me.

He marched out into the hall. Justet waited until Sanderford had rounded the corner before speaking.

"Okay, Kris. I know you think I'm the bad guy right now, but I want you to listen for a sec."

Kris again. My stomach did its traditional jolt.

His watchful eyes crawled up and down my body. A colony of creepers shivered across my skin. I exhaled an irritated breath and managed to take another step.

"We found aliens." Justet didn't seem to notice my progress.

I stared. "Say again?"

"Yeah. Out in the Sonoran desert, not far from Fort Huachuca."

Cold swept my body.

"Fort Huachuca? Like in Arizona?"

"Where else?"

I swallowed. "So like—uh, Retha?"

"What do you know about Retha?" Justet remained completely still, aside from the gentle bob of the flashlight.

I shrugged. My hands curled into fists. "Just what I found in your office. That coin."

"This coin?" Justet held the silver coin between two fingers.

I wanted to snatch it out of his hand, but I just clenched my fists tighter. "Yeah."

"So?"

"So," I said, trying not to yell, "a foreign-looking, silver coin was found at the crime scenes of over a dozen missing military personnel and police officers, stamped with those same five letters!"

"So?" he repeated.

"So!" I forced the anger back, closing my eyes for a brief moment and rubbing my hands together. "So I'd like to know what R-E-T-H-A stands for. And how you're connected to that coin."

Justet came closer. I retreated down the wall a few more paces. A partially-stable Justet in a room full of witnesses was one thing. A completely unhinged one alone with me in the armory was something else entirely. I was quite suddenly aware of just where my obsession had landed me.

"We tried. We called homeland security, the secret service, the CIA, the FBI, everyone we could think of. They didn't . . . they don't . . . It wasn't a credible threat, they said. Not enough evidence. We'll look into it. The shove off basically."

"What?" Why did I think I was going to get actual intel out of him?

"You asked." He shrugged.

"You're a nut," I said.

I hated him. His stupid, earnest expression and the way he leaned intimately toward me. I slid cautiously along the wall, trying to imagine an escape route besides the latrine, with its small, high windows and single door. I supposed I could make a break for the front doors, but that would leave me wide open to a bullet in the back.

"You think *I'm* the nut?" I froze. Justet's voice sounded more like a threat.

"Meaning?" The door to the latrine was in reaching distance now. I could smell the ammonia.

"Meaning that you've put us in a tough spot."

"*I* put *you* in a tough spot?"

"You saw the ammo. What do you think ammo's for?"

"Firing ranges—?"

"Killing people, smartass."

I was dead.

He pointed his pistol at my chest. I cringed and slowly raised my hands. If the military had taught me one thing, it was to respect a loaded weapon.

"We're going after them. The Rethans. They've set up this thing on an electrical tower outside of Fort Huachuca. The question is, are they stealing electricity or sending something else through it? What if this is the first step to their take over?" Justet went on. "But we can stop them. We can stop all this before it's too late! We even have a source that's paying us top dollar to go down to the base and grab their stuff for evidence."

I felt for the handle to the latrine. "Wait, this is about money? Noble."

"No, it's not about the money! It's about," Justet turned back, his voice taking on an oddly reasonable tone. "It's about protecting all those people out there from the fancy big wigs who don't believe a threat like this is credible." His eyes locked on mine. "And we don't need you screwing everything up with your big mouth and overdeveloped sense of morality." Justet shook his head. "So the question remains: what the hell are we going to do with you?"

"Dammit, sir! What's taking so long?" Sanderford suddenly appeared in the CTA. Several other dark figures eased behind him. Justet turned to look.

I thrust the latrine door open, lunged inside, and tried to slam the door behind me. A shoulder thrust it open, throwing me back. I scrambled for the plunger in stall three.

"Where does she think she's going?"

"Grab her!"

A half a dozen men followed me into the latrine. I managed to get my hands around the splintery handle of the plunger before being yanked backward by my collar. My uniform cut into my neck, choking me. I tried to get my feet under me as I was dragged out of the stall. Sanderford shoved me against the wall. I coughed, running my fingers under the collar of my shirt. My tags clanked together.

The small room was cramped with so many bodies inside. The only light was Justet's flashlight flickering across faces and walls.

"Quit stalling, L.T." Sanderford said. His sandy hair looked thin and balding with the flashlight behind it.

"Okay, but I was thinking—" Justet reverted back to whining.

"Shut up, Justet. Give me the damn pistol."

Justet's flashlight strobed the walls and faces as they argued. I saw a flash of the pistol between them. I gulped oxygen and started to push myself to my feet. The handle of the plunger pressed into my palm.

Private Luginbeel suddenly leered over me. His half-rotted front tooth gaped against the black of his mouth. I fell back in surprise. "Should've let me buy you that drink, Rose."

"Get away from me," I rasped the words, and tried to push him away. He leaned out of my reach with a nasty laugh.

"Always wanted to know what it felt like to kill someone. Why else would anyone put up with years of this shit?" The words whistled between his teeth. He pressed two fingers gun-style to my forehead and pulled an imaginary trigger. "Kapow!"

I swung the plunger and it splintered against Luginbeel's face. He went down with a howl. The rubber end of the plunger flew in the opposite direction. I pushed to my feet, clutching the small ragged end as another figure rose to my left. The other private leapt back, barely avoiding being impaled by my plunger stick. I chucked the stick after him. A solid clunk and a surprised "Gah!" told me I'd hit my target.

Luginbeel clamored to his feet. I smashed my fist into his nose. Cartilage crushed under my knuckles. My already mangled hand seared with pain. Luginbeel squealed and collapsed on his side.

Arms wrapped me from behind, pinning my arms to my side. I kicked into open air, bashing back my head at the same time. The back of my skull connected with a face, and the arms released me. I shoved Sanderford away. He stumbled against the sink, hand at his cheek.

"Rose, stop!"

I whirled to face Justet, my fists raised.

He pointed the pistol at my face. "I said, stop."

I opened my hands slowly.

"She hit me!" Luginbeel got to his feet, his voice nasal. One hand covered his nose.

Justet coughed. "Yeah, she does that."

"Not quite like killing someone," I said, searching for another avenue of escape, "but, yeah, it *does* sorta feel good." The taunt surprised me with how true it was. "Hey, Private, have fun telling your pals how your nose got busted."

Luginbeel pulled his hand from his mangled nose and looked at the blood on his fingers.

"I'll kill her!" He sprang at me.

Justet caught Luginbeel by the arm and forced him back. The pistol was now pointed in the general direction of Sanderford. I raced for the door.

I didn't make it two steps before pain shattered through the back of my skull in a flash of blue light. The floor rose before me. My knees hit the tile with twin thuds, and my hands felt weighted. My cheekbone smashed against the floor. A vapor of darkness congested the single clear bulb of light shining in my eyes.

"Hand me that pistol, sir," the hollow voice bounced an echo into the distance. "No loose ends."

My fingers curled, trying to drag me somewhere—anywhere but the painful now as a "loose end." A foot jammed under my stomach and heaved me onto my back. Sanderford leaned over me, his face fading with the dimming light. He reached for me.

"What's this?"

I felt a tug and the chain of my dog tags chafed my neck. The vapor solidified into blessed nonexistence.

CHAPTER 5

Caz
Retha
20 years pre-RAGE

Lightning pulsed deep within the threatening electrical storm, brightening the elegant arches of Vislane Academy. The trees of the rare and protected envirophylum cast a sharp relief around the tall building. Smaller buildings bowed to the left of the academy, low and squat as though cowed by the magnificence above them. Lightning shattered the sky again, bringing deep rolling thunder. The metallic surfaces mirrored back the lightning, striking light across the collection of children.

Caz's breath misted before her. A cold, dry breeze lifted the silvery curls of her hair, bringing with it the strange, earthen scents of the phylum. She stood apart from the group, with her back to the academy and her feet planted wide on the slick, coppery ground. Her hands clenched near her sides. The clouds rolling overhead mimicked the darkness welling in her chest. Using her shoulder, she rubbed an ache above her left ear.

A handsome boy, standing head and shoulders above the group, held her attention. Vin. His white teeth gleamed in the failing light as he laughed at the words of a smaller friend. A chorus of laughter from the group warmed the air about them, leaving Caz alone in the cold outskirts. She narrowed her eyes to slits of silver and ground her teeth.

She was going to kill him this time, no question.

Caz shoved children aside and lunged. Her shoulder buried in the softness of Vin's solar plexus. The air went out of him in a *humph*. His head made a ringing sound as it struck the copper surface of the ground. Caz sat on his stomach, managing to pin his arms to his sides with her knees. His eyes crossed, his perfect lips parted in surprise.

Three times Caz's fist rose and fell: to his cheek, his ear, and his neck. A silvery curl of immaculate hair bounced on his forehead with each strike. Her pulse pounded loud and angry in her ears.

"You never . . . ! Don't ever . . . ! How dare you, Vin! How dare you!" The words came out as gasps, catching against the fury constricting her throat.

"Get off me, Caz! Get off!" Vin sounded whiney and winded. Gone was his self-assurance. His insane composure. This was a boy scared for his life.

A shiver of voltage raised the hair on her arms. Hands circled her waist and pulled her away. She shoved at them but they clenched into her stomach, yanking her up. She stumbled for footing and came around, fists raised.

Xander stood before her, his hands up to ward off the strike. His face held a mixture of concern and frustration. Simple signs of growing weakness.

"Don't do it, sis." His voice had deepened in the last couple of months, making the two years separating them seem like decades. "Vin's not worth it."

Vin, not worth it? Caz opened her mouth to respond, then settled for cutting him a look of utter disbelief. She let that marinate for a moment, relishing the droop of his head, and then widened her eyes and tossed her head so he knew she was in control.

Of course Vin was worth it. Vin, her best friend since she could remember, was the most infuriating person on the planet—and worth every minute of her time. It was Vin's room she snuck into almost every night so she wouldn't have to listen to her parents bicker in their mind-numbing, passive aggressive way. She even forgave him over and over when he flirted with the other girls at the academy.

But this? This was totally different.

The very fact that Vin even nodded in agreement while Zak Faras slandered her family name turned Vin into Ben Attikin, Retha's most infamous traitor. She really was going to kill him this time.

"He said . . . they said . . . They called Mom and Dad m-mutineers." Caz wiped her mouth to dispel the filth of the word. She jabbed a finger at Vin, letting the slur turn to power. "Mutineers!"

Shocked giggling from the crowd.

"It's not mutineers!" Xander turned on Vin and Zak. He never could refrain from correcting this very personal offense. "Munitioners. As in munitions artisan."

"I didn't say anything!" Vin rubbed his jaw. The skin was red, definitely bruised. He turned his large, pretty eyes on Caz. His shoulder sloped in her direction. "I never called them that, Caz."

"You nodded. I saw it!" Caz said.

Vin fell back a step and looked around at the crowd. His face went from apologetic to a steely expression.

"So what?" Vin hooked his thumbs in his pockets. "My dad says they make weapons. What's that sound like to you?"

"It sounds like they're doing what your dad told them to do," Caz snarled. "Not that you would know a pico-amp about it!" Who was he, besides the spoiled kid of the dimensional congressional commandant himself? "You or ol' Zak Flak."

Zak Faras's pale face glowed scarlet, but he took courage from Vin.

"Doesn't matter what you call them," he said. "They're still the ones making weapons. And weapons are for . . . killing." Zak whispered the last word. He scooted next to Vin, drowning in his tall shadow. "What's that sound like to you?"

"It sounds like you need to shut up!" Caz took an aggressive step. Xander wrapped his arm around her shoulder and pulled her back.

With a sudden scuttling movement, the circle of children broke ranks. Caz noticed the startled face of Vin's shabby little brother, Ricks, among them. The headmistress of the academy, Madame Vislane, strode calmly toward them amidst a swirl of metallic fabrics and striking blue voltage. Her silver eyes caught the light, her eyebrows held aloft in condescending composure.

Caz released a hiss. The Queen Drone herself, here to put them in their places. She wouldn't shout, she wouldn't scold. She wouldn't even punish them—at least not in her mind. That would go against the rules of etiquette and serenity. That would put her on the same level as a mutineer—a *munitioner*. As Caz's parents.

All the children wandered purposefully away, pretending they'd taken no part in the moment of hostility. They were innocent bystanders who found it all so very beneath them. Ricks buried himself in the crowd. Caz was surprised he'd been watching at all, the coward.

"Cazandra. Xander," Madame Vislane addressed them in a soft voice with a gentle bob of her head.

She touched their hair with small, elegant hands. A mild crackle of voltage traveled down Caz's scalp and entered her mind. Unnatural peacefulness enveloped Caz's wild emotions, molding them and softening them into the Rethan standard.

Caz closed her eyes. This was where she had to comply. This was where she forced herself to allow the manipulation—to become a drone. This was what it meant to be Rethan. It was not only expected, it was required.

Required. Caz opened her eyes, finding the headmistress's face inches from her own. The headmistress seemed to sense her gaze and her eyes fluttered open as well. They stared at each other.

Queen Drone wouldn't sway her today. Better a *mutineer* than a drone. Caz shoved the hand away.

The headmistress curled her poor, wrongly-abused hand and placed it under her chin. Her eyes settled on Caz.

"I can't say that I'm surprised at you. The both of you." She included Xander in her look. Xander dropped his head in shame. "You are, after all, Fisk children." And with a wave of her hand, she dismissed them as hopeless cases. Not that that would stop her from zapping the abnormality out of their brains whenever she felt the need. She smiled. "Come and see me in my office after classes today, Cazandra."

Xander wasn't looking at the headmistress but at Caz. His lips pressed together. She was going to get it when they got home, that was for sure. Not that it mattered. Xander would forgive her. He had to.

Madame Vislane turned disappointed eyes on Vin. "Vincent, I expect better of you."

Vin's head dipped. Every student cowered under this gaze, distressed at falling from the headmistress's good graces, forlorn at the thought of ever failing her again. Drones.

With that, the headmistress glided away. Caz glared at her back, remembering the stupid, smug look on her face. Her work was done, her students pacified. All was right in her precious academy. Caz shoved her hands into her pockets to keep them from doing something she was sure to regret.

Vin looked apologetically at Caz. She narrowed her eyes. She should make him suffer for this. In fact, anyone else but Vin would suffer for the rest of their lives for making her undergo a serenity lobotomy. She already had something special planned for Zak Faras.

But Vin was, well, he was Vin.

Caz swiped at her mouth and dropped her eyes. A small, gray spider scurried across her shoe, a deserter from the envirophylum. Anger and resentment welled inside her. Spiders didn't inhabit Retha naturally. They were protected, along with the other lower-dimensional elements residing in the nearby envirophylum. In fact, the spider was a trespasser in her world, every bit as much as Madame Vislane had been by entering her mind. Caz allowed the depths of her emotions to rise to her eyes, and trained them on Madame Vislane's retreating figure.

Caz stomped her foot once. The spider flipped off her foot. She crouched and snatched it from the ground by one leg before it could scurry away. Xander and Vin argued quietly above her, their words lost behind the angry swish of blood in her ears.

She couldn't allow her emotions to override her good sense. There was no place on Retha for those who couldn't conform to the rules of etiquette and serenity. The spider turned and curled, trying to escape. One of the spindly legs gripped her finger. Caz delicately plucked the leg from its body, rolled it between finger and thumb, and then cast it to the ground.

A person who couldn't conform was exiled to a lower dimension, their bodies scoured of the metals that allowed them to wield electrical currents. Like former commandant Ben Attikin. Caz shuddered. How could a person live without metals—without voltage? The very thought must be what kept the drones in their places. Caz released a frustrated breath.

She pulled the remaining legs from the spider and dropped the body near the legs. Caz stood and was met by a revolted look from Xander. The corner of Vin's mouth twitched upward in a furtive smile.

That was all that it took. She gave Vin a cool smirk. She could fake things a little longer. For Vin. Better a fake than a drone, anyway. She crushed the still-wriggling body of the spider with her heel.

Take that, conformity. Long live the mutineers.

CHAPTER 6

Rose

My body lay heavy against a rocky surface. I was fairly certain I had arms, legs, and a torso, but that was the extent of my knowledge. There was a nudge against my foot. Then another. I blinked. The bright sunlight made my head cry for mercy, and I squeezed my eyes shut again.

Nudge, nudge. Harder this time. Something in my mind warned me against opening my eyes. I pried them open anyway and grunted in pain. My hand went to the base of my skull, and I tested a tender, grenade-sized lump. The muscles in my face worked into a grimace, informing me that my cheek was terribly bruised.

Something bright flashed in my eyes. My vision went in and out of focus before solidifying on a set of swinging dog tags. A small, half circle pendant about the size of my thumb shone against the duller metal of the tags. My hand went to my throat, touching the naked skin. My tags. My dad's pendant. I grabbed for them.

"Wakey, wakey, Kris." Justet pulled the tags out of my reach.

Memories of the night before crowded my brain. I groaned and rolled myself into a sitting position. Dry dust stirred in the air. I coughed, but stopped immediately when it sent my head throbbing in mighty pain. I held perfectly still, willing the feeling to subside before my stomach emptied its contents all over my uniform.

"Kris?" Justet persisted, making me want to punch him in the face. "Kris. Rose. Rose!"

"Shut up a minute. Sheesh!" I held my breath, and then let it out slowly. I pressed my head between my hands, clenched my eyes shut, and then winked them open. My pounding head pulsed its way to a dull ache. I brushed at the dirt covering my uniform. One of my pant legs pulled out of my boot, and the laces curled in the dirt. I glanced around to get my bearings.

The sky was a brilliant blue, the sun not too high but already blistering hot. Dry dirt and scrubby junipers created the majority of the landscape. along with the occasional spike of desert grass. We could only be in the hills to the west of the base, the home of the rappelling tower and an uncounted number of firing ranges, land nav ranges, war games ranges, leadership training ranges. The gas chamber.

The heavily populated Salt Lake Valley sloped away to my left, meaning we were somewhere in the north ranges. The outskirts of the city of Herriman were much closer than the base. These ranges were usually used as a last resort, for the sake of the homeowners. No one would find me all the way out here. There were a thousand foxholes to choose from for a burial site, and a single brass casing wouldn't be thought of as amiss. So why had they let me wake up? Why wasn't I already dead and buried somewhere?

Justet backed up a few paces. Only Justet? Where was everyone else? Sometime during my forced night sleep, he'd taken the time to change out his pistol for an M-16, which he held under his arm. His face was splotchy and red in the mid-morning heat and his usually immaculate uniform was rumpled, his cap was crooked.

"You hit me." I squinted up at him.

"I guess that makes us even." His tongue flickered out to taste his split lip.

"No it doesn't. Not even close." I tested the contusion on the back of my head. Yep, still there. Still hurt.

"Sanderford clocked you. Not me." Justet scuffed his toe in the dirt and put his hand in his pocket. The rifle hung lazily under his arm. "He was all for finishing you off too. I stopped him."

"My hero." I curdled the words with sarcasm so they couldn't be misconstrued. Justet smirked.

"Actually, Kris—"

"Rose. My name is Rose," I snapped. I rubbed my eyes and forced myself to take a calming breath. If I was going to make it out of here alive, I was going to have to use my brain rather than my temper. "What do you want, sir?"

"On your feet, Kr—Rose." Justet motioned with the rifle.

I groaned my way onto my knees and then my feet. I braced my hands against my knees. Blood rushed away from my brain and the world fuzzed, but I was still standing. First good thing that had happened to me today.

"Rose! Rose!"

He was back to shouting. My poor head. At least he'd stopped calling me Kris. I pressed my lips together and gestured with a hand to shut him up. I stood with a deep inhalation to help the oxygen circulate but held my head between my hands to keep it from falling off.

"What do you want, Lieutenant?" I repeated, keeping my eyes on him. Well, one eye. I couldn't get both eyes to stay open at the same time without seeing double. One Justet was more than enough. Justet raised his eyebrows but let me go on without interrupting. "Because after being assaulted last night, you can imagine how anxious I am to return to the base and get you and your poor-excuse-for-army-dropouts court-martialed."

Justet laughed, brushing at the corners of his mouth. I glanced over my shoulder. The shrubs scattered across the terrain provided only the bare minimum of cover. There were no boulders big enough to shield me from bullets, although an outcropping of rock down the hill might be of some use, if I could get there without being shot first. Add on the heavy slope and I was left at a clear disadvantage. Running was a really bad idea.

"I just want to ask you some questions," Justet said. I forced my attention back to him.

"And then shoot me?" I retreated a couple of steps. Justet adjusted his rifle.

"Stop right there."

I lifted my foot to take another step. Justet brought the rifle to his shoulder.

"I said stop!" Justet sighted along the barrel of his rifle, cheek resting against the stock.

Energy jolted down my leg. I took an unbalanced step to the side.

The sun beat on the back of my neck. Sweat erupted from my pores and dripped between my shoulder blades. I raised my hands.

"That's better." He lifted his cheek from the stock and pulled the rifle tight against his shoulder so that he could release the hand-guard with his other hand, and put his free hand in his pocket. "Now tell me, Rose, what is this?" He held my dog tags and pendant out as though offering them to me.

An unusual emptiness hollowed out my brain, sending the extreme emotions of the past twelve hours dispersing into the atmosphere. Gone in the wink of silver catching the sun.

Then rage drove needles into my nerves.

"That's mine! Give it back!"

The ache above my left ear exploded with pain, washing out every other discomfort. My breath quickened, and my vision tunneled onto the single glimmer of silver light that was my pendant. I took an aggressive step with the intention of snatching the tags from his hands.

"Nuh-uh, Rose," Justet said. My view widened to include him. His other hand went back to steady the rifle. The tags clinked against the hand-guard. "Not another step."

I found that I was on the balls of my feet, fingers curled into claws. My heart raced, and it was all I could do to not launch myself at him and tear out his eyes.

"What do you want with my tags?" My voice was sharp with a serrated edge.

"Tags? Why would I want your tags?" Justet maintained his smirk but the lines around his eyes tightened. He flicked his little finger at my pendant, making it dance in the sunlight.

The thundering pain above my ear shivered tension through my limbs. Energy raced into my extremities until my fingers prickled. I couldn't drag my eyes away from the bright curve of silver against the black of the rifle.

Justet went on, "See, I thought when you asked about Retha, it was just some squint question, ya know? Something you read about in the message traffic. But it goes deeper than that, doesn't it?"

I shook my head and pressed my lips together. All thought of flight was gone. He had my pendant. He was talking about Retha. And one little rifle was not going to stop me.

"Retha?" I asked. There it was again. That strange feeling as I said the word, like I'd said it a million times before and loathed it.

"Right, Rose. Retha," Justet said patiently. "The boss recognized this little charm thing." He nodded toward my tags. "Said it was a key used by Rethans to activate their weaponry, so that they can invade Earth. And lookie here, you've been carrying it around on your tags since I've known ya."

Alien invasion again? Oh please.

"I don't know anything," I blurted.

The smile dropped and Justet's face seemed to flatten. He had a stake in finding out whatever his "boss" thought I knew about my pendant. Whether out of fear or for a pat on the head, I couldn't tell. A jolt of energy ripped down my spine. I backed up a few steps. Justet followed.

"We've looked in your wall locker, Rose."

"You what?" I whispered. I was beyond screwed. I felt violated.

"Yeah. That's quite an obsession you have. I even learned a few things. But it's more than just an obsession with Retha, isn't it?"

"I swear, Lieutenant, I don't know anything," I persisted, only partially truthful. "You've been in my wall locker. You know as much as I do."

"You zapped the hell out of me last night." Justet moved closer. His lips pulled against his teeth. "You nearly took out my entire team with that damn plunger. You! You have a shitload of information about Retha and you're carrying around a key to one of their weapons. Who the hell are you?"

"I'm just Rose. Specialist Rose." I couldn't believe I had resorted to pleading.

Attikin's ass! A voice snarled with venom. *Just Specialist Rose? Stupid child.*

I jerked around, searching for the voice. It was almost like it had come from inside my head. My jacket caught on a shrub, and I stumbled on a rock, going to one knee. I breathed in and out through my nose, only partially aware that Justet had followed. I wanted to yell back at the voice, tell it to help instead of offering a lot of worthless advice. I squinted up at Justet.

He looked confused. Like I was the crazy one. And yet I wasn't the one training a weapon on an unarmed comrade.

There was something about staring into the muzzle of a loaded rifle, with a killer at the other end, which obliterated my fear reflex. Anger reared inside my chest. Determination. Cold logic. Energy raced through my body. I felt a nod of approval from the location of the voice. I pushed myself unsteadily to my feet. Justet's rifle followed.

"You know me, sir. You think I haven't noticed you, watching me day in and day out? Think I haven't seen you creeping around behind my back, checking my files, studying me for who knows what? You know me better than anyone. So tell me, Lieutenant, do I look like a threat to national security?"

Justet's face contorted in thought. He adjusted his finger on the trigger and licked his lips. "So where'd you get this little key thing?"

My chest tightened at the thought of Dad pressing the small, poorly wrapped box into my hands. He said it came from my previous home, probably from my birth parents. There was solemnity in his eyes as I opened it. I remember touching it for the first time, letting the slick curve fit perfectly to my thumb. I'd felt an instant attachment, all the more meaningful these days because of Dad's absence.

"It was just a gift," I whispered, glancing to the left. The heels of my boots hung over the slope. My fingers found a spiky branch of the shrub and I clung tight. "From my dad."

"From your dad?" Justet seemed to miss the gravity in my tone. "Where'd he get it?"

"If you can find him, you're welcome to ask him," I said bitterly. "I haven't seen him in years."

"That it? That all you know?"

"Yes, sir."

Justet paused and then nodded. He dropped the rifle to his side and stepped back. With one hand he shoved my tags back into his pocket, then pulled out an old flip phone.

He pressed one button with his thumb and lifted it to his ear, his eyes on me. At that moment, I realized just how off-book these people were. No military walkies. It was hard enough believing that these men I'd worked with for years were willing to break the military code of conduct. It was even worse realizing they were operating under no code of conduct whatsoever.

"Hello?" Justet spoke into the phone. "Yeah, it's me . . . No she doesn't know anything, just said she got it from her dad . . . No, well she seems sincere. I scared the hell out of her so . . . Okay then . . . Yes, of course . . . No. I can handle it."

Who was he talking to? Sanderford? Someone else I hadn't identified?

Justet shifted uncomfortably, his eyes flicking from me to the rifle and back. The implication didn't look very promising. "So you want me to . . . Of course . . . No, I don't need Sanderford . . . Yes, ma'am . . . yes, ma'am. Of course. Will do."

Justet took the phone from his ear and stared at it, his mouth partially open. Ma'am? That could only be . . . I cleared my throat, more from the sudden dryness than from an attempt to get his attention. Justet snapped the phone shut and shoved it in his pocket.

He licked his lips and adjusted his rifle. "I'm supposed to bring you back with me."

"To the base?"

"Hell, no." He shook his head. "I hate to say it, but things don't sound good for you."

"What doesn't?" My breath caught.

"The boss wants to take care of you personally."

"Take care, as in . . . ?" He was right. It didn't sound good. "Oh, come on, sir!"

I couldn't seem to react properly. I should be pleading for my life, or running headlong into the bushes, or even just feeling incapacitating fear and wetting myself. Instead, I saw myself from his perspective. My small head framed in the center of the rear sighting circle, the barrel sight stabbing upward into my throat. Hair fraying from my braid. One cheek bruised, eyes narrowed against the pulsing throb above my ear.

My face burned. I raised my hands. A shiver of energy raced up and down my spine. My hands hovered in front of me, trembling slightly. The open wound on my knuckle from punching Justet gaped a bright, dirt-coated red.

So volt him. The voice in my head instructed. *Volt him, volt him, volt him.*

Volt? The thought drew me upright. Could I do it? Conjure the electricity from last night? A slight tingling moved from my fingertips to the open skin.

Awesome. I could static shock him into submission.

"Who was on the phone?" I snapped, delaying the inevitable. "You called her 'ma'am.' Are you talking about the commander?"

"Shut up. It doesn't matter." Justet lifted his rifle, with some hesitation, to his shoulder.

"Tell me something, Justet." My words sounded coarse and angry in my ears. I wasn't going to cower here, waiting for him to take me to someone who'd blow my head off. I fixed him with an icy stare. "What do *you* know about Retha? You keep talking aliens, so I want to know what these *Rethans* want with seven small-town police officers and nine enlisted soldiers, missing from their homes or places of work over the last six years."

"What are you talking about?" Justet dropped the muzzle of the rifle, genuinely curious.

"You heard me. Taken. Kidnapped. Abducted. Whatever you want to call it. Their places trashed, like in an explosion, and a single silver coin left at the scene stamped with the letters R-E-T-H-A."

Justet's eyebrows shot up. "Oh, the coins. Why's this matter so much to you?"

"It matters." I took a single step toward Justet and his rifle. I was going to find out what he knew, even if it killed me.

"You think they're taking our people too?" Justet asked.

"What do you mean, 'too'?" I narrowed my eyes.

"If they're invading Earth with their weapons of mass destruction, it only makes sense that they've studied us first," he mused, turning his back to me.

I'd done enough ride-alongs with Dad to know when someone was three-sheets-to-the-wind, or just plain raving mad. Justet was neither. I rubbed my eyes, looked at Justet's back, and glanced behind me. If I was going to run, now was the time. My hesitation cost me one of my alternatives. Justet rotated so rapidly that dirt kicked up around him like a billow of smoke. He flicked something shiny and silver toward me.

I ducked, covering my head with my arm as though the expected bullet was speeding toward me. The silver coin landed near my feet. The word RETHA, stamped across it in raised letters, shone in the sun. Shaking and breathless I plucked the coin from the dirt.

"Where'd you get this?" I turned the coin over, testing the weight and balance, checking for imperfections in the surface that might afford me some clue.

The one left at Dad's crime scene had been squirreled away by the police as evidence before vanishing with everything else, taken by a mysterious government agency called the DLA. I'd only gotten a small glimpse of it when they'd shown it to me, obscured in a plastic evidence bag. They'd asked if I knew anything about it. I hadn't, at least not then. The image was imprinted in my mind. Someone was taking cops and soldiers and leaving this calling card. Why?

"They're not all bad." I looked up. Justet's eyes were wide, and he nodded conspiratorially. "Some just want to help us prevent the invasion."

It took all I had not to roll my eyes. Invasion? Aliens? It all sounded so . . . But then again, he had a coin. A RETHA coin, exactly like the one left at Dad's crime scene. And he and his minions were planning something. Something that involved twenty-seven cans of stolen ammunition, and probably a lot more I didn't know about.

"Justet! Where the hell are you?"

The voice floated toward us from the south, and I jumped. Stomping boots followed. A jolt of energy ripped down my spine and out into my extremities. Justet turned in the direction of Sanderford's voice.

"Lieutenant!" Sanderford called again, closer this time. "I swear, if you're stalling again, I'll pop you myself."

I didn't so much dive for cover as panic for cover. Both feet tried to be the first to start running and tangled, driving me hard to my knees behind a large juniper shrub. The exquisite, zapping pain of voltage surged into my limbs from some bizarre, unknown source within my body.

The shrub graced the edge of the slope and I found myself sliding backward. I rolled twice, letting gravity help me along, and then scrambled to my feet. I was vaguely aware of shouting somewhere near the top of the hill. Two large, dusty strides carried me a good distance down. I changed direction on the third, taking me toward the outcropping of rock I'd noticed earlier.

An M-16 chattered a three round burst. My step turned into a leap and I rolled over the top of the rocks before falling to my knees on the other side, out of the line of fire.

I lay there for what seemed like an eternity, my breath a sharp wheeze in my ears. The tingling in my body did a rapid circuit, quivering into my fingertips and then racing into my torso and legs before making it back into my fingers. I held my hands away from my body, afraid that I might electrocute myself. I almost expected to see a thin, blue line of electricity jumping between my fingers like some weird, five-pronged stun gun. I shivered, biting down until my molars ached. The coin pressed a circular indentation into my palm. With trembling fingers I shoved the coin into my pocket.

The furious rise and fall of an argument floated from a short distance. I peered around the boulder. The sound waves were almost visible in the summer heat. A set of boots stomped closer. Moments later, a camouflaged body pushed through some shrubs fifty feet away. Sanderford stopped, his rifle loose against his shoulder.

Justet stumbled out of the bushes behind the Sergeant, batting ferociously at a branch when it snagged his shirt. I was struck with the odd sense of shifting power. I guess on a rogue mission such as this, military rank could feasibly go out the window.

Lieutenant Justet tried to stop, but slid a few inches down the slope before bumping into Sanderford. Sanderford threw him off with his shoulder, and Justet found a more level spot for his feet. He held his rifle by the pistol grip, aiming it pointlessly at the ground.

"The boss isn't going to be happy you nearly killed her," Justet said.

"This is Rose we're talking about." Sanderford examined my track on the ground in front of him, his eyebrows drawn. "She's not going to lie down and let us do our thing. She tattles on us, and you can kiss your hundred grand goodbye. I guaran-damn-tee it. She's better off in the ground."

"There's a footprint." Lieutenant Justet's voice was small. He waved a hand at the ground. "It's a shame, really. About Rose. She's a hell of a soldier."

"A helluva pain in the ass, maybe. The boss is thinking too much about this. What's so special about Rose anyway?"

Justet shrugged, his face troubled. Fine, dry dirt exploded around Sergeant Sanderford's boots. Sanderford crouched, touched the ground, and looked up. I swear he was staring right at me. He narrowed his eyes and pulled the M-16 strap from his shoulder.

"Maybe you should hang back this time, L.T. I can't imagine you've grown a pair since you were out here with her ten minutes ago. I'll take care of it."

"You mean kill her?"

"If that's what it takes." Sanderford stood, pulling the rifle casually to his shoulder.

Lieutenant Justet didn't answer and I realized, with a certain amount of surprise, that I was feeling an unusual affection for his weakness. He remained stock still behind Sanderford, his rifle hanging at his side.

I let my breath out slowly. My hands trembled. I looked at my fists. Could I really kill Sergeant Sanderford? I tried to remember the mantra my drill sergeants put into my head. Kill one enemy, save a thousand friends. Sergeant Sanderford was an enemy—my enemy.

Kill Sergeant Sanderford.

A chilly calm swept my body. An odd sense of amusement lifted the corners of my mouth. I pictured the shocked look on his face as electricity from my fingers coursed over his body, blistering him with burns. I saw him fall to his knees, screaming as smoke poured from his eyes, his sandy hair scorching into black, smoldering curls. I saw myself laughing—

My stomach heaved. I pressed a fist to my mouth and breathed through my nose. The image repeated with different ghostly levels of clarity.

Was it better to be dead than a killer? My dad would say, "Defending yourself is a God-given right. Only you can decide if you can live with the consequences."

Voltage, volted, volting.

Sanderford's camouflage flashed through the branches of a nearby juniper. He crouched next to my boulder, examining the scuff marks in the dirt. Almost within reaching distance.

My lips pulled against my teeth, every muscle stressed. With desperate swiftness, born of years of military training, I kicked out.

The bottom of my boot crushed into the side of Sanderford's knee. His legs went out from under him and he landed on his side, catching himself with a hand, then an elbow. The rifle fired three bullets zinging against the boulder. Chips of rock flew everywhere as the bullets ricocheted off in other directions.

Sanderford swung the rifle toward me. I crabbed forward and crunched the toes of my boot against the back of his hand. The weapon flew from his fingers, banging and skittering out of reach, while the magazine ejected and flew in another direction.

Sanderford clutched his knee with one hand, groaning and swearing, while clawing his way toward his rifle. I clambered to get there first. Our fingers met on the trigger and the rifle fired a single shot. The blank burned past my cheek. Sound was lost behind the blast of the rifle, turning everything into a hollow echo on my left side.

The taste of metal filled my mouth, and a sizzle of energy escaped from my skin. Sanderford withdrew his hand with a bellowing cry, only to come at me an instant later and smash his fist into my ribs. I curled my body to protect my screaming side, at the same time backhanding Sanderford across his cheek with a blessed release of energy.

A zapping sound hissed through the air, raising the hair on my scalp. Sanderford's head thumped to the ground. Dust covered one side of his face. He didn't move. Blood leaked from his nose and ears.

My torso cramped. I tripped away from his body. Was he dead? Had I killed him? My knees shook, but I managed to get to my feet, pulling Sanderford's rifle up as I stood.

Lieutenant Justet didn't move except for the toe of his boot resting on the magazine from Sanderford's rifle. He held the hand guard of his M-16 loosely in one hand. His expression was surprisingly neutral.

Justet raised his rifle a hair. I jerked my attention back to him and lifted my own rifle to point at his chest.

"Don't do it, sir," my voice rushed softly across the several feet separating us.

"There's no ammo in that rifle."

"You sure about that?" The bolt filled the chamber, telling me either that there was a round still in the chamber or that the bolt release had been hit. I was hoping for the former but was pretty certain it was the latter.

Justet tapped his toe on the magazine, probably wondering the same thing.

"Is he dead?" he asked.

"Don't know. Don't care."

That wasn't true. I did care. Quite a lot, in fact.

"How'd you do that?" His chin quivered.

"Do what?"

He pointed at Sanderford but then dropped his hand back to steady the rifle. "Last night, and that . . . that—"

"Where're my tags?" I set the rifle to my shoulder and sighted down the barrel with both eyes.

"It's more than my life's worth to give 'em to you."

My finger found the warmth of the trigger. All I needed to do was put the smallest amount of pressure on the little curve of metal and, if there was a round in the chamber, I could take my pendant and tags from his bleeding corpse.

So very easy. The slightest pressure.

A chatter of voices sounded from the direction Sanderford had come from. My mind cleared, like a wind blowing away a lethal fog bank. My finger lifted from the trigger. I gulped.

"They're not coming to help you, Rose."

I took a backward step. My finger touched the trigger again and then jerked away.

"Don't I know it." I retreated another step.

Justet didn't move. The muzzle of his rifle dropped. I stumbled, righted myself, and allowed a rock outcropping covered in scrubby bushes to come between us.

The second Justet was lost from my line of sight, I ran.

CHAPTER 7

Branches tore at my shirt, and the pungent smell of sage followed me as I crushed smaller bushes under my boots. I couldn't think. I wished I couldn't feel. Voltage coursed through my body, threatening to tear me apart from the inside. The contusion on my head and bruise on my face pulsed with the beat of my heart. I pulled one arm close to my body, trying to protect my side as my ribs jabbed pain into my lungs. I clung to the rifle with my other hand.

I tried to listen for pursuit, but my left ear was giving me sketchy, hollow-sounding information and my right was jammed by the whoosh of my own breathing. My course took me dead east toward the base. But then, with a burst of ingenuity, I turned southeast—in the direction of the road where I hoped to be able to hitch a ride with some unsuspecting convoy.

It had to have been more than a mile before the rumbling of a distant vehicle penetrated my bubble of white noise. The road showed through the brush several yards to my right. I threw myself to the ground, and crouched beneath an enormous tumbleweed in the nearby ditch.

I'd pushed my body way past what it felt was fair, and my lungs were letting me know. Darkness edged my vision. I forced myself to stillness and concentrated on getting a breath all the way down to the bottom of my lungs. I heard the rumbling of the vehicle again, closer now. The engine roared low and slow. I dragged myself up until I could peer over the incline.

A brown, cumulous dust-plume from the vehicle turned to cirrus as it rose into the still air. At least it was coming from the direction of the base and not of my pursuers.

Without any ammo the rifle was only good for a bludgeoning device, which wouldn't help with that Humvee . . . except . . .

Oh, of course! The round! The stupid, little round that I'd taken from Justet's office. A live round. I reached into my pants pocket, frustrated with my shaking fingers, and discarded my hat, a waterproof notebook, and a tube of ChapStick before finding the small brass cylinder. I pulled back the charging handle with stumbling fingers. No round popped out. I guess that answered that question.

Sweat stung its way into the corners of my eyes. I pressed the round into the hot, black chamber, snapped the bolt back into place, and rested the rifle on a rock so it was aiming down the road. The Hummer droned into view. It could belong to anyone on the base. All Hummers looked the same, as did the high and tight haircut in the driver seat.

I breathed in and out through my nose, willing my hands to still, and lined the driver's head in my sites. I moved the rifle by fractions as the vehicle drew closer. My finger hovered over the trigger.

The driver swiveled his head this way and that searching for something. Closer. The Hummer was directly across from me before I recognized the man inside.

"Thurmond," I whispered. I knocked my elbow against the stony hill in my haste to get to my feet. Ignoring the stab to my funny bone, I waved one arm above my head. "T! Hey Thurmond! Thurmond!"

The Hummer skidded to a stop several yards up the road. I crawled up the embankment. When I looked up, Thurmond was already out of the Hummer. The door hung open, creaking on its hinges.

"Rose?" He paused near the taillight, shielding his eyes. A few stumbling steps brought me next to the opposite taillight. I paused in sudden trepidation, my throat tight.

I searched his face. Was there deception hidden in the concerned slope of his mouth, the familiar lines around his eyes? Up until last night I'd had full confidence in my military comrades. Liked some more than others, but I didn't fear them. Thurmond was my best friend, my battle buddy. Of course, I'd never thought the events of last night could happen either.

"What the hell happened to you?" Thurmond's words rang with a hollow sound. I touched my left ear and rotated my jaw.

"You working with Justet?" My legs shook, and for a moment I was sure they would abandon me.

"What?"

"Justet and his freak squad." I let the butt of the rifle rest on the ground and leaned on the weapon for support. I should probably have been aiming it at him instead. "Are you working with them, T?"

"Justet did this to you?"

"Just answer the question."

"I would if I knew what the hell you're talking about." His expression was so confused and words so sincere that there was a painful release in my chest.

Of course he wasn't working with Justet. He was the Thurmonator. I pressed a palm gently against my puffy eye, barely restraining the desire to wrap my arms around his solid torso.

"Rose?" Thurmond reached out to touch my cheek. I flinched away. He drew his hand back, surprise on his face.

"I'm fine," I lied, looking up the road. How long did I have until Justet started hunting me down in his vehicle?

"The hell you are."

"What're you doing here?" I asked, turning back. Thurmond put both hands in his pockets.

"Wichman sent me."

"Wichman?"

"Yeah. I went to the barracks looking for you last night, you know, after the commander took you out of the club." Thurmond ran his hand across his mouth. "When you didn't answer the door I figured you were already racked out and didn't care to talk. But when you didn't show up to formation this morning Wichman dragged me out of the line, and suddenly he's shoving me toward this Hummer and telling me to take the north road up toward the firing range." He wouldn't stop staring. "Said I'd find you with Justet and Sanderford and he'd be right behind me."

"We need to get out of here," I said, barely listening. I stepped around the side of the Hummer to the passenger door. Thurmond spoke at my back.

"What's going on here, Rose? Did Justet—?"

"No, he didn't. Well he did, but it's not like that."

"Then tell me what it's like because this whole thing is screwy."

I didn't respond immediately. Thurmond touched my side. "Hey, talk to me, Rose."

The bruising where Sanderford's boot had made contact sent pain shooting into my lungs. I turned and shoved him with a furious release of anger and tension. Thurmond took a surprised step back and rubbed his chest where I'd struck him.

"They tried to kill me!" I shouted. The whole experience condensed into five brusque syllables made my stomach flip-flop. Anger surged through my limbs. My head pounded. "Is that okay with you?"

"What? Why?" Thurmond retreated another step.

"They . . ." I swallowed to hold back a sudden desire to punch something else.

"What'd they do?" Concern etched lines in his face. He hesitated, and then brushed soft fingers against my cheekbone. I forced myself to stand there and not assault him again.

I had to trust someone. This was too big for me to carry alone. But doing that would open a door I'd closed when I'd lost Dad. I looked into Thurmond's honest blue eyes and took a breath.

"Justet stole ammunition from the armory," I said. Thurmond raised his eyebrows. "And it wasn't just Justet either, in case you think I'm being . . . Anyway, Sanderford, a couple of privates, and two people I didn't get a good look at are in on it too." Now that I was committed, I couldn't stop the words. So I vomited the story all over Thurmond. The abbreviated, thirty-second version that ended with me omitting the fact that I had probably killed Sanderford with a freakish volt of electricity from my fingers.

"They beat the hell out of you over . . . aliens?" Thurmond looked murderous.

"The beating was mutual." I frowned. "Though I definitely lost."

"But over aliens?"

"Apparently." I touched my cheek. The skin was hot and puffy under my fingers from where I'd struck the floor last night. A breeze cooled my sweaty scalp.

"Let's get you out of here," Thurmond said, reaching around me and yanking open the passenger door.

I stared up the road. A plume of dust rose not more than a mile away. My stomach leapt. Thurmond was already climbing in the driver seat as I slammed the door.

He squeezed the steering wheel, whitening his knuckles. I ran a finger gently across the blood scabbing my own knuckle. After a moment he shook his head, popped the gear into drive and made a tight U-turn. Dust flew up next to the open window. He pushed the speed higher than the Hummer was made to go, making it moan in protest. Wind whipped through my hair.

Thurmond pulled an elbow up to rest on the back of the seat. His eyebrows lifted in question as he alternately watched me and the road.

"You serious about this alien thing?" he finally said.

"Yeah. It was a freakin' awesome start to my day." Anger churned my stomach. I pressed a hand to my suddenly splitting head. "Especially when Corporal Thurmonator entered from stage right to save the day." I was appalled at the sudden sarcasm twisting the words. "Hoo-freakin'-rah!" I couldn't hold his look anymore. I glowered into the side mirror, watching the road behind us.

Silence stretched between us, a long and heated thing that only cooled when Thurmond spoke.

"You hurt? Besides what's on your face?" Thurmond asked.

"You should see the other guy." The dead other guy.

A smile flickered at the corners of his mouth.

"And they really said they were going after aliens, huh?"

I suppose I went through a similar moment of disbelief and humor when Justet told me, but having it followed up with physical violence had a way of dampening the hilarity. And after what I'd done to Justet and Sanderford, aliens seemed downright plausible.

"Rose, maybe this is all just a big misunderstanding."

"They want to kill me! Does that sound like a misunderstanding to you? I'd think if you were going to kill someone you'd have a really clear understanding as to why."

Thurmond shook his head. I couldn't tell if he was angry or simply perplexed.

"Fine. What the hell do you want to do then? Go to the MPs?"

"And tell them about the aliens? No thanks." If Thurmond thought I was off my rocker, what would the MPs think? Not to mention that an investigation would be in order, making my wall locker public domain.

"I was talking about the ammo theft."

He had a point. I pulled my hands close to my chest and stared down at my open palms. My nerves pulled taut. Tingling voltage raced into my fingers. I suppose I *could* go to the police. There was a certain amount of security at the thought. They were the heroes of our urban world, the ones you went to when you had a problem such as this. And Justet was delusional.

That shivery, electrical feeling crawled through my hands. A delicate blue thread of light leapt between my finger and thumb. I shoved my hands between my knees.

I was delusional too.

"What about the commander?" Thurmond suggested.

My stomach twisted, remembering Justet calling someone "ma'am" on the phone.

Before my thought could come full circle Thurmond jerked his head to look in the side mirror. I looked in my own mirror. An enormous Deuce and a Half military transport truck bore down on us.

Thurmond mashed his foot on the accelerator. The Deuce smashed the Hummer from behind, flinging me into the dashboard. I caught myself with my hands and shoulder. Thurmond swore.

"What—?"

"Get down!" Thurmond shoved me to the floorboards.

The Deuce struck us again and the Hummer slewed recklessly to the side, lifting for an instant on two wheels before it slammed back on all four. The back passenger wheel dipped into the ditch, jarring everything to a violent stop.

Dust rolled through the air in hot, sun-streaked clouds. The world seemed too still, the quiet too long. The smell of motor oil and gasoline fill the air. I turned my head, trying to bring coherency to the moment, and found Thurmond's face. His mouth moved and the world sped up with a rushing sound, focusing into a distant echo of words.

"Rose, did you hear me? Get outta here!" Thurmond held his side with one hand, crushing his uniform into little mountains and valleys. He shoved at my shoulder with his other hand. "Get out! Don't let them see you!"

I fumbled with the latch. The door fell open, exposing the dirt in the ditch. I tumbled out, my hands hitting the ground first. The rest of my body followed, landing with an unsightly flump and sliding down the incline a few inches. One foot caught in the Hummer, halting my descent. The strap of the M-16 hooked around my ankle, the rifle itself wedged against the floorboard and seat. I twisted to get free. Desperation clouded my reason.

A vehicle door slammed.

I closed my eyes, took a frantic breath, and with abrupt efficiency, pulled the muzzle of the rifle up and away from the seat. I yanked my leg out of the Hummer, dragging the M-16 with me.

I braved one more glance at Thurmond. He hunched over the steering wheel, hand clutching his side, frantic eyes on me.

"Don't let them see you. You hear me, Rose?" he whispered.

I nodded. He scrunched his eyes shut and pressed his lips together. I wanted to go to him and call for help. Instead, feeling like a coward, I untangled the strap from my ankle and kicked the door shut.

Voices lifted over the top of the Hummer. "Should've been on our way to Air Guard base by now to load the C-130. She's not going to like it if we're late."

From the way the Hummer was slanted in the ditch I could see only the soles of several pairs of boots on the other side. I pressed my back against the slope and wormed my way upward until I was beside the back wheel.

"She'll like it even less if she finds out you didn't take care of this." Sergeant Sanderford's gruff voice brought a peculiar mixture of exultation and terror trilling through me. He wasn't dead. But on the other hand— he wasn't dead. "We've got time anyway. Wheels up at twenty-three-hundred hours."

"He doesn't know anything." Justet this time. "We're wasting time, not to mention that now we have to do something about him."

"He knows something all right. Thick as thieves, those two. We'd have to take care of him anyway."

My thumb found the safety switch of the rifle and flipped it to the off position. I wondered if I'd be able to find a single clean shot quick enough to save Thurmond. The racking of a pistol made my finger freeze on the trigger.

"Where's Rose, Corporal?" Sanderford barked. The boots scuffed up a great deal of dust, muting their individuality.

Door hinges complained. A moment later, a grunt of pain sounded from inside the Hummer. My head pounded. I could barely make out the words through my hollow left ear.

The scuffling of feet. A dragging sound. The boots stepped quickly back and a camo-clad body fell onto the ground. Thurmond's blue eyes stared at me for one second, tight and angry, before he was yanked upward. Only the backs of his boots were now visible.

"Don't make me ask again, Thurmond." A soft thud and oomph of air released from his lungs. Thurmond's hand and knee appeared. "Where's Rose?"

"W-why would I know w-where she is?" Thurmond wheezed and coughed, a painful wracking sound.

"I'm telling you, Sanderford, he doesn't know anything," Justet said. "You think she's hiding in his cargo pockets or something?"

"Or something. Lewis, check inside the Hummer. Make sure she's not under a tarp or a blanket."

The Hummer rocked and the wheel above my head slid further into the ditch. I slid with it. Thumps pounded over my head and a minute later a voice spoke.

"Nothin' here, Sarge."

"W-why do you want Rose anyway?" Thurmond said.

"Dust coming!" The nasally, broken-nosed voice of Private Luginbeel called out from farther away.

"Last chance, Corporal."

"Come on, we've got to go. Someone's coming!"

"Where's Rose?"

Another thud sent Thurmond gasping and coughing again. I pressed a hand to my mouth.

"If he'd seen her she'd be in the Hummer with him, Sanderford!"

"Tell me where she is!"

"Bring him with us—"

"Where is she?"

I clenched the grip of the rifle. I could take the shot. Any shot to stop this.

"Sergeant Sanderford!" Justet seemed to remember his officer's rank and dragged it out from where it had been hiding with his backbone.

"Tie him up. We'll take him with us. That's an order! Let the boss decide what to do with him."

A moment of silence and then Thurmond's hand and knee disappeared. The boots scuffed up more dirt and thumped out of sight.

Somewhere in my mind I saw myself rising from behind the Humvee and placing a bullet into the back of Sanderford's head. My fictional self then raced around the vehicle and beat the snot out of Justet and the rest of his cronies, after which Thurmond and I would turn over the survivors to the MPs for the court martial—a great heroic act that remained dormant in my mind.

I remained where I was, a single soldier with a single round. Even if I made the perfect shot I would still have a half a dozen other soldiers and their dozens of rounds to contend with. I know what I'd do in their boots. Put a gun to Thurmond's head and threaten to kill him. That's what my heroics would get me. That's what it would get Thurmond.

I stayed under the Hummer, hands tight on the rifle. The stench of motor oil burned my nose and something else burned my eyes. The rifle seemed to weigh a thousand pounds, my legs a million. It took everything I had to force myself to stay still, to avoid the easiest, most violent option. My head hurt.

Somewhere out there a motor started with a rumble. Voices argued. The old, loose gears of the Deuce ground into drive, and still I didn't move. Tires crunched on gravel. The vehicle picked up speed and the sound diminished in the distance.

Nothing. Silence. Still I stayed under the Hummer, my mind rattling over the insanity of my plan. Again and again and again and again.

A breeze lifted a curl of hair and brushed it against my cheek. Startled, I batted it away. My foot jerked. Then the rest of me moved. I slowly slid out from under the Hummer and crawled out to the road, dragging the rifle along behind me.

I gazed down the empty road in the direction of the base, my thumb absently circling the rifle's forward assist. The plume of dust that was supposed to be the approaching vehicle turned before reaching me. The small convoy of Hummers unfurled onto a road to the south.

Air guard base? That's what they'd said. It could only be the base connected to the Salt Lake International Airport that we'd flown out of on our last annual training run to Alaska. It was the only place within a hundred miles that could fly out a C-130.

Wheels up at twenty-three-hundred hours. And, unless I was very much mistaken, they were taking Thurmond and flying to Fort Huachuca in Arizona. Home of the "alien base" and information about Retha and Dad.

I had a flight to catch.

CHAPTER 8

Caz
Retha
10 years pre-RAGE

Caz lay on her bed, subdued. She should have been sobbing her eyes out. Instead, she clutched the pillow tight under her chin and methodically pulled threads from its decorative, metallic tassels. *One-twenty-one, One-twenty-two.* One hundred and twenty-three threads. The same number as the members on the Dimensional Congressional Council. Caz rolled onto her back, taking the pillow with her, and stared at the black ceiling.

The Dimensional Congressional Council. They, at least, were a large, cold entity she could blame everything on.

Vin was gone for the rest of the year. A business trip of sorts arranged by his esteemed father, DC Commandant Paliyo himself, to teach Vin the ins and outs of what would one day be his honorable position. What wasn't there to love about a trip to one of the lower dimensions? To engineer a peaceful overtaking before the Heart could destroy them? In fact, it was just the thing to break in your young, impressionable son. The one who'd been spending too much time with the wrong girl.

It might not have been so bad if Vin had put up a bit more of a fight about it. But he'd talked in circles, trying to convince Caz of how important he was. This was why he'd been asked. This was why he needed to go. And of course the distance would be good for their relationship in the long run.

It was fortunate they'd been nestled in their usual meeting place, a small natural cave in the middle of the Vislane envirophylum, when he'd broken the news. Caz had thrown a tantrum capable of blowing every conductor within twenty grids.

The only consolation Caz had was the plain silver ring circling her finger. Vin had given it to her yesterday before he officially left. There was genuine sadness, even regret in his eyes as he'd placed it on her finger. Using her thumb she rotated it around her middle finger, taking pleasure in the feeling of ownership it gave her.

Caz breathed out a sigh and curved her fingers around the tassel. She released the smallest amount of electricity from her fingers into the tassel. The metallic threads jumped and danced, sparking a vibrant light across her dark walls. Her door squeaked. A sliver of brightness cut across her face. She severed the current and dropped the pillow to her chest.

"What do you want, Xan?" She didn't have to look. Who else would it be? The door opened a bit wider.

"Vin really left, huh?"

"Yep."

"Do you want to talk about it?"

"Nope."

"Okay then." The light on her face narrowed.

"Wait." Caz rolled onto her stomach. "Do you know anything about the LRM?"

Xander paused in the doorway, one hand on the knob.

"The what?" He stared blankly at a silver disk in his other hand.

"The Liberated Rage Movement," Caz said. "Some extremist faction that wants to take over Retha. Make us free or something."

"Yeah, sure. Heard of them." Xander shrugged. "What about it?"

"Vin was just . . ."

"Just what?" Xander opened the door a little wider, a concerned twinge contorting his voice.

Caz expelled a breath and sat up. "It's just that he wouldn't stop talking about it. Asked me to look into it while he was gone." Bitterness crept into her words, and she realized that she was going to ignore his request deliberately. The pure spite of the decision would keep her warm at night in his absence. "Never mind." she slouched against the bed frame. Her mind circled the track of resentment that their last few moments together had been to talk about something as idiotic as the LRM. Retha's two laws would prevent the infant faction from ever gaining traction anyway. She hoped Vin wasn't taking them too seriously.

After a moment she realized that Xander was still darkening her doorway. He looked exhausted. Sometimes she believed he never slept. When would he have found the time, between fighting to stay in the top five in his academia classes and being a constant buffer between his bickering parents and impulsive sister?

"What do you have there?" she asked, hoping for something truly spectacular.

He looked up. A smile lit his face and he waved the silver INFOD, an information disk she had come to crave anytime she saw it in his hands. "Only the latest and greatest problem Mom and Dad haven't been able to solve."

Caz's heart thumped heavily in her chest. "You mean for the Heart—!"

"Shhh!"

She heard a door open and close from deeper in the house, and then their parents' squabbling voices. Xander shut the door behind him. Their parents wouldn't check on them. They never did.

"You mean for the Heart of Annihilation?" Caz whispered, making room for Xander on the bed.

"What else?"

"Show me, show me!" It was all she could do not to shout.

If there was one thing that could take her mind off Vin it was the endless puzzles, broken road maps, and unsolvable problems her parents ran across with their newest and most devastating weapon. This was the one, her mother said, that would allow them to retire. This was the one that would end even the idea of war with the Thirteenth Dimension. But they didn't know if it could work.

That was where Caz and Xander came in. Xander had been sneaking information from their parent's lab for the last several years and feeding it to Caz. Caz would then work the problems in secret, reveling in the emotionless nature of numbers before having Xander send it back. Her parents would then proceed as if they did the work themselves. No one ever spoke of it. Plausible deniability and all that. What Caz needed now was to get the equations right.

Xander inserted the INFOD into the wall receiver and applied a charge with his hand. The bare wall opposite the bed lit up, revealing lines of numbers that scurried from left to right in tiny, neat rows.

Caz sighed, losing herself. Occasionally she'd reach out a finger and cast one aside or replace it with a hastily tapped out row. Xander sat beside her on the bed, part of the background.

She didn't know how long she worked before Xander startled her.

"Did you hear about Zak Faras?" he asked.

Caz paused for a miniscule moment, and then pretended he hadn't spoken. How could Zak Faras be more important than this problem? She almost had it if she could—

Xander went on. "He overdosed on Direct Current."

Caz ignored him.

"His parents think he took Azshatath. You know, that drug that helps with voltage asthenia. Nearly took out his entire grid," Xander paused before continuing, "Except I know Zak, and he wouldn't."

Xander shifted beside her on the bed.

"There it is!" Caz found the hole in the equation. A few flicks of her fingers rearranged the numbers. This was what she lived for. Making order out of chaos. Filling in that gap. Shuffling the twelve and the three to the power of . . . oh! No, they shouldn't do that. If they subtracted to allow for the storage of energy, taking into account the covariant formula and electromagnetic force, it would make the quantum mechanical effects negligible thereby stabilizing what remained of the . . . Ah ha! Her fingers flew across the wall, and it all came together.

There it was. She sat back. As clear as Retha on a moongrave night. How could her mother have missed it?

"Look, Xan!" She practically shouted. She couldn't take her eyes from the blissful harmony of the equation. "It's not about detonation and expansion of the core, it's about—"

"Did you hear me, Caz?" Xander's voice penetrated her euphoria. "Zak Faras is dead."

Voltage erupted from her fingers, overloading the receiver and plunging them into darkness.

She muttered her most injurious cuss words and felt around on the wall for the reset. Her hand felt the imprint, and a blue light scanned her palm. The receiver lit the wall again, driving black numbers across Xander's illuminated face.

"What do you mean he's dead?" Caz kept her voice cool, calm. She locked eyes with her brother.

"I mean *dead.* Fried to a crisp."

"Dad takes Azshatath. At the most it would—I mean, come on! It's never killed anyone before."

"That's because no one would take it unless they had to. Zak didn't." Xander stared at her with his most irritating, all-knowing expression.

She dragged her eyes from him and examined the problem on the wall. Hopefully the overload hadn't wiped out her alterations. She was in luck. There they were, perfect, harmonious.

"What a shame." She coughed into her hand. "Too bad nobody cares a picoamp about a drone like Zak Faras."

Xander made a noise in his throat.

"Look, Xan. Look at this. It's the piece they've been looking for!"

"Tell me you didn't have anything to do with what happened to Zak." Xander's voice was quiet and probing, with much more intensity than he usually directed at her. She wished he'd go back to walking on eggshells.

Caz leveled him a cold stare.

Xander closed his eyes. When he opened them she saw the retreat. He gave Caz a thin smile, and turned to look at the wall.

This would *finally* enable her parents to begin production of the prototype. Now all she had to do was make them see that she was needed in the lab.

She flicked her eyes away from the equation. Her thumb rotated the ring on her finger.

CHAPTER 9

Rose

I jerked myself awake. The tips of my fingers touched the ground, keeping me from falling over.

I must have dozed off again. It wasn't surprising, considering everything I'd been through in the past few hours. But leaned up against a building? I gently touched my puffy eye, encouraging it to open a bit.

The ride from Camp Williams to the Air Guard base, a nearly straight shot down Redwood Road, was slow considering that the bruised Hummer hadn't wanted to reach speeds higher than thirty miles an hour. Fortunately, getting onto the Air Guard base was as easy as showing my military ID at the gate and dropping the commander's name. The young security police had jumped at mention of the commander, and waved me past the barricades with flustered efficiency. Apparently my suspicion about the commander had some truth, and she was expected. I wondered, as I parked my Hummer in a more southern parking lot and walked up the narrow, nearly deserted streets, how much the guy at the gate was getting paid. Maybe he was just concerned that his face would end up like mine.

I'd gotten here well ahead of Justet and his troops, leaving me ample time to sit out of sight in the weeds between two buildings just off the runway, fingering my bruised ribs, and going through every piece of paper and scrap of information I'd committed to memory about Dad.

The C-130 Hercules hulked on the tarmac, a dinosaur of a plane: simple, pale, and gray as a ghost in the darkness. I remember a civilian telling me once how the C-130 was her favorite plane, with the cute pug nose that looked like it needed a smiling mouth painted under it, the low plump body and high tail to accommodate the rear hatch. However, no one who had ever flown in one could call it "cute." Not with its notoriously loud, turbulent rides and uncomfortable seating conditions. The rear hatch lay across the ground, a hospitable ramp waiting patiently for the commander, Justet, and, hopefully, Thurmond.

The quiet drone of a motor hummed into the silence. I dropped to my chest, wide awake now. Headlights raced across the buildings and the plane before the tires squealed to a stop beside the ramp. I pulled my rifle closer to my body.

After a moment, the Hummer clunked into reverse and moved in a backward arc until the front was lined up with the ramp. The gears changed again, and the Hummer disappeared into the belly of the plane. Headlights danced in the puny windows of the C-130, and everything went dark again.

A few moments later a couple Deuces, with braced canvas tents covering the gear in the back, grumbled from behind the row of hangers. They parked in a neat diagonal row near the hatch of the plane. The headlights glared in my direction, as though to flush me out. Soldiers swarmed from the vehicles, muffled shadows behind the lights.

I counted figures as they unloaded duffles, boxes, weapons, and crates from the vehicles and carried them into the plane. The accuracy of the count was sketchy at best, and there was no sign of anyone looking remotely like a POW.

It took everything I had not to fall prey to the guilt over my role in Thurmond's abduction. It would be fine. He'd be fine. He was a soldier.

One of the Deuces started with a hefty roar. It lined up with the plane's ramp, headlights sweeping the tarmac, and eased after the Hummer into the belly of the plane. Red taillights winked against the torsos of the men as they followed it.

I swung the sling of my M-16 over my head, so the rifle hung down my back, and got to my feet. My knees inquired shakily if I really, truly wanted to do this. The transport aircraft roared to life with a sudden, jarring rumble. I dropped back down.

I couldn't see the red painted flight line, the one guarded by the SPs, but I had to assume it wasn't being watched. Not on an off-book mission such as this.

Another Humvee rumbled up next to the plane and screeched to an angular stop. There was just enough light coming from the National Guard fire station a few hundred yards away to highlight a pair of long legs strapped in combat boots as they stepped from the missing front passenger door.

The tall, slender form, the stern cut of the hair hanging at a precise angle from under the beret, the slashing scar across her eye, and the sharp features bringing to mind a resolute hornet—there was no mistaking Major Kuntz, the commander.

My focus deteriorated. I wasn't surprised. Angry, maybe. My confidence in the chain of command and belief in the inviolability of military leadership was scarred beyond redemption. But her hard, irrefutable presence was still hard to swallow.

No wonder she'd been so mad when I'd socked Justet in the mouth. Was that why she'd sent me into the armory when Justet was about to show up? For an offense as small as that?

Unless there was something else. Something she'd hinted at last night when she was setting me up for a beating. I couldn't remember the precise words she'd used, what with being assaulted and marked for death and all. But it itched in the back of my mind, like the memory of a memory you can't pin down.

The commander's mouth pressed in a hard line. She placed one hand on her hip. The other hung stiff at her side, long fingers twitching to the beat of some abrupt tune in her head. She rotated slowly on the spot, taking in everything around her. She paused, her eyes burning into my location. I couldn't have felt more vulnerable had I been standing in the middle of the runway waving my arms and shouting.

A movement from the plane made her look away to regard the man coming down the ramp. I crouched low, my boots crunching softly on the weeds. I couldn't hear Lieutenant Justet's voice as he shouted to the commander over the roar of the propellers. Major Kuntz nodded with a smile. Justet hooked a finger next to his collarbone, drew a chain away from his neck, and pulled it over his head.

I knew what it was before I saw it. I couldn't take my eyes off the chain as it changed hands. The commander shined a penlight on the swinging tags.

The half circle pendant caught the light, flashing a dancing reflection onto the damp runway. She gave Justet another of her curt nods, slung the chain around her own neck, and dropped the tags down her shirt. The driver of the Humvee pulled a duffle bag out of the back seat and handed it to her. The commander clutched the carrying strap of the duffle and, with one brief but comprehensive surveillance of the runway, she followed Justet up the ramp.

Electricity crackled through my extremities and collected in my fingertips. The propellers of the plane slowed, and then resumed their thundering wind.

I forgot about Justet and the aliens, about Sanderford and the guns, and even all about Thurmond. I saw myself striding up to the commander and snatching the tags from her fingers before plowing a voltage-charged fist into her face. The violence of the idea coursed pleasure through my body. She had no right to touch my possessions.

No right, agreed the voice.

Like a junkie wanting nothing more than the next fix, my focus zeroed in on the commander.

The pendant. The plane. The pendant. The plane, the voice in my head chanted.

My vision tunneled. Without another moment of hesitation, I made a crouching run toward the plane.

The plane's engine revved from an idle to a higher pitch. My mind flashed to the image of the commander holding the penlight on the glimmering pendant, and an irresistible need for the object overpowered any second guessing. I was to the ramp in a few seconds.

My brief peek into the plane's interior showed mostly the beefy back end of the Deuce, but I also took in a portion of the faces and their locations. The majority of the people lined the walls far to the front, and they were busily settling into the pull-down mesh seats. Major Kuntz stood toward the front of the plane, listening to an airman.

My eyes went to the thin line of tiny, duplicating, silver beads around the commander's neck. With a single glance behind me, I abandoned any more thoughts of an alternate action.

The ramp pressed against my belly button. The toes of one boot scuffed across the tarmac. Then I was on the ramp. My knee hit the rough traction. I rolled once, putting the bulk of the Deuce between the people and me. I stalked forward in a very low crouch to reach the Deuce, dropped to my belly, and crawled under it.

A pair of combat boots and the olive drab pants of an airman thumped past the front tires. I drew my feet to my body, trying not to think.

The deafening noise of the aircraft muffled slightly. The gears to the ramp groaned in tune with the plane's rumbling as the hatch raised in preparation for takeoff. The plane moved.

The finality of the ramp rising, my irrevocable permanence aboard the aircraft, was almost more than my nerves could stand. I pressed my hand to my mouth, and a tiny thread of blue light stung my cheek. I jerked my hand away from my face. Electricity snaked between my fingers. The hypnotic glow shivered an exquisite ache through my hand and down my arm.

I had only a moment to consider that stowing away right under the noses of my enemies might be considered a derailment from rational thought before acceleration punched me in the side. The plane raced forward. I slid backward.

I scrabbled my fingers across the wheel of the Deuce. The nails of one hand dug into the tread while my other hand gripped a grime-covered pipe above my head. With an abrupt lift that left my stomach on the ground, the plane cast off the demands of gravity.

We banked. My hand ripped away from the wheel. I smashed into the opposite wheel, my face and shoulder taking the impact, before being thrown out from under the Deuce against the rear hatch. I scrambled for cover.

I considered making my way to the front and turning myself in, in exchange for a seat with a seatbelt, some earplugs, aspirin, and possibly a barf bag or two. We had to reach cruising altitude at some point though. I could hold on until then. I hoped.

I was dragging my battered body back under the tailgate of the Deuce for the fourth time when something heavy struck me atop my back, flattening me onto my belly. A duffle bag rolled off to the side and slid with a shushing sound against the hatch.

A flash of movement. The dim lights in the plane flickered and went out. At least I didn't feel the need to check the faces at the front of the plane every few seconds for fear I'd been seen.

I pulled myself into the Deuce, gripping the splintery wood to keep my feet as the plane dropped and then rose. The scent of mildew brought to mind every military vehicle I'd ever ridden in. I stumbled across other duffle bags and equipment—it was amazing that I hadn't been bludgeoned to death by the entire load.

A sudden drop. I smashed my head into the canvas ceiling and then fell onto something warm, soft, and moving.

My chest lay across a muscled shoulder, my forearm pressing against a nose and mouth. A knee ground into my thigh. I pulled myself off the body I could only assume belonged to Thurmond. A profound feeling of relief washed out a hollow pit in my stomach.

I swallowed back the greeting I really wanted to give, which would include a non-awkward hug and something that didn't sound sappy in my mind but would certainly come out that way. Instead I kept one hand on his arm, afraid if I stopped touching him for even a second that he'd somehow vanish. I felt around with the other until I found the warm, coarse skin of his face. Blocky plastic indicated tape across his mouth. I caught a sticky edge with a fingernail and pulled gingerly. He jerked his head, leaving the piece of tape in my hand. The lights flickered back on with an additional hum.

The dim light filtering through the canvas gave Thurmond's face a sickly green tinge. He lay on his side, hands taped behind his back and feet strapped together with more duct tape. The skin around his mouth looked darker from where the tape tore away a layer of skin cells. His eyebrows furrowed angrily at me.

"What the hell are you doing here, Rose?" Thurmond's voice sounded loud even against the plane's roar.

"I came to . . ."

I'd come to save him, that's what I was doing here. The tape finally came away, curling into a thin, tight roll with Thurmond's assistance. He pushed himself into a sitting position, and I sat back on my heels so he could free his own legs. Thurmond had finished removing the last of the tape when the lights flickered out again.

Except that you're not actually here for your soldier friend.

The voice was loud between my ears. My head throbbed. I pulled my knees up to my chest, wrapped my arms around my legs, and rested my head on my knees.

Something that belongs to me.

The whisper drew me out of my slouch. Like a compass finding north, my eyes searched through the darkness for the commander. Was the pendant warm against her skin as it always was against mine? Was she sitting quietly in her seat, earplugs protecting her from noise and approaching intruders? Was she dozing at this late hour, blissfully unaware that I would be pleased as punch to remove her head to retrieve the tags?

A hand gripped my arm. I jerked away. Red spots blotted against the vision of blood and reclamation.

"Rose?" Thurmond's hand squeezed my shoulder. "Hey, I'm sorry I snapped at you."

I didn't say anything. My mind continued to roll over the image of the commander's decapitation. A combination of delight and horror duked it out for my attention. The confliction wasn't helping my already woozy stomach. I closed my eyes, trying to help the picture find an exit from my brain before it settled in for good.

Thurmond spoke in my ear again. His lips brushed my skin. A shiver ran up my arms. The red spots faded, along with the ache above my ear.

"I'm not mad, just worried. Okay?" His fingers tightened on my shoulder. "Did you bring help?"

"I'm the help, Corporal. Sorry." I almost hoped the blunt sarcasm would be lost in the roar. Almost.

Oppressive darkness pressed on all sides. I bounced into Thurmond. He threw an arm across my shoulder to steady himself, then left it there as we leveled again. After a moment he pulled me tight to his side. I stayed there, too anxious to be alone.

CHAPTER 10

Cold, green light appeared as the first hints of morning brightened our little, canvas prison. I rubbed my eyes and found Thurmond wide-awake. His stubbled jaw was tense, the side of his face bruised. One hand clutched his side.

"You hurt?"

"A bit." Thurmond shrugged. "Bashed my ribs up pretty good in the crash, and Sanderford wasn't exactly subtle about his interrogation. What about you?"

"No, I'm fine. I think." I wasn't. The memory of Sanderford's boot striking my ribcage made my side ache, among other things. I waved toward the hatch. "I'm a bit concerned they're going to throw us from plane when they find us."

I wasn't trying to be funny, but Thurmond's face relaxed into a grin. "We could probably use some parachutes, then."

I blanched. "There aren't any—"

"Actually there are." He poked my shoulder. "I saw them bring in a whole pile of them."

"Oh."

It was nice to know there was an alternative to a chute-less free fall from twenty thousand feet, even if it meant trusting my life to a bit of fabric and some shroud lines.

"Come on." Thurmond groaned, getting to his feet. "We're going to get a couple."

He made his way carefully across the scattered gear and dropped out of the back of the truck. I pushed myself up as well. A nervous hammering pained my gut. It was too easy, sitting quietly in the dark, to believe that things weren't as grim as they truly were.

I lowered myself out of the Deuce to where Thurmond crouched. His hands were balled into fists as he watched for movement from the front of the plane. When he saw me next to him, he dropped onto his belly and crawled under the Deuce. I followed. My belly jarred against the floor. Thurmond glanced back once and then pulled himself out the other side.

I was about to follow when I felt a touch of air from my right. I jerked my arm next to my ribs and sucked my body into a solid, rug-like statue. A second pair of boots marched past. The leather brushed my sleeve. The hatch ground open. Light and a fresh, cold wind poured into the plane. I'd flown a C-130 enough times to know they were either disposing of several dozen full barf bags or taking a gander at the scenery. Maybe doing reconnaissance.

I made to follow Thurmond, feeling oddly incomplete without him, when I felt a double-nudge against my leg. My stomach leapt and I bashed my head on the underside of the Deuce. Eyes watering, I faced the pair of combat boots standing next to the vehicle.

Fear turned a hard fist in my stomach. Maybe someone accidently kicked me while moving past. Maybe they were trying to get something out of the Deuce. Maybe—

The boot nudged my leg again, more insistent this time. I heaved out the air in my lungs and, with great reluctance, pulled myself partially out from under the vehicle.

My eyes traveled up the camouflage-covered legs, thick hands clenching next to the pockets, past the torso and chest, pausing on the staff sergeant rank and nametape before landing on the face. My eyebrows hit my hairline.

The usually friendly face of Sergeant Wichman stared back. He pressed his lips together under his bristling, salt and pepper mustache.

I thought about pulling myself back under the vehicle, hoping our friendship spanned from alien-hunter to stowaway. Then another figure slithered up next to him. The ruddy skin of the second man paled when he saw me. The girlish lips made a round, red O.

Wichman glanced over at Justet and then grabbed the collar of my uniform. He dragged me from under the truck. I gripped the barrel of the rifle slung across my back and scrambled my way to my feet.

"Rose?" Justet shouted. "How the hell did you get here?"

I wanted to think up a really good response, the kind that would shock them to their boots. Something really remarkable that implied I had a different army, a better army, like F-16s and Chinooks bearing down on their lumbering sky bus, prepared to do them in.

My fantasy made me feel like a cockroach—annoyingly hard to kill and not even worth their time.

"What the hell were you thinking?" Sergeant Wichman's very presence scuttled my last remaining confidence in my military leadership.

"What was *I* thinking? What were *you* thinking?" I yelled. "You . . . you—!"

Stray strands of hair flicked around my head, and I heard as much as felt the cool emptiness to my right. I pressed myself into the side of the Deuce, attempting to pry Sergeant Wichman's fingers from my collar. The pistol grip of the weapon pushed a reminder into my spine. My fingers tightened around the rifle.

The commander appeared a few paces behind Justet. Her expression went from curious to blank.

"Very good, Lieutenant." Her small eyes bore into me. "Take her into custody."

"Remove that weapon from her, Sergeant," Lieutenant Justet ordered, gesturing to Sergeant Wichman.

Wichman hesitated, his eyes locked on me. Justet turned toward the commander, possibly to plead for her support, as a large package flew past my head.

Justet and I both wrenched to the side. The parachute plowed into Sergeant Wichman's face, throwing him against the stack of ammo cans behind him. The band securing the cans came loose, and the olive drab canisters tumbled across the floor.

I used the truck to find my balance and yanked the rifle up under my arm, my hand clenched on the pistol grip and my finger on the trigger. The shoulder strap pulled tightly across my back, but at least the muzzle was aimed at the commander's face.

Justet's hands were the first to rise. The commander's smile disappeared, but it took her another full minute before her hands went up. The gesture was so unperturbed that I could have been holding a super-soaker instead of an M-16. Sergeant Wichman got to his feet, cursing under his breath. One hand touched his nose. Blood flowed across his mustache.

I flicked the barrel of the rifle at him, encouraging him to join Justet and the commander. Most of the other passengers were on their feet now, staring in unabashed surprise. Where was Sanderford? He had to be there. I needed to keep him in sight.

"Don't anyone move!" I yelled. My finger trembled on the trigger. My thumb froze over the safety.

"Everyone relax," Justet hollered. "There's no way she has any ammo in that rifle."

He didn't lower his arms, and I knew what he was thinking. How much ammo did I really have? One shot. But I wasn't sure they believed even that.

Thurmond inched his way between the two vehicles. Multiple straps and buckles crisscrossed his chest and around his legs, his uniform bunching here and there. He held the straps of a second chute. I could see myself simply backing into the thing before fighting our way to the hatch. A few eyes turned on him but then went back to me. Without a weapon he must not have appeared much of a threat.

I tried to keep everyone in sight, analyzing each movement and micro-expression. They were all beyond hostile. I don't think I ever felt so much hatred directed at me in my life.

In your life maybe, said the voice. My head pounded. My eyes locked onto the commander.

Her pulse beat a rhythm under the chain around her neck, the little beads popping hypnotically toward me. I pictured the chain descending down her boney chest, the tags resting under her breasts, the pendant hooking across the bridge of her bra.

Flaming rage burned up my throat. I flipped off the safety.

"Give me my tags," I said, the words a guttural snarl. "Now!"

The commander reached slowly into her shirt. Her thumb drew the chain out with cool precision.

"Private Luginbeel." Justet's voice worked its way into my conscious-ness. "Get that nine mil. Quickly!"

My intense focus evaporated. My finger eased off the trigger. Private

Luginbeel sat in the seat closest to us, a duffle bag between his knees, pulling a 9mm handgun from the bag.

Attikin's ass! He's going to kill us!

Tension turned my muscles into hard knots. A raging ache pounded above my left ear. In one rapid movement, I swung my fist, releasing the tension in an agonizing, knuckle-crushing wallop across Justet's jaw.

He collapsed, a heap of camouflage and carroty hair, his legs in an unattractive sprawl. Time to go. My eyes went back to the commander, zeroing in on the tags hanging against her uniform. My head split with pain. Lights popped into my vision.

Get the key . . . get the key . . . get the key . . . The chant in my mind surged energy into my limbs. I couldn't look away from the pendant. I'd never wanted anything more.

I stepped across Justet's body to reach the commander. My fingers closed on the tags and snapped the chain from her neck. I felt the welcome, warm curve of the pendant, a blissful moment of contentment.

The commander's hand clamped onto my wrist. Our eyes locked. I pressed the muzzle of the rifle against her abdomen. My finger depressed the trigger just a hair.

I wanted to kill her. Pull the trigger and feel her blood spill across my hands. The desire was so strong it burned my mouth. I couldn't breathe.

Kill her, kill her, kill her.

No I didn't. I didn't! I didn't want to kill her. Except that I did.

With superhuman effort, I took a step back. The plane lifted and then dropped. My balance shifted. The ache in my head retreated.

A single gunshot echoed through the plane.

I jerked backward and slammed into the side of the Deuce. Agonizing heat burned down my arm. A spot near my shoulder pounded for attention. My upper body collapsed over in an effort to protect itself. Only the support of the Deuce kept me on my feet. I watched in a daze as my left hand reached over to staunch the flow of an astonishing amount of blood. The thick crimson fluid dribbled over the chain entwined in my fingers.

I staggered, the left side of my body scraping against the Deuce. Every harsh line of the plane's interior became surprisingly sharp. Scars of sunlight moved across the walls of the aircraft as it banked.

I clutched the rifle, my hands forgetting how to let go. My gaze traveled from the blood . . . *so much blood* . . . to Luginbeel and the pistol he was pointing at me. Wind whipped away a delicate trail of smoke. The commander kicked Lieutenant Justet's leg out of her way and took a step in my direction.

An arm circled my waist. Thurmond yelled near my ear. I was dragged back several paces. My legs refused to work. In fact, my whole body was going numb. Wichman lunged at me.

A shout. Pressure at my back. Then emptiness, accompanied by the sensation of falling.

CHAPTER 11

Caz

5 years pre-RAGE

Caz tapped the tiny, red-hot shard of metal with her hammer, curving it around the stone anvil. It had been smelted down from the promise ring Vin had given her, not because she no longer needed or wanted it, but because it was the only metal she'd had on her when she descended into the lab two days ago.

Ash flecked her lap. It dirtied her dark, formal dress and glowed white in the darkness. She continued her methodical *tap, tap, tap* with the hammer, turned the shard by microns and *tap, tap, tapped* some more.

She was more than late. In fact, she had most likely missed it. *Tap, tap, tap, turn.* It was better this way. Who wanted to attend the interment of Retha's most infamous munitioners? Who wanted to hear Xander's sad words echoing in the vacant chamber?

The door clicked open. Unwelcome warmth blew at her back from the outside. The lab was kept cold for a reason. Not the sterile, metallic cold that encompassed the entirety of Retha but a foreign, damp, earthy cold.

Her parent's lab was buried deep underground, and consisted of materials only found in the Third Dimension. Everything about the lab screamed the excessive amount it was costing the DC Council. No one had owned a room this extravagant since the days of former Commandant Ben Attikin. Nowadays equal distribution of capital, and the rules of etiquette and serenity, kept everyone on the same economic level. Except for government-funded munitioners, of course.

Tap, tap, tap. Caz drummed her teeth together in time with her hammering. Footsteps followed the clack of the door closing and the deliberate turning of the key. The flames from the forge revealed a shadow of another person.

The walls were a deep brown, made of some kind of wood. Everything in the lab was either stone or wood. Nothing that could conduct electricity, except the tiny shard of metal held between her nichrom tongs and the matching hammer in her fist.

The archaic lock on the door only reinforced to her the dependency and helplessness of the voltage-wielding Rethans. They could unlock any door on Retha with an electrical charge, but would stand in complete bewilderment at the sight of a key. They were such drones. Caz smiled at the word she'd used as a child. As true today as it was then.

"You promised you'd be there." Xander's voice was flat.

Caz continued her work. *Tap, tap, tap.*

"Did I?" After a moment of silence she couldn't help adding, "How'd it go?"

"Vin spent the entire service making wild excuses for you, chatting up everyone he saw, and trying to pawn your kid off on sympathetic relatives. Even spoke with an LRM representative, if you can believe it."

Caz paused for one irritated second. Even reference to the Liberated Rage Movement set her teeth on edge. Especially since it was gaining such support from her passionate husband. Freedom from the two laws was tempting, she had to admit, but there was a feverish intensity to their actions that hinted at an escalation she was sure would end in violence. It was better if Vin stayed far, far away from them. She went back her work, pounding out her frustrations on the fragment of metal.

Xander went on. "He's very diplomatic, that husband of yours. But what do you expect from a council member?"

"Did he manage it?" Caz asked. *Tap, tap, tap.*

"Manage what?"

"To pawn the baby off on a relative?"

"Yes." The word was clipped. Xander let out a huff. "You know, between having him as a father and you as a mother, it's a wonder the kid doesn't shrivel up and die from neglect."

Caz stiffened, and then turned slowly. The handle of the tongs cut into her palm. Xander stood behind her. The silver of his eyes caught the flickering of the flames. His breath misted in the cold, damp air. In his arms he held a small bundle. The softness of the blue blanket contrasted with Xander's nicest, mourning metallics.

He stomach lurched. There was that feeling again. What was it about this tiny, immature Rethan in Xander's arms that made her perfectly aligned world seem askew?

She reached for the child. *Her* child. Xander offered him up with a sigh. She was sure he hadn't expected her to show any interest. That was where he was wrong. When the child was born, she was surprised to discover that she liked nothing better than feeling the helpless warmth in her arms.

The baby was still so tiny, but getting bigger every day. He would take after her father, intimidating everyone with his size and stature. He would make her proud.

She held him close, inhaling his scent: a mixture of storm clouds and milk. She was held captive by the connection she felt for him. It didn't make sense in her ordered mind. In fact, nothing about him made sense. And yet here he was, so tiny, so helpless, and so very powerful.

She became aware of Xander, staring at her with those damnable omniscient eyes of his. His gaze never seemed to leave her when she was holding the child, searching for the motherly instincts he swore she was hiding somewhere.

Caz stood, and brushed Xander aside. She held the baby tightly with one arm, the tongs still in the other, and made her way to the forge. She nestled the curve of metal deep in the coals, and turned to Xander. The fire heated her back.

"Did you really come all the way down here to accuse me of bad parenting, Xan?"

Caz bounced the baby even though he hadn't made a sound. She wanted to squeeze the tiny form, make him a part of her again. The disconnect had been painful, like losing a precious possession without the ability to ever retrieve it again. Xander stared at her. The deficient light made his eyes black holes.

"No."

"Oh, that's right, now that's the lesser sin." Caz gave a brief bark of laughter, turned back to the forge, and picked up the tongs.

She loved the way the fire seared her face in an unpredictable dance of heat. The cold lab kept the stockpiles of volatile chemicals and explosives stable. The forge was unable to penetrate such bio-crafted cold, but right here it scorched and burned in such strong contrast to the chill she felt herself divided in two.

"Say it," she said. It was coming. Why delay the inevitable?

Xander shook his head, unable to verbalize his thoughts. Then, "Did you do it?"

"Do what, Xan? Be specific." He wasn't going to get away with a passive, partial accusation. If he wanted anything from her, he was going to have to say it.

Xander heaved out a resigned sigh. "Did you kill them? Did you kill our parents?"

She kept her face expressionless, although inside her chest a random bubble of laughter threatened to escape. She batted it down, and when she answered it was with the cool, overly composed voice she used to bully Vin into getting what she wanted.

"How can you even ask that?"

"Because you were fighting with them hours before it happened—"

"I always fight with them—"

"And you know as well as I that they were never going to let you here into the lab."

"Xander, I'm wounded by the insinuation." She said his name with condescending affection. Xander, who knew everything. Xander, who stood by her side no matter what. Xander, with his staggering and limited view of the world. She narrowed her eyes. "Have you voiced this to anyone else?"

"Caz—"

"Because with the marshals asking questions about the deaths, what are they going to think of you naming your little sister—"

"Caz—" Xander's voice was insistent.

"—as a suspect?" She turned from him and worked the tongs deep into the coals. "The work here is too important to allow it to be sullied by conspiracies and false accusations!"

"Gauss's law, Caz! The baby!" In two strides he was at her side and wrested the baby from her grip.

She tried to hold onto him at first, but then let go. What was the point? Xander stumbled back. The heat from the forge had melted the corner of the blanket near the baby's feet into a black mound. A curl of rancid smoke rose from the charred spot. Xander ripped the blanket off and dropped it on the floor. The baby gave a surprised squall. Xander checked the little feet to make sure they were unharmed. Her son gave another cry, a whimper, and then sucked his upper lip as he fell back into contented sleep. Xander curled him close and stomped to the door.

The moment she'd shared with his little soul was lost again, just like every time she stopped holding him; stopped trying. She reached for her tongs and removed the tiny curve of metal from the coals. It glowed white-hot. She strolled back to her stool and fitted the curve of metal to the anvil. The key clicked in the lock behind her. Warmth flooded the room again.

"You'd better watch yourself," Xander's voice was a quiet hiss.

Caz whirled on her stool. Xander stood in the open doorway, gripping the baby to his chest to keep the small limbs warm in the absence of the blanket.

"Is that a threat?" She raised her eyebrows. He wasn't one to walk such a dangerous line.

"No!" Xander lowered his voice. "No, Caz, it's not a threat, it's . . ." He stroked the baby's head and looked Caz in the eyes. "It's me warning you that losing your temper and getting yourself exiled will only succeed in causing your work to fail. Completely! Do you understand?"

Caz rolled her eyes and turned back to the anvil. She was too smart and methodical to ever get caught.

"Enjoy the rest of the memorial, Xan." *Tap, tap, tap, turn.* "Give everyone who was brave enough to attend my excuses."

The door slammed, leaving her with only the tell-tale tendrils of warmth touching her hands. As she tapped away she vaguely wondered who would care for her child until she got home later that night. Vin? No, not Vin. Of course not him. Vin would have important council-member work to catch up on. Or perhaps LRM extracurricular activities. It would be Xander.

Thinking on everything Xander said, Caz had to admit to herself that he was right. Again. But she took solace in the knowledge that he couldn't be right about everything. It was the Heart of Annihilation or the child. Too much work had gone into the Heart to abandon it now. Xander would have to make up the difference in the meantime if he truly wanted to be right.

CHAPTER 12

Rose

I couldn't understand why my face was burning. I wasn't even sure if my heart was beating.

Then there was pain.

A nauseating thrumming centralized near my right shoulder and burned across my entire arm. My mind wanted to retreat into oblivion. Flashing images of Deuces, rifles, airplanes, pistols, and parachutes trampled out another memory clinging to the surface.

I clenched my eyes and then slowly blinked them open, terrified of what I might see. The sun blasted hot rays onto my face. I squinted, turning my head to the side. Brown sand covered everything. The only life visible was a handful of scrappy plants scattered helter-skelter. Dark sand. Darker sand. A scorpion standing on wet, bloody sand.

I felt a strange detachment to the fact that my blood was leaking unchecked across the desert. The scorpion, on the other hand, made me severely uncomfortable.

Without thinking, I lifted my hand to direct a small electrical bolt into the creature. It popped backward with a fizzle, landing on its back a foot away.

A jolt of surprise spasmed my body with pain. I stiffened and stopped breathing, afraid to move. Slowly, I let my breath out in shuddering increments.

I opened my eyes, finding myself face to face with the dead scorpion. Its legs curled over its abdomen where a trail of smoke rose.

Did I just fry that thing? No . . . yes. That was new. Wasn't it? I tried to remember.

The plane. I remembered the plane. The angry faces.

And Thurmond.

Where was he? Why was I here alone? I clenched my fist. Something confined my fingers in a sticky claw. I lifted my hand to see a blood-stained chain entwined around my hand. Twin tags clinked quietly together, and my half-circle pendant flashed a reddish-golden color in the sunlight.

I wanted it. Wanted it so desperately that I had boarded a plane full of hostiles to get it back. No, no. I boarded the plane to save Thurmond. Right?

Don't be ridiculous. The cold voice spoke into my mind with calm reasoning. *Only one thing on that plane mattered. And now you have it back.*

"Who are you?" I shouted, my voice a hoarse croak. A serrated cackle in my head and then silence.

In a sudden moment of frustration I tore at the chain with my teeth, gagging on the rusty taste. It didn't budge. I was alone in the middle of the desert with a bullet in my shoulder.

You stupid, weak child. The voice hammered the ache above my left ear. *Get up. Get up and find help. Save yourself. Save me!*

"Get up," I whispered. I could do this. I had to.

All I really wanted was to sleep. *No.* I wrenched my eyes open. If I slept now there was a good chance I wouldn't wake up.

More for something to do than an overwhelming curiosity over my condition, I gingerly touched the moist fabric of my right shoulder. A jagged hole just below my clavicle oozed blood across my chest and shoulder. The entire sleeve of my uniform clung to my skin with sticky, hot blood. If I were to guess, the bullet was still somewhere inside. But as long as I got medical attention in the very near future, I wouldn't die. I lifted my head with a groan, trying to examine the injury, but the strain of using my neck muscles pulled at the wound. Darkness edged into my vision.

I couldn't die. Not here. Not all alone. Not without answers.

"Dad," I whispered.

Your father is not here. No one is here. No one will save you. They'll all abandon you in the end. There's only you and me. Get up and save us.

Some trembling breaths held the darkness at bay. The voice was right. Well, right and wrong. I wasn't a damsel in distress. I'd gotten myself into this mess. I could get myself out of it.

First things first. Stop the bleeding. Easier said than done. If I could take off my camouflage top I could use it as a bandage. Of course, that meant pulling it off over the wound. The thought made me sick. What else did I have? My pants? Forget it. I felt the bulges of each of my pockets using my left hand. The search yielded my cap and the brown army handkerchief I used to wipe the sweat from my face. I held my breath and rested the folded cap over the injury. I then worked the handkerchief under my armpit. With every ounce of determination and willpower I possessed, I looped the ends over my shoulder and tied it, using my teeth to pull it tight.

I rolled onto my side, gagging and coughing as my body tried to expel the pain through my mouth. When I felt like I would not be dying within the next few minutes, I blew out a breath and swallowed. The bloodied chain slipped from my fingers, where I promptly forgot all about it.

Tears burned my eyes.

Now get up!

Yes, get up. I could do that. I didn't have to save myself. I just needed to get up. As long as I could move, I wasn't dead. *Get up*! I pushed myself onto one elbow, drew my knees under me, and held my injured arm close to my side. The weight of something hung down my back. A quick flip through my memory reminded me that it was the rifle. That was good. A rifle and a single round. I was armed against the commander or Justet's aliens as long as my injury, or the desert, didn't kill me first. I pulled the shoulder strap gently over my head so as not to brush against my makeshift bandage and gazed at my surroundings.

To the left everything was flat desert, broken only by subtle hills. In the distance to the right, dry mountains shouldered dark storm clouds. An aggressive breeze flapped my uniform against my body.

Left or right? According to the sun, left would be south, either taking me toward the Mexican border or Fort Huachuca. The right at least gave a hint of civilization. Electrical towers lined a narrow dirt road, their wires scalloping off toward a substation somewhere. One of the towers standing on a hill looked different from the rest, lopsided with blocky obstructions surrounding it. Something Justet had said niggled at the back of my mind. When he'd spouted about their plan to get the alien's portal, he'd mentioned that they were using an electrical tower as either a power supply or something else.

What would I find when I got there? Aliens? Rethans? Dad?

Keeping the tower in sight, I used the rifle to push myself to my feet. Blood throbbed through the wound. The fingers of my right hand were numb. The sharp edges of the rocks and the individual blades of desert grass fuzzed together into a mesh of color. I used every ounce of concentration to get a lungful of air all the way down the bottom of my lungs. I knew I was still standing simply because I hadn't fallen, but I couldn't feel anything but shivery cloudiness.

Each step was a greater challenge than the previous one. The assistance of the rifle became a burden. I wasn't sure when I discovered that it was no longer in my hand. My vision grew hazy, but always I kept the electrical tower on the hill in my line of sight.

CHAPTER 13

Caz
1 year pre-RAGE

Vin's office in the DC Council building was an extension of everything that drove Caz nuts. The elegant architecture and immaculate décor, with nothing was out of place. Caz stood in the outer office, staring at the blank doorway. She heard Vin's voice on the other side, engaged in the rise and fall of an argument.

It had been months since Caz had been to the office. There was no reason for her to show up. Vin didn't have time for her at home. Why would he have time for her at work?

It didn't matter. She didn't have time for him either.

Today's visit, however, had a purpose that was everything to do with the pretty little thing sitting at the outer desk. Her silvery, light-blue uniform specified her as the young marshal assigned to Vin, responsible for everything from the councilor's paperwork to enforcing the Two Laws when Vin required it. Caz simply knew her from the four other times she'd seen her—spied on her really. A dark surge of loathing filled her stomach.

"New here," Caz checked the name on the desk, "Deputy Veella?"

It was good to finally have a name for her target. Deputy Veella stood upon seeing her, surprise on her narrow face. She slapped her hand to the doorframe, applying a charge to the doorway of Vin's inner office. A web of electricity leapt across the doorframe, cutting through the voices with a zap. The web was more to control sound than actually keep anyone out. There was too much *etiquette* floating around to ever warrant the need for protection.

Caz followed the girl with her eyes.

"Yes." Deputy Veella turned to her. "Sort of. I've been here a few months, actually." The girl's face had been a mask of pleasant neutrality. Now her lips tightened, blunting her surprise. "You can call me Zell. And you must be Mrs. Paliyo."

They stared at each other, a cold surge of energy passing between them as intense as the quiet zapping of the web. What had Vin said about Caz that would make this girl hate her already?

"Ms. Fisk, actually." Caz repressed the wholesome urge to rip this pretty girl's skin from her face. Instead she smiled sweetly. "But, yes, Vin's wife. Had to keep our dear councilor's name separate from that of the *mutineers* didn't we?"

The girl gave a tiny squeak at the shameful slur, her eyes widening. Caz sat down on the corner of the desk, leaving the girl with a choice: stay awkwardly near the door, or sit back at her desk with Caz uncomfortably close.

"Oh, I'm sorry." Caz stood and giggled apologetically into her hand. "This is your desk. Please, please. Sit. I'll take that chair."

The girl frowned, keeping her eyes on Caz but not moving.

"Do you know how long Vin's going to be?" Caz settled in a chair across the room.

She'd met the girl, sized her up, and discovered why Vin would risk her displeasure—again. She tried to feel grateful that he'd chosen to put his efforts into infidelity, rather than the dangerous track he'd been heading down with the Liberated Rage Movement. Of course he'd no longer have his prestigious job if he got too deeply involved, especially now that the idiotic faction had staged a riot that had destroyed a RAGE portal, just so they could "rescue" a few condemned Rethans. That a marshal had lost his life during the incident destroyed any hope of the movement ever gaining the support of the common citizen.

But apparently in Vin's eyes it was better to destroy your spouse than your career.

She glared at the web covering the entrance to his office. She could deal with his perky little mistress later.

"He won't be long." Zell reclaimed her desk. "He's in with his esteemed father, the commandant, but the commandant has a meeting in a few minutes. They'll be out soon."

"Thank you." Caz placed her hands in her lap. She curled her fingers together, forcing them into stillness. A young male marshal entered the office. He placed papers in front of Zell and they chatted pleasantly while Caz stared at the web covering the door, straining to make out the argument. Nothing. Time ticked by. The crackling voices from the other room intensified, and Caz was able to pick out the word "annihilation." Or maybe that was just the word she heard everywhere. She absently drew a half circle on her knee with her finger and then tapped the spot where the center should be. The Rethan symbol for annihilation.

"Mrs. Pa—I mean Ms. Fisk?" Zell startled her.

The marshal had left, and they were alone again.

Caz turned to the girl, her eyebrows high. A smile played on her lips. "Please, call me Caz."

"Caz. Um, right." Zell pushed some hair out of her eyes. "Councilor Paliyo needs to leave shortly after this meeting. I can only give you a few minutes with him."

"*Give* me a few minutes?" Caz smirked.

"Well, a meeting concerning munitions is not on the schedule—"

Caz stood abruptly, causing Zell to lean back in her seat. Her eyes widened in alarm.

"I understand. Believe me. There's such a stigma attached to being a mutineer. But you know, people aren't always what they seem." She arched an eyebrow. "Wouldn't you agree?"

Zell opened her mouth, but before she could respond the net of voltage covering the doorway brightened, and Commandant Paliyo stepped through. He brushed shivering strands of electricity from his shoulders before catching sight of Caz. He halted.

"Cazandra." Deep-seated hatred lay in the cold acknowledgement.

Caz returned the gaze. The feeling was mutual. "Looks like you could use a charge of serenity, *Commandant.*"

Zell leapt from her seat and rushed over to close the door's circuit. The web vanished. Vin stood in the doorway, a younger, thinner, and more handsome version of his father. Beside him another figure slunk out. Vin's younger brother, Ricks, clutched a pile of devices most likely belonging to his esteemed father. The commandant wrenched his gaze away from Caz to glare at his son.

"This is non-negotiable, Vincent. Do it!" Commandant Paliyo turned and exited the outer office, trailing crackling threads of electricity from his robes.

Vin watched his father leave. Ricks went to follow, his shoulders hunched. He was usually hunched for some reason that no amount of serenity could penetrate. Poor lad had fallen through the utopian cracks.

"Hey, Ricks," Caz said cheerily.

He jumped, as though a million amps had shot up his spine. The load in his arms fell to the floor and clattered in every direction. Caz gave him a wide smile, loathing him with the same amount of passion that she loved Vin.

He didn't answer but knelt to gather his scattered items. Caz folded her arms, prepared to goad him a few more times. Vin stepped through the door, inadvertently saving his anode-kissing brother.

"Caz, what in Gauss's law are you doing here?" Vin looked flustered and aggravated. Not himself.

"Can we talk?" Caz kept her voice neutral.

Vin harrumphed noncommittally and turned to Zell. "I have to leave in ten minutes. I'm sending the information to your monitor. Get the specs in order." Vin kicked an IFOD closer to his brother. "Get it together, Ricks." He turned without another word and disappeared into his office.

Zell smiled at Vin's back, glanced at Caz, and then dropped to her knees to help Ricks. Caz followed Vin into his office and set a charge to the door. The web brightened the room. Vin hunched over his desk, meticulously packing a silver case.

"Where's his honor, Esteemed-Unto-Himself, sending you this time?" Caz asked.

"Ather."

She grabbed Vin's arm and yanked him around. Zell, the new deputy. Their romantic dinners on the shore. The sweet way they'd leaned together. The complete disregard for Caz and her claim on her husband. All of that was forgotten.

"The hell he is," Caz snarled.

They glared into each other's eyes with an intensity only possible those who have shared a life.

"I don't have time for this." Vin pried her fingers from his arm and turned back to his case.

"Make time."

Vin answered into his desk. "There's been some damage to the dimensional fabric. That's all. Ather's as safe as any lower dimension."

"Are you serious?" Caz wanted to shout, but the last thing they needed were the marshals in here. She lowered her voice. "They're already under level thirteen surveillance and now you're telling me they have dimensional tears? They're as good as dead."

"My father feels there's a diplomatic solution."

"Diplomatic solution my ass!"

Vin slammed the case shut with a growl. He pressed his palms to his desk, shoulders high.

In an angry sweep he cleared the top of his desk. Com drives, INFODs decorative dishes, lamps, lighters, and even his silver case clinked, clattered, and crackled against the walls and floor. He turned on her, his eyes sparking.

"This is my job, Caz! The commandant orders me to save a dimension and that's what I do! And guess what, sweetheart, I'm damn good at it!"

"Damn good at abandoning your family every chance you get!" Caz fed off of his anger, turning it back on him. "And for what? For some scrawny quean with lips like a coaxial cable?"

Shock jolted through his face. This wasn't the first time one of Vin's indiscretions was discovered. Just the first time Vin had gone to extreme lengths to hide it, or reacted badly when faced with the accusation. Caz narrowed her eyes. This wasn't the way they played the game. There was something more to his deception this time.

"Don't talk to me about abandonment." Vin jabbed his finger at her. "What do you do every single day? Abandon Manny? Hide out in your lab?"

"You want me in the lab! You told me so yourself. 'Get the weapon done.' 'Is it done yet, Caz?' 'When will that weapon be done?'" Caz felt as if her heart were going to burst from her chest. It was usually about this point their personal silentiary marshal was called in to pry them apart and dose them with serenity.

"I can't do this right now." Vin turned away from her and knelt. He brushed aside the scattered debris to retrieve the case he'd packed. He set it back on his desk, opened it, and checked the tossed contents.

He was really leaving again. Caz could deal with the infidelity. She could deal with the lies and even the distance growing between them every day. What she couldn't deal with was losing the other player in the game. She exhaled her animosity and softened her voice.

"Don't go, Vin," Caz said. He turned and leaned against his desk. "What makes you think Ather isn't going to end up like the other six?"

Vin scrubbed his hands across his face in uncharacteristic indecision. Then he looked Caz in the eyes.

"If there's a diplomatic solution, I'll find it."

Of course he would. He was Vin. Nothing was impossible to him. He was so assured, so confident. So *perfect*. And yet she could feel the tension in him, telling her that something was wrong. This was something bigger than an affair. Something that would keep them apart. She raised her hand, hesitated, and then brushed a lock of his hair back into place.

With a half sigh, half growl, Vin rolled his eyes, grabbed her shoulders, and pressed his lips roughly to hers. She wrapped her arms around him and set her teeth to his bottom lip, tasting the metal of his mouth. Caz pulled away first.

"Caz." He rested his forehead against hers, caressing the lobe of her ear between his finger and thumb. "I'm asking you, no, pleading with you. Finish that weapon, whatever it takes."

He released her, slammed the case shut, and locked it with a charge. In one movement he swung the case from his desk and disappeared through the crackling web.

Finish the weapon? Caz pressed her hands against her head until an ache started in her temples. No, "take care of our son?" No, "I'll be back before you know it?" Not even an, "I love you." It was, "finish that weapon whatever it takes."

Caz slapped her hand to the doorframe, absorbing the energy of the web. She paused in the doorway. Vin's shoe vanished around the corner. Only then did she realize she wasn't alone with Zell.

Xander stooped in the center of the room, holding Manny's hand. The five-year-old's fingers were dwarfed in his uncle's hand. Zell crouched before them, her uniform pulled tight against her scrawny ass, an adoring smile stretched across her insipid face. As she spoke to the boy in sticky tones, Xander reached up and touched Zell's face.

Caz's stomach dropped, adding weight to the load already there. How could she have missed this? They were too familiar with each other. Not familiar—familial.

She felt apart. Already abandoned by Vin, and now by the one person she never thought possible.

Only Manny saw her standing there. Did she still have the dregs of anger on her face? It didn't seem to matter to her son, because he pushed past his uncle and raced to her. She caught him under his arms and squeezed him to her. He giggled in her ear, rubbing his chubby cheek against hers.

She didn't deserve his love, and her guilt nearly overpowered her affection for this little creature. She squeezed him tighter. It would be all right. He would never abandon her. Not like Vin. Not like Xander. The liars.

CHAPTER 14

Rose

"Rose!"

The word drew me away from the darkness. Light and heat scorched my eyelids. Dad?

"Rose! Dammit, where are you?"

The voice raced across the unknown, responding to my silent question. No, not Dad. Dad wouldn't call me Rose. Or swear. There was quiet again.

"Rose!"

"Thurmond." My voice croaked. I pried my eyes open and found myself staring into a bush, body leaning against a large boulder.

My limbs were rigid and achy. My cheeks felt wet. I brushed a hand across the moisture on my face. My other hand hung limp and numb beside me.

"Rose!" Thurmond finally came into sight. I rolled my eyes upward to see him better, blinking rapidly to clear my vision. Dust covered one side of his uniform, clinging to what looked like a lot of blood. He held a rifle in his hands. My rifle? I dropped my eyes to my empty hands.

"I'm so sorry. The wind caught the chute and dragged me way in the other direction, and when I got back to the place where I dropped you . . . I've been tracking you for hours. Where the hell did you think you were going?" He fell to his knees beside me. Thurmond lightly touched the blood-saturated handkerchief.

"Ah—" I exhaled in anticipation of his touch.

"Dammit, Rose, you're bleeding all over the place." He retracted his hand, his eyes wide. Then his brows descended and his voice changed to deep anger. "What'd you let that little ass shoot you for?"

"What?"

"You couldn't have shot him first or something?" He pulled off his camouflage jacket with angry yanks, balled it up, and pushed it none too gently against my shoulder.

"H-hold on—" I gasped, clenching my eyes shut.

"That's what rifles are for, you know."

I wanted to cry, but I could barely swallow.

"And here we are, out in the desert without so much as a field bandage." He took a deep breath and released it noisily. When he spoke again, it was with the cool calm I associated with Thurmond's military efficiency. "Let's get this bleeding stopped."

I peeked from under teary lids to see Thurmond pulling his t-shirt over his head. He pressed it flat across his lap, folding it over several times.

Some distant, semi-conscious part of me wanted to admire his flat stomach, with its hint of a six-pack and well-defined chest, sun glistening in the beads of sweat nestled among the trivial amount of chest hair. It was nice here in semi-consciousness. Nice and toned.

Thurmond removed the wadded jacket from my shoulder and pressed the neatly-folded, brown t-shirt on top of my saturated handkerchief. Fiery shards of pain brought my fingers to life, burning up across my chest, returning me to full consciousness.

"Ow! Thurmond. Ow. Ouch," I whimpered my way into a pained silence.

"Hold this here."

My hand was shaking but I managed to locate the folded shirt and hold it in place. Thurmond pulled a knife off his belt. He cut and tore the sleeves off of his camouflage jacket and then ripped them into long strips.

I was aware, in an abstract way, of Thurmond tying the shirt to my shoulder with the strips of fabric he'd cut from the camouflage.

"Th-thanks." I rubbed my eyes with a finger and thumb. "You know, for the bandage, and the lecture."

"After following your trail for damn near eternity, I figured it couldn't be so bad . . . even after all the blood you left. I mean, you made it this far." That sounded suspiciously respectful. His tone softened. "Sorry I yelled."

"S'okay."

Thurmond sat back on his heels, an uncertain twitch at the corner of his mouth. His hands were covered in blood and lay palm up on his knees, as though he didn't know what to do with them. After a moment he rubbed his palms on his pants and then rose to his feet. He slid his arms through the gaping holes of his sleeveless camouflage jacket and fastened it with unhurried, meticulous fingers. I blinked away the haze and started to push myself to my feet.

"What do you think you're doing?"

"Getting up."

The world fuzzed and darkened. Thurmond called my name from somewhere at the end of a long tunnel, his voice growing louder and louder. The earth under my feet became concrete, the sun hot atop my head, and the arms around my back more than an ethereal presence. My face was pressed against a solid, warm body. I opened my eyes to find myself leaning against Thurmond's chest, one of his arms tight around my back and his voice loud in my ears. I breathed in his scent of soap and sweat.

"S'all good. S'okay." I pushed away from his chest, and he released me with the greatest reluctance. One of his hands remained tight on my arm. I held my other close to my body. "Where're we?"

"Sonoran desert. Somewhere in the vicinity of Fort Huachuca, if I were to guess." Thurmond sounded worried. "We fell out of the plane. Don't you remember?"

"Of course I remember." The words came out clearer now. "I was just wondering how close we are to the tower?"

"Oh. Yeah, it's right there." He rubbed his hand across his scalp, turning his eyes to the left. I followed his gaze. Storm clouds behind the tower swathed the tops of the mountains, roiling deep and close. "Once I figured out that's where you were heading, you were easier to track. I'm gonna go see what I can find."

You want answers? You'll find them there, said the voice.

"Okay, then. Let's go. Just, you know, don't let me fall and bash my head open or anything." I made to move, but Thurmond held me back.

"You're not going anywhere, Rose."

"I'm fine. It'll be fine." I blinked away the fog. "I'll just walk with you 'til the ambulance arrives."

"I'll be much faster if I don't have to drag you along." He wasn't looking at me anymore but studying the landscape, his mind making the heroic trek for help.

"I told you, I can walk."

"We're wasting time."

"I just—"

"What?" He finally looked at me. Irritation and worry tightened his mouth.

I felt about ten years old, pestering Dad to get him to take me with him on his business trip to California, rather than having to stay with a sitter. "No, Krissy, the DLA's not a place for little girls. Too scary," he'd said, his expression stern, his eyes distant. "I'll only be a few days." The few days turned into an unprecedented few weeks, and my grudge lasted a few months beyond that. His face was haunted every time I'd brought it up, and he'd never left me that long again.

Even the memory brought the taste of abandonment to my tongue. Would I find a RETHA coin in Thurmond's place after he'd left? Would I be left wondering where he'd gone for the rest of my—granted, probably short—life?

Wait . . . DLA? I shook my head. Why hadn't I recalled this memory before now? *The* DLA. I squinted over at Thurmond, trying to remember our argument.

"I just don't want to be left alone here, in the desert—" I tried to smile through the encroaching anger "—with Justet's aliens and scorpions and stuff."

"There's no such thing as aliens," Thurmond said slowly, as if he wanted to yell but didn't think it was appropriate to yell at someone who'd been shot. I had no such reservations.

"Well I wish you'd been around to tell Justet that back in the armory!" Anger flushed my cheeks. The spot above my left ear throbbed.

"Give me a break." Thurmond rolled his eyes.

"Not to mention that Justet and the commander are probably going to be driving around, looking for us."

"And you want to expend your remaining strength climbing that damn hill when I could—"

"Why do you get to be right? Why can't I be right this time?"

"Because I am!" Thurmond was yelling now too, his face red.

"What are you, my father?"

"That depends. Do you listen to your father?"

"Hey, I know. Why don't we stand around and argue while I bleed to death?"

The two feet separating us seemed to widen even while our heads butted together in uncompromising conviction. My resolve wavered. A tear tickled down my cheek. I brushed it away and dropped my eyes.

I hated the clinging whininess of my voice. The desperate pleading. My mortality loomed over me, a giant red-eyed monster, waiting for Thurmond to look away long enough to drag me to hell.

"Fine," Thurmond conceded in irritation. He hitched the rifle more securely onto his shoulder. Then, as if remembering something, he turned back and reached into his pocket. A bloodied chain raked across the edge of the fabric. My dog tags and pendant followed.

My first reaction was surprise that Thurmond was holding it when I very clearly remember it entangled in my fingers. Then fury scorched my throat. I snatched for the tags like the strike of a cobra.

"Holy shit!" Thurmond drew as far away from me as possible without letting go and clutched the tags close to his chest.

The sudden movement caught up with me. I wheezed in breath after breath. The maniacal desperation receded, but I still wanted them.

"Sorry. I'm sorry. I—"

"What the hell was that?"

"I . . . what was? Nothing . . . it was nothing. Can I . . ." I held out my hand for the tags.

We stared at each other for another few seconds. Thurmond cocked a cautioning eyebrow and released me to the care of the boulder. He removed the broken section of chain, wrapping the remaining chain around my neck, and reconnected it. The chain was much shorter now, fitting snugly against my throat. The warmth of the pendant contrasted with the coolness of the tags. I rubbed it between two fingers, the way I always did when I was in need of my father's comfort. Then I pulled up the neck of my sweaty shirt to hide the tags.

Thurmond's fingers grazed my cheek, his lips pressed together. He turned toward the tower and immediately dropped to his knees, pulling me down with him. I groaned my disapproval. Thurmond stared over the boulder and drew the rifle from his shoulder.

"Someone's coming," he murmured.

"Really?" My stomach gave a hopeful jerk. "Someone as in . . . ?"

He pulled the rifle up. His thumb flicked the safety.

"What?" Worry replaced the hope and settled deep into my chest. I pictured the commander and Justet charging in to finish us off.

"Okay, you know how Justet was talking about aliens out here?" His finger hovered over the trigger.

"Yeah?" I drew out the word.

"Well, there's someone coming—and I think . . . I'm thinking it might be them."

CHAPTER 15

"Them who? Aliens?" I leaned around Thurmond, trying to see what he was seeing. "There's no such thing as aliens. Remember?"

At first glance it looked like the sun reflecting off a line of shiny objects, until I realized the objects were moving. Figures sorted themselves out like a mirage shimmering in the hot desert air. Their legs flickered in and out of oblivion, becoming more solid as they descended the hill. The four figures stretched out in a long parallel line, a good ten feet separating each one.

Arms and legs, heads and torsos, all with the correct proportions to be human. Each was relatively normal-sized aside from a singular figure standing head and shoulders above the rest. He was so enormous that Andre the Giant came to mind. They approached with silky steps, their legs moving so rapidly that my mind struggled to make the leap. The sun glinting off of their silver, metallic-looking hair and white, almost translucent skin also gave them away as something different—something alien.

They wore metallic blue uniforms of sorts, their pants tucked into white boots military style. As they came closer, I was able to discern a distinct jogging pattern over the shoulders and descending across of the uniform that looked like silver lightning bolts—rank, if I were to guess.

A shiver stole through my body, drawing tingling voltage from every cell. Electricity ran across each individual nerve ending, intensifying every sensation. Sunlight blinded me, scents of dirt and heat assaulted my nose, and the crunching of distant footsteps were as loud as if they were walking right by my head.

One of the visitors spoke. I jumped. The sensory-overload vanished, and the voice became as distant as they actually were.

"She's around here somewhere. Deputy Hoth obtained a visual not more than ten minutes ago."

The person's soft face and curving figure gave her a feminine appearance, and the way she spoke clearly identified her as their leader—not to mention the five stripes of lightning across her shoulder. Her voice croaked in a harsh, raspy, crackling tone, reminding me of electricity. And of anger, and mayhem, and an inexplicable act of violence I somehow knew I didn't want to remember.

I wanted to hold my hands to my ears to block everything out, but I couldn't move. I couldn't look away. I couldn't hide.

Two males flanked the female, one the Andre the Giant-sized one and the other a small, ratty individual holding some sort of white instrument. The fourth, a male of average height, with a ponytail, trailed behind the others. Their heads moved this way and that, searching.

Thurmond lay the barrel of the rifle across the rock and sighted down its length.

"Don't waste my round," I whispered. I had an indeterminate plan for that round, and I didn't see how it could help against a bunch of strange folk with powers yet unknown.

"Can't you pinpoint her exact location?" The female said, hand on her hip and expression impatient.

"Well, uh, no. Her dimensional camouflage has rendered the signal unreliable. But she's here." The rat-like male said, and if the timbre of his voice wasn't so bizarre, I would have thought he sounded frightened.

"Spread out!" the female commanded, and her troops peeled off. The only one left was the female, and she seemed to be staring at our boulder.

The ache above my ear split my head with pain.

Kill them before they find you. Kill them. Kill them!

"Shoot her," I said in a soft guttural tone.

"What?" Thurmond glanced at me.

Icy calm spread through my limbs, bringing with it the tingling sensation of voltage. Anger surged from the ache above my ear. I had no doubt at that moment the female would have a bullet between her eyes if I'd had the rifle and the ability to fire it. I flexed my fingers. A movement in my peripherals jolted the anger out of me.

Silver, pupil-less eyes stared into mine from the right of the boulder. They were set deeply into a thick head and rimmed with silvery-white lashes. Silver stubble covered a square jaw, which sat atop Andre the Giant's body. He crouched, eye level to me, with one of his hands rested on the boulder and the other lay clenched on a muscled thigh. A deep, tangy odor, like the smell of the earth after the rain—*ozone*—washed over me, filling me with a hint of familiarity and a sensation I could only describe as affection. Then I tasted fear.

"Here!" His rumbling voice was as enormous as his body.

I rose slowly. Blood pumped in my ears. He also stood, towering over me, silver eyes locked onto my face.

"Step back, sir!" The butt of the rifle rested against Thurmond's shoulder as he aimed at the guy's chest.

My legs ceased to exist. The rock scraped my back as I slid down onto my butt, my shoulder throbbing. I had only a vague perception of what was going on around me. Shadowy figures blocked the blazing sun while voices rang hollow and indistinct. Deep breathing of the hot desert air helped my vision clear, and I found that we were surrounded by a tight circle of Justet's aliens.

"Is that really her?" asked a tall thin man. Not man. Alien. His long hair was tied back in a ponytail. Revulsion twisted his face.

"Looks like her." The small, rat-like male said. His apparent fear of me was almost as strange as everything else about him. Ponytail Guy threw an arm across the female's chest, pushing her back a step.

"All of you! Back off!" Thurmond shouted.

Andre the Giant released my gaze, flicking his eyes toward Thurmond. There was a minute tightening of his lips and, in a flash of movement, he smacked the rifle out of Thurmond's hands.

Thurmond tripped backward, striking my shoulder with his leg and jarring pain through my body. I clutched my arm, unable to suppress a whimper as the rifle clattered to the ground near my feet. Andre the Giant pressed a large ham-like forearm against Thurmond's neck, holding him against the boulder.

With Thurmond disarmed, the female approached. Her look was cold and penetrating. An involuntary shudder spread to my extremities, and

I felt as much as heard a retreating hiss within my mind. Two more cautious steps put the female at my feet. She crouched before me, stared for an eternity, and then extended her hand.

"Get away from her!" Thurmond shoved at his captor.

One of the dish-sized fists plowed into the side of Thurmond's head. His breath exploded in a gasp, his eyes crossed, and he clutched the arms of Andre the Giant to keep himself on his feet.

Aggression channeled through my arms and into my hands in a blinding burst of energy. With a crackle of jagged, blue light, the burst of electricity struck the female in the shoulder. She barreled over backward, smashing into Ponytail Guy and the little rat-like fellow.

Ponytail Guy shrugged the female out of his arms and lunged at me. With an agonizing stab to my shoulder, I discharged a second burst of voltage at him. The volt sizzled a jagged knife of light across his arm. He wrenched his whole body to the side.

A movement to my left had me redirecting my other hand. Andre the Giant rested his fingertips lightly on Thurmond's chest. My eyes traveled from his unreadable expression to Thurmond.

Thurmond's mouth hung open, but as he saw me looking, his jaw slowly clenched and his eyebrows furrowed. This look was one I had no trouble interpreting. The ache in my head retreated, leaving me empty and cold. I lowered my hand.

Ponytail Guy pulled himself to his feet and reached over to help the female. The rat-like one stayed on the ground where she'd flattened him, the rapid rise and fall of his chest the only indication he hadn't been crushed to death. The leader's fingers clenched the shoulder of her uniform. She drew her hand away for a quick glance beneath it. A black scorch mark marred the silver lightning and blue fabric. Her eyes flashed back to mine.

"All the violence of the Slayer in a brand new package," her rasping voice dripped with disgust.

"What're you talking about?" My mind felt sludgy and rumpled.

The female rubbed her hands across her neck, softly touching some red indentations, like finger-sized scars. I wondered if the scars had anything to do with her rough voice.

"Inmate two-three-six, you are currently in violation of code two-twenty-two stating that no felon shall approach closer than five hundred grid lengths of—"

"What?" I interrupted her lawyer-esque ramblings before my brain imploded.

She narrowed her eyes. "What in Gauss's law are you doing here?"

"Fell from a plane." I leaned my head against the rock. The effort of trying to make sense of anything was almost too much. But something nagged at my mind. "Did you call me . . . inmate? You said felon too."

I caught Thurmond's eye. A wad of saliva caught in my throat. There was distrust in Thurmond's face, and it bothered me more than the less-than-friendly aliens or even my tortured body. I pictured what it would be like for me if he suddenly sprouted a cape and flew through the air. Or maybe it was more like sprouting tentacles.

The female snapped her fingers.

"Inmate would be a polite term for someone like you, but yes, inmate. Your sentence here precludes contact with any Rethan of non-convict status. So you can imagine why we're not necessarily happy to see you so close to our base of operations."

A shiver raised the hair on my arms before tremoring down my spine and across my buttocks and legs. I swallowed.

"R-Rethan? As in Retha?" I attempted to rise. The female ignored my question and reached for me. I slapped her hand away and fell back, breathing heavily against a shock of pain. I forced the words between clenched teeth. "What'd you freaks do with my dad?"

"I don't know what you're talking about." The female rubbed the back of her hand.

"My dad, Benjamin Rose. You're Rethan, you have to know . . . you have to know." The pain was too much. Tears rose to my eyes.

The female ignored the question, her expression cool. She offered her hand to me again. Did she want me to shake it?

Don't let her touch you. Don't let her touch you.

"I'm the officiate here," she paused. "Please, we need to confirm your identity." When I still didn't move she blew out an exasperated breath. "I don't intend to harm you."

"Get away from me!"

Her lips tightened, and she snatched the fingers of my right hand. Pain warped up my arm. Her skin was chilling, a cold foreign feel that only exacerbated the shivery feeling I couldn't banish despite the heat of the desert. I tried to retract my hand, but she held tight.

Something silver flashed between her fingers, and she pressed it into my palm. Cold seared my skin, followed by an electrical jolt. She released my hand and stepped back, taking the silver torture device with her. Rat Face appeared at her shoulder. Ponytail Guy crowded on her other side. Together they stared down at my hand.

My fingers curled over my palm. A quiet hiss and then a miniscule trail of smoke rose from my palm. I gasped and jerked my hand off my lap, my fingers spreading apart to distribute the intensity. Rune-like characters appeared in a silver, glowing sequence across my palm.

As quickly as it set upon me, the blistering decreased to a faint burn and the glowing of the silver muted to a black, tarnished look. A quiet hiss of sound filled my mind and quickly graduated to angry mutterings.

Damn marshals . . . RAGE . . .

What was this? A trick of some kind? Some alien trick to make me think I was someone else, to throw me off kilter?

"That's her!"

"The DCC Slayer!"

"Gauss's law!"

Clenching my teeth against the pain, I grabbed the rifle and used it to drag myself to my feet. Yellow spots popped out in my vision. I scowled at the four of them to prove I wasn't weak and with an arch of my eyebrows, I hitched the rifle to my shoulder. Left shoulder, left hand, awkward as all get out, but it was up. I couldn't muster the energy needed to raise the muzzle to point anywhere but the gaggle of white boots. Not to mention my hand was shaking so badly I didn't think touching the trigger was a good idea.

"Stand back!" Ponytail Guy spread his arms wide to push everyone back.

Their hands disappeared into pockets, making me wary of hidden weapons.

Andre the Giant released Thurmond and stepped back with his comrades. Thurmond pulled himself upright. He rubbed his knuckles across the purpling bruise on his jaw where he'd been struck.

I groaned, losing my grip on reality. Somewhere voices continued to argue.

Watch your mouth. Watch your mouth, the voice inside my head sounded more like a warning than a threat. Colors and images whirled around me. *Careful now. Don't let her touch you again. Don't let her touch—*

"Looks like she's found a companion here."

The words came from a muddy, fuzzy someone who didn't look remotely real. I swayed on my nonexistent feet. I squeezed my eyes shut to hide from the blackness surrounding me.

CHAPTER 16

Caz
9 months pre-RAGE

It was one of those rare, early evenings home. Caz's work on the Heart of Annihilation had come to a standstill thanks to some red tape from the finance council, and Caz couldn't find anything else in the lab to justify her time.

The seat in Vin's personal vehicle was stiff, the interior dark and cool. Caz brushed her hands across her lap in an attempt to remove a few stray flecks of ash, then gazed out the tinted window. Attikin dome towered above the city on her left, visible even through the cold smog covering the city grid. She flicked a stubborn spot on her knee and then removed a cloth from her pocket. She touched the cloth to her tongue and scrubbed at the spot with sudden fury.

Vin had been gone for three months now, exactly eleven days late. That in and of itself didn't bother Caz. He'd been gone for lengthy periods before and she'd always used that time to torment, torture, and basically destroy whatever newest girl-toy Vin had fallen for.

What did bother her was how Zell was doubled-dipping in the family pool. She'd become engaged to Xander within the last few days, which was bad enough, but the real trouble was Caz's own son. Caz twisted the cloth around and around her finger while staring unseeing out the window.

Manny had developed quite the affection for her. Almost like hero worship. She was pretty and sweet, kind and soft spoken. Everything Caz wasn't. Manny still found it in himself to greet her when she approached, but with much less passion than he used to show.

A delicate touch was needed to pry his affection away from Zell before Caz destroyed her. Caz hadn't had the time nor energy to give to such an endeavor. Until today.

The vehicle hummed to a stop, and Caz shoved the door open. She stepped out, waving off the driver before he could attempt to help her with her bag. He looked relieved, and pulled away as soon as she was out.

Caz stared after the vehicle, hefting the bag in her hand. It was light, only containing some INFODs she'd lifted from her parent's impossibility file. She was sure with a few tweaks she'd be able to find a solution to each concept and create a usable weapon. A little something to occupy her hands while letting her mind work out the Zell problem.

Caz's shoes zapped against the coppered road, drawing in the energy from the grid to fill her body. She was used to the electrical deficiency in the lab, but not so much that she didn't enjoy filling her bodily reservoir upon reentry into the real world. She applied a charge to the high gate surrounding the mansion Vin had built for them before Manny was born. Government officials weren't held to the same economic standard as the rest of Retha, although with the amount of time Caz and Vin spent there, she wondered if Vin hadn't gone too far.

The gate swung open, revealing the long curving walk up to the steely structure. A rare ray of sunlight filtered through the sullen clouds, illuminating a spark of light and movement.

Caz slowed. Xander bent over the walk below, examining a smattering of silver beads covering the ground. Manny stood to beside him, a black Pyk Styk in his hand, a smirk lifting the corners of his mouth. Xander knelt on the ground, looking closer at the beads, and then stood. A bright grin stretched across his face. He picked up his own Pyk Styk, positioned it next to a bead, and applied a charge into the handle of the Styk. A pink jolt of electricity powered into the bead, popping it to the left. It rattled and then magnetized to the ground several inches from the intended target, a silver circle.

Xander dropped his chin to his chest and groaned. Manny chortled, thumping the Pyk Styk against his shoe. Another giggle sounded from the portico, followed by brief applause.

Caz's eyes zeroed in on the sound. She didn't even realize she'd been smiling until her grin vanished, making her face feel oddly flat.

Zell lounged on the bench under the window, the collar of her blue marshal uniform pulled loose at the neck, a command screen forgotten on her lap as she applauded Manny's victory over his uncle.

Manny applied two charges to his Pyk Styk, sending first one then other bead into the circle. Zell cheered each new point. When he finally missed, giving the turn back to Xander, Manny mounted the steps and collapsed next to Zell. She brushed her fingers through his hair, and they laughed as Xander tried and failed again.

Caz took a moment to imagine the players changed in this little scenario. She saw herself on the bench, Vin holding the childish Pyk Styk. Manny was the only character who remained the same, turning his delighted, silvery eyes on her for approval, cuddling close and interlacing his small, cool fingers with hers.

Caz shivered away the image and clenched the handle of her bag. She looked away from the happy group and inhaled to govern her emotions.

"Manny!" she called, letting her voice lilt in false pleasure.

"Mother?" Manny sat up straight, his eyebrows disappearing into the shaggy, silver hair covering his forehead. He was off the bench in an instant. He leapt across the beads and brushed by Xander, covering the distance in the rapid, yet clumsy strides of a young, growing Rethan.

"Mother! Is Father coming home today? We heard he was coming so we came here to wait."

Manny grabbed her hand and led her toward the house, chattering all the while. Caz let him drag her along, only half comprehending his words. Had he always spoken so well?

"Did you hear the sirens earlier? They didn't last long so Uncle Xan says it couldn't be an entire dimension, just a storm or something. The sky's been crazy though, and I absorbed enough energy to defeat Uncle Xan five times at Pyk Styk. Will you play? Can we play with Father when—"

Caz shook his hand free of hers. "There were sirens?"

Manny suddenly looked unsure. He turned to his uncle.

Sirens. The early warning systems set in place decades ago to warn Rethans of voltage fluctuations that might interfere with their lives. Usually they sounded when a particularly bad electrical storm loomed, but it didn't negate the real reason they existed. The last time the Thirteenth Dimension destroyed a lower dimension almost a century ago, the voltage fluctuations had created massive damage to the power grid and infrastructure and caused an untold number of deaths. She'd heard first-hand accounts of when Thera, the Fourth Dimension, had been anni-hilated, and the panic the voltage fluctuations had caused. The sirens nowadays simply warned the public to shut down any device using over ten thousand amps and pay attention to the voltage in their bodies.

Of course, most Rethans didn't have a loved one on an unstable dimension already under level thirteen surveillance and experiencing dimensional tears.

Caz's hands tingled.

"Xander!" She left Manny behind and strode as quickly as she could to where Xander was collecting the beads into a small bag. Her voice was angry and hoarse. "What sirens?"

Clouds closed over the sun, leaving them in standard Rethan half-light. The amiable atmosphere that had permeated the space was gone, blown away by a frigid breeze. Zell was on her feet, her expression con-fused. Xander stood, rattling the beads in the bags.

"Yeah, Caz, there were sirens. Don't worry, they only lasted a few min-utes." Xander frowned, retrieved the Pyk Styks and set them on the steps. "What are you doing here?"

Caz shrugged, "What are *you* doing here?"

"Like Manny said, we heard Vin was coming home today. We're wait-ing for him."

Caz nodded slowly. She glanced at Zell, who had gone completely still, her expression cold. Caz narrowed her eyes. A sound behind drew her attention. She turned, finding that she'd forgotten to close the gate. A blue marshal vehicle slunk into the yard. Electricity sparked against the bot-tom of the vehicle in a sharp blue light. It didn't shut down. A half a dozen uniformed Rethans made their way out of the vehicle and up the walk.

Caz didn't like being caught off guard, but she liked the particular marshal leading the group even less. Marshal Lafe's white boots and light blue uniform with triple silver stripes of lightning across her left shoulder specified her rank. Rumor had it she would be the next high officiate, but Caz only knew her as the one who pried her and Vin apart when they were at each other's throats. She was their unofficial Silentiary, hired by the commandant himself to preserve Vin's reputation.

Her soft features effectively hid her darker, more serious nature. Quite an anomaly by Rethan standards. Caz had made the mistake of underestimating her only once. Her eye twitched at the memory.

In the past Marshal Lafe had always come alone. So why now was she accompanied by so many deputies?

The deputies, wearing low-ranking white uniforms, trailed shreds of electricity from the still running vehicle as they fell into formation. Marshal Lafe made her way to the front of the group. Caz gave Manny a gentle shove toward Xander. She held up a hand to stop the marshals.

"Gauss's law, Lafe," Caz kept her voice low. She didn't need any skeletons expelled from her closet in front of her son. "What are you doing here?"

"Cazandra Fisk." Marshal Lafe let her voice carry. She wasn't looking at Caz, rather at the group near the steps. "There has been an incident on one of the lower dimensions that warrants your immediate—"

"Don't talk down to me."

"Keep your voice down, Cazandra," Marshal Lafe stated, this time more confidentially, and locked eyes with hers. "I'd hate to have to charge you with a breach of the Two Laws, today of all days."

"Then screw the fanfare and tell me why you're here, you simpering—"

"It's Ather." She didn't soften her delivery of the information. "All intelligence states that within the next few minutes they will—"

A siren wailed in the distance, instantly sparking echoing wails from closer warning stations. Surges of light pulsed in the sky, altering the flow of the current within Caz's body. Her legs and torso were suddenly absent. A Rethan would say it was a result of the voltage fluctuations, but Caz sensed the significant absence of something else.

"I tried to tell you, Cazandra." Marshal Lafe remained expressionless. "We lost contact with Councilor Paliyo, and now that Ather's gone," she gestured at the sky with a nod, "we have no way of knowing if he made it out in time."

With her other hand Marshal Lafe removed an INFOD from a pocket and held it out to Caz.

Caz couldn't move. Her hands were now missing along with the rest of her body. A thin arm reached from somewhere beside her. Zell retrieved the drive. There was a brief lilt to her lips but the expression was gone a second later, replaced by dramatic sadness. Zell had done up her top button, making her look much more official.

"I'm sorry, Ms. Fisk." Marshal Lafe's voice was clinical and detached. "Councilor Vincent Paliyo was the most inspiring leader we've had in years. He lived the laws of etiquette and serenity as an example for all of us."

"What does that mean, Mother?" Manny's voice came as from a great distance. "What does she mean?"

"Retha will mourn him as they did your parents," Marshal Lafe continued.

"Is she talking about Father?" Caz felt a tug on her arm. "Mother! The sirens! Father is on Ather! What does she mean? Mother!"

The distress in Manny's voice, the insistent tugging on her arm, the wild fluctuations of the new voltage within her body slammed into her, a million amps shocking her into motion.

Caz shook free the hand tearing at her sleeve. A scream threatened to escape her throat. Certainly the marshals were here at the request of the commandant to smooth over any rumors that might have surfaced about Vin and his unstable wife. Save his son's image, where he couldn't save his life.

"Mother!"

"Xander, take him!" Caz snarled. Manny sobbed, reaching for her as Xander carried him to the house.

Caz snaked out a hand and grabbed the front of the marshal's uniform. She dragged her close until she smelled the sour ozone of her breath.

"Marshal Lafe," she whispered so no one else could hear. "You can go back and tell the commandant that if he doesn't free up my funding I'll make damn sure he ends up on a cenotaph with his son. Now get the hell off my property."

Marshal Lafe maintained her cool indifference. She pried Caz's fingers from her uniform. "I'm not going to warn you again, Caz. Maintain propriety, or my deputies will need to apply a charge of serenity."

"And I'm warning you, if I don't have my funding cleared in the next hour *no one* will need a charge of serenity."

"Deputies!" Marshal Lafe barked the command. "Marshal Veella!"

Zell jerked to attention. Rage scorched through Caz's veins. She plunged her fist into the side of Marshal Lafe's face and felt something break under her knuckles. Her other hand gripped the thin throat, holding the soon-to-be high officiate on her feet. Her fingers clawed into the cool flesh. Bright blood dripped from her fingers.

Demands and cries reached her ears. Hands crawled across her body. Her fingers raked across Marshal Lafe's flesh. Caz was forced to the ground, face down. Her own screams filled her ears, an animalistic sound full of pain and fury. A palm and fingers crowned her head. A charge plunged through her scalp.

Unnatural calm attempted to brick the rage into a contained space in her head. She screamed again, fighting for control of her mind, wrestling against the hands that held her. Another charge, more intense this time. Her limbs stiffened in a spasm. Her eyelids fluttered. Tranquility flooded through her, drowning the screams, eliminating the fight in her body, obliterating who she was.

She retreated from the pain and unnatural confliction devouring her mind. As she was drawn into unconsciousness, Caz's last thought was to wonder how she was going to get to the lab when she couldn't seem to stay awake.

Vin told her to finish the weapon. His last words to her were to finish the weapon no matter what. She had to finish the weapon. No matter what.

CHAPTER 17

Rose

"Rose." Thurmond's voice cut through the haze of unconsciousness. "Rose! Come on, wake up."

I forced my eyes open, blinking heavily. I panicked for a moment, not knowing where I was.

Thurmond held me tight to his chest, one arm under my knees, the other putting pressure on my back. He tromped up the hill toward the electrical tower, his breath heavy under my weight. He glanced at me, saw my eyes open, and grunted, his mouth pressed in a hard line.

"Wha-appened?" I asked, my mouth dry, my foggy mind refusing to fill in the blanks.

"Well," he said. "We are officially being abducted by your aliens."

The one who'd called herself the officiate led the way, the shadow of the electrical tower cutting large stripes across her body. Her pace was slow, and she didn't look behind her to see if we were behaving. The ratty Rethan stumbled along just behind her. He walked in a weird, crabbing, sideways manner, refusing to remove his eyes from us for even a second. I looked over Thurmond's shoulder to see Andre the Giant trailing along behind us. He held my rifle slung across his shoulder and when he saw me looking, I caught the briefest lifting of his lips that could have been a smile.

"They're Justet's," I said, looking away.

"What?"

"They're Justet's aliens," I repeated, the words coming a bit easier now. "Not mine."

Thurmond grunted again.

"What'd I miss?"

"Well, these Rethans are taking us up to their creepy camp so they can fill out paperwork or some crap."

"'Kay." That didn't sound too bad.

"Also, thanks to my mad negotiation skills, they know about the commander and Justet coming to do them in."

"Oh—"

"And now they think the commander is responsible for their portal being down and they want you to charge it."

"With what?"

Thurmond paused, huffing, and fixed me with a cool look. I bunched the shoulder of his uniform in a tight grip and he started walking again.

"Like, with . . . electricity?" I asked, hesitant to say the word. "What do I look like, a giant, friggin' car battery?"

"What the hell's going on here?" Thurmond said softly, questioning rather than angry.

"How should I know?" Distance yawned between us even though we couldn't physically be any closer. My limbs trembled. I thought I might be sick.

"I saw you zap them with your fingers. That's not exactly normal, you know." The accusation was direct, the suspicion biting. "If your hair were a different color I'd assume you were one of them."

"That's completely unfair! I'm on your side, okay? I-I never did anything like that before yesterday, I swear. But then when Justet . . ." I couldn't finish. I didn't have a good explanation anyway. "I'm not an alien—or a Rethan—or whatever. I've lived on Earth my whole life. You can ask my dad." Realizing I'd made a mistake, I closed my mouth.

"Yeah . . . about your dad—"

"Forget it, T," I said. "I don't want to talk about it."

He didn't say anything, making me feel worse. If I weren't so certain I'd do a face plant, I would have jumped out of his arms and made my own way up the doggone hill.

"You know," I said. Why couldn't I just be quiet? "I could understand it when you got mad at me on the plane for coming after you. I even got your anger when you were bandaging me up, even if it was just the panic talking." I was rewarded with a quiet grunt. "But I thought volting those guys back there was helping. I kinda hoped you wouldn't hold it against me."

Thurmond maintained a blasé silence, not even providing another grunt of acknowledgement. His step remained steady. I rubbed at the pendant underneath my shirt and closed my eyes. Anger and tension churned the silence and suddenly it burst from my lips.

"Dammit, Thurmond, say something!"

Thurmond was so surprised he swung my feet to the ground. I wobbled there for a moment, but he held me steady. I looked up to see a perplexed, half smirk on his face.

"Did you just . . . ? You never swear."

I ground my teeth, regretting my outburst. "My dad always said swearing was the effort of a feeble mind trying to express itself."

"Yeah?" Thurmond returned a deadpan stare. "Well, my dad always said if he didn't know any cuss words he'd never have anything to say to me."

"Why are you doing this, Thurmond?" I asked, desperate to know where we stood.

"Doing what?"

"Helping me. Being my friend. You've as much as said you don't trust me."

Thurmond was silent. His mouth pulled into a hard line.

"T?"

His lips parted for an instant before he pressed them together again. Ponytail Guy shouted for us to keep moving. Thurmond glanced back and pulled me into motion. My legs responded unwillingly, but after a moment I found I could walk, sort of. When Thurmond spoke, his words were almost lost in the scuffling of our boots.

"When I was nine my mom decided she wanted to leave my dad. She said things had been rocky for years, and she couldn't take it anymore. The thought terrified me more than I could stand, and I begged her to try to work it out. I even talked to our pastor and had him call her in to meet with him. Well, guess what? She stayed. She listened to the pleading of a small boy desperate to keep his family together—even though that little boy didn't have all the information."

I opened my mouth to ask him a question when my arm jerked in a sudden spasm. I squeezed my eyes shut until the pain passed, and when I opened them I couldn't remember what I'd been about to say. Thurmond looked at me in concern, then turned away, his face tight. He continued.

"It wasn't long after that my dad widened his circle of abuse to us children as well."

"Thurmond—"

"After a few more years, my mom lost her willpower to leave. I swore after that I'd never overstep my bounds again unless I had all the information."

"You—you don't have to—"

Thurmond pulled me to a stop, and we locked eyes. His expression was reserved but thoughtful. "Whatever the hell is happening here, you're still Rose. I know that much at least. I have your back until I have a damn good reason not to." He shrugged and turned away. "Maybe when I get all the information I'll need to reevaluate my opinion, but I doubt it."

A crackling voice from behind reminded us to keep walking.

We fell into a more companionable silence this time, puffing up the last few feet to the top of the hill. Something about the exchange made me feel he had forgiven me for doing something as weird as volting.

"How come I'm getting the impression you had a conversation in your head as to whether you're going to trust me?" I asked.

"Probably 'cause I did."

"So despite thinking, 'this chick is responsible for me being kidnapped, making us fall nearly to our deaths, provoking the aliens, and then volting the daylights out of them,' you're totally cool with that."

"Yep." Thurmond grinned.

"Outstanding."

We passed between two buildings and into the circle of thirteen small stone structures. Each was about the size of your average tent trailer, and they made a perfect circle around the electrical transmission tower. Sand sloped up next to buildings that were either painted the same color as the desert or had blended through time and exposure. Sand also shimmered over the slanted rooftops, their empty, cave-like doorways facing inward.

The tower itself rose a good couple hundred feet above us. Four heavy-duty legs supported the sturdy mesh of metal, the steel beams widening into a latticed mess as they rose to meet in an upside down V at the top of the neighboring legs. The very top of the tower resembled a giant, geometrical cat head, with thick black cables strung from the tip of the ears and several other protrusions of metal, slinging toward the next tower. It was one of hundreds standing sentinel over a rural road leading to a sub-station somewhere. The difference with the tower at the Rethan's base camp was that cables also cascaded down to the rooftops of the buildings.

Saturated storm clouds rolled overhead. Lighting pulsed within the blackness. The mountains were obscured behind the angry depths. Thunder rumbled, and the insistent wind plucked at my uniform.

Aside from our four-Rethan welcoming party, there seemed to be no more than twenty others. Those twenty bustled around, not in a state of urgency but with heightened efficiency. Silver hair glinted dully in the deepening light. All wore the same uniform: subdued blue with the silver lightning across the shoulders, pants tucked in white boots military-style. One team carried large metal crates about the size of your average coffee table, while others carried two or three smaller crates ranging down to the size of a lunch box. The crates were scattered at the base of one side of the tower, giving the entire camp an unbalanced look.

Upon closer examination, I realized it was more than their baggage that made things seem lopsided. One of the upside-down V-like open-ings of the tower appeared to be covered in enormous silver scales. The platter-sized plates overlapped each other, rising up to the highest point and descending down the other. They also lay across the ground below creating an unbroken circle, like a doorway—or a portal.

"Marshal Rannen," the officiate called to Andre the Giant. "You can hold the prisoners by building twelve until we're ready."

The officiate pointed to the nearest crate and snapped her fingers impatiently for the two closest Rethans to bring it to her. I suspected she'd already forgotten all about us. Fine by me. She wasn't the one I wanted to interrogate anyway.

Marshal Rannen gave a beckoning toss of his head and led us around to the far side of the camp. Thurmond kept me on my feet until we finally stopped near one of the structures, indistinguishable from the others.

Thurmond expelled a tired huff. I looked back to find that Ponytail Guy had followed us. He leaned against a building, arms folded but with his weapon still trained on us. He looked as though his eyes were attempting to bore holes into my soul. He only managed to come off as grouchy and irrelevant. With a stupid ponytail to boot.

When he saw me looking he gave the weapon a little wave.

"Deputy Hoth!" the officiate yelled. Ponytail jumped and ran to join her.

I tracked him with my eyes before examining the terrain for a possible avenue of escape. That the tower was sitting on a hill put us at a disadvantage. The far side of the portal had a gentler slope and was littered with large boulders. They could provide just enough cover to get us pretty far. Except that I didn't know the range of their weapons. And I didn't know which way led us back to civilization.

Deciding the direction with the boulders would be our best bet, I eased myself to the ground on the eastern side of the building and leaned my head against the hot wall. I pulled my knees closer to my chest, exhausted beyond measure. I could barely think any more. I just needed a moment. Just a small moment to gather my thoughts. My eyes closed and my mouth opened to expedite the flow of oxygen to my lungs.

"That's their portal?"

I slit my eyelids open to see Thurmond staring straight up at the complicated mesh of metal towering above the camp. He glanced around, looking for something perhaps a bit more Star Gate-ish.

"Dunno," I replied.

"So they want you to use some kind of special skill they know about, because of those weird symbols on your hand, to fix it?"

"Dunno." I closed my eyes. "I suppose."

"And I suppose this all needs to get done before the commander, Lieutenant Justet, and the rest of the crew arrive to take these guys out?"

"Sure."

"Well then, let's get this thing fired up so we can get the hell out of here and find you some medical attention."

I peered between half closed lids to find Thurmond glaring at Marshal Rannen. The enormous Rethan leaned against the corner of building twelve. His silver eyes were alert, and focused with alarming captivation on my face.

"Yeaaah," I said. Sort of. Marshal Rannen's face blurred. "An-drugs. I cad-use morphine-er-even assspirn."

That morphine word was a bear. In fact, enunciation in general seemed outrageously overrated. My eyes drooped, shutting out the intense gaze of the marshal.

"Rose? Dammit, you're white as a sheet." Thurmond patted my cheek, then shook my chin. I blinked my eyes, trying valiantly to keep them open. "Stay awake."

"Her lips are turning blue! Rose, you're . . . Take some deep breaths. In and out. Come on!"

I attempted to comply, but everything seemed disconnected. I couldn't pin down what was important and what wasn't. Thurmond pulled the collar of my shirt away from my neck and tugged at the laces of my boots. I hadn't realized my feet were numb until my toes tingled. Blood flushed through my legs.

"Don't you have meds you could give her?" Thurmond's eyes were trained on me, his head turned a little to the side, directing the question at Marshal Rannen.

Rannen's eyebrows lifted. He shrugged and looked away. I let my eyes drift shut but forced them open again. Rifle drills with my eyelids. This sucked.

"No. Well, yes. Deputy Boderick is bringing over a little something."

"Tell me it's a pain killer of some kind."

"That's not the kind of medication we generally have on hand. And the officiate needs Specialist Rose awake."

Voltage . . . The word hissed through my mind.

"So?"

"So, pain medication of the necessary strength would most likely put her to sleep, and we're going to need her before long."

"Oh right. To power your *portal.*"

Volted . . .

"That's correct."

"Bullshit!" Thurmond rose to his feet and faced the marshal.

Volting . . .

Marshal Rannen pushed away from the building, his expression going from casual observation to something more wary.

Voltage, volted, volting.

"I'm not the one in charge."

"And if you were, would it make a difference?"

Voltage, volted, volting. Voltage, volted, volting. The mantra quivered through my nerves in an eerie intensity. It erased the argument and obliterated any thought trying to surface. The storm didn't help matters. The ions in the air exacerbated the tingling, heated feeling, biting through the pain and bringing out a magnified alertness that my consciousness was trying to hide from. The voice peaked, putting pressure on my hollow-sounding left ear and pounding head.

Voltage, volted, volting. Voltage, volted, volting. Voltage, volted, volting!

"Rannen?"

The word made me jump, and it took a moment before I realized it came from my mouth. The gears in my brain creaked into action, silencing the mantra. I rotated my jaw, trying to pop my ear.

"I mean, Mister . . . um, Marshal Rannen, sir?" I continued. Rannen and Thurmond turned from their argument. My words were no longer slurring, and now that I'd started talking I couldn't seem to stop. "Hi, uh, yeah. It's me. Kris Rose. I was wondering if you wouldn't mind clearing a few things up for me—us? I mean, since we're sitting here."

"Kris Rose?" Rannen asked, his expression curious.

Thurmond touched my cheek with the back of his hand, then turned to Rannen.

"Yeah, or Specialist Rose. Or just Rose. Whatever. You pick." I shook my head, trying to force myself to stop babbling.

Rannen drew his shoulders to his ears, then dropped them with a sigh and nodded. He grabbed the handle of a metal crate a few feet away, grated it across the ground, and dropped it. Dirt puffed around the base. He cast a fleeting glance around the camp as if noting the locations of each Rethan before sitting on the crate. Thurmond crouched beside me, his muscles taut and eyes vigilant.

"What would you like to know?" Rannen seemed relaxed, but his hands balled into tight fists and rested on his knees.

I worked my hand into my pants pocket, felt around for a moment, and then with some difficulty pulled out Justet's RETHA coin. My fingers fumbled the coin onto the sand. Rannen stared. Thurmond plucked the coin from the dirt and looked at it curiously before placing it in my hand. I caressed the coin with my thumb, and offered it to Rannen.

"Do you know what this is?"

Rannen's eyes widened. He took it hesitantly. His mouth opened and closed as he turned it over in his hands. He looked from the coin to me, closed his mouth, and handed it back.

"Yes," he said. I waited for more.

"And?"

"Where did you get it, Kris?"

My stomach jolted at the use of my first name. "Tell me what it is."

"It's a dimensional catapult. Clearly Rethan." He pressed his lips together.

This was getting us nowhere. I didn't have even a basis of understanding of what he was talking about.

"Okay," I said, clearing my mind and trying to find a stable base to start again. "So dimension, erm, dimensional." I blew out a breath. "I keep hearing about this dimension stuff. What exactly are we talking about? Dimensions like one, two, or three dimensional objects, or are we talking dimensions, like . . . like other worlds?"

A smile tilted the corners of Rannen's mouth. It made him look, despite his enormity, like a little boy.

"You really don't understand even the basic integrity of our planet?"

I tried not to take offense. "I understand that the Earth rotates around the sun and the moon around the Earth. I understand about the ozone layer and gravity and all the stuff in between. I just don't understand dimensions."

Rannen leaned away from me, and his hands relaxed for the first time since we started talking. "Our planet is made up of thirteen planes, or layers. They wrap around each other in a sort of ethereal sense."

"You're not aliens, then?"

"Well, yes. Alien to your dimension."

"But not from outer space or anything?"

"No, not from outer space. We share the same planet. Terra. The third planet from the sun and one of the nine in our solar system."

"Eight. Pluto was demoted."

"So say the humans." Rannen grinned.

I almost smiled back.

"So, the dimensions?" I prompted.

"Yes, the dimensions." The grin wilted from Rannen's face. "For example, the center dimension, or Thirteenth Dimension, is called the Heart. Retha, as the twelfth, wraps the Heart while Ather, the eleventh, wraps Retha."

"And Earth?"

"Earth is considered an outer dimension. A lower one. Bottom three, only above Ehtar and Tareh in regards to technological advancements. Each dimension was colonized one at a time by settlers from the original three dimensions: Heart, Retha, and Ather." Rannen gave a brief smile, and then puckered his mouth to suppress it. "Earth is a colonization of Retha, so I guess that makes us relatives."

Yeah right, and I was a Rethan criminal. A shiver coursed down my arms and legs. I closed my eyes, waiting for it to pass. When I opened them again, Marshal Rannen's face was the first thing I saw. He glanced around the camp again, chewed the inside of his mouth, and offered us a stern stare.

"You have to understand, this is all very hushed. Humans, as a general rule, are not privy to this information for obvious reasons. I trust you'll keep it to yourself."

Thurmond shrugged, as though he couldn't believe he was being asked by our captors to protect a secret the world would scoff at anyway. I lifted the coin again.

"So, a dimensional catapult would be something that catapults you across dimensions?"

Rannen nodded but looked baffled.

"However, what you're holding is a rarity. Those are only used after making a dimension jump from the Dimensional Congressional's portal chamber. Unlike our other portals," he waved his hand toward the tower, "you don't need a matching portal on the other dimension. You simply use a dimensional catapult to jump you back from where you came. You just need a very specific electrical charge to keep you from jumping dimensions accidently."

I squinted my eyes, trying to put all the information into a box that would help me understand Dad's disappearance better. "You don't have any more of these little coin thingies? I've got to jump start that massive thing over there instead?"

"Correct. Those," he pointed at the coin in my hand, "haven't been used in over twenty years that I'm aware of. They are housed in the portal chamber which has been locked since . . ." He looked at his hands, "Since your sentence."

"Sentence?" Thurmond broke in. "Yeah, you guys were talking about that earlier. Care to explain?"

"Kris was sentenced to RAGE over twenty years ago." Rannen kept his eyes on Thurmond. "Although not Kris exactly."

"Sentenced, like, for committing a crime?" I said, suddenly nauseous. I looked at my imprinted palm. My right hand rested on my lap like a dead thing, blood crusted across it in dried, brown stripes. I uncurled my fingers enough for the tarnished symbols to be visible. "Is that what these mean?"

Marshal Rannen reached out and traced the symbols on my palm with fingers. My fingers closed around the symbols, and he jerked his hand back.

"They indicate your crime, your sentence, and the Vizshathain dosage . . . um, a dimensional camouflage of sorts—which makes you look like your human friend here."

I rubbed my thumb across my palm, wishing it would erase the numbers, and exhaled in frustration. "So I was sentenced to a crime over twenty years ago—ya know, when I was a baby—imprinted with some letters on my hand, and dosed with camouflage. Even if this did make any sort of chronological sense, I'm going to believe you because . . . ?"

Rannen's eyebrows rose, as if the answer couldn't be more obvious. I answered with my best facial sarcasm. He sat back.

"Because, as I said, you were sentenced to RAGE."

"RAGE?" Thurmond said.

"What's 'rage'?" I asked.

"The Reverse Aging Gateway to Earth. R-A-G-E. RAGE. It's an incarceration portal between our dimensions." He gestured at me. "For those exiled."

"Reverse aging?" I asked. "So, like you stick some grownup in that portal and they come out the other end as a-a—"

"What, like a baby?" Thurmond finished with a snort.

Up until now I had been treating the whole thing like a big misunderstanding, some stupid mistake that neither the symbols on my hand nor the volting could prove. Now Rannen had thrown out a chunk of information that made the whole thing plausible on some weird, alternate-dimensional level.

I wanted to laugh. Mostly because it was ridiculous. Partially because I was desperate for Thurmond and Rannen to join in so this whole outrageous conversation would vanish into talk of college football or the weather.

Rippling lightning brightened the deep clouds. A grumble of thunder answered a few seconds later.

It wasn't true. It couldn't be. This whole thing was a nightmare, a hallucination brought on by shock. I mean, I'd been shot. I could be in shock, right? Yet the pain, the wind, the alien faces before me all seemed so real and . . .

Familiar?

No. None of this was familiar!

Then run. Run and they'll hunt you. Hide and they'll find you, the voice whispered in a sing-song voice. *They'll find you. They'll find you.*

"Okay, so let's *imagine* for a second what you're saying is true," I said, with as much skepticism as I could. I opened my hand again. "What's my crime?"

"Kris," Rannen closed my hand, engulfing my dirty fist in his massive white paw. The personal use of my first name, the look in his eye, and the sad droop to his mouth combined into an expression so desolate it made my heart falter. "I don't need to read your inscription to know your crime."

A jolt of electricity passed from his hand into mine, but instead of causing me discomfort it raced across my arm and into my head. An image solidified before my mind's eye for a millisecond, not giving me enough time to examine but leaving behind the trace of an intense personal connection to this complete stranger.

I narrowed my eyes, examining his face. The pleasant mouth, the straight nose, the thick brows. Every tiny feature hid a clue, a tool in helping me pin down the memory that hovered like a gnat just outside my present recollections.

"We've met before."

"We have," Rannen said.

"What'd I do?"

"You brutally murdered two hundred thirty-six Rethans," Rannen whispered.

The two of us froze in an icy box. His eyes held no anger. Nothing hinted at the despair from before. He might as well have been an icicle for all the information his face contained. And yet the accusation hung between us. A black, ugly thing, riddled with cause and consequence.

Killed them. Killed them all. Forty thousand volts of Earth amperage and an elegant blade of silver. The voice laughed with a breathy sigh.

Lightning flashed across Rannen's face. A clap of thunder answered, making me jump. I blinked. The otherworldly tension connecting us lifted. I pried his fingers from my hand. He leaned back quickly, pulling his hand away and rubbing his knuckles. I turned to Thurmond, hoping he'd bring me back to Earth where I belonged.

But where I hoped to see humor, disbelief, and skepticism, I found instead a grim, thoughtful expression.

"So." I kept my voice light in an attempt to bring the mood back to my originally planned interrogation. "Why have all these little dimensional catapult thingies been left all over the US in the last several years?"

"They have?" Rannen looked genuinely surprised. "I don't know. As far as I know, the portal chamber is locked tight. With no jump through the portal, no coin is needed to get back. We use that one over there because we can't mimic the technology of the chamber. It's been thousands of years since it was created. You think we'd have figured it out by now."

My gut tightened. Retha, coins, dimensional aliens, and portals. The one thing I understood, though, was that if a coin were left at the site of the crime, a dimensional jump would have been made. Did that mean Dad was in Retha?

I dropped my eyes to the coin in my lap. I barely listened as Thurmond picked up the questioning.

"Retha is the twelfth dimension and you said Earth is the third?"

Rannen answered, "Yes."

"And there are thirteen?"

"That's correct, but dimensions six through eleven no longer exist. I guess you could say there are only seven now."

"Where'd they go? The ones that don't exist anymore."

"The Thirteenth Dimension, the Heart, as the governing power of the entire planet, reserves the right to exercise genocidal authority over the lower dimensions."

"What the hell does that mean?" Thurmond asked.

"It means they can and have destroyed entire dimensions to maintain the planet's balance. I remember when the eleventh dimension was destroyed. Too corrupt, or something."

His answer was vague enough that he probably knew exactly what had happened but didn't want to reveal it. Pretty bad then.

"They are the center dimension. The original dimension." Rannen went on. "It is their right as our forefathers."

"Sounds like one hell of a God complex." Thurmond finally relaxed enough to sit against the wall. "Not something you should just let them get away with."

Rannen sat back, his face thoughtful. After a moment he spoke. "There was a group once who tried to stand up to them. They believed that even the most intelligent and advanced governors need to be governed. We chalk it up to mythology now. A warning to the rest of us. No one wants to become like the Ehtar." He frowned. "It's not something we like to talk about."

"Ehtar's right under Earth, right?" Thurmond said.

"No, Tareh. Ehtar is—*was* the first dimension."

"Was?" I scoffed, shaking my head.

"Oh," Rannen's eyebrows shot up. "Don't misunderstand. The Thirteenth Dimension is simply protecting the rest of us. They're quite benevolent."

Oh yes. Quite benevolent, the voice offered.

"Sure they are." I let it go. I was barely interested. I looked toward the tower, where the officiate shouted orders.

"So, there are different societies in each dimension?" Thurmond asked.

He talked in the background as I studied the route to the tower. Would I be detained if I got up and walked over there? Would I even make it, or pass out cold?

"Yes," Rannen said. "In the dimensions that are populated, that is."

"How come we can't see or sense each other?"

"Sometimes we can. There are places where the dimensional fabric is so thin a presence can be detected. I understand this is where your ghost stories come from."

"Or we have ghosts," I said, my eyes still following the officiate.

Rannen shrugged. "It's the simplicity and primal nature of your dimension that allows you such thoughts. It's a way of understanding something outside your realm of technological comprehension. This is why Earth makes such a perfect prison system. There's less mischief for the inmates to get into."

"Why go to all this trouble?" Thurmond asked. "With exiling and everything? Why not intern your inmates in your own dimension, or put them to death, or something?"

"Put them to death?" Rannen sat back, astonishment at this notion printed plainly across his face. "We could never do that. Rethans are a strictly non-violent society. We don't exile many, but the ones we do are those unable to conform to the basic standards of etiquette and serenity. They are too violent to be allowed to stay in Retha."

Great, we were back to that. Me, the too-violent-to-be-Rethan inmate type. My limbs buzzed with energy. The spot above my ear pounded venom through my veins. I turned on him.

"Okay, so answer me this, Rannen. *If* I was such a hard-core person back on Retha, then why do I do everything now from paying my taxes and obeying the speed limit, to—to not swearing. Shouldn't I be running around murdering people?"

Rannen chewed on his bottom lip. "Most of Earth's genocidal dictators and serial killers have been RAGE inmates."

"And you keep sending them here?" Thurmond sounded offended.

Rannen scratched his jaw. "The percentage is small enough to keep our contract intact."

I agreed with Thurmond on this one. But what did that mean for me? Volting, anger, voices in my head. Either I was coming apart at the seams, or there was truth in his words.

"But I'm not a serial killer, or a genocidal dictator. "

"It will be interesting to see what happens in your future," Rannen interrupted.

"Oh please." Thurmond rolled his eyes. "She's had twenty years for a test run."

"Twenty-one," I corrected.

"It's easy for a person to maintain a moral persona when there is nothing to challenge them," Rannen said. "It's quite another when the circumstances are more—extreme."

"Yeah, well they've been extreme in the last twenty-four hours and I haven't seen any bodies piling up under Rose's murderous little thumb."

Rannen sat back and folded his arms. He didn't seem to know how to respond to that. I didn't either. I'd wanted to kill Justet and Sanderford back at the base. I'd wanted to kill the commander on the plane, and I'd had my heart set on putting a bullet through the officiate's head. The bodies may not be piling up under my thumb, but they were certainly piling up in my mind.

Thurmond took my fist and smoothed my hand open across my knee. I loved the warmth of his skin after the cold of Rannen's. So very human.

We sat quietly for a few minutes, the conversation hitting a dead end. The working Rethans continued to chatter. The camp looked much less cluttered. The wind plucked at my hair and uniform. I couldn't seem to stop shivering.

"Okay, so what do you guys need this lowly, psychotic inmate for?" I sighed. "And don't just tell me your portal's busted, because that doesn't explain anything."

Rannen didn't move but his eyes locked back onto me. "In the Twelfth Dimension our society and technology is powered by electricity—"

"Sort of like here," Thurmond interrupted.

"Not exactly. In fact, it's not even a close comparison." Rannen shook his head. "The currents in our dimension are very different and much stronger. Our bodies can store up to well over five hundred thousand volts of electricity. We power our society, not the other way around. The majority of your dimension is made up of earthy materials that cannot conduct electricity. *Everything* in our society can."

"Okay, so what do you need Rose for if we are all so very beneath you?"

"The type of electricity in your dimension is not the same as that used in Retha. You think of it as one dimensional—amperes, voltage, resistance. This is scientific fact. However, on Retha, electricity has a variation not included in Earth. Kilvran: output by any object determines how much energy our bodies need to expend in order to power it to its maximum potential."

"Okay." I was pretty sure my brain had exploded. "I didn't understand a word of that."

"Our bodies don't understand the kilvran deficiency here in Earth, and are therefore unable to either absorb your currents or wield them.

However, with an extended amount of exposure to Earth currents, we've discovered that a Rethan body is able to adapt and channel it. Although it's more like throwing a round from one of your weapons into a fire versus shooting it from a gun. It's clumsy and inelegant." Rannen gave a thin-lipped smile. "But as an unintentional flaw in the dimensional camouflage, it will be enough for what we need from you. Your twenty some years of acclimatization may very well save our lives."

Rannen nodded, trying to get me to approve. I watched him, wondering if I should agree with him or not, and I realized I couldn't pin down his age. My mind had created a first impression for me based on the silvery hair and translucent skin, telling me that he was much older. Now as I studied his face I saw the smooth skin, the taut muscles of his jaw and the clear, silver eyes, and realized he could barely be considered middle aged. Definitely older than Thurmond and myself, but not by much. This made me feel less threatened by him. He was also a young soldier. Almost a peer.

But from another dimension. And despite his soft voice, honest face, and explanations that almost made sense, he was still holding Thurmond and me captive.

"Rannen, you said I was given some kind of drug to make me look human."

Marshal Rannen sighed, rubbed his eyes with the palms of his hands. He glanced over to where the officiate was scolding a Rethan over the contents of a spilled crate, and stood. Thurmond stood as well, but less defensively this time.

"Yes. We are not so different, Kris. The continual charge in the air on our dimension has leeched the majority of the pigment from our bodies, which is why we look different from your human friend here." Rannen sighed. "When a Rethan is sentenced, a pigment enhancer and memory inhibitor serum called Vizshathain is injected before the sentence is carried out." The wind flipped up Rannen's collar against his jaw. His eyes captured my attention. Like he was examining me for some sort of physical evidence the numbers on my hand had supposedly proven. He smoothed down his collar. "You don't have to believe anything I say, Kris. But the fact remains. You are a convicted inmate from Retha. You were sentenced to RAGE and grew up in Earth as a human."

All my bluster and hope deflated in a tired whoosh of air. I felt dirty, contaminated. Something filthy in hiding. An alien to the place I loved and considered home.

I fingered the makeshift bandage around my arm and found Thurmond staring at me, his mouth open.

"Don't look at me like that, Corporal." I was trying to sound angry, but the words came out sad. Resigned.

Thurmond closed his mouth slowly. Before he could respond the shuffling of feet and a quiet "ahem" made us look around. The rat-like tech guy stood a few feet away, shifting from foot to foot, his hands hidden behind his back. Marshal Rannen ran a hand across his short-cropped scalp, sent me one last piercing look, and gave the tech guy his attention.

"What is it, Deputy Boderick?" Rannen asked.

"The officiate asked that I give this to the inmate." He opened his hand.

Where I hoped to see a cell phone or a set of car keys, I was supremely disappointed if not downright disturbed to see a huge hypodermic syringe filled with an opaque, light blue substance.

"Oh, no you don't." I pulled my feet closer so I could stand up quickly if needed.

Deputy Boderick took a step back "It's just human-grade epinephrine combined with Azshatath—"

"What's it do?" Thurmond folded his arms, letting his biceps bulge. Deputy Boderick's eyes left my face.

"Epinephrine? It's adrenaline to help with," he waved a finger at me, "that. It's a vasoconstrictor to slow the bleeding and stuff." Speaking to Thurmond seemed to be easier for him anyway. No sense in engaging the psychopath if you didn't have to.

"And the ash—whatever?" I asked.

"Azshatath?" He glanced at me and then back to Thurmond. "On Retha we use it to help with voltage asthenia. It increases the metallic mass, strips away current inhibitions brought on by bodily abstruseness and—"

"It suppresses the dimensional camouflage, Kris Rose." Rannen took a formal tone. "It will help you better absorb electrical currents."

Boderick glanced at Rannen. Rannen gave an almost imperceptible headshake. Boderick spoke fast, in a breathless voice. "I'm afraid the

Azshatath will also lessen the amnesic effect the Vizshathain produces, so we'll need to reinject you before—"

"Amnesic effect? So, I could start acting like . . ." I couldn't finish.

There wasn't a chance in the world I was taking this weird, other dimensional camouflage junk, vasoconstrictor or no. I widened my eyes and pursed my lips to show everyone how serious I was, and then looked to Thurmond for support. He rubbed the back of his neck, his face thoughtful. My eyebrows shot up.

"You don't actually think I should take it, do you?"

"Would that stuff hurt someone who's human?" he asked Boderick.

"No. Well, the adrenaline would react the same on anyone, but only someone who's been injected with Vizshathain will be affected in any way by the camouflage reducer."

Thurmond held out his hand. Deputy Boderick clutched the syringe and then handed it reluctantly to Thurmond.

"I'm not taking that, T." I cringed as far away from him as the wall would allow.

"Knock it off, Rose." Thurmond crouched in front of me. "You heard what he said. The adrenaline will help control the bleeding."

"What about the dimensional—camo—azz—whatever it's called?"

"Come on. At best it will help you stop losing so much blood. And at worst," he paused, and I could see his mind churning on how to continue, "it will help clear things up a bit."

I scowled at him, furious that he was siding with anyone other than me.

"You want me to take it first?" he asked, and for a moment I hated him for being so noble.

"No," I grumbled. "No, I don't want you to take it at all." I wasn't going to last forever especially if I kept losing blood like this. I drew in a sharp breath, holding my arm close to my body. Thurmond's face was a controlled mask of neutrality but with a dash of now-will-you-listen? I brushed cold sweat from my lip.

"Bodie. Can I call you Bodie?" I asked. Boderick shook his head. "You got any alcohol swabs or disinfectant of any kind?"

He gave me a blank stare, which I took as a no. I held my hand out to Thurmond for the syringe. "I'll do it."

"Fine." Thurmond took off the cap, looking pained. The needle was much smaller than I'd expected. I took the syringe. He didn't stop me.

"So, Bodie, what side effects can I expect? Vomiting, rash, trouble sleeping, increased risk of cancer, premature graying, or maybe the uncontrollable urge to shoot electricity from my fingers and kill people?"

Boderick tripped back with a little squawk. Thurmond gave me a brief, gratuitous smile that didn't touch his eyes. With only a second of hesitation, I jabbed the needle through the fabric into my thigh. Everyone around me jumped. I depressed the plunger, choking back a groan. The blue liquid emptied into my body in a chilling wave. An enormous rush of electricity tore through my body. My heart raced in frantic, pounding bounds.

"Holy . . . ow!" I put my head between my knees with a violent shudder.

"You okay?" Thurmond asked.

"That stuff has quite a kick." My knees muffled my voice. The needle dropped from my hands. I pressed my knuckles against the injection site and raised my head. "How's my camouflage looking?"

Thurmond shrugged, his face unreadable. I must have still looked the same. The pain from the bullet reverted to a secondary discomfort. Jitters shivered up and down my body, tightening and loosening my muscles with racking tension until I felt I would tear apart in a thousand directions. I slid my back up the wall, ignoring Thurmond's protestations.

The landscape lost its warm tints, becoming a cool azure that was like seeing through blue-lens glasses. The wind, the lightning, the very air intensified, blistering me with a swath of sensations that my body struggled to process. I braced my hand on the building.

Thurmond touched my arm. I shook it off. The electricity in the heavens. The sheer power enveloped by the clouds. I tilted my head to sense it better. For the first time I saw streaks of light and surges of power, much deeper and more intense than anything I had witnessed before. The temperature dropped several noticeable degrees.

A deep, pressurized ache started at the usual spot above my left ear and spread across my skull. My chest tightened until I could barely breathe. Dark, bloody anger washed through my mind, swirling in a whirlpool of hatred before exploding from my mouth in a liberating cackle.

A whisper of voices. Conspiratorial, exclusive. I whirled toward them. Rannen and Thurmond stood shoulder to shoulder, or shoulder to elbow as it were. They stared at me like silenced gossips.

Thurmond: a nobody. My gaze settled on Rannen in his blue marshal uniform.

"You!" The word hissed from between my teeth. One menacing step and the power of hatred and fury boiled into a scalding inferno of violence. "Is this what you've become? A fluxing Rethan drone!"

Thurmond and Rannen retreated, knocking into each other.

"Stop right there, Kris." Rannen raised his hand. The other went behind his back.

"What the hell's going on?" Thurmond said.

"You should have cut your own throat rather than become this— become one of them! *I* should have cut your throat!"

I advanced on him, shoulders hunched. Nothing penetrated the blistering anger, the absolute rage, the murderous intentions. *Drone!*

CHAPTER 18

Caz
10 days pre-RAGE

Xander sat behind Vin's desk, forehead resting in his palm. He leaned over the small command screen in front of him. The outer office was empty, no surprise. It was early. So early that the city hadn't begun to stir. Zell had probably been called in to watch Manny so Xander could come into the DC Council building this morning. Or perhaps he'd come in last night.

Caz vaguely wondered when she ceased having any responsibility for her son. Perhaps because of her outburst that had nearly killed a marshal? It was a wonder she was currently free to finish her work. Having a brother on the council had its perks.

Caz shook her hands out of their fists. It was good that Xander had been offered Vin's seat. At least the commandant's aversion extended only to her, not the Fisk family in general. That in itself gave her license to hate the commandant all the more, and it would serve her purpose— *their* purpose—now that Vin was no longer here.

Sometimes she wondered if Xander had forgotten who he was. He had accused her of the same thing in the past, when Vin kept her out of the lab for too long. *Don't forget who you are,* he would remind her, *what our purpose is here.* But thinking about it now, she realized it had been years since he'd mentioned it.

Caz hadn't been to the council building since learning of Vin's death. All she would run into were memories and emotions. Vin had died in large part due to his father and the council. The rage simmering in her veins kept her warm at night but confronting the council, or more specifically her father-in-law, would only cause her to boil over. Calm and control were called for if she was going to accomplish her goal.

Coming here today was a necessity. As much as she loathed the hypocritical extravagance around her and all it entailed, it was time for Xander to use his influence with the council. It was worth him becoming a Rethan drone for this.

Caz slapped her hand against the doorframe to energize the web and enclose them in the office. It crackled to life with a razor zap. Xander jerked his head up.

His eyes were rimmed in dark shadows, his hair tousled. He didn't say anything but had a resigned look. He'd expected her. He raised his eyebrows in question. Caz nodded. He nodded along with her and then heaved a sigh.

"When did you finish?" he asked.

"I tested the eight millimeter prototype last night."

"Where?"

"The envirophylum near Vislane Academy."

Silence. Xander ran his hand across his mouth and stood only to sit back down. He leaned across the desk toward her.

"And?"

Caz released her excitement in a breath.

"It was amazing. You should have seen it! All twelve kilometers within a matter of seconds. The plants, the grasses, everything in a perfect circle." She stopped. This wasn't what Xander wanted to hear. In fact, she knew it was only with the greatest restraint that he hadn't already interrupted her to have his say. She tapped her nails on Xander's desk, unable to hold back her excitement. "This is it, Xan! It's ready!"

"All twelve kilometers?" He didn't move from his seat but his eyebrows contracted. "Did any of it leak over to the city?"

"Come on, Xan, do you really think I'm that careless?" A snarl rose in her throat. It caught, making a lump she couldn't swallow.

"Because a report came in a few hours ago of a freak storm that raced through the Vislane Envirophylum and Academy—"

"They're calling it a storm?"

"—that decimated the entire phylum as well as the academy and the eight adjoining grids." He flipped around the power screen so Caz could see it. It was an image taken from high above, showing the shimmering lights of a block of standard Rethan grids. At the very center was a blackened hole. No lights. No dark, blocky symmetry implying the location of an envirophylum. Just a perfect circle of darkness.

Caz shoved the screen back at him.

"And that's not all," Xander went on. "Ten days ago a similar storm popped up at a phylum twelve-hundred grids to the south, although that one only destroyed about a square kilometer of the phylum—"

"Xan—"

"And another one thirty days ago in a phylum to the east. At least that time the surrounding grids had been empty, or the death toll would have been enormous."

"I needed to test it." Caz waved a hand at the power screen. "The Heart of Annihilation can only be condensed so far, as you can tell with that first failed test. I made it as small as possible for the second which was about as effective as a firecracker. The third had the most consistent response, but I'd never have been able to contain it to a single envirophylum."

"If you'd gotten a permit from the council for the test we could have found you a suitable location."

"Oh please. The council?" Caz tossed up her hands and paced before the desk. "Sure. As if every single council member weren't under the imperial thumb of our esteemed commandant."

"I'm on the council now, Caz." Xander thumped his fist on the power screen. "I could have pushed it through, like Vin would have."

"Attikin's ass!" Caz stopped pacing. "You don't have the same authority as Vin. Commandant Paliyo desperately wants me to finish the weapon, but he doesn't understand the complex necessities involved in testing. He would as soon give me permission for a test as he would hug me. It had to be this way."

"And so the Rethans within the neighboring grids are what, casualties of your own personal war with the commandant?"

"You're forgetting the higher purpose here, brother," Caz hissed. She pressed her knuckles to the desk, her eyes hard. "If this weapon isn't admitted into the arsenal, the Thirteenth Dimension will continue to annihilate dimension after dimension until the dimensional fabric is so thin the slightest infraction will cause an irrevocable rift. Is that what you want?"

"That's on their heads, while this," he picked up the power screen and pushed it back under her nose. "This is on yours."

Caz shoved it off the desk. It cracked, causing the image to vanish.

"It's not just mine, Xan." Caz folded her arms. "Don't think because you're not turning the key or applying the charge that the blood won't stain your hands as black as mine."

Xander sat back down, his eyes wide.

"What if it's not enough to introduce the Heart to the Rethan arsenal?" Caz walked around the desk and perched on the edge as close to Xander as she could. "I mean, what's that really going to do?"

"Caz, don't—" Xander looked scared for the first time.

She inched closer. "What if the only way to free the planet from the Thirteen Dimension's oppression is to annihilate them first?"

"That's not our purpose and you know it!" Xander leapt to his feet. Caz thrust him back into his seat. She leaned over him, her lips pulled against her teeth.

"You and your little, impotent council are welcome to debate amongst yourselves. But know this, Xander," Caz bent forward until their noses touched. His breath was cool and fast on her face, "this Rethan serenity—this passivity—will not stop me from destroying the Thirteenth Dimension myself if I have to. And you won't be able to stop me."

Her fingers circled Xander's collar while her other hand trailed a thin curl of electricity down his cheek. He slapped her hand away. Caz laughed and released him. She got off the desk and moved toward the door. Xander's voice stopped her before she could leave.

"This isn't about revenge, Caz. Don't let Vin's death blind you. You have a mission. Create a weapon that can take down the Thirteenth Dimension. You've accomplished that. Now it's time to turn it over to the council, and let them decide how best to use it. If you try to set it off on the Thirteenth Dimension and fail . . ." He left it hanging, but it was no secret the consequences that would rain down on the remaining dimensions for such an infraction.

Caz turned her head toward Xander. "You're not going to tell the council, right? About the tests?"

"Of course not." Xander looked frightened at the thought.

"Okay then. Set up a meet with the council." She chewed her lip and then nodded, agreeing with herself. Laughter bubbled up from deep inside and spilled out with her next words. "Yeah, let's do that. Set up a meet. I'll meet with the council. Yeah. We'll do that."

She was still laughing to herself as she walked through the web. Electricity trailed from her clothes. Out the door, past the council chambers, down the stairs to the empty vestibule. She ran her fingers along one of the pillars and made her way out of the dark, quiet building. A meeting with the council was just the thing.

CHAPTER 19

Rose

I blinked against the blackness encroaching on my vision, the rage bursting from me in a homicidal wave. I staggered forward, murder on my mind.

Rannen's leg bumped against the crate as he backed away. He put out a hand to keep his balance. Fear shimmered in his eyes. His hand came up, and I was staring into the muzzle of his weapon. I narrowed my eyes.

"Put that away." Thurmond attempted to push the weapon away. "Knock it off, Rose!"

The hatred leaked away, taking with it the pressurized ache in my head. I sagged against the wall, drained and sick. I recognized that voice, the one that had come from my mouth. And it wasn't mine.

Rannen dropped the weapon to his side, unaware that Thurmond's hand was still on it. Both of them stared at me open-mouthed.

Too ashamed of myself to speak, I turned away. I stood at the edge of a steep embankment looking in the direction we'd arrived.

Miles of empty desert stretched before me. Trapped on an island in the middle of a sandy ocean. Trapped and dying. Trapped and losing my mind. I didn't know which was worse.

My eyes followed the line of electrical towers and the thin track of road running alongside it. A dirt cloud rose not more than twenty miles away. The sun retreated behind the glowering clouds and the whole valley was cast into a dark, stormy shadow. The dust cloud was only barely visible now, but I knew what I'd seen.

"Hey," I called over my shoulder, "someone's coming!"

Thurmond stepped to one side of me. Rannen's hip brushed my other shoulder. They followed my gaze. No one spoke. Not about the convoy of vehicles, and not about me going off about drones and cutting throats and such, although I caught a wary flick of the eyes from Rannen.

"What do you think the chances are that's the commander coming to do us in?" Thurmond said.

That was my first guess too, but I couldn't seem to put the timeline together. Get shot, fall from a plane, blah, blah, blah, stumble across miles of desert, find aliens, be accused of mass murder, blah, blah, get some weird injection, threaten to kill someone, blah-diddy-blah. Yeah, I guess they might have had time to land, unload the plane, gear up, and drive all the way out here.

"How far out would you say they are?" I asked.

"I'd say they're driving between twenty-five and thirty miles per hour." Thurmond looked at his watch. "A generous guess would put them here around twenty hundred hours. That's less than thirty minutes from now."

"Are they coming for us or these other guys?"

"Probably both."

A shard of lightning cut the sky, followed instantly by a boom of thunder. My insides bounced.

Energy surged throughout my body, increasing exponentially with every moment. It refused to hold still, racing throughout every cell like a child on a newly discovered playground. I rested one hand on my knee. I couldn't stop shivering.

Thurmond's voice continued to intone somewhere to my left; Rannen joined in a moment later with a quiet rumble. I lost track of the conversation. In fact I lost track of everything.

Lightning, thunder, electricity, ice. Icy cold.

"It's all right, Rose." Thurmond rested his hand on my back. "We'll be fine."

I opened my mind and eyes back to the outside world. Thurmond stood by my side. Deputy Hoth, a.k.a. Ponytail Guy, had joined Rannen at some point. The Rethans chattered and worked in the background. A drop of water landed on my cheek, then another.

Something sparked on my skin. A flash of light. Then another. I blinked. Water plus electricity equaled . . .

"Rannen?" I called. Fear clutched my throat.

I turned my face to the sky as the clouds released their heavy load. A sopping deluge saturated my hair, skin, and clothing. Water filled my eyes. I brushed it away only to have it obscure my vision again.

Rannen and Hoth stood together, their shoulders lifted in an instinctual defense against the sudden watery assault. Water dripped from Hoth's ponytail onto his shoulder.

"The officiate is ready for the inmate over at the portal," Hoth hollered over the rapid-fire of thunder and accompanying rain.

"How long is this going to take?" Thurmond left my side to join them. "Marshal Rannen, those people are coming to kill you."

"Rannen?" I tried again.

No one looked at me. The three of them grouped together in a tight, arguing fist. Blood trickled in watery rivulets down my arm. Electricity sparked through the crimson streams, like power pouring from the injury.

"I realize that," Rannen said. "But the safest thing for us is to get through the portal."

"The safest thing for you guys maybe, but what about Rose and me?" Thurmond swiped water from his face.

"What are you talking about?" Rain flecked from Deputy Hoth's lips.

"It appears that the government soldiers Specialist Rose referenced are on their way." Marshal Rannen gestured behind him. Hoth stepped to the edge of the hill.

Headlights were now visible, tiny twin penlights repeated over ten times, fading in and out as the rain overwhelmed the vehicles. Hoth was suddenly at my side, wrapping his cold fingers around my wrist.

If he'd been holding my left arm, I would have yanked it away. As it was he took my electricity-riddled right arm that was attached to a leaking hole in my shoulder and pulled me in the direction of the portal. He didn't seem to notice or care about the snakes of electricity crawling down my arm.

"G-get off me!"

Thurmond blurred through the rain. His fist met Deputy Hoth's jaw in a squelching thud. Hoth went down, dragging me with him. I hurt enough when I was holding still. Moving, falling, and landing was a friggin' mother.

I was vaguely aware of Thurmond going in for a follow up. Rannen snagged his arm and yanked him back. Snarling voices. My hip and a rock doing the tango. Hoth's hand jerking on my arm.

I blinked over at Hoth's angry face, then at my arm, where electricity danced over his hand. A sharp ache clamped my head in a vice.

"Get off me!" I shouted, sending every amp of power collected within my body out of the hole in my shoulder, through the streams of water and into Hoth's fingers.

A spasmodic pop exploded in a crackle of blue light. Hoth yipped in pain, releasing me. I scrambled away, my hands splashing in the mud. Electricity crawled across my soaked skin, clothing, and through the rainwater collected on the ground. My back hit building twelve. I slid down the wall and my body sprawled across the ground, head propped up. The electricity jerked my muscles in uncontrolled spasms.

Marshal Rannen crouched before me.

"Stay calm, Kris." His voice was intense but calming. "You have the control. The power does not. Sense the power. Draw it in. Contain it to the water in your cells. Master it. Control it."

"Gah!" I breathed out. I couldn't concentrate on anything but the fact that I had long since lost any control.

"Kris, listen. If you can't draw the power, at least contain it. Think of it like shutting off a valve."

I sensed it. The valve he was referring to. Unfortunately the valve included a giant hole in my shoulder that I was far from able to patch at the moment.

You stupid child, growled the voice—louder and stronger.

I felt something akin to a switch being flipped, and the electricity stopped its mad steeplechase. The world was too dark. I was very cold, but my muscles were at least still. Rain pattered on my head.

Lightning flashed across the faces of Thurmond and Rannen.

"Whoa," I breathed out. "That was weird."

"Damn, Rose," Thurmond said. Rannen almost smiled.

My vision adjusted. At least it wasn't quite so dark any more. Hoth held his wrist to his chest, his fingers curled across his palm.

"Officiate Lafe needs her *now*, Marshal Rannen," Hoth sounded winded.

"In a minute," Thurmond snapped over his shoulder.

"No. Now!"

Something white flashed in Deputy Hoth's hand. A warning caught in my throat as he jabbed the weapon into Thurmond's neck.

"Get out of the way," Hoth snarled.

Thurmond flinched. He raised his hands and got slowly to his feet.

"Deputy Hoth, this is contrary to our laws." Rannen was up now also.

"What's the matter, Rannen? Losing your edge?"

"We don't need an edge when we abide by the Rethan standard." Rannen's voice was cool.

"The Rethan standard doesn't apply to them."

"These two have been cooperative since we arrived at the camp. There's no need for your weapon."

"Cooperative. Is that what you call what they did?"

"They were antagonized."

"The officiate needs inmate two-three-six right now and if I recall, this one is expendable."

"Holster your weapon!" Marshal Rannen ordered.

Deputy Hoth looked surprised. He glared at Rannen for another moment, and then lifted the weapon from Thurmond's neck with a reluctant jerk. Thurmond rubbed at the spot on his neck but didn't move otherwise. Rannen drew himself up to his considerable height.

"Now then. I will discuss an exit strategy with her friend, if you can manage to get Kris Rose to the officiate without another incident."

Deputy Hoth's lip curled, but he retreated. His weapon disappeared in his pocket or holster, or wherever he kept it when it wasn't at Thurmond's head.

Rannen followed him with his eyes. "Do you think you can handle that?"

"I can handle it!"

"Good." Rannen stepped over to me. He held out a hand, his face gentle and expectant. "We do need your help, Kris. In the meantime I'll work with your comrade on an exit for the both of you."

I swallowed, hesitated, and then took his hand. He put his other hand around my waist and hoisted me to my feet. I blinked the rain out of my eyes, swaying but standing.

"Rose?" Thurmond took my arm.

I couldn't look at him. My embarrassing and downright sinister moments were stacked precariously high. A wrong look from Thurmond was sure to topple any of my remaining dignity. And even now, among alternate-dimensional aliens, injuries, and imminent death, it somehow still mattered what he thought.

"I'll be right back," I mumbled, and pushed past Thurmond.

I weaved toward the center of the camp. The adrenaline seemed to be wearing off, because my energy and clarity of thought wavered. I focused on the silver plates of the portal shimmering with every flash of lightning and the officiate standing next to the southernmost leg.

Lightning illuminated each drop of rain in brilliant white. Static on a television screen. Uncontrolled chaos. The Rethans had piled their metal crates not far from the portal: the large ones two or three high in several different clumps, the smaller ones in short pyramids. The crackling chatter of the mingling Rethans made the air itself seem electrically charged—an assessment not too far off considering the storm.

They quieted as I approached, conversations ending with a sharp look in my direction. Feet stopped mid step, and hand gestures hung forgotten in the air. The occasional Rethan flinched out of my way, but other than their eyes following my every step they might have been part of the desert.

At the sudden silence, the officiate looked up from a glowing, dripping screen lying on her arm. Her eyes went directly to mine, and then she glanced at her troops.

"Get back to work!"

The Rethans jumped. In a flurry of movement and noise, their tasks were resumed, their conversations remembered. I slumped onto a single crate a few feet from the officiate, thankful for even that much of a luxury. Deputy Hoth arrived. She spoke before he could.

"That will be all, Deputy. I'll take it from here."

"But, Officiate, the government soldiers—"

"Are on their way. Yes, Boderick already informed me. Go help Marshal Rannen."

Hoth gave me one more dark look before striding away. The officiate's fingers flew across the screen, flicking water this way and that, her eyes glowing in its light. I rose a little out of my hunch to get a better look. Whatever the thing was looked very twenty-first century Earth to me.

"I thought we were in the Jurassic era compared to you guys," I said.

Officiate Lafe huffed but didn't say anything immediately. She opened a panel on the leg of the tower, just to the left of the portal plates. She pressed her palm to a bright blue pad of light and waited while it scanned her hand.

"Our technology doesn't work well in this dimension. We've assembled what we need from your primitive equipment to create a Third Dimension border."

The enormous armadillo plates pulsed with a faint blue light, turning the officiate into a silhouette. I put my hand in my pocket and rubbed the coin with my thumb. What would she say if she knew I had this rare dimensional catapult? Would I suddenly become unnecessary and expendable? I tightened my hand around it and kept my mouth shut.

The officiate handed the screen over her shoulder to Deputy Boderick, who had magically appeared to retrieve it.

"Here, finish up the coding for the first five," she said without looking at him. Boderick vanished again. She clasped her hands behind her back and turned to face the increasing glow of the portal plates. "Inmate two-three-six, I know we have not gotten off on the right foot in either dimension, but our survival as well as yours depends on your cooperation right now."

I didn't say anything, although I might have nodded if she'd have bothered to look at me.

"The storm is putting out a great deal of electricity," she said. As if to prove her point a jagged shard of lightning split the sky, making her hair look like liquid metal. "Can you feel it? Have you been able to absorb any since your injection?"

"Yeah, I had a whole bunch about ten minutes ago. But that nasty, little deputy with the ponytail got a little handsy, and I had to use it to volt him into the next dimension."

She did a snazzy, Rethan-style about face. "You what?"

I stared her down. "Don't worry, it's starting to come back."

"Starting to come back?" She massaged her throat. "You know you're powering a portal, not a vacuum, right?"

"I'll manage."

"Fine," she snapped, and was about to continue but I cut her off.

"Uh, Officiate." I chewed my lip and she gave an impatient shrug. "You seem to know everything that's going on around here." She gave no indication that flattery affected her. "I was just wondering if you've ever heard of Benjamin Rose?"

"Benjamin Rose?" Her tone was sharp and surprised. She did know something! "Of course I know of Benjamin Rose. Now concentrate on the—"

"Wait, that's it?"

"We don't have time for this, inmate."

"Rose. My name is Rose," I snapped.

Her face was hard. After a moment she blew out a breath and unclenched her jaw. "Rose," she conceded. "Yes, I know of Benjamin Rose. As far as I know he was last seen on Retha. Now, really—"

"Recently? I mean, when? Did you see him?" I couldn't keep the excitement from bubbling out."

The officiate's eyes hardened. "I have had no contact with Benjamin Rose, and only know him from gossip and rumor."

"What rumors? Just tell me what you know."

"No." Her answer was nonnegotiable.

"But—"

"I said no." She pressed two fingers to her eyes, took a breath, and then fixed me with a stern stare. "How about this . . . Rose, do your part to get us through this, and I'll give you what little information I possess." With that the conversation was over. "Now concentrate. Feel the currents and draw them toward your body."

"I don't need a lesson in controlling the electricity in *my* dimension." The words came out snottier than intended, in a downright bitter wave of malice I should've seen coming. The officiate clacked her teeth together.

It actually wasn't true. I didn't have the first idea what I was doing. Electrocute a weasely First Lieutenant? Check. Throw a volt out of desperation? Check, check, check. Power a portal?

"Just tell me what to hold so I can charge the stupid thing," I said. My eyes pricked with frustrated tears and I swiped rainwater from my face to hide them.

"Have it your way. Over here."

Getting up from the crate required willpower I didn't know I possessed, and thirty seconds or so to clear the wooziness from my head before I dared take a step. The officiate waited patiently. Once I was successfully standing, she gestured to two coils of metal below the panel that had scanned her hand. Tesla coils? Slinkies, maybe? She said they were using Earth technology. The coils pulsed with a bright blue light, surging a faint ripple through the portal plates. Thick cables ran from the coils, rising to the cables near the top of the tower. On a normal day I could see how it would provide the portal with enough energy to send Rethans across several dimensions.

"So I hold them, or . . . ?"

Officiate Lafe stared at me, unspeaking, her face tight. A flash of movement, a glint of silver, and my left hand was captured between her fingers. I felt a sting on either side of my hand. It didn't hurt, at least not compared to getting shot, but I yanked my hand away.

"What'd you do that for?"

"Currents flow better through broken skin."

"Broken like my shoulder?"

"The currents go where you tell them to."

"No, they won't." I held my pierced hand close to my body. The lightning illuminated a small bead of blood on either side. I was imagining all the power escaping through the cannonball sized wound in my shoulder compared to her little pinpricks.

Lafe flipped a sharp silver instrument between fingers. Her lips were thin. "Your injury shouldn't cause a problem," she said, reading my mind. "We can deal with that in a moment if you would—"

"Seriously? You have super healing powers? Because I'm not going to lie, that would—"

"If we need to we can use some non-conducting material to fool your body into thinking the only open skin are those points on your hands," she paused. "I can't heal your injury. That's Thirteenth Dimension power."

"Oh." The small tremor of hope that I might not die on this Godforsaken, muddy hill washed away as quickly as the rain washed the beads of blood from my hand. I lifted my right hand as far as my injury would allow and Officiate Lafe pricked both sides without apology.

"Place your fists within the coils, and open your hands wide so you are touching as much of the metal as possible. Then simply release the charge within your body through your hands. You can manage that, right?"

"Sure." I didn't move. "If you get me that non-whatever-it-is material for my shoulder. You can manage that, right?"

We stared at each other in the pulsing, blue light. If my face looked anything like hers, this was a battle for the record books.

"Just put your hands in the coils," she finally said, and marched away.

I didn't watch where she was going, instead dropping to my knees with a sigh. Water saturated the already wet lower half of my pants. An exhausted ache shivered through me.

I needed to grab my right hand with my left to be able to place it into the coil, moronic invalid that I was, before jamming my left hand in the other coil.

Something cold and heavy slapped onto my shoulder. I grunted, raising rain-bleared eyes to Officiate Lafe. She adjusted a bright white swatch of non-conducting fabric and stepped back.

I closed my eyes and tried to wipe away the tension and fear, the debilitating pain and trauma. I tried to distance myself from the booming thunder and the drenching rain and focus on the currents flowing through my body. I was surprised at the masses of electricity I'd accumulated since volting Deputy Hoth. They crackled to life all along my nervous system, racing across the nerves like copper wires. Shivery threads of current made their way at my urging toward my hands. They tried to make a rapid and painful exit through the entrance wound in my shoulder, hardening for a moment where I imagined the bullet was lodged. The electricity pooled against the Rethan fabric, splintering pain into the damaged flesh. I sagged against the tower, my forehead coming to rest against the cold wet metal. I bit my tongue to suppress a whimper.

It was only with extreme concentration that I forced the mass to unravel and work its way down my fingertips. A burst of burning power exploded from my hands in much larger amounts than I thought the tiny pinpricks of broken skin could accommodate.

Once the flow of electricity started the coils drew the energy away, sucking it from my body as neatly as slurping liquid through a straw. A loud, whirring hum pulled me out of my focus. Bright blue light penetrated my eyelids. I fluttered them open, squinting into a dazzling array of zapping energy. Currents bounced in diagonally jerking masses across the opening, going from one plate to another until they created a solid-looking screen of light. The screen brightened at the edges and expanded into a perfect circle.

Through the electrical screen, I could see a landscape so dissimilar in geography to the one on which I knelt that it might as well be a different planet. Everything appeared smooth and solid, made of shining stone or metal—had to be metal, I concluded—and was housed in an enclosed arena of some sort giving no evidence of what might lay beyond.

My limbs trembled. My mind muddied. I collapsed with a watery squelch, and my limp hands slid from the coils. I leaned my shoulder against the leg of the tower, the peel of an orange, every nutritional bit extracted to power the monstrous display of light before me. My lips tingled in an I-need-oxygen sort of way, but I couldn't seem to get air any farther than the very top of my lungs. A slow and certain suffocation I didn't have enough energy to prevent. I should've given her the coin and taken my chances with her good will.

Officiate Lafe stood over the top of me, her focus on the hand-scanning panel. She didn't bother to look at me or offer any gesture of appreciation. Her fingers brushed across her reacquired monitor and adjusted something near the panel. I didn't expect a party or tears of gratitude, but was a murmured thank you too much to ask for? If I'd had even a spark of energy I would have given her a matching scorch mark for her other shoulder.

"That's it, right?" I asked, hoping.

"Not quite."

"I charged your portal. What more do you need?"

"I need you to be quiet while I finish this."

The energy of holding my hands in my lap became too much, and I let them drop to the wet ground. Cool rain hammered on my head. Water drizzled through my hair and ran down my back. The night deepened as the sun set, the storm no longer the only thing making the Sonoran Desert dark. Rethans splashed around with white-booted feet doing their unknown jobs. More seemed to be congregating closer to the portal, speaking to each other in soft, lighting tones. An eerie cacophony.

I would have given anything to be sitting on the back porch at home, eating watermelon with my dad and watching the deer scamper through the back field. The air at home always seemed to be the right temperature, the setting sun giving off a dazzling array of Technicolor brush strokes. We would spit melon seeds across the lawn in a brilliantly pointless battle of aim and distance.

A shudder brought me back to the miserable present. My eyes focused, unfocused, and then unscrambled two figures from the rain. Thurmond and Marshal Rannen walked side by side, speaking to one another like comrades rather than prisoner and warden. Thurmond halted, staring open-mouthed at the portal, and then hurried to catch up with Rannen. Rannen carried an extra-large crate, and he set it down on top of the crate I'd been sitting on earlier.

My camouflage must have been doing a supreme job, because without so much as a glance in my direction Rannen unlatched the lid of the crate, and Thurmond helped him lift the lid to the ground. The brilliant light from the portal illuminated rain-spattered variations of the unusual snakelike weapons with which the Rethans had threatened us. Most were small, the ones that wrapped around your wrist and fit into the palm of your hand. Several others were only slightly smaller than my own M-16, but looked more like a twisting coil of white stone than an actual weapon.

"What's the range on these smaller ones?" Thurmond asked. He glanced uncomfortably over his shoulder at the portal. The light turned his face pasty.

"On Retha it depends on the amount of electricity you can draw from your body, but on Earth we need to depend on the temporary charge." Rannen picked up a weapon, "See, here's the charge indicator. This charge is nearly gone, but you could still get up to a hundred meters for a stunning shot. Fifty meters if you want to kill."

"Only one shot?"

"For this one yes, but look here. This one has a higher charge. If you leave it on stun, and keep the shot close, you should be able to get as many as five shots. This one," he held up the longer weapon. "No, you'd get only a single shot with this one."

"I get it," Thurmond said. The weapons rattled against each other as human and Rethan sorted through them. "How many do you have? Is this it?"

Rannen nodded. "And the majority of them aren't even charged. You can thank Hoth for that—him and his target practice all week. Rethans are, for the most part, noncombatants, so our company has little or no training in the use of arms. Hoth is considered our weapons expert."

"We need to set up some ambush locations at the south of the camp." Thurmond gestured in the general direction he meant. "Rannen, why don't you grab Hoth and anyone else who can fire one of these things."

"I think Deputy Boderick might be able to give us a hand."

I thought the little guy was more likely to collapse in a dead faint than shoot someone. The sorting of the weapons, the tactical manner of speaking as these Rethans—these aliens—planned to stun and kill human beings, felt suddenly wrong. Never mind that said humans had already tried to kill me. Never mind that they were descending in an unprovoked attack. We would be fighting humans. Humans wearing the uniform that sported the stars and stripes. Justet told me aliens were here to overrun Earth. Unreliable or no, what if it was true? As a citizen and a patriot of Earth, I felt a duty to ask before committing treason.

"Hey, uh, Rannen?" My voice barely made it past my throat manifested by the fact that neither of them turned around. I tried again, louder this time. "Rannen?"

They both looked up and around, squinting into the portal, before their eyes finally found me.

"Oh, crap. Rose!" Thurmond was over to me in two brisk strides. He squatted and chafed my hand between his to return the nonexistent warmth. "You look like hell." He pressed his lips together, examining my face. "But still pretty human-looking."

Rannen approached. The officiate stepped aside, calling for Boderick like she'd been about to do that anyway.

"Rannen," I said again.

"What is it, Kris?" Rannen shuffled one of the larger weapons from his left hand to his right and back.

"You," I swallowed. "You guys aren't here to take us over, are you?"

"I'm sorry, what?" Rannen's head cocked. A tilt of his lips.

"One of the soldiers told me y-you guys were aliens, come to take over our planet."

"That's ridiculous," Rannen said. Creases of laughter circled his eyes.

It had sounded much better in my head. I persisted. "So what are you doing here?"

"The officiate and I had some private business to attend to, but otherwise we're wardens doing our yearly check of the inmate population."

"Oh."

The Rethans were lining up near the portal now, whispering and crowding together. Wardens on peaceful terms with our government. Innocent people—even if they were aliens.

"T, wha-time's it?"

He snapped a look at his watch. "Twenty-oh-eight. You done?"

"No." Water dripped into my eyes. My body shuddered in misery. I rotated my jaw in an attempt to get the words to come out better. "Officiate says she needs me . . . but won'-say why."

Marshal Rannen's silver-white eyebrows dripped water onto his cheeks. "The portal is supposed to be powered constantly, and can only hold a certain amount of charge with the kind of power you're giving it." I sensed his irritation was not directed at me. "It will need another charge or two to be able to get everyone through."

"Ah." The bitter realization settled deep in my chest. I let out a bark of mirthless laughter. "I guess I ought to go *recharge* myself then."

Rannen glanced at the officiate working a few feet away and then said softly, "Why don't you just give her the dimensional catapult?"

I shrugged. "Why aren't you making me?"

Rannen's face went blank, and he didn't respond. Thurmond studied me, his jaw muscles taut. I stared back, trying to look strong and in control of myself. After a moment he addressed Rannen.

"You have any more of that serum?"

"No!" Water sprayed from my lips. "No way!"

Thurmond ignored me. "Rannen?"

"Thurmond," I pleaded. "Didn't you see what it did to me?"

"Yeah. I saw you could walk around and get out more than two words without sounding like an eighty-year-old smoker."

"And I almost volted . . . I was . . . I—"

"Rose." Thurmond rubbed water from my cheek with his thumb. "You charge that portal again in your current state, and it'll kill you. I don't understand what weird attachment you have to that coin thing, but you're going to have to pick between the coin and the serum."

My will to fight flattened into a one-dimensional object of no substance. I didn't respond.

"I'll have Deputy Boderick bring another syringe." Rannen nodded. "You can decide."

"It's going to be fine," Thurmond said to me. "Rannen has a plan. We're going to get you to a medic, and everything will be okay." He released my hand and pushed back to his feet, gathering a few weapons from the crate before disappearing into the rain.

I dropped my eyes away from the intensity of Rannen's look. My gaze landed on his thumb, which was hooking under a familiar-looking black strap strung across his shoulder. As if sensing my focus he pulled the M-16 off his shoulder, and held it by the muzzle.

"D'ya know how'ta use that?" I asked.

He grinned and shook his head. Water sprayed from his hair.

"Can . . . c-c-could I?"

He laid it across my lap. "Stay safe, Kris."

Without another word he grabbed several weapons from the crate and followed Thurmond. I watched the rainy darkness, catching a glimpse of his silver hair over by building twelve as lightning flashed. Then nothing but rain.

I hitched myself straighter against the tower leg. I lifted the shoulder strap of the M-16 over my head and drew the butt of my rifle under my injured arm. I clicked off the safety and flicked the switch to a single-round shot as opposed to the semi-automatic function.

One shot. I had one shot. One shot. One shot.

I couldn't think of anything else. What if I used it too early, or worse, too late? How do you decide that it's *the* moment?

A banging noise drew my attention to the hand-scanning panel. Officiate Lafe was once more at work.

"All right, Shevla. You first." She gestured to the huddled line of Rethans. An older female broke away. Officiate Lafe almost tripped over my knee. She gave me a scornful look before returning her attention to the portal. Shevla placed her hand on the panel, allowing the light to scan it. Then, without a backward glance, she walked into the blue screen of light. Her face and knee disappeared first, making her look like she'd been cut in half vertically. Then she was gone. The metallic world rippled through the blue of the portal, but no figure showed on the other side.

"Next!" The officiate hollered. Her fingers flew over the screen again. The next in line stepped up. I dropped my eyes. This was going to take forever.

The roar of motors could suddenly be heard over the zapping of the portal. For the first time the heroic rumblings of US military vehicles filled me with dread.

Here we go, laughed the voice. Hollow, delighted. *Bring on the blood.*

CHAPTER 20

Caz
6 hours pre-RAGE

The dome of the Dimensional Congressional Council building, the very heart of Retha, rose above Caz. Its multi-metal stripes glistened in the overcast light. She didn't marvel at the design as everyone did, not the shear enormity of the structure nor the massive amounts of foreign materials needed to complete it.

This was former Commandant Ben Attikin's greatest accomplishment. His glory. It had even been named Attikin Dome in its day. Of course, that was before the laws of etiquette and serenity. Before he was exiled. Before it was turned into a simple government building for the self-important council. Now it was the centerpiece of the plaza, housing building upon building of offices, museums, assembly halls, and theaters. A veritable cathedral to all the refinement, culture, and etiquette Retha could afford.

Caz stared at the DCC building's entry doors, sheathed in electrical webs designed to keep out the weather and little more. Her heart maintained a calm, steady beat; her breathing was a quiet rush in her ears. The history of the building, the magnificence, none of it mattered to her. What mattered was that this was the last place she had seen Vin alive.

Rethans flowed past her, going about their important business, placid smiles pasted on their stupid faces. What Caz wouldn't give for them to drop their pathetic masks and show the emotions she knew were screaming to get out.

They wouldn't. They'd been too controlled their whole lives. Brainwashed into believing that *etiquette* and *serenity* kept the world from falling apart. And yet even here in utopia, someone you loved could still betray you or die, and no amount of serenity could make it right again. She'd see if they could maintain their uniform composure when they were running for their lives.

Caz picked up the larger of the two almost identical bags resting near her feet and took a step toward the building. With a jolt she collided with a passerby. The older gentleman's bag thunked to the ground and tipped, spilling the meager contents.

"Oh dear," he said, offering a stiff smile. "My deepest apologies, madam." He bent creakily over his cane in an attempt to reach his bag. "Rough day."

"Am I having a rough day?" Caz looked at the time indicator imprinted on the inside of her wrist. She had four minutes.

"No. *I'm* having a rough day. The roughest. Do you call a marshal when you're feeling rough? No, ma'am. They give you the shuffle off, tell you to meditate, talk to a friend, visit the market of tranquility." He managed to snag the handle of his bag, but a half a dozen round packages of standard fare soy protein rolled away from him. "Don't they know that all that doesn't work when you get to be my age? You need a quick fix of serenity or you end up screaming into pillows, or kicking your pet, or scaring your wife until she starts to talk about getting you exiled." He abandoned his escaped packages with a shuffling kick. He stared at her in what could have been construed as a glare, if his eyebrows hadn't forgotten over the years to contract in anger. "They give you attention then, oh yes. Threaten you with RAGE, and I look at them and say, 'fine by me.' I could use a do over. And then I get a fine for back talk, a shove off, and a few minutes later find myself run over by a pretty lady who wants to tell me how she's having a rough day. You don't know what rough is, sweetcakes! No one does anymore."

Caz grinned at the old anomaly of a Rethan. She retrieved his squishy spheres. The wrapping crinkled in her hands. She shoved them in his bag and then brushed past him. She was halfway across the plaza before she turned back. He was watching her.

"You might want to clear out, grandfather." She adjusted her fingers on her larger, much more important bag. "Your day will only get rougher if you don't."

His lips puckered, but Caz turned away before he could say anything more. She was almost to the door of the DCC building when she heard his voice again, carrying over the chatter of the flowing crowds.

"You left your bag, sweetcakes!"

She grinned over her shoulder, touched her chin, waved it toward him in a gesture of thanks, and then pushed through the web covering the entrance.

Another glance at her wrist. She stepped through the lesser crowds of busy congressional workers and positioned herself behind one of the twelve stone columns adorning the dark vestibule. The stone was cold on her back. Stable, secure, protective. She would be safe here.

Exactly one minute and four seconds later an explosive boom heaved her from her feet. Electricity burst around her, leaping in jagged currents through the air. The power crackled out of the building, searching for the source in Caz's abandoned bag. There would be casualties within the localized blast radius, but other than those few the greatest damage would be to the surrounding infrastructure. That device was a basic, miniaturized prototype of the one in the bag she cradled, and yet held none of the elegance and subtlety.

Screams echoed around her, and sirens from the outside. Caz crouched behind her column. As the hall emptied Caz closed her eyes, letting the horrified sounds of terror fill her. Outside the building any vestiges of Rethan serenity had been obliterated. With the loss of this control, perhaps anarchy would finally reign.

Caz heard a dragging sound coming from the front doors, heavy breathing, and then a thump from the other side of the column. She'd thought she was finally alone. Apparently not.

A deep red pool crept toward her from beyond the column. She watched in fascination as it spread. Caz touched the pool with two fingers. She tapped the blood with her thumb and rubbed it into her palms, where it etched deep crimson lines into the folds of her skin.

She hadn't expected blood, at least not this close to her—not yet. Caz stayed where she was, listening as the breathing panted along. Then, with a gasp and a sigh, silence.

She rose to her feet, calmly rubbed her hands together to disperse the blood, and then wiped the remaining blood onto the legs of her pants. She looked at her wrist and picked up her bag.

It was time to meet the council.

CHAPTER 21

Rose

A single gunshot shattered the air.

My eyes flew open, the natural instinct to duck forcing my shoulder to slide off the tower leg. My hands and rifle splashed in the mud.

The line of Rethans condensed into a roaring mob. Hands reached over me, trying to get to the hand-scanner first. Cold treads of white boots struck my arms, legs, and chest. I protected my head with one arm, unable to move or even cry out as my damaged body was knocked and pummeled. A rather vicious kick to my mouth, and I tasted grit and blood.

"Enough! That's enough!" The officiate bellowed, a hammer of sound that demanded respect. "I said enough!"

The feeling of churned waters settled. Boots shifted from foot to foot. I peered past my arm. The officiate gave two Rethans a prompting shove and waved off the rest.

"Get back in line, or I'll send you to help Marshal Rannen and Deputy Hoth!"

The Rethans submitted, although with a great deal of complaining. An especially baleful-looking fellow stepped backward, his chin thrust out. Not angry exactly—his face couldn't seem to unflatten—but perhaps angry for a Rethan.

I pushed myself from the mud, drawing my rifle closer to my body. Warm, coppery blood filled my mouth. I spat. The officiate reached into an inside pocket of her uniform and drew out two large, identical syringes.

"You might want to use one of these right now." She stretched out to hand them to me, not bothering to lean over far enough for me to reach. "We're going to need another charge before too long."

I struggled onto my knees, swiping my sleeve across my chin, and spat again before fumbling with cold, wet fingers for the syringes. The second they left her hand, the officiate turned away.

"Next!"

Several Rethans jostled, and one broke free. He put his hand on the panel before the others could untangle themselves. If my mental count was correct, this Rethan made only three that had gotten through so far. Three out of twenty.

I squeezed the syringes. Hateful darkness saturated my mind as thoroughly as the rain drenched the rest of me.

Forget about the drones, snarled the voice. *Worry about yourself.*

I muttered under my breath, "Shut-up-stop-talking-to-yourself-I'll-do-what-I-want," and yanked off the cap of one syringe with my teeth. I let the other fall onto my lap. The enormous needle shook like a twig under gale force winds. Once—twice—three times I tried to jab it into my leg. I succeeded on the fourth. At once I felt the overwhelming rush of not only electricity and adrenaline, but also the ferocious anger stabbing into my brain.

Damn that Marshal Lafe. Curse her to hell.

"Marshal Lafe?" I whispered. "The officiate?"

Officiate. Marshal. Whatever she's calling herself these days.

I had to stop talking to myself. Although it didn't feel like a one-sided conversation.

The heavy *bam-bam-bam-bam* of an M-249 SAW silenced my thoughts. A hum and a strange zipping sound from the Rethan weapons responded. The M-16s were getting in on the action now. Quite a few by the sound. The bursts from the south of the camp were still far enough away that I knew they hadn't taken the hill yet.

A grenade exploded somewhere not far from the southern buildings, spraying up a funnel of mud. The Rethans hit the ground, crying out in terror. The fear of leaving the line again and being sent to fight was apparently stronger than their fear of being shot here. Aside from the scattered piles of crates, not close enough to be useful, the entire line of Rethans was woefully exposed. The officiate sent another Rethan crawling through the portal.

The weapons fire was so close now that flashes of fire could be seen exploding from the rifles. A single bullet dinged into a stack of crates not far from us. I ducked. The face of the closest Rethan came into focus. He was an older male, with a lined face and wide, frightened eyes. His silver hair was plastered against his head. Mud spattered his face, but his lips were set in a curve that hinted at frequent laughter.

My mind flashed to the time my dad had gotten his leg stuck under his truck. A tire had blown when he'd been working somewhere out in the field. When he'd tried to repair it, the truck had tilted off the jack, trapping him under the axle. I'd panicked only after he'd missed dinner, and I hadn't found him until he'd been stuck for several hours already. I remembered his eyes peering into my flashlight as it swept across his face. The fear had drained from his face, and his mouth had pulled into a pained grin. From fear to hope.

I blinked at the face of the frightened Rethan, his mouth a grimace of fear. A good ten or eleven Rethans still needed to make it through the portal. They wouldn't all survive at this rate. To emphasize the point, the portal flickered and went out with a distinct hum.

Don't bother, said the voice.

With stumbling fingers I pulled the coin from my pocket, rubbing my thumb across the letters. Rannen said it was a catapult that would open a portal through to Retha. Would we all be sucked through? Would there be other Rethans who could help fight off the commander? Would Dad be there?

Will you cry like an infant if you see him?

I closed my eyes to block out the voice, and searched through my mind and body for the energy the coin needed. A certain type of voltage, Rannen said. A certain type. Different from what I had used on the portal. Different from anything I'd used before.

I felt it. Like an element hidden within the energy from the storm. As though we were finally speaking the same language, the coin between my fingers called to it and drew it from my body.

The coin flew from my hand with a deafening zap. I wrenched my eyes open as a jolt of electricity exploded from the coin and shot toward the sky. The electricity grew and expanded, almost directly in front of the other portal. The new portal solidified into a perfect circle, taller and wider than what was left of the scrapped-together version. But unlike the portal on the tower, there was nothing to see on the other side. Just blackness, like a void. No weapon-wielding Rethans. No Dad.

I collapsed onto my side, my body an exhausted, empty shell. A bitter taste filled my mouth.

Officiate Lafe appeared beside me. Her eyes and mouth were wide as she stared at the newest portal hovering before us. She recovered in an instant and gestured the last of the Rethans forward.

"Into the portal now, everyone!"

Rethans leapt through the circle of lightning one at a time and vanished on the other side. A tentative touch on my shoulder startled me. I knocked the hand away before looking up. The older Rethan who'd reminded me of my dad recoiled a step.

"Are you all right?" He held out a hand to me. "Can I?"

With hate exploding around us, the innocent helping hand seemed like a foreign object. He must have sensed my trepidation because his fingers curled over his palm.

"Th-thanks," I said, lifting my muddy hand for help.

His hand felt brittle, the translucent skin papery thin. He helped me to my feet and assisted me the few yards to a safer spot behind a crate, not far from the tower. I collapsed and rolled onto my side.

Here, in a subconscious realm of thought, things were so simple. There was nothing I could do, so I would do nothing.

Get up! the voice shrieked. *Don't just lay there. Go through the portal before you get us killed!*

My head ached so badly I almost moved to get away from it. Rain hammered my face, a not-so-gentle reminder that I was still alive, if only just.

"Miss?"

Only two Rethans remained. Officiate Lafe and the one kneeling in front of me, a syringe held between two fingers. The older Rethan patted my face. "Miss? Would you like help with this? I can if you want me to. I don't think you're going to last much longer if—"

I blinked at him, trying to speak.

"Please, I've got to go." He jabbed a thumb over his shoulder at the portal where Officiate Lafe was beckoning to him, her expression incensed.

"You did us a big favor here, and another personal favor for me years ago. I want to help you, if I can. A story to tell my grandbabies, how the DCC Slayer saved—"

An explosion rattled the crate at my back. The Rethan ducked, cowering next to my leg.

"Do you want the injection, miss?" He was breathless.

"Rose." Such a small word and yet so important.

"What?"

"M-my name is Rose. Kris Rose."

"Oh, okay. Um, Rose." He nodded, seeming to understand.

I nodded back and closed my eyes.

There was a soft touch to my chest, a stab, and then agony burst through my heart. My limbs stiffened in a torturous spasm. Vivid splashes of colors, emotions, thoughts, memories—

Dad tossing me a dinner roll from across the table, two already on his plate . . . the chow line overrun by a group of overambitious lieutenants . . . Xander's head thrown back, laughing at his nephew's childish joke . . . irritation turning to worry that Dad wasn't home yet from police work . . . annoyance that Drill Sergeant Williams wouldn't let the smudge on my uniform go . . . the Rethan drones' contented smiles, like a lifetime of brainwashing could actually have made them happy.

I gasped and pried my eyes open. Energy pulsed through my body in such strong increments that I couldn't bear to sit still.

My eyes lingered on the portal for a second. The elderly Rethan was gone. Only Officiate Lafe was left. Why hadn't she gone through yet? I pulled the rifle's strap over my head so I could hold it better and dragged myself through the mud until I was beside her behind a barricade of crates. She didn't even glance at me.

A grenade exploded inside the circle of buildings. We ducked toward one another. Mud burst outward. When it settled I rested the barrel of the rifle on the crate, sighting down the length with my finger on the trigger. My pulse pounded in my shoulder. I watched for movement.

A particularly brilliant flash of lightning illuminated a camo-clad figure racing past building twelve. I lined him in my sites before I recognized Thurmond. In one bound he disappeared behind a barricade of crates.

The firing stopped. An oppressive silence pressed on the camp. The pinging of the rain on the roofs of the buildings, the watery splashes in the puddles made the uncanny hush downright frightening.

Where were they?

A dark figure materialized next to Thurmond's position. The white patch on the nose identified Luginbeel. A limping figure appeared a building over, had to be Sanderford.

The way Luginbeel strutted in, his rifle weaving back and forth for a target, was so primetime SWAT I would have shot him myself if I'd thought he was worth my round. But this was not *the* moment. Of that much I was sure. Luginbeel passed Thurmond's location. Thurmond rose up from behind the crate, slashing out. His knife caught a flash of lightning and disappeared into Luginbeel's shoulder. A boom of thunder muted the cry. Luginbeel disappeared into the muddied shadow of the building. Thurmond wrenched the rifle out of his grip, and it rose and fell twice against Luginbeel's head.

The officiate shifted beside me.

"I need Deputies Boderick and Hoth, and Marshal Rannen."

That's why she was still here. I couldn't help feeling grudging admiration toward her. We hunched low as bullets pinged off the barricade, some zipping through the openings between crates or spraying up small funnels of mud. Rifle fire answered from Thurmond's location thanks to Luginbeel's stolen rifle.

"Where are they?" The officiate hissed.

The militaristic bulk of two Humvees roared from between buildings. One slowed to a stop twenty feet from us. The headlights beamed blinding eyes on our location.

Thurmond sent bullets pelting into one side of the Humvee. The passenger door of the Hummer was thrown open. A red-haired figure rolled out and scrambled for cover behind the back tires. Justet lined up nicely in my sites, and I wished I could have stitched my initials in his scrawny rump. He seemed to decide Sanderford's location was his best shot, and he high stepped away. Bullets from Thurmond's rifle threw up mud at his heels.

"Attikin's ass! I need those three now!" Officiate Lafe pushed me to the side and peeked between the crates.

"You should go, Officiate Lafe," I said. She snapped me a look. I held her gaze. "I'll hold this position until they get here." I wished I had anywhere near the confidence in myself I was trying to express.

She turned away, glaring between the crates, and suddenly her mouth fell open in a formulaic, shocked expression. Slowly she stood, a hand going to her gaping mouth.

"What are you doing?" I tugged at her pant leg. "Get down!"

My brief glimpse between the crates showed a single figure standing within the circle of buildings. The commander's tall, angular body and stern-cut hair was instantly recognizable.

From behind her, Justet's white hand launched a grenade toward us. The spoon disconnected from the top and flipped away. The automatic count started in my head. The grenade arched. *One thousand.* I dropped the rifle. *Two thousand.* I grabbed both the officiate's legs and yelled, "get down," trying to pull her behind the crates. *Three thousand.* No time. *Four thousand.* I buried my face next to my arm, curling my legs up to protect my abdomen.

The grenade exploded on the other side of the crates. Thousands of bits of shrapnel tore into the crate, smashing it into me. I bounced once before coming to a stop, a crate resting on my back. Stinging, oozing warmth melted across my face. I touched a jagged gash on my hairline.

I threw the crate off my back. My vision fuzzed. It took a moment to locate Officiate Lafe. She had been blasted against the crooked leg of the tower but was, unbelievably, still standing. The light from the portal lit her hair from behind. Her arms still shielded her face, but the fabric was shredded away. Shards of metal glistened in an enormous amount of red, very human-looking blood. Blood also flowed from gaping wounds in her chest and mingled with the rain. I couldn't tear my eyes away, finding it so peculiar that a Rethan could be just like a human inside.

Adrenaline in a tube was nothing like the natural adrenaline flowing through me now. I dashed water and blood from my eyes, rose onto my knees, and pulled up my rifle.

Thurmond fired over and over again from the eastern end of the camp. The rest of the commander's crew ducked out of sight. I pushed painfully to my feet, using Thurmond's cover fire to get me over to the officiate.

"Come on ma'am, you've got to go back to Retha!" I yelled, my hand going around her waist. With a painful wheeze, she locked her knees, refusing to move. Silent words fell from her lips.

I didn't have the strength to force her and took a knee, motioning with my rifle for Rannen and Hoth to come. Thurmond held back the soldiers with his cover fire. I didn't see Boderick. Marshal Rannen ran at a crouch toward me with Hoth behind him, Rannen's head moving side to side as he watched for a target. He had a Rethan weapon wrapped around his hand and fired blue electrical bolts toward the enemy to keep them down.

Five, six, seven shots from Thurmond and silence descended again. Thurmond ejected the magazine, looked at it, and cast it aside. He wasn't holding a Rethan weapon anymore either.

Marshal Rannen passed the first Humvee, a mere twenty yards away. Hoth paused and rose from his crouch. What was he doing? Water dripped from his ponytail. His lips became a thin line. A Rethan weapon glimmered in his hand. He aimed at Rannen's back, blinked, and squeezed the trigger.

The bolt curled into Rannen, wrapping around his torso and throwing him forward onto his face into the mud. He didn't move.

"No!" The scream tore from my throat.

I brought the rifle to my hip, forgetting everything else, and fired at Hoth. The trigger clicked the firing pin into place, but no bullet exploded from the end. I smashed my fist on the forward assist and fired again. Click.

Hoth gave me a cursory glance and leaned over Rannen to touch his neck. Red, bleeding rage eclipsed any fear or pain.

The commander stepped from the shadows. She made no attempt to crouch or hide. The corners of her mouth lifted in amusement. Her boots sloshed in the mud and water. Rain dripped from the brim of her hat. Lightning illuminated her face, leaving her eyes black holes of shadow. She eased a 9mm out of a drop-leg holster and tapped it against her thigh.

Deputy Hoth rose from his examination of Rannen. He turned his head and opened his mouth to say something. In one fluid motion, the commander raised the pistol to his head and squeezed the trigger.

My whole body jerked in revulsion. The crushing sound of Hoth's collapsing body sent waves of nausea through me. My fingers numbed. The rifle dropped from my hands and splashed near my feet.

"What are you doing?" Justet yelled. His dripping white face arrived at the commander's shoulder. He couldn't seem to look away from Hoth's body. "I thought you said he was working for us?"

"No loose ends." The commander stepped over the corpse.

"We just need to get the portal, right? We don't actually have to kill them!" Justet's voice reached a high note.

The commander ignored him. Sergeant Sanderford and over a dozen other soldiers came out from behind the buildings. The rain, wind, and thunder beat a metronome against the weighty quiet.

I spotted a glistening white object on the ground near one of the overturned crates and dropped to my knees. This wasn't over. I rotated the Rethan weapon, trying to remember how Rannen held it. Egg thingy in palm. Snake thingy around wrist. Thumb on trigger. With a zinging sound, energy was drawn from my body into the weapon. Easy, peasy. I aimed at the commander . . . lemon squeezy . . . my thumb squeezed the trigger.

A blue bolt zipped out, hitting Lieutenant Justet in the hip. He was thrown back with a yell and landed on his butt. His feet went up over his head, and he belly flopped into the mud. I adjusted my aim and squeezed the trigger again. It hit another soldier on his elbow and sent him spinning. Everyone else split.

The commander alone stood her ground. I squeezed the trigger again. A spark fizzled from the muzzle. I pressed the trigger several more times, and then chucked the weapon at her. It only flew a few feet before landing with a squelch of finality. The commander raised the baretta and pointed it between Officiate Lafe and me.

The last of my energy leaked quietly away. My legs weakened. I leaned against a crate. A whisper of words from behind and I finally understood what the officiate was saying.

"My men first . . . my men first . . . my men first . . ."

I thought about her simply stepping backward through the portal. Surely someone on the other side would be able to heal the shrapnel wounds with their highly advanced technology. She rubbed at the blood flowing from her abdomen as though if she brushed enough away it would clear the problem. Her eyes never left the commander.

How Officiate Lafe remained standing so long was a mystery, but whatever it was suddenly deserted her. She dropped to her knees. The commander shifted the aim of her weapon to me.

A revving motor shredded the night. Headlights bore down on me as one of the Hummers raced forward to cut me down. I only had time to cover my face with my arm.

"Rose! Get out of the way! Get out of the—"

A blur of Thurmonator sprinted past the commander just as a bullet exploded from the muzzle of her pistol.

CHAPTER 22

Blood sprayed from Thurmond's head, misting my face. His body slammed into my chest. I landed on my back. Thurmond's body was heavy and limp on top of me. All the air went out of my lungs. Jagged shards of pain ripped through my shoulder.

With a gasp and a desperate grunt of effort, I rolled with Thurmond. The Hummer hurtled over the top of us, the front tires barely missing my face, and smashed into the tower. It jolted up on its front wheels where it balanced precariously long enough for me to throw Thurmond off my chest.

With a groan of Kevlar on metal the Hummer dropped, the back wheel landing its crushing weight onto the back of my thigh. I cried out as my leg, chest, and the side of my face pressed deep into the sludge.

I gave one weak effort to free myself and fell still. Mud seeped into my ear.

The light from the dimensional catapult portal vanished, laying a blanket of darkness on the battlefield.

The commander stood dimly in my line of sight, one hand rested on her hip, the other holding the pistol at her side. The rest of the camp was a smudge of movement behind her, unimportant worker ants scurrying to do the queen's bidding.

The Hummer door creaked as it opened, and a pair of boots dropped down next to the vehicle. He limped toward the commander while offering me a smug glance. Sanderford's thin, sandy hair was plastered to his head.

In a quick, rough movement, the commander grabbed his collar and dragged him toward her. His expression changed to surprise in the second before only the back of his head was visible.

"If you've damaged the portal, you'll pay for it with more than your life." She put her face right in his, snarling with such venom I felt as though my skin were crawling with spiders. "Now go get the others to help disassemble it."

The commander shoved him. He stumbled away from her, and disappeared from my line of sight.

"Specialist Rose." The commander approached with languid steps, like a dorsal fin gliding above bloody water. She crouched next to me. A long finger traced through the blood from the gash on my hairline and made a wide circle that ended on my chin. Then she touched the tip of my nose.

"But it isn't really 'Specialist Rose' is it?" She exhaled an almost nostalgic sigh. "It's a pity you don't remember anything. There was a time when your brilliance was infamous throughout the entirety of Retha, with a flashy title and everything. Now you are simply irrelevant."

She took my chin in her hand and pulled her face close to mine, looking at me with molten silver eyes.

"There was a time when I thought I'd like to be the one to finish you, Caz. Pull the trigger or wield the knife. But then I realized I'm *not* you."

She pushed my head back into the mud. He finger hooked around the chain of my dog tags and she yanked them from my neck.

"You kept the key." She raised it to eye level and examined the pendant. "You had no idea what you had here, and yet you kept it. Fascinating."

She pulled something small from her pocket. Lightning flashed on a tiny, silver object not unlike a ball bearing. Holding my half-circle pendant between two fingers, she placed the silver BB next to it. With a zap it snapped together, and she released the pendant. The BB hung suspended, somehow, where the center of the half-circle should have been.

I reached for it, my arm shaking with the effort. She rose to her feet, pulling it out of my grasp, and stared down at me. Cold humor etched her face. With a scornful snort she turned away.

"Marshal Lafe." The commander made her way past the scattered crates over to the mortally wounded Rethan leader.

The officiate hunched over her injuries. Bulging eyes glared through strings of shimmering silver hair. Her mouth opened and closed. The commander ejected an empty magazine and allowed it to splash to the ground before snapping in a new one. She pulled back the slide and released it with a metallic snap.

"You should have listened to me when I said she was unhinged. You should have done something. But to condemn me to the new council? You knew I had nothing to do with the murders. You knew!" The commander ran her hand over her face to expel the anger. When she looked up again, her expression was calm. "None of it matters any more. I fluxing well don't know where she hid the Heart of Annihilation, and of course she doesn't know. They never remember anything do they, *Officiate*, these RAGE inmates? I blame you for the loss of the weapon more than I do her."

She shook her head and tapped the pistol against her leg. Without another word or expression she raised the pistol, pointing it at Officiate Lafe's head.

"I've spent over twenty years trying to find another source that will lead me to the Heart of Annihilation and now, finally, I am close. So very close." The commander looked to her left. I followed her gaze until my eyes lit on the still form of Marshal Rannen. She looked back at Officiate Lafe. Her finger tensed on the trigger.

"And," the commander swung the pendant in front of the officiate's face, "I have the key. I want you to die knowing you failed your mission here, and that I destroyed Retha's last chance at finding the device."

The commander's face tightened, not in pleasure but cold, hard, premeditated justice. I closed my eyes the instant before the shot fired. The sound ricocheted through my mind—a heavy thump and a splashing sound. The busy voices of the soldiers in the background became perceptible only as they silenced. Rain pounded into the puddles, cheerfully fulfilling the yearly moisture quota.

The rumble of a motor cut through the rain.

"Sergeant Wichman, there you are. So good of you to finally join us."

I forced my eyes open. A Deuce was now parked inside the circle of buildings, with the driver's side door hanging open. Dark streaks covered Sergeant Wichman's shoulders, and water beaded on the brim of his hat. The commander didn't look at him while she holstered her pistol, but I got an eyeful of the shock on his face as he surveyed the scene. The expression was gone when the commander looked up.

She nodded in the direction of Marshal Rannen. "I'll have the other men get the portal and load that one in the Deuce." She jabbed her thumb at me. "Make sure the rest are dead."

She shouted orders to the milling figures. The rain lessened for the first time since it started, and I was able to see the carnage in vivid detail. The headlights of the vehicles illuminated the twisted bodies of Hoth, Rannen, and Officiate Lafe. Lieutenant Justet was being helped to his feet while someone else slapped Luginbeel's face.

I gripped Thurmond's leg, grateful that my near-paralyzed state didn't allow me to see the way his stomach refused to rise and fall.

Sergeant Wichman was suddenly crouching beside me. His eyes roved down my body to my trapped leg, and he placed two fingers against my throat to check my pulse. When his eyes made it back to my face I gave a slow, accusing blink. He jumped.

"Hey, little buddy," he whispered.

I blinked a few more times. My tongue glued to the roof of my mouth.

"Where's Thurmond? What happened to him?"

I tightened my grip on the motionless leg.

"Oh, shit." He glanced around. "You've got to hang tight here for a bit. Don't let them know you're alive."

"Wh—" I swallowed and tried again. "Wh-where am I g-going ta-go?"

"Sergeant Wichman. Sometime today!" The commander called. Wichman leapt to his feet. "They're either dead or they're not. Finish up. We need your help over here."

"Be right there, ma'am." He crouched next to me again, slipped something white into one of my muddy pockets, and whispered, "I'm really sorry about this."

Wichman drew a 9mm from a shoulder holster, and for a moment I believed I'd used my last life.

Wichman aimed, and I jerked as he unloaded two rounds into the mud not far from my head.

Then he disappeared from my line of sight to answer the commander's beckon. Rannen's enormous body was rolled over and lifted by a team of no less than seven soldiers, who struggled to wrangle him into the back of the Deuce. Camouflaged figures moved past me, pulling the silver plates off the tower. No one noticed the simple silver coin they were churning deep into the mud. They jostled Officiate Lafe with irreverent feet as they worked off the hand-scanning panel and disconnected wires.

The pieces were piled into overturned crates and loaded into the Deuce with Rannen. Every eye avoided looking at me.

Luginbeel, his head lolling, was helped into the Deuce by another private I vaguely recognized. Sergeant Sanderford gave me a hard, unreadable stare as the commander spoke softly in his ear, her back to me.

Everyone climbed into the vehicles with juvenile whooping and cheering like they had scored a victory, not murdered a bunch of guiltless alien visitors and two former comrades. I included myself in this count, since there was no doubt I would be following Thurmond shortly.

Sergeant Sanderford finally looked away, nodding to the commander as she climbed in the passenger side of the Deuce. Doors slammed and headlights flickered around. They maneuvered the vehicles between the buildings, all except the Humvee parked on my leg, and trundled off into the darkness.

The officiate's body lay directly in my line of sight. She was twisted in an unnatural heap, her blank silver eyes staring at me. The bullet hole in her forehead oozed a trickle of blood that the rain washed down her nose.

"Daddy," I whispered.

I was painfully aware of my isolation, my utter aloneness on this bloody hilltop surrounded by corpses. Corpses of enemies. The corpse of a friend.

Shoot me. Cut me. Crush me. Anything but be responsible for a friend's death.

Please let me die, I thought.

You die, I die. The angry voice in my mind snarled. Caz. That's what the commander called her—called me. *Dig yourself out of this you stupid, selfish little girl.*

I couldn't feel anything but sorry for Caz. She would die with me, angry and vengeful to the end.

Something shifted under my fingers followed by a groan. I gripped Thurmond's pant leg, only to have the fabric ripped away. Movement, muttering, and swearing. A face hovered inches from mine.

"Hey, Rose." A soft touch to my head.

The moon shifted out from behind the clouds. I couldn't tell where the mud ended and the blood began, but there couldn't possibly be a bullet through Thurmond's head if he was talking to me. My lips parted to take in a shallow breath. He pressed two fingers on my neck, checking my pulse, and then vanished.

A moment of panic. Had I imagined him?

Thurmond staggered around the Hummer, bracing his hand on the side for support. I closed my eyes, maybe even took a snooze, because when I opened them he knelt next to me. He gathered my face in his hands. His thumbs wiped the blood and grime from my cheeks.

"Come on, sweetheart, you're in shock," he said. "Can you talk to me?"

His voice, a composed rumble of sound, penetrated deep into my injured soul. Soothing. Quiet. My consciousness wavered. A light slap to my face. A shock of breath shuddered through me.

"There you go. Good girl. Deep breaths."

Tears jammed up somewhere behind my eyes.

"Say something, Kris. Come on now, talk to me."

"There's a H-Hummer on m'leg."

Thurmond barked out a brief explosion of humorless laughter. "I know there is."

He pulled a sticky strand of bloodied hair from my face and smoothed it back. His eyes flitted to the wheel of the Hummer. I couldn't imagine how he was going to get it off. I don't think he knew either.

"You're going to be okay, but you need to stay awake for me. Can you do that?"

For him? Sure. My body, however, rebelled, quietly shutting off the lights and closing the doors.

Indistinct flashes of events paraded before of me, Thurmond's voice a constant soundtrack. Sometimes he seemed to be camped out near my head, patting my cheek to force my eyes open. Sometimes he was a shadow, moving around the Rethan camp and assembling a pile of debris. Sometimes I didn't see him at all, although the Hummer rocked on my trapped thigh.

I wasn't sure when my leg came free of the tire, but with a release of pressure my flattened limb curled toward my body. The coolness of the mud on my chest spread to my back. The moon and stars, fringed by wispy clouds, rolled into view. Strong arms cradled me like an infant.

"Come on Kris, wake up. Please! I need you! God, I need some help!" Thurmond's voice whispered in my ear, desperate, pleading, and prayerful. "Please, she needs a doctor and I don't know how to get that for her! I don't know what to do!"

I remembered my dad saying, *When you've done all you can do, God will make up the difference.* My mind cleared and I saw a possible solution.

"Let's take the hummmm . . ." Too many m's. My lips wouldn't move beyond that.

"Rose?"

"Hmm mmm?" That was almost clear.

"The battery on the Hummer's dead. I don't know what to do." Discouragement poured from his words.

"Use hummman jummm jummm-per . . ."

"Jumper cables?"

"Me."

"You can't even walk."

"You haven't . . . you . . . given me a chance." Blackness crept in. The small window that opened long enough for me to communicate a solution began to slide shut.

"Didn't you use all of your energy on the portal?"

"Dunno."

Thurmond's face disappeared as my eyelids fell shut. The problem with the Humvee suddenly didn't seem so important.

"Rose? Hey! Come back!"

Movement. A warm touch of skin to my hands. Cool metal under my fingers. My despondency lifted for a brief second as a jittering surge of electricity erupted from my fingertips. The hazy roaring of an engine. The musty canvas smell of a Humvee.

CHAPTER 23

Caz
*5 hours and 40 minutes pre-*RAGE

Caz had never taken the opportunity to step inside the council chamber. Few did. Not that it was forbidden. Just looked down upon. For a government with the sole purpose of keeping their population peaceful and content, they allowed little if any participation in decision-making. Everyone was always happy with their decisions, thanks to the serene enforcement of the marshals.

One would think that the council chamber would be housed beneath the extravagant, gaudy dome that could be seen from thousands of grids away. Attikin's dome. It wasn't. But the council chamber was legendary in and of itself. An enormous half-circle amphitheater descended before her, the roof open to the sky. A zapping, multi-colored electrical web usually covered the arched entrance. The web was now missing, absorbed by the blast in the square. A chatter of frightened voices from deep in the chamber filled the air in the web's absence.

Caz trailed her fingers across the archways and came to a stop inside the chamber. Each step of the amphitheater was made of a different metal: the ones closer to her were alloys, making them more resistive to electrical conductivity; the lower ones, pure metals such as copper and gold. Highly conductive. Highly valuable. Exactly one hundred and twenty-two elaborate seats, staggered across the different steps, were filled with either aging Rethans who would most likely die in their seats or the younger sons or daughters of dead council members, groomed their whole lives for the position. Like Vin.

The very epicenter of the chamber was a stage made of the most precious of Rethan metals, the most highly conductive pure silver, which had been tarnished through the ages. The hundred and twenty-third seat, a huge, garish throne, was occupied by the commandant himself.

Caz stood above them all, looking down at the silver heads. Some were already out of their seats, gathering their things in preparation to leave. Others stood in tight groups. A cold wind whipped through the chamber, scattering their tense, frightened chatter.

Caz took the time to count. *Attikin's ass.* All the seats were filled except one. And she knew exactly who was missing.

Xander.

She shrugged, knelt, and opened her bag. Several items were laid neatly side-by-side. Caz touched the melon-sized orb in the very center. The yellow glow warmed her fingers. It was so lovely. She sighed, and moved her hand to the two items beside it.

She'd spent her whole Rethan life obsessing over weapons. The cold, hard mathematics; the elegant engineering, the thrilling potential of killing capacity. What she never considered, until the last few weeks, was the artistry essential in taking an individual life.

Fire a weapon, set off an explosion. None of it had that personal touch. The cool of the other person's skin. The flicker of terror in their eyes. The recognition of her complete power.

All the mathematics and science in the world were no match for the most basic of weapons. She already had the materials in her lab: the anvil, the forge, the nichrom hammer. And silver. Alloy silver with lead, and strength was added to the weapon's high conductivity.

The blade sang against the Heart of Annihilation and whispered across the fabric of the bag. Caz held it before her eyes. Twelve inches of glistening, untarnished silver alloy, sleek with a graceful curve. A handle of polished copper fitted perfectly to her hand.

Caz draped her bag's long carrying strap over her shoulder and adjusted it so it hung down her back. She stood. Her eyes went straight to the lord of the room, sitting on his throne.

The commandant stared back at her.

"Cazandra, what in Gauss's law are you doing here?" Commandant Paliyo's voice echoed all around the chamber, silencing the other council members. The one hundred and twenty-one other faces turned on her.

The commandant pushed himself to his feet. Caz hadn't seen him since before Vin died. He'd aged in that time, adding at least another ten kilos to his weight. His face was splotchy, and cavernous circles shrouded his eyes.

"We have an appointment," Caz said into the silence of the room.

"The hell we do. I told council member Fisk not to allow it." Commandant Paliyo gestured to the side. A half a dozen marshals materialized from the shadows and came her way. "Get her out of here. And will someone *please* get me a report of what's going on out there!"

"I can tell you." Caz adjusted her fingers on the blade.

"You?" The scorn in the commandant's tone worked a twinge of anger past Caz's cool façade.

"Yes sir, your honor. Or I could show you." Caz sighted down the blade.

The marshals climbed the steps toward her. Caz set her feet, bent her knees, and grinned at the closest marshal. He was young. Not much older than Caz was when Zak Faras died. Too young to carry the vacant mien of all Rethans.

He reached for her. Caz slashed the blade across his arm, cutting through flesh and bone with ease.

The world silenced. His mouth opened, his tongue as red as the blood flowing from the missing appendage. She recognized that noise should be filling her ear—screams, perhaps a spattering sound. It was lost behind the *whoosh, whoosh* of her own singing blood and the deafening song of adrenaline. Of rapture.

The first marshal hadn't even fallen before her blade moved on. A slice to her left, a stab to her right. She felt the blade penetrate flesh. The catch of bone. The tug of fabric. She counted as they fell. She danced down the steps, her feet light upon the alloyed daises, the melodious whoosh in her ears.

Pure, tarnished silver brightened beneath her feet. The rushing sound faded and sounds penetrated. Screams. Running feet, cries of supplication, chaos. The quiet zap of the energy surging up and down the dripping blade.

"Silence!" Caz whistled the blade through the air, projecting energy into a sizzling lightning bolt that swept the chamber and spattered those closest in blood. "I said silence!"

The screaming melted into whimpers, and the council as a whole froze where they were. An ancient male wiped a crimson spot from his cheek. Caz scanned the doorways, nooks, and corners for evidence of other marshals. None appeared. Her path could be mapped by the blood and bodies.

Caz's boots squeaked as she turned on the silver daises. Commandant Paliyo cowered behind his oversized throne.

"My esteemed commandant," Caz said quietly. "Would you be so kind as to ask everyone to take their seats?"

He came out from behind his chair, shuffling on his knees, his hands clasped prayerfully.

"Cazandra."

Caz cocked an eyebrow. He stood hastily.

"Everyone, take your seats," the commandant said in a hoarse whisper.

The council members, for the most part, obeyed. Hesitant and shaky, they managed to get to their feet and either collapse into the closest chair or perch precariously on the edge, so as to take flight at a moment's notice. A few were unable to move in any direction.

"My dear council." Caz ran the blade of the knife across her arm, revealing the weapon's shine. Blood saturated her sleeve. "We are gathered for a plenary session to discuss the inclusion of weapon number one-twenty-three to the public arsenal."

No one moved. No sound was heard except a groan of pain from one of the closest fallen marshals. Caz swung the blade around, directing a powerful charge of voltage into the copper handle and down the blade. White lightning curled out, striking the prone figure atop his head. The body jerked, then lay still and silent. Gasps exploded from the council members. Half rose from their seats. Caz silenced them with a look.

"However, your graces, I would like to submit that it is no longer enough to add a weapon to the arsenal. The public record may state its presence. It may hold at bay those lower dimensions who would like to invade us for our technology." She raised her voice. "But it will *never* deter the Thirteenth Dimension."

Caz allowed a pause for emphasis, then continued. "As requested— nay, as forced upon my dearly departed parents—the Fisk family has completed the weapon in which we will be able to combat the Thirteenth Dimension, the Heart of our beloved planet."

Caz reached into her bag and palmed the orb. She withdrew it with one hand and held it aloft for the council to see.

"What I am proposing is not simply adding this magnificent feat of engineering to the arsenal, but using it to eliminate the threat to Retha and the remaining dimensions."

Some gasped. A few muttered complaints. At least she had gotten a response of some kind. Not favorable, but then she hadn't expected it to be.

"Cazandra," Commandant Paliyo's voice broke over her, angry and disbelieving. "You can't possibly think we would ever be willing to start a war with a dimension so far beyond our capabilities to combat. This not only goes against the rules of etiquette and—"

Rage boiled her blood in a sudden burst of heat. Caz slammed the Heart of Annihilation into his lap. He choked on a gasp. Caz put her face in his, pressing the tip of the blade against his throat. He shrank from her as far as his seat would allow while pushing against the orb.

"Do I look like I give a damn for the rules of etiquette and serenity?" she snarled. "The Thirteenth Dimension has destroyed billions of lives, including Vin! Your son, Commandant! My husband!"

Caz inhaled and exhaled through her nose, forcing the rage back to a manageable place. A drip of blood welled from the point of the knife. She withdrew the blade and wiped her mouth with the back of her hand. With the other she retrieved the Heart.

"I think we should put it to a vote. Wouldn't you say, Commandant? That is, after all, what this council is for, right?" Caz looked around at the assembly of Rethans, most staring at her in terror. However, enough anger still encompassed the room, giving her the opposition she craved.

"All in favor of including the Heart of Annihilation in the public arsenal, where it will perish in disuse and anonymity while the Thirteenth Dimension lays in wait to destroy us all, say, 'aye.'"

Only the groan of a dying marshal could be heard. Caz scanned the room for signs of affirmation. Nothing.

"Okay then," Caz said. "All in favor of allowing the Heart of Annihilation to reach its full potential and eliminate the Thirteenth Dimension before it can destroy us, I repeat, say, 'aye.'"

Muttering and whispering. Some council members even leaned toward each other, while others remained frozen in their seats.

A quiet "nay" echoed from the back of the room.

Caz searched for the perpetrator, but before she could locate him another voice answered, "Nay." Then another and another. Soon the room rang with nays. The deep voice beside her, so unbearably like Vin's, echoed, "Nay."

Caz rotated so she was facing Commandant Paliyo. He seemed to have gained strength with each nay, and now sat up straight in his throne.

"You see, Cazandra," he said. "The rules we have created are not just a nice thing to keep everyone happy and compliant. We hold peace in our hands when we follow them. Murdering an entire dimension over rumors of their genocidal capacity breaches the etiquette and serenity put in place to not only protect our way of life, but our hearts and souls." He shifted in his seat. "You may come in here with your weapons of anarchy and terrorize us into your absurd way of thinking, but you will never get these fine council members to agree to something so brutal, so beyond everything we've dreamed for our dimension. You have been voted down, Cazandra Fisk."

He clenched the arms of his seat. His eyes, sad and weak, scanned his comrades, connecting with each of them. Caz felt the unity of the chamber, the companionship. The utter rejection of everything about her.

Caz scraped the tip of the blade along the Heart of Annihilation and nodded her head. She looked at the orb, felt the warm yellow glow penetrate her skin, and then calmly tucked it back into her bag.

She turned on Commandant Paliyo and touched the tip of the blade to the drip of blood on his neck. She gave him a vapid smile, her head still bobbing as if in agreement.

"Wrong answer, Commandant." Caz thrust the blade downward.

CHAPTER 24

Rose

Agony arched my back, every muscle rigid. Someone was screaming. Disease churned in my organs, burning through my blood vessels. Hands gripped my body. Each point of pressure exponentially increased the sensation of my nerves tearing apart.

"She's crashing!"

"Paddles!"

A bright explosion of light mimicked a burst of electricity in my body. My heart ripped from my chest. Screaming drowned out the beeping, but not the voices.

"Hold her down! Let me get this IV in!"

The stinging scent of alcohol bit my nose. I couldn't breathe. The tug at my hand might as well have been a tank driving over it.

Then the pain retreated into soothing sleepiness, warmth, and comfort. Silence and emptiness.

An incessant beeping roused me from a world of nonexistence. My eyelids felt as heavy as Dad's homemade bread. I pried them open, blinking at the semi-darkness. It was too much, and I gave up without an effort. My lids dropped, shutting out the dark, foreign-looking surroundings. I didn't even try to imagine where I might be, nor did it seem very important. I relaxed. The beeping faded.

The beeping penetrated my consciousness again. This time I opened my eyes to sunlight streaming through a tiny window above my head. I blinked heavily but managed to keep my eyes open this time. The small room was covered with fine wood paneling, an overwhelming amount of cupboards, and limited furniture. My hand rested on my stomach. A luscious-feeling fabric covered me to my armpits. I examined a red-lit clip on my forefinger, and a clear tube leading into a vein taped securely to my skin with transparent tape. My eyes followed the tube to a blood pressure and heart rate monitor near my bed. Squiggly green lines measured my heartbeat. Ah. That horrible beeping sound. A bag of clear liquid hung from a metal pole. I tried to read the fine print to discover what was being pumped into my body. My eyes tired of the challenge almost immediately, and the bag went out of focus. I dropped my hand back to a champagne-colored, brocade quilt.

The movement jarred into my other shoulder. Achiness and shadowy echoes of pain drew my eyes open. I rolled onto my side with a groan and pushed myself into a sitting position. My IV-restricted hand tried to tug me back into place. I fingered the thick, white bandage covering my shoulder. I wanted to peel back the dressing to see the damage underneath—but then again, I didn't really. I rubbed my eye.

The image of blood spraying from Thurmond's head jolted through my mind, so vivid that my whole body lurched. I could still feel his dead weight on top of me. I tore back the covers and threw my legs over the side of the bed.

I used my thumb to flick off the heart rate monitor. The beeping turned into a long drawn out squeal. I growled and sent a volt into the machine. It sparked and went silent.

Frustrated, shaking fingers tore at the tape holding the IV in place until I finally caught an edge, grimacing as I yanked out small hairs, a layer of skin, and the needle from my hand. I dropped it on the bed. Clear liquid with a curl of watery blood leaked across the quilt's bright white monogram—a very swirly X.C.

I put pressure on the small, bleeding hole in my hand. My bare feet curled in the plush carpet. I glanced down at myself. Then stared. A black, lacy nightgown barely covered the most important parts of me. The spaghetti straps did a great job of keeping the bandages clear but other than that I couldn't imagine why I would be wearing something out of a Victoria Secrets catalogue.

At least it gave me a fine view of the enormous bruise wrapping from the back of my left thigh. The majority of it was a deep wine color, although the edges were already yellowing.

That's what happens when your so-called comrades decide to put you in the ground.

I shook my head to dislodge the voice.

Sure, shake me out. That will work. If I hadn't been there you would have been the hood ornament for a Hummer.

I could almost feel the rush of air as the Hummer's wheel missed my face, the jolt of the massive vehicle slamming onto my thigh.

If you'd put up more of a fight the key wouldn't be gone. Rannen as well. Lafe with a hole in her forehead.

Nausea twisted my gut into a tight mass of agony. I pressed a fist to my mouth and breathed through my nose. Not nearly good enough. I stumbled to my feet and yanked open the door hoping to find a bathroom. Instead I found myself staring at a small kitchenette, some very nice leather couches and recliners, and—a steering wheel?

Throwing open a door to my right in a wild guess, I finally found the toilet. I slammed the toilet lid up. Again and again my stomach tried to expel nonexistent contents, as though it would also eject the images from my head.

Sweat beaded on my forehead and upper lip. In an attempt to force my mind somewhere, anywhere else, I hummed the Beach Boys song about the Salt Lake City girls. Dad loved to break into that song at the most inconvenient times, because he knew he could get it stuck in my head. As true today as then.

Slowly my stomach settled. My throat felt tight and sore. I spat, wiped my face with toilet paper, and spat again. I rested my head on the toilet seat and let the words of the song tickle my lips.

Even with the song I found my thoughts focused on Thurmond. He was alive, I was sure of it. Hadn't my last memory been of talking to him? About what? I couldn't remember much, just his face. Muddy, bloody, but very much alive.

When I was sure the toilet would no longer be requiring my services, I pushed myself to my feet. All the aches and pains I'd ignored in my mad rush to the bathroom crept up on me with sharp hands. My leg, of all things, hurt the worst. Putting any weight on it made it feel that perhaps the muscle was more than simply bruised. I limped to the sink to splash cold water over my face and rinse out my gummy mouth. I felt like I hadn't opened it in over a week. How long was I down?

I stared at my hands as the water ran over them. I pictured blood soaking the skin instead of water. Not my blood. Not Thurmond's. Blood, splattered onto the handle of a knife. A silver blade pressed against a white throat. Silver eyes peered at me, pleading. A Rethan in another dimension. A Rethan at another time. I rubbed my hands together, wondering why I could feel the stickiness of blood even when my hands looked clean.

Soap.

I grabbed the scented bar of soap from the lip of the sink, ignoring the stab of pain in my shoulder. I lathered quickly, running the soap between my fingers and all the way up past my wrists. Again and again I rinsed and lathered, desperate to rid myself of the Rethan blood. I felt the resistance of the knife against bone. The slipping as my fingers tried to grip the slick handle. The squelching sound as it pulled clear.

Again and again. Soap, lather, scrub, rinse. My hands turned raw and my shoulder ached with the strain.

Movement in the mirror above the sink finally caught my attention. I froze. Burning water ran across my hands. I rested my hands on the lip of the sink, staring into the mirror. Steam rose past eyes I barely recognized.

The irises could probably still be considered hazel, but were now flecked with silver spots. The inner edges seemed to be fading into lightened pupils.

A scoff burst from my throat that sounded wrong—the wrong reaction to something very clear.

Very Rethan.

"Shut up!" I rubbed my face with wet hands and then scrubbed my nails through my hair.

My hair. *Damn.* The long, auburn thatch cascaded across my shoulders and down my back, shimmering with a hint of metallic, silver—*Rethan*—highlights.

No, not silver. Gray, or white, or something. Trauma equals white hair. It had happened before. I'd read about it somewhere. It was nothing a little Clairol couldn't fix up. Gray—not silver. I pulled a multifaceted strand in front of my eyes, repeating the words to myself.

Sure, Kris. Make sure you follow through with your textbook denial. That usually fixes everything.

I slammed my hand on the faucet to shut off the water and braved one more look in the mirror. My face looked almost as foreign as my eyes and hair with the multiple scrapes, cuts, and bruises. I turned my head this way and that, witnessing small flashes of memory of how each one occurred, ending with the shrapnel wound on my hairline. The hair parted around thirteen stitches. I glanced at my eyes again, and the silver in my hair, before sinking to the floor with my back against the door.

They told me I was a Rethan. Some kind of murderer. I rubbed the barely-visible, tarnished symbols burned on my palm. Proof, they called it. And hadn't powering their portal been proof as well? But I wasn't! How could something of this magnitude have escaped my notice or knowledge for the entirety of my life? I supposed being a Rethan in and of itself might not be so bad, but a mass murderer? No, I couldn't be *that* person!

Caz, the acidic voice whispered. *That person has a name.*

I rubbed my raw, wet hands together, looking at them with fresh eyes. Just hands. Clean hands. Not murdering hands.

Murdering? Sure. That would put us right up there with Ben Attikin, Genva Lunas, and the commander herself. There was a brief burst of laughter inside my head. *What are you going to do about it?*

Shut up, Caz, shut up! You're not real. I can't be hearing this. I clenched my hands in my hair. Terrified that the madness from the battle had carried itself over to wherever I was, I slipped from the bathroom and slammed the door behind me. My back pressed against it to trap the monster inside, my breathing loud and heavy in my ears.

I touched my neck with trembling fingers, searching for comfort from my dad. The instant I felt the bare skin I remembered the commander lifting my tags and pendant away, the silver BB suspended from the center. A key, she'd called it, but the only thing that mattered to me was that I didn't have it anymore. The commander did. She had the key, and she'd taken my last lead in finding Dad.

Who knew she had it in her. Damn her.

Apparently I hadn't trapped the voice in the bathroom. I squeezed my eyes shut, pounding the back of my head against the door.

I needed Thurmond. I opened my eyes, glancing down at my clothes— or lack thereof. Thurmond would ground me. He always could. But not like this.

Back in the tiny bedroom I rooted through the closets and cupboards, finding pillows, blankets, t-shirts, handkerchiefs, and even socks adorned with the same X.C. monogram. I paused once to examine an oil painting of a very tan man with overly white teeth.

I finally spotted a hint of camouflage poking out from a neatly folded mesh of tissue paper on the bedside table. The paper crinkled as I pulled it away, finding my uniform with the Rose nametape indicating ownership. It was washed, ironed, starched, and I fingered an almost invisible patching job on the right shoulder. I shook it out and dropped it on the bed before grabbing the starched pants, a black t-shirt that wasn't mine, and a small pile of white underclothing that looked new.

The black nightie I shoved under a pillow. I worked on the pants one-handed, buttoned one-handed, pushed my right arm into the shirt sleeve without trying to move my shoulder too much, all of which very nearly tested my patience for the year. I tucked in my shirt simply because it was the one easy thing to do one-handed, and was reaching for my boots when something gold under the tissue paper caught my eye.

I picked up the M-16 tracer round, my round, and rolled it between my fingers. It was buffed and polished to a high shine. Not the slightest dirt was visible in the tiny imperfections of the surface. The last time I'd seen it was before inserting it in the rifle. It hadn't fired when I'd needed it. I ran my thumbnail along the red-painted tip and wondered if the rain had dampened the gunpowder. I folded it in my fist, allowing the tip to bite into my palm, before placing it in my pants pocket.

I jammed my feet into my boots without socks and left the bootlaces hanging open. There was something downright liberating about going into public with my uniform completely out of whack.

I made my way past the comfy couches. Blinds covered all the windows, even the windshield, giving the whole area a muted, shady look—bluish even. Although hadn't everything kinda gone blue after my first Azshatath injection?

An overabundance of framed photos of a single man covered the walls and cabinets and sat on every available counter space. Tanned skin, white teeth. The same man in the oil painting in the bedroom. A twinge of familiarity touched my mind, but aside from the fact that I was using his RV as a recovery room, I didn't really care who he was.

Mid-afternoon sunlight blinded me as I swung the door outward. I used the rail for support down the three steps. My feet hit hot black asphalt, and I shielded my eyes. Several other RVs like the Winnebago were scattered across the pavement. Other temporary buildings also sat neatly in rows, spaced so close together the doors would hit if they opened at the same time. Uniform trees farther to the south hinted at a more permanent infrastructure, but everything else around me screamed short-term. People strode past, talking importantly on cell phones or making their way toward some critical appointment or another. No one paid me the least bit of attention.

I didn't notice Thurmond at first because he was nestled in a shady spot not far from the door. He lounged in a camp chair, his legs stretched out and crossed at the ankles, looking very relaxed except for the tightly folded arms across his chest. He wore his uniform, although his mutilated camouflage jacket had been replaced with a black t-shirt adorned with the symbol of some punk-rock band. A long, thick gash slashed toward his temple and was held together by a large number of stitches. The blood had drained across the entire side of his face, and his left eye and cheek were mottled in a symphony of colors. His eyes followed the progress of one person after another, but his head only turned to scratch his ear with his shoulder.

"Hey," I said, leaning causally against the stair railing.

One faded glance of indifference, and then Thurmond was on his feet. The camp chair fell backward and folded with a clatter. He covered the distance between us in two strides and stopped. His eyes searched my face with his wonderfully normal, gray-blue eyes.

I lowered my chin and lashes in a sickening moment of self-consciousness.

Thurmond exhaled. His hands lifted to my cheeks. His fingers trembled against my bruised skin.

"They said you might not . . . they weren't sure if . . ." Thurmond's eyes flitted away from my face before returning with lowered brows. "Dammit, Rose, do you have any idea how long I've been waiting to talk to you?"

His gruff anger trailed away and he pulled me into a rough embrace.

"Sorry," I said, a little surprised at the warmth of his welcome. My voice muffled against his shirt.

"Sorry doesn't cut it." He pressed his cheek against my hair. His breath was hot and fast on my scalp.

I ran my hand across his back, trying to smooth away his tension. Maybe smooth away a little of my own discomfort at his lack of uber-army toughness. His breathing mellowed. My contrition went up a couple of notches. He drew away, stared hard in my face for a moment, and dropped his eyes.

"So," I let the word trail out. "What did you want to talk about?"

He set the fallen camp chair back up, motioning for me to sit while he pulled another chair from under the RV. I lowered myself gingerly into the seat.

"Just wondering how you're doin.'" Thurmond said, slamming open the second chair on the asphalt. He ran a hand across his mouth and chin, hesitated, and then sat down as well. His elbows rested on his knees. He glanced over at me before looking away in obvious discomfort.

"Pretty good, considering." I rubbed my palm on my leg. "How's your head?"

"Fine. Thirty-six stitches."

"Really? That's pretty decent."

"Should be a nice scar by the looks of it."

"Yep."

We sat in silence. Not uncomfortable, but heavy with the weight of a traumatic experience neither of us wanted to discuss. The sun heated my legs. I narrowed my eyes in contentment and let the world stand still.

Thurmond watched me from the corner of his eye when he thought I wasn't looking. The setting was so bizarre compared to what I'd expected that I finally couldn't contain my curiosity.

"So, where are we?" I finally asked.

"On a movie set."

"Really?" I scratched my head. Interesting. "I woulda guessed another dimension."

Thurmond snorted. He appeared to be highly engrossed in a spot on his palm, which he kept rubbing with his thumb. "Well, not actually the set. More the base camp for the movie."

"What movie. Are we in Hollywood or something? Rethan Hollywood maybe?"

"No. We're on the base. You know, Fort Huachuca." He cast me a fleeting look and then clasped his hands together, letting his eyes wander over the setting of bustling people and temporary buildings as though he hadn't already been watching them all morning.

"T." I tapped his arm to make him look at me. "What happened?"

"To what?"

"After I passed out, or whatever, at the Rethan camp."

"Oh, yeah. I guess you were sort of out of it. I wasn't sure when you were actually conscious." He stared at his hands. "You were sort of . . . some of the things you said—"

"Like what?"

"It was nothing, really."

"Then why'd you mention it?"

"Can we just drop it?" he snapped.

I rubbed my eye, uncomfortable that whatever I'd said in my delirium was too embarrassing for Thurmond to talk about.

"You could at least tell me how we got out of there."

Thurmond nodded, relief washing over his face at setting foot back on solid ground. "After you charged the battery on the Hummer—"

"I did? I don't remember that."

"Yeah. Totally saved our asses." He expressed his gratitude by giving me the slightest glance. I offered him an encouraging smile. "So after you charged the Hummer," he continued, "I put you in the back seat and started heading south. I knew the base was somewhere in that direction, so I followed that road along the power lines. The damn road was such a mess from the commander's vehicles and the rain that if we'd been in anything but a Hummer you never would've made it. I kept second-guessing myself, you know? Stay on the messed up road, or take one of the hundreds of little sidetracks and hope for some hermit in a cabin with a cell phone or something. Finally, Boderick points to this invisible turn—"

"Wait, Boderick? As in Deputy Boderick? Little Bodie?"

"Yeah, that ratty little Rethan—"

"I know who Bodie is. Where'd he come from?"

"He freaked out after the commander showed up. Little twerp hunkered down and waited out the fight."

"Smart, I guess."

"He resurfaced just in time to give me a hand with you. So he points out this track, and ten minutes later we see all these bright lights and equipment and stuff. At the time I thought I'd driven into the twilight zone, but come to find out it was this movie crew filming a night scene."

"Really? You drove right onto the movie set?" I wondered if they had gotten our arrival on film. "So what happened next?"

"Next? I get out of the Hummer, yelling my head off for help. Boderick thought you'd stopped breathing, so I'm racing around to the back seat to check on you. Then all these people start gathering around, pulling out cell phones. You can't imagine how pissed I was when this one guy started taking pictures!"

"Really? Did you break his phone?"

"Yeah. That and his nose."

"You busted his—" A giggle bubbled out of my throat, a choked, burbling sound I couldn't stop. Thurmond jerked his head up, his expression confused.

"I can picture it—" The words battled with the laughter, tripping over each other and chopping my sentence into pieces. "—a bunch of pampered Hollywood folk with their makeup and fancy clothes having to deal with all our mud and blood. And you, you flattening some guy and freaking everyone else out."

Thurmond laughed softly. The strain and stress drained from the lines around his eyes. Dad always said, why cry when you can laugh? I buried my face in the crook of my arm and let it all out.

"Oh, man," I said, running the back of my thumb against my watering eyes. "I bet that was awesome!"

"Yeah." Thurmond chuckled. "Sure."

"Miss Rose, it looks like you're feeling better."

I pressed my hand to my mouth as the humor faded. The voice belonged to a gorgeous woman who had appeared a few feet away.

Highlighted blond hair, tight black skirt, and red stilettos made her legs look five feet long—everything about her screamed super model. I pulled my unlaced boots up closer to the chair, feeling very plain and clunky.

"I'll have to tell Dr. Tolman you're finally up." She put a cell phone to her ear before continuing. "You really shouldn't be out of bed. Mr. Coy gave specific orders. He wanted to know immediately when you wakened. I'll need to find what happened to your nurse as well. Excuse me—" She lifted the phone closer to her mouth, turning her head away. "Dr. Tolman? Yes, that's right. Come right over. No, there was nothing I could . . . Yes, yes, of course. I'll tell Mr. Coy you're on your way. Thank you."

She snapped her phone shut and turned her heavily made-up eyes on Thurmond.

"Devon."

"Hi, Angie." He sighed her name. I frowned, surprised at the jealousy rising in my chest.

"Is there anything I can get for you?" Angie asked. She dropped her eyes back to her phone, dialed, and held it to her ear.

"No thanks." Thurmond looked at me briefly, pressed his lips together, and turned back to Angie. "Wait, actually, could you have someone get us something to eat?"

"Of course. Just sit tight. I'll be right—" She pulled the phone closer to her mouth, strutting away, her heels clip-clopping across the asphalt in short, brisk steps. "Xavier. Yes, she's awake. Right. Outside your . . . All right, see you soon."

Angie called out to the occasional person she passed and collected quite the following before she rounded the corner of one of the far trailers.

"Wow." I followed the last shining glint of red, patent leather kicking around the corner. "Friend of yours, Corporal?"

"She's been really helpful." Thurmond lifted his shoulders to his ears.

"How helpful?" I looked at the branded hand in my lap, my self-consciousness graduating to full-blown insecurity.

"Rose?"

"Forget it," I muttered.

"You look great as a Rethan, by the way."

"I'm not a Rethan!" The words thundered out like a defensive linebacker.

"Sure you're not." A smile played at the corners of his mouth. He tried to hide it under a finger and thumb. I rolled my eyes and lounged back in my seat.

"I'm not a Rethan. I'm—" Did I really sound that panicky?

"Do you want to talk about it?"

"You think it's true. You believe everything Rannen said about me."

"I think maybe you should look at the facts."

"I don't want to talk about it." Agitation worked its way into my nerves. A shiver of electricity made the hairs on my arms stand on end. I hunched in my seat, willing the sudden, angry pounding in my head to not warp my good feelings toward Thurmond.

"We're going to have to talk about it sooner or later." Thurmond turned away, his face serious.

"Why? Because hanging out with a creature from another dimension totally creeps you out?"

"It doesn't, actually."

"Of course it does. You can't even look at me!"

"That's not true. It's not like that!" He stood up with a frustrated huff and locked his hands behind his head.

"Then what's it like? As you can imagine I'm feeling a bit insecure right now. "

"Dammit, Rose! Have you seen yourself?" Thurmond turned to face me. His hands dropped to fists at his side. "Do you have any idea how responsible I feel?"

I didn't realize my mouth was hanging open until a hot breeze dried my throat.

"Responsible?" I coughed and moistened my mouth with my tongue. Memories crept into my head, little demons I'd been trying to shut out. "T, you saved my life . . . like, a whole bunch of times."

"Do you know how many times the doctor said, 'If only you'd gotten her to us sooner'?" Thurmond gestured at me, anger tightening his eyes. "Your temperature was through the roof. Your heart was a mess because of all that damn adrenaline, and you exploded the defibrillator when they tried to use it on you. Nobody had the first idea of what kind of blood to transfuse, not to mention they finally had to induce a coma because you wouldn't stop screaming!" He scrubbed a hand down his face. "Two days I've been sitting outside this trailer, waiting for some indication you were going to pull through, all the while racking my brains to figure out what the hell I was going to tell your dad!"

I leaned back in my chair as his words steamrolled me, realizing for the first time that I'd never told him about Dad. Quoted him, sure, but never let Thurmond in on the greatest tragedy of my life.

I pressed my hands to my ears. I didn't want to hear any more. It was all in the past, one of the darkest moments of my life. Here on the other side of things I felt that it didn't belong, something obscene that was best left to rot in forgetfulness.

But Thurmond's face held no forgetfulness. For him this hadn't happened in a subconscious, dreamlike world. This was the constant of his life, something vivid and horrifying. Something he hadn't had the luxury of sleeping away. It could very well have been one of the darkest moments of his life.

He turned away, rubbing the sides of his face. I didn't move. Movement would imply that something actually happened.

Except this moment wasn't about me. I'd been lost in my own fear and pain for so long. How could I deny someone else, someone I cared about, the sympathy and compassion he so rightly deserved?

I pushed out of the chair. Veins stood out on Thurmond's arms. I wrapped my arm around his waist and rested my cheek on his hot back.

He didn't move for a moment, then rotated around to face me. His arms enfolded me in a tight embrace. He nuzzled his face into my neck, his breath steady and warm. I don't know how long we stood like that, two people reveling in the fact that we were both still alive and relatively well.

I sighed. Thurmond drew away, but only enough to pull me over to his chair and onto his lap. I leaned against his chest. It wasn't comfortable, but the warmth and security of his arms around my waist more than made up for it.

"So what happened next?" I prompted. "After you drove onto the set?"

"Next?" Thurmond said. "There was talk of calling an ambulance until this one guy walks up. You could totally tell he was the star of the show by the way people deferred to him. So he takes one look at you and starts barking orders. The next thing I know, he's having you loaded into this orange Ferrari and driving away. They had Boderick and me follow with Angie in an Escalade."

"A Ferrari? On that road?"

"Naw, the main road was thirty seconds in the other direction. With pavement."

"So Bodie just kinda blended with all the other people? What do people think of him? As a Rethan, I mean?" I tried to convince myself my concern was simply for his welfare.

"Do you really think a bunch of Hollywood people even think twice about a guy with silver hair and eyes?" Thurmond asked. "Hell, half the people in this place look like aliens themselves."

Aliens. I didn't like that word. It seemed inaccurate, even derogatory.

"'Kay," I said.

"You don't look *that* different, Rose."

"I wasn't talking about me."

"Sure you weren't."

"Finish the story, already." I nudged him.

"That's pretty much it. We met up with you here on the base, where they had a makeshift hospital set up in that RV."

"Why here? Why not a real hospital?"

"You really want me to answer that?" Thurmond tugged my hair.

"Oh, you mean because of the whole Rethan thing?"

"Mr. Coy took charge. He called in his personal physician and paid a load of other medical personnel off the books," Thurmond explained. "He said he didn't want you under the microscopes of any unknown doctors. Not to mention how we are now officially AWOL."

"Oh." I watched my previously unblemished military record take a belly flop into the swamp. All I needed now was a stint in the pit of some military prison to top everything off. "Who's Mr. Coy anyway?"

Thurmond looked past me with a nod.

I turned to see a man with jet-black hair striding up. He wore some very classy Ray-Bans, a white, button-down shirt open wide at the chest; a white pair of pants with an accented silver and black belt, and shiny black shoes. He looked to be in his late forties, his skin tanned and his teeth unnaturally white.

Thurmond helped me off his lap and stood with me.

"Xavier Coy." The man extended a hand with perfectly manicured nails. His voice was strong and cocky with a hint of an unidentifiable accent.

I narrowed my eyes, hesitated, and then jammed my hand into my pocket. I didn't know if it was the cold, subtle tension in his jaw, the microscopic curl to his mouth as he looked at me, or from the back of my mind, but there was something about this man I heartily loathed.

"Mr. Coy." I nodded.

He arched an eyebrow as he waited for me to say something else. When I didn't, he dropped his hand.

"It's *Xavier* Coy," he said.

"You want me to call you Xavier?"

"I'm just wondering if you know who I am?"

"Sure. The guy who loaned me his trailer and his personal physician," I said. "Thanks, by the way."

Even that much gratitude stuck in my throat. Xavier shifted his weight to one leg, and I was struck with an odd sense of uncertainty coming from someone who otherwise seemed to have everything together. Then it came to me. The hair, the voice, and that annoying aura of the untouchable celebrity—of course, Xavier Coy!

"I remember who you are now," I said, recalling the lame date I'd gone on a lifetime ago. Xavier took a step back. His smile faded. "I saw you in that one movie once. Um, *The Omniscient Observer.* Definitely two stars in my book but my date liked it."

His shoulders dropped, and he exhaled. The toothy smile returned. Clearly he'd expected me to say something else.

Traitor. The harsh whisper made me look up and around. I pushed Thurmond's hand off my waist.

"Rose?"

I jerked back around to face Xavier. Hatred flared in my chest. My cheeks grew hot. His smiling mouth was moving, saying something to me while his gaze was directed somewhere over my left shoulder. A perfect moment. A perfect target. Who could stop me? Why would they think they needed to? Electricity shivered into my fingertips.

"Rose." Thurmond repeated my name right in my ear. He might as well have stabbed me in the side. A crackle of electricity leapt from my hand into my thigh with a sizzle. I gave a tiny squawk. The anger and hatred, so poignant moments ago, vanished in a sickening wave.

"Ow. What?" I pressed my hand above my ear. The ache in my head thudded away. "What do you want?"

Thurmond's eyebrows lowered. Xavier Coy paused. When I finally looked at him his eyes tightened.

"I was saying, Miss Rose, that *The Omniscient Observer* is one of my favorites. A real classic, if I do say so myself." His grin looked forced, and he went on with a hint of reciprocal dislike. "The critics gave it five stars, not two, and I was even nominated for an Oscar in the role of Davis Clay."

Xavier beckoned to someone behind me. Angie strode up with a veritable army of people carrying items ranging from trays of food and hangers of clothing to stacks of papers and folders. I was shunted to the side as the people surrounded Xavier, asking him to sign this and approve that. He answered with confidence, often giving orders or speaking harshly to someone who seemed to have done his or her job less than perfect. Fascinating, and a bit disgusting.

I stepped back to avoid being trampled, until I bumped into someone. Pain jarred through my shoulder. I blinked up at Thurmond.

"Come on." He held a tray of food. "Let's get away from this circus."

Thurmond's hand supported me at the small of my back as we made our way up the steps of the Winnebago, escaping Xavier's entourage.

I slid onto the soft leather couch behind the table with a tired groan. Thurmond placed the tray on the table and sat to my left. His arm relaxed on the seat back, and he leaned in to take the lid off the food.

"Thanks." I picked up a black plastic fork, examining the food in front of me: curls of bean sprouts amid a mystery meat and other veggies. I grimaced. Hollywood health garbage. I stabbed a piece of broccoli, smelled it, and put it in my mouth. Not bad. Of course, just because I was hungry enough to eat tofu didn't necessarily mean it was good. I ate in silence before striking up the conversation again. "What do you think of Mr. Coy? You've probably talked to him more than I have."

"I haven't, actually," Thurmond picked out a bean sprout and stuck it in his mouth. "He asked me a few personal questions, but he seems more interested in you."

"Why? Because I'm so alien?" My sarcasm annoyed even me.

"Maybe because you needed medical care, and I knew you best."

"Or thought you did—"

"Give me a break, Rose. Stop acting all misunderstood. Do you *want* me to treat you differently?"

"It's easy for you to say." I pushed the bowl away and fingered the tines of the fork. "If I kept telling you that you were some—some mass murderer from another dimension, you might get up in arms too."

"Well, let's say for a moment it's true," Thurmond said. I opened my mouth to protest. He held up a hand. "That's not who you are now, is it?"

I folded my arms across my chest and examined the table. Of course that wasn't who I was. I nodded slowly, and then shook my head.

There's just that little matter of those homicidal tendencies, Caz snickered. I clenched my eyes and rubbed my temple, wondering if driving the fork into my eye would shut her up.

"And I'll finish signing those in twenty minutes, Angie." I opened my eyes. Xavier backed up the steps. "No, make sure we're ready for the shoot and I'll talk to you after lunch. And Ang, send Dr. Tolman right in when he arrives."

He slammed the door and turned to face us. "Being me can be so exhausting!"

I glared. Phony bleached grin. Phony tan. He didn't take off his sunglasses and, compounded with the other things Thurmond told me about him, I was struck with a sudden suspicion. I watched him carefully as he made his way up the stairs, adjusted a picture on the wall, and peeked at his reflection in a mirrored cupboard. He pulled something out of his pocket, and with a rapid flick of his wrist he showed me exactly what I was watching for.

"You're a Rethan!" I said.

Xavier's hand gave a startled jerk. The accusation colored the air between us.

"Now hold on, Rose—" Thurmond started to say.

Xavier's lips tightened, and he slowly removed his sunglasses. Silver, Rethan eyes, with barely a pinprick of pupil in the center. "As are you, Miss Rose."

Thurmond slid away from me and stood as though an enemy had presented itself.

"You guys just keep popping up, don't you?" I lounged back, my muscles tense.

"Why do you think I was so interested in your personal medical care?" Xavier's tone took a sour edge. "I didn't like the idea of being outed by you."

"Or maybe we know each other from Retha."

"Of course we don't." Xavier dropped his eyes.

"You're lying," I said.

"So you're both Rethan. Who cares?" Thurmond held his hands up between us as though we might start brawling. It wasn't far from my mind. "There's got to be at least as many of you guys in Retha as there are in Earth. What are the chances you two actually know each other?"

"Because he's lying." He was *so* lying. I knew him from somewhere, and it wasn't from another stupid movie.

"I think you should listen to your friend, Miss Rose." Xavier lifted between two fingers what he'd pulled out of his pocket moments ago, giving me a clear view of a white business card. Half of it was stained brown, but the small black lettering on the one side was clearly visible.

"This was found in the pocket of your pants." He set it on the edge of the table and stepped back to sprawl on the couch across from me. He crossed his legs and curled a lock of hair around his finger. "I thought maybe you could explain it."

I picked it up. Mud had been wiped off the border, and a bloody fingerprint covered the words.

Dimensional Liaison Agency
Special Agent Jim Wichman
703-555-0236

My breath caught. Dimensional Liaison Agency would be DLA for short. *The* DLA? And Wichman was a part of it? A shadow crossed the card, and I didn't have to look up to know Thurmond was reading it also.

"Do you want to tell me, Miss Rose, why you have a contact in the DLA?" Xavier's voice was cool. "I was under the impression, thanks to Boderick, that you've only just been made aware of the fact you're Rethan."

"I don't—I mean, I did—I mean . . ." I recalled the memory surfacing in the desert, the one about Dad going to the DLA when I was young. This little acronym was associated with abandonment in my book. I narrowed my eyes at Xavier. "You know what this Dimensional Liaison Agency is?"

"Every Rethan in Earth knows who they are." He studied his fingernails, flicked something off his pants, and returned my look. "For those sentenced," he gestured at me. I scowled. "They take care of the infant RAGE inmates and make sure they get into the foster care system. They also watch them throughout their lives, and eliminate them should they show signs of memory recall or violent tendencies. For those of us here under our own volition—the denigrated entrepreneurs—they are tasked to track us and make sure we do not cause any problems. They are a specialized dimensional police force for the Third Dimension. Human, and ruthlessly dedicated to protecting Earth."

"Sergeant Wichman must've been undercover." I tossed the card on the table and massaged my left temple. "He must've been watching the commander."

"Why would he watch the commander?" Thurmond asked. His eyes hardened. I could tell he suspected what I already knew.

"She's a Rethan. A renegade of some sort." I rubbed the card with my thumb and forefinger.

"How do you know that?"

"Because she told me. She said she knew me from Retha. She also took my pendant. Said it was a key or something. Then I remember her saying something about being close to finding the Heart of—something or another—" A warm glowing orb and a bloody knife tugged at my memory.

A loud thump shattered the image. Xavier was on his feet. His face sagged.

"What?" he whispered.

I sat back and folded my arms. What was this mysterious Heart the commander was willing to kill over? And what did Xavier Coy know about it?

"You obviously heard me. The question is, what does that mean to you?" I slid out of my seat. My fingers tingled. I felt lightheaded.

"Nothing. Why would that mean anything to . . . don't be ridiculous—"

"Don't give me that!"

"When did you talk to the commander?" Thurmond asked. His arm brushed mine.

"Right before Sergeant Wichman left us for dead."

"He did what?"

"Well, he said he was coming back."

"So this Agent Wichman is not your friend?" Xavier cut in.

"I don't know," I admitted.

"He left us for dead, of course he's not!" Thurmond slammed his fist on the table.

"He left the card. He had to have some motive for that," Xavier argued.

"Everyone shut up for a minute!" I held up a hand. The lights flickered.

Thurmond and Xavier stopped talking. Xavier glanced around at the lights. Thurmond stared hard at me.

"Okay, now here are the facts. One: the commander is looking for something called the Heart, which Mr. Coy will be explaining to us in a minute. Two: Sergeant Wichman needs to be contacted to find out if he knows where the commander has taken Marshal Rannen; and three—"

"Rannen? Rannen's gone? He was taken? Is he all right?" The tan leaked away from Xavier's face. A dirty gray took its place.

"Okay, rewind. Mr. Coy will be explaining two things to us—what the Heart is *and* what he knows about Marshal Rannen."

"I'm just concerned this *commander* might do something to a fellow Rethan, that's all." Xavier's sputtering wouldn't have convinced his most brain-dead fan.

"And the Heart?"

Xavier's hands trembled, and he folded them together to hide it. "If I even thought that . . . if anyone were to find . . . no, there's no way. No way. I don't know anything about this."

I opened my mouth to call the movie star a big, fat liar.

"Wait a second," Thurmond interrupted. "Why the hell do you need to know all this, Rose?"

Do humans not understand loyalty?

I dug a knuckle into my aching temple. This had nothing to do with loyalty.

Call the DLA and ask them for Rannen's file. Or your file. Don't you want to know who you are?

Sure. Ask them for a bunch of files. The DLA didn't even technically exist. And even if I did get some files, what would they tell me? Information about Rannen? Or what about the truth behind Dad's involvement with Retha?

Is it about finding Rannen, or your father?

I rubbed my eyes. It took a moment before I realized Thurmond and Xavier were staring at me with contradicting expressions.

"I need to talk to Sergeant Wichman," I said.

"Rose, you almost died. If you think I'm going to let you—" Thurmond took a step in my direction.

"Let me?" I jabbed my finger in Thurmond's chest. It hurt to breathe.

I understood that my reaction was wrong, my attack on Thurmond one person off. I couldn't rein in the anger. The lights hummed a blinding white. Bulbs exploded in a shower of sparks. Thurmond bumped against the counter behind him.

"Caz, that's enough!" Xavier's voice pushed against the rage.

The shrill, humorless laugh inside my head diminished to an echo across an expansive chasm.

My breathing was loud in my ears and I found I was kneeling, my eyes on the carpet. The cream-colored fibers looked like fluffy little soldiers standing in formation.

"Rose? Are you okay?"

"Of course she's not okay. She's insane."

"She's not insane. She was just given too much of that damn serum." A shadow crossed my carpet soldiers. "Rose?"

Thurmond crouched beside me. His eyes were concerned but not angry.

"Sorry," I whispered. "I didn't mean—"

"Don't worry about it. Can you stand?"

A tiny flinch marred his face when he took my arm, but at least I didn't electrocute him. I allowed him to pull me to my feet and lead me over to a couch, where I collapsed. I smoothed my hair with shaking fingers.

Xavier watched me with narrowed eyes. One hand hid his mouth. I looked between the two faces but stopped on Xavier.

"Mr. Coy, could I borrow your phone?"

"You planning to order pizza or something?" Thurmond's mouth set in a hard line.

"No, I'm calling Sergeant Wichman."

"Why?"

"To find the commander." I'd held onto the secret about Dad so long, I couldn't bring myself to tell Thurmond about it even now. But if I were really honest with myself, at this moment I wanted to find Rannen almost as much as Dad, even if I didn't completely understand why.

"Rose, we're in big enough trouble as it is. We've got to report this."

"To who? Our chain of command? I don't know if you noticed, but they tried to kill us."

"The police, or the FBI, or something."

"Sure. I'll let you explain the dimensional angle."

"Someone has to know about this!"

"Yeah. I was going to start with Special Agent Jim Wichman from the Dimensional Liaison Agency."

"You've got to be kidding me." Thurmond threw up his hands. "He left us for dead!"

"It doesn't matter! Don't you get that?" My face flushed hot in my attempt not to yell. "The commander has Rannen and whatever information he has in his head!"

"He's dead! Hoth shot him! I saw it!"

"He's not dead!" I was on my feet again. Blood drained away from my head. Thurmond's angry face became fuzzy and the argument unclear. "He's not dead."

"Why is this so important to you?"

"Because it is! There's something . . ." The reason was on the tip of my tongue, a maddening little motive that would convince Thurmond without a doubt if I could only spit it out.

"And when you find the commander you'll, what, ask her to hand him over? Put her under citizen's arrest?"

"She's looking for that Heart thing." That might convince Xavier, at least. I put as much pleading into my eyes as my words, pushing away a twinge of guilt. "T, remember what you told me back before we got to the portal? This is definitely one of those moments where we need all the information."

"I can't believe you even remember that," Thurmond grumbled.

"There's something going on here that goes beyond the commander getting her hands on that portal, or the key, or even Rannen. What if we're the only ones who know about this? What if we're the only ones who could stop her? I'll follow this lead by myself if I have to."

I could see Thurmond's natural protective instincts fighting against my risky, illogical, and unreasonable option. He turned away, and for one solitary moment I thought I'd lost. When he faced me again he held Wichman's business card.

"Any chance we can go about this with some common sense and a plan?"

Relief swept through me, no less poignant than if he'd promised to save my first born.

"Sure."

He gave a tiny, resigned nod, which I returned. He turned to Xavier. The movie star placed his hands on top of his head, his face lost in bewilderment.

"Mr. Coy, can I borrow your phone?" Thurmond held out his hand.

Xavier's eyes flitted to Thurmond and then back to me, but he didn't reach for a phone.

"You know, I should probably call him," I said, "He knows I was still alive when he left, but he was under the distinct impression you were dead, T. That may come in handy."

"Or I could call him," Xavier cut in. He pulled a cell phone out of his pocket. "You know, use a little star power. I don't know, I could offer him money or something."

"I thought you didn't know who Marshal Rannen was?" Thurmond rubbed the edge of the card on his palm. "Why would you want to throw some money at a guy from the DLA to get information about him?"

"I—I just want to help."

"Give me the phone," I said.

"Dammit, Rose, would you just—" Thurmond turned on me.

"I'll make the call," said a squeaky voice from the door.

I hadn't heard the door open, but Boderick was suddenly standing behind Xavier. His Rethan face looked so foreign in these modern, Earthly surroundings that I cringed. After all that had happened, my mind still didn't want to accept what was right in front of my eyes. His tan slacks, red button-down shirt, and baseball cap only succeeded in making his silvery hair and skin look more peculiar.

An older, distinguished-looking gentleman stood behind him. Dr. Tolman, I assumed. The doctor pushed past Boderick and Xavier. Without a word he pressed his stethoscope to my chest, then flicked a penlight across my eyes. I resisted the urge to fend him off.

"I've had contact with Agent Wichman before," Boderick continued. His shoulders hunched, and his hands opened and closed in an obsessive gesture. "He knows I'm no threat, and he'll at least know who I am without having to risk the identities of you three."

"That's enough for today, gentlemen," Dr. Tolman broke in. He took the stethoscope out of his ears and tapped my hand where the IV had left a scab. "Miss Rose needs some liquids. And rest."

I wondered if Dr. Tolman was the type that could be bullied. His expression was relaxed, but as I opened my mouth to speak his eyebrows lifted, and his lips thinned.

"Bodie." I turned to Boderick. "Make the call. Set up the meeting for as soon as possible."

CHAPTER 25

I awoke with a scream, batting my hands through the air. I could feel the heat of the orb in my hand, the cool of the blade, the stickiness of the blood spattering my skin. I couldn't see anything other than face upon bloody face filled with terror, anger, and hatred.

"Whoa! Hey, hey!" Arms tried to contain me. I fought them away but they persisted. "Hey, Rose, calm down. You're okay. It's okay. It was just a bad dream."

Thurmond swam into focus. I stopped fighting and clenched my hands into fists, every muscle in my body aching and tense. Thurmond wrapped me in his arms. I trembled against his chest. He brushed his hands up and down my back and slowly I relaxed, breathing in the tang of his soap.

"Same dream?" Thurmond asked.

"No. Yeah," I said.

I pushed away. I rubbed my eyes to block out his concerned face. We sat in the back seat of a large custom van parked on the street. I must have dozed off during the drive from the airport.

Thurmond didn't ask more questions. I was grateful. I suspected he didn't believe me but didn't push the matter. The one that really bothered me was the bloody knife that replayed over and over, like the favorite movie of a sadist. Only it wasn't a movie. And it wasn't a dream. Caz made sure I knew that.

Thurmond was watching me. "Do you need a few minutes?"

"No, we're still a go." I checked the clock on the dashboard. Twenty minutes before the meet. No time for a conniption. Boderick sat in the passenger seat looking flustered. Thurmond had been driving and must have plowed past him to get to me when I'd started screaming.

"You and Bodie head out," I said. "Just like we practiced. I'll be right behind you."

Thurmond squeezed my shoulder. "Copy that. See you in a bit."

Boderick was out of the van before Thurmond could get the door open. Both doors slammed shut at the same time, and they walked away side by side. Thurmond leaned over to give Bodie last minute instructions, probably in regards to acting more human.

I scrubbed my hands up and down my face, trying to banish the images of the dream. I'd come to dread sleeping, staying up late and waking early, thanks to my nightmares. I even stopped taking the pain medication I still desperately needed, because it made me drowsy.

I'd taken some today, though. It was a choice between having a completely clear mind and a partially functioning body. Dr. Tolman and I agreed on a mild pain killer that would make me woozy, but not overly.

Opaque curls of fog rolled away from the rustic walkways of Cannery Row, reaching cool fingers back toward the ocean. The boardwalk was nearly empty this time of the morning with the occasional local walking a dog or hurrying to open their touristy Monterey, California shop.

I rubbed goose bumps from my arms, checked the clock again, and exited the van. I placed my hat on my head, and stepped off the curb. Thurmond stood across the road with his back to me, his face mirrored in the large display window of an herbalist's shop. His eyes roved across the reflections, searching for anyone remotely suspicious.

We'd raided the racks of costume clothing on the set, and Thurmond looked good wearing the stylishly faded blue jeans and a high-necked, short-sleeved shirt. A black cap hid his awesome scar. The shirt in particular hugged his pecs enticingly, making him look for all the world like a magazine model.

I pushed a light pair of sunglasses onto my nose, trying not to feel irritated that my eyes were becoming less hazel every day. My hair was also much more silver than yesterday. I'd had someone braid it early this morning before the flight, and at the last minute stolen a black and white fedora from Xavier's Winnebago.

I adjusted my sleeve over the bandage on my shoulder and held my arm close to my body to compensate for the lack of a sling. Dr. Tolman would never have consented, so I'd left it in the first garbage can I'd come to outside of the airport. My dark jeans and tight, cream shirt clung to my skin. That was Angie's idea, saying something about how a garbage bag on a cute girl like me would only get me noticed. Someone should make Angie wear a cotton t-shirt and sweat pants so she knew what comfort felt like. At least I'd been able to pick my shoes, flatly refusing anything open-toed, heeled, or missing some other vital part. I'd ended up with some high-top gray trainers almost identical to a pair I'd worn in high school. Something I could run in, if it came to that.

Thurmond was a block behind me now. I crossed to the other side of the street, trying my best not to limp. I feigned interest in the window dressings of the shops while thumbing the zipper of my purse. I would have felt much more secure if I could have carried Xavier's short-barreled .357 Magnum out in the open, or at least in a holster. A purse seemed like such a hurdle when you might need to shoot someone before they shot you.

A good ten minutes of walking put me in a shabbier area of Monterey. The sidewalk steepened, and my pace slowed. Weeds grew between the cracks in the sidewalks, and peeling paint now seemed a requirement for the majority of the buildings.

The little pub café I'd picked out came into view. It sported an old-fashioned hanging sign above the door proclaiming it "The Brewer's Swill," accompanied by a washed-out picture of what looked, oddly enough, like a chamber pot. They were open twenty-four hours a day and made fabulous eggs Benedict.

However, the reason I'd picked the place was for its slow yet steady local traffic, dim, private booths; and most importantly, two entrances with doors that always remained open, as well as a back exit through the kitchen.

I looked down a side street at a flash of movement. Boderick skirted around two older women before flattening himself against the wall of a shop. They stared at him with a mixture of curiosity and bewilderment. I snickered. I should've been concerned about him drawing attention, but he was like a naughty puppy you can't bring yourself to scold for chewing your shoes. He'd been so determined to come along and blend with the humans that he'd even dyed his hair black like Xavier's.

I made a slight motion with my head, and he melted into a doorway. The two women kept an eye on him over their shoulders before rounding a far corner. At least Thurmond was a natural; practically invisible to the growing pedestrian traffic.

My CI training only became second nature to me after months of practical field experience. Teaching two other people basic techniques, including one who was only partially familiar with the culture in the Third Dimension, was frustrating; especially since it was done mostly in the cushy confines of Xavier Coy's private Gates Learjet 55 on the way to California. Xavier himself opted out of our scrappy mission, though he accompanied us to Monterey before giving us a bogus line about some ambiguous appointment.

I stopped next to the door of the café, scraped my finger across the peeling brown paint, and watched the reflection in the window for movement behind me. I caught sight of my own face.

Thurmond said I didn't look *that* different. I had to disagree. The makeup Angie made me wear to cover the bruises altered my look to a significant degree, but it was more than that. My cheeks were sunken in from lack of food, and my skin had paled to a translucent white. Include the silvering of my hair and eyes and I looked faded, frail, and washed out. Alien.

I turned around and took a cigarette out of my purse. I didn't smoke, but it gave me an excuse to stand outside the door until I could get a report from Thurmond.

My fingers trembled on the cigarette. I hoped the painkillers weren't wearing off already. Dr. Tolman had been grumpy enough that I refused to stay in bed, and practically livid that I was planning to go gallivanting off on some mysterious mission. He was a good man.

I tapped the cigarette against my leg. Thurmond and Boderick passed each other without talking. Boderick touched the brim of his hat before strolling almost human-like across the road. Thurmond continued in my direction. He gave me only the briefest glance when he passed, adjusted his cap, and strode out of sight.

At the all-clear signal, I dropped the cigarette and crushed it with my foot. I didn't remove my glasses or hat as I stepped into the café, giving a cheery wave to the older waitress heading my way.

"Hey, uh," I read her nametag, "Linda. I hear you make a fantastic eggs Benedict."

"Well I don't make it, sweetie, but sure. It's the best." Her voice croaked in a pleasant way, reminding me of my late Aunt Brenda.

Linda tried to sit me near the front window but, after a little prompting, showed me to a corner booth of my choosing. It gave me a view of the entire room as well as both entrances.

"Coffee too?"

"No, but I'd love a glass of orange juice."

She brought the juice to me within a few minutes, then left while the rest of my breakfast cooked. I sipped my juice and watched the doors. Any second Wichman would show his face, which I'd last seen on a rainy, muddy hilltop surrounded by gun-toting enemies and bodies of Rethans. His presence would not only bring it all back, something I wanted very much to forget, but there was the possibility he would bring with him the very people who wanted me dead.

Linda bustled from the kitchen and placed a steaming plate in front of me.

"Thanks so much," I said.

"You're welcome, hon. Anything else I can get for ya?"

"Nope. This looks great. Oh, and hey, I'm meeting someone here this morning." I gave a giggle I hoped didn't sound too phony. That was me with the hat and the sunglasses—phony through and through. "He's an older guy I met on the Internet. Real cute in a bald head and mustache sort of way. When he gets here will you make sure we get a little privacy?"

"Sure," she drew out the word. Concern wilted her brisk demeanor. She paused with the tray balanced on one hand. Shaking her head, she headed toward the kitchen. She paused and turned back to me. "I don't like to meddle, but you sure he's safe, sweetie?"

"Not really." I exhaled a determined huff. "That's why I'm meeting him in a public place. I'll give him a chance. He might just be the connection I'm looking for."

"All right, hon. I hope you know what you're doin.'"

"Me too," I whispered to myself as she walked away to help an older couple sitting several booths down.

Thurmond was supposed to circle the block and then take up residence on a bench across the street and facing The Brewer's Swill. I couldn't see him from here, but it was comforting to know he was close by.

It was another ten minutes before Sergeant Wichman strode past the large front window. Sunlight glinted off his bald head. He stood in the doorway, letting his eyes adjust. His face displayed a two days growth of graying beard, and his button-down shirt was bunched and wrinkled. A tight fist gnarled my stomach.

"Jim," I called out, with an enthusiastic wave.

His reaction was comedic, complete with a jerking of his head that must've cricked his neck and a dropping jaw that put his chin on his chest. He was very good at recovering from shock though, because he was sliding onto the bench opposite me before I could put my hand down.

"Sonuva-bitch! Rose? Is that really you?" He smoothed his mustache with two fingers, leaning back to examine my face.

"Yep, alive and kicking."

"I can't believe you're here. That you're okay." His genuine surprise and pleasure took me aback.

"Yeah, I know. Big surprise."

Sergeant Wichman glanced over his shoulder, clearly uncomfortable having his back to the door.

"How'd you get out of there?" he asked.

"You mean after you left me for dead?"

He stopped fidgeting and gave me a deadpan stare. "Leaving you there was the only way I could think to save your life, Rose."

"I bet it was."

"So?" he prompted.

Like I was going to tell him. "I bench-pressed the Hummer off of my leg, resurrected Thurmond, and we double-timed to the nearest hospital." I pulled off my sunglasses, laid them on the table, and looked Wichman in the eye.

His skin paled, and his mouth fell open again.

"Damn, Rose. They gave you Azshatath didn't they? A pretty heavy dose too, by the looks of it. They should've given you enough Vizshathain to bring you back to normal though. You can't be walking around like—"

"Shut up, Sarge." I lifted my hat to scratch the healing skin around my stitches. "Don't talk like you're not a part of whatever the commander's up to. Maybe you didn't hear me? You. Left. Us. For. Dead."

Wichman sat back. "I came back the first chance I got, but you were already gone. What the hell was I supposed to do?"

I was reasonable enough to understand the logic of what he was saying. If the commander had known I was alive there would have been no misfires into the mud. However, I wasn't going to let him walk away without taking any responsibility.

"Oh I don't know—not allow it to happen in the first place? Bring in your DLA troops before the commander even got on the plane?"

"You don't understand the half of what's going on." Wichman rubbed an eye in clear exhaustion.

"Then enlighten me," I said.

"I was under the impression I'd be talking to Boderick."

"That was the idea."

"What are you doing here, Rose?" Wichman absently dumped salt into his hand and tossed it on my untouched eggs. "You could've gone into hiding and no one would ever come looking."

"Hiding from the commander, or from you and the rest of the DLA?"

"The commander, of course."

"Because if I'm really who everyone says I am, I'd think the DLA would want to make good and sure I wasn't about to kill a million people. Or maybe they'll just rush in and cover it up, so no one knew anything ever happened."

"What are you talking about?"

"Staff Sergeant Mary Chatting. Corporal Jeremy Toon. Officers Kyle Ferguson, Casey Wright, and Benjamin Rose." As I rattled off the list Wichman's face went from confusion, to understanding, to a blank mask. "Do you want me to go on?"

"Stop it, Rose. This isn't the time or the place for any of this."

I released a frustrated growl. "Come on, Sarge. How about we stop playing games here."

"That's a great idea. You can stop pretending to be someone you're not, and I'll stop pretending I don't have information far above your clearance."

"Oh, that's rich! Pull out the whole need to know act. I'm a counterintelligence agent in the US Army. I happen to have top-secret clearance, and I should think my obvious appearance change would cover the dimensional angle. As a concerned daughter I definitely have the right to know."

Sergeant Wichman looked behind him again and then scratched at a dirty spot on the table. I hoped he was just being cautious and not actually expecting someone. He rubbed his eyes with a finger and thumb.

"You want some intel, Rose? I guarantee you won't like it."

I leaned forward. Wichman's face hardened, and I almost retracted my request.

"My original assignment wasn't anything more than to do an O and I," he said.

"What's that?"

"Observe and interact. I was assigned as your squad leader to keep an eye on you."

"Why?"

"There's been some . . . stuff happening in the inter-dimensional community over the last seventy-two months, pointing directly to your involvement."

"What?" I wasn't involved in anything until the last week, except . . . "I didn't—"

"I know that." Wichman held up a hand. "I've been the one on your tail. You've always just been US Army Specialist Kris Rose."

I rubbed my knuckles on my cheek. I barely remembered who that was anymore. "So what's been going on?"

"It's complicated."

"I can keep up."

"Let's say that the plan 'you' put into motion twenty-two years ago, the one that you murdered all those Rethans over, appears to once again be in the planning stage."

"You can't be any more specific than that?"

"I *won't* be any more specific than that."

"Why not?

"Because with all that Azshatath in your system, your mind has got to be pretty unstable."

I shrugged off that very real truth. "Okay, then tell me why the commander wants me dead."

It was Wichman's turn to shrug. "I thought at first it was one of those 'wrong place, wrong time' instances, until you followed us onto the plane."

"You guys took Thurmond. What was I supposed to do?" An ache pounded above my ear. I fingered the blade of a butter knife.

"Now hold on, Rose." Wichman held up his hands, his expression telling me he was prepared for a bad reaction. I thought I was holding it together quite well, considering. "I know you were friends, and it's destroying me what happened to him, but you've got to believe me. I thought I was sending him to give you a ride back to base, not getting him killed."

My knuckles whitened around the knife and I reminded myself that, despite Wichman speaking of Thurmond in the past tense, Thurmond wasn't dead. He was right outside on the bench. I set the knife back on the table with some effort and pried my fingers from the handle.

"If you were tasked to follow me, how did you end up on the commander's crew?"

"It didn't take much to identify her as a Rethan. A Rethan in the military is unusual enough, but one who comes out of nowhere, who's not a RAGE inmate or a registered denigrated entrepreneur, throws up a lot of red flags. Now compound that with her proximity to you and all the other bells going off in regards to your past, and we had a serious problem. My workload suddenly doubled."

"So who is she?"

"We know she's not really Major Jamie Kuntz."

"No duh."

"She's been impersonating the real Major Kuntz for at least a year, maybe more. The investigation was still underway when we flew out on the C-130."

"What's her connection to me?"

"Well, that's the million dollar question, isn't it?"

"There's nothing about her in my DLA file or anything?"

"Nothing." Wichman shook his head.

"Does it have anything to do with my Dad going missing?"

Wichman went still and silent.

"Come on, Sarge! He's my dad!" I pleaded.

"Rose."

"Please, just tell me something. Anything!"

Wichman rubbed his eyes. "Rose, all I can say is that, yes, your father worked for the DLA years ago. He was a good friend of mine, actually. His disappearance shook our whole agency to the core, so believe me when I say we have our best people on it. But now isn't the time to be worrying about him. This is about you and the commander, and the sooner we understand more about the both of you, the sooner we can move past it to other important things. Like finding your father."

A million questions piled up in my mind. Dad in the DLA? The confirmation hollowed out my stomach. Did that mean he knew who I was? Was I the reason he was gone? Gone to Retha, if I believed the officiate. I rested my face in my hands and, with superhuman effort, mentally pushed the questions aside. For the first time since Dad went missing, I looked beyond my loss and saw something more important. Something bigger and badder that definitely required my immediate attention. I ran my hand across my forehead and looked up at Wichman.

"She knows me," I said with a nod. "The commander. She called me Caz. Said something about Retha losing its last chance to find the device, whatever that means." The memory surfaced unexpectedly, and I shivered at the successive image of the gunshot to the officiate's head.

"What?" Wichman's eyebrows shot up. "What else did she say?"

"I don't remember." I shrugged. "I was half dead at the time."

"Hmmm." He scratched his whiskery chin and looked out the side door. "Someone who not only knew you but knew about the device. That narrows things down considerably."

His voice trailed off, his thoughts somewhere else.

"So who is she?"

"No idea. We'd have to do some digging."

We were going nowhere fast. "Listen, Sarge, the commander obviously has some diabolical plan in the works, and she needs Rannen to accomplish it." Wichman turned his head, his eyes slowly following until they locked on mine. I continued, "You're in her inner circle. What is it?"

"I don't know." He averted his eyes. He was still hiding something.

I slapped my hand on the table. The lights flickered with a loud hum. My head pounded. The other patrons of the café looked around, but as the lights returned to normal and the humming quieted, the clicking of forks against plates and the soft buzzing of conversation continued.

"Don't you think enough damage has been done?" I hissed across the table. Wichman flinched.

"If I tell you, she'll know it was me—mission over, Rannen dead. And you and me as well."

"So you *do* know where Rannen is."

He shrugged and rested his back against the seat. My fingers tingled.

"What does she want with him? If you know you've got to tell me. Please!" I hated that this tight-lipped song and dance routine had forced me to resort to pleading. My head hurt.

Sergeant Wichman looked over his shoulder and then flattened his mustache with his hand. He cleared his throat, hesitated, and then pulled a napkin from the napkin holder. He tugged a pen out of his back pocket, drew a simple image on it, and pushed it across the table to me.

A half circle and dot where the center should be stared back at me in an amateur etch. My pendant—the key.

I touched the shrapnel wound on my head and ran my hand down to my chin before touching my nose with my finger. The commander had drawn the same design on my face with my own blood.

What in Gauss's law is he doing with that information! Caz said. I rubbed at the ache above my ear.

"What is that?" I hissed.

"*That* is the Rethan symbol for a device created by a very capable Rethan over twenty years ago. Up until a few months back I was under the impression it was only a myth, a tale told to keep the lower dimensions in line. It's called the Heart of Annihilation. Supposedly it has the capability to destroy an entire dimension." He crumpled the napkin and pushed it deep into my glass of orange juice before shaking off his fingers.

I traced the brand on my hand. The last symbol was the same half circle and dot. The ache in my head intensified. My eyes watered. I squeezed my head with both hands, clenching my eyes to shut out the pain.

Look. Look! You simplistic child! Caz's voice became louder. Louder. Her shout rang in my ears. My head split in agony. *Look!*

CHAPTER 26

Caz
10 days pre-RAGE

The envirophylum near Vislane Academy was one of the largest in the world. It spanned twelve grids and was home to plants and creatures from all thirteen dimensions. It held over four thousand different varieties of plants and trees, thirty-six mammal families, two hundred forty-eight species of birds and reptiles, and three million insects.

As beautiful, time-honored things praising a simpler time and the still-simplistic lower dimensions, the envirophylums were spread across the globe. They were as precious and protected as they came. Committees and funding and round the clock care were provided to keep all the living entities within, well, *living*.

Caz stood outside Vislane Academy. She hugged her bag to her chest. The last light of the sun brightened the clouds, casting the high swaying trees of the Vislane envirophylum into sharp relief. The school sat less than a quarter of a grid away from the dark, creeping vines that continually threatened to touch the school.

Caz looked carefully to the left and the right, then searched the darkness of the trees for a phylum patrol. No movement. She'd stood here for the past hour and had yet to see anything other than plant and animal life, and not even much of that.

Caz checked both ways once more and stepped across the vines. Caz and Vin had made this their special place while growing up. They'd skirt the patrols to get to the tiny cave they'd found on one of their first explorations. Then they would squish in side by side to discuss the latest gossip at the academy, or talk around whatever was happening at home while watching the insects or the occasional animal.

It was years since they'd come here together. Caz was sure Vin had forgotten about it, and she'd missed her chance to ask him.

The cave was nowhere near the center of the phylum. Caz would have to hike all night if she wanted to get to the center, and she simply didn't have the patience for that. She was amazed that she remembered how to get there. Vines covered most of the entrance, but enough light seeped across the weathered scrapings—V & C—carved deep into the rock.

Caz yanked open the bag. She looked cautiously around and then settled to her work.

The eight-millimeter Heart of Annihilation prototype fit into her palm, no bigger than a pebble. It gave off a faint yellow glow, warming her fingers. She rotated it in her hand, examining every millimeter for flaws she knew weren't there, before finding the keyhole. She drew the chain from around her neck and rubbed her thumb across the half-circle—all that remained of Vin's promise ring.

Her first creation in her parent's lab was the key that would one day belong to the Heart of Annihilation. Everything that came after that was secondary and made to fit the key. It slid comfortably into the slot. Caz rotated it twelve times, then pulled it out.

Someday there would be higher security measures for the actual device, but for today this was enough. She gave it a gentle roll across the grass, putting the prototype at the mouth of the cave. Caz touched her fingers to her lips and then pressed her hand toward the device in a final farewell—to her past, to her present, and to Vin.

And so the countdown began.

She didn't hurry from the phylum. No need. She'd given herself enough time. She even slowed, perhaps hoping in the darkest part of herself that she might be caught in the deadly wave.

She made it out of the phylum with no trouble, passed the academy, and kept going. It wasn't until she was almost a grid away that she paused. A quick glance around showed her the reddish door leading to a narrow set of stairs inside an abandoned high-rise apartment building.

Caz climbed up the stairs. She was completely devoid of electricity, a necessary precaution for what was about to happen. She didn't think she was in danger, but she didn't want any accidents.

The roof of the building was higher than anything else close. Vislane Academy was the next tallest with its gaudy spires. The only thing higher were the trees from Vislane envirophylum, reaching for the stars against the indigo sky. Caz glanced at her wrist to check the time, pulled a command screen from her bag, and settled in to watch.

Golden light bloomed from deep in the phylum. It was a bit bigger than Caz calculated, but not by much. The light reached serpentine fingers through the woods, expanding in a perfect circle.

It was the moment Caz had worked toward all her life. The fingers of light glowed brighter with their progression and seemed to be retracting at the same time, or rather drawing all the energy they touched back to the device itself. The glowing light expanded not only outward but upward as well, climbing the towering trees and bleeding them of their life force. Vislane Academy was now in its graceful claws, and still it expanded. Outward and upward.

A breeze plucked at Caz's hair. She brushed it away impatiently, and then watched the same breeze touched the closest tree and blew it away in a gray cloud. And the next, and the next, until the sky was thick with ash.

Exactly two minutes and thirty-six seconds later the light suddenly sucked inward on itself and vanished.

CHAPTER 27

Rose

You're going to need to get to that first. Get it first. Get it!

I pressed my face into my hands. The pressure in my head intensified and then retreated into nothing. The image vanished.

"Rose, what happened?"

I rested my forehead on the table, my stomach churning. "I'm going to be sick."

"Rose?"

I allowed myself a moment between two worlds before forcing myself back into the real one. When I was sure I wouldn't be adding my stomach's contents to my cold eggs, I lifted my head. Wichman's face swam into focus.

"What's going on with you? What happened? Did you remember something?" Wichman battered me with questions.

"Rannen mentioned something about several of the dimensions being destroyed." I flicked my finger at the cup of juice, where tendrils of ink spread from the napkin. "Is that the device that would do that?"

"Tell me what you remembered." Wichman's expression was hungry.

"Just answer the question, Sarge."

"Theoretically, yes. That device could destroy an entire dimension." He huffed the assent.

"How does it work?"

"You would know better than I would."

"Me? Why?"

"Because, you created it."

Not you, exactly. Caz corrected with a little laugh.

I didn't bother to question the accuracy of his statement.

"And I, uh . . . I suppose you need a key to operate it?"

"Two pieces of a key combine together to make one, but yes." Sergeant Wichman narrowed his eyes. "Do you know where the key is, Rose?"

A complicated trilling from my purse made me jump. I reached for my phone as a clatter of dishes and a scream from Linda shattered the midmorning calm. A popping sound extinguished all the lights.

The commander filled the closest doorway. She wore all black. Her hair was streaked with silver, and the backlight cast her face into shadow. Lieutenant Justet slunk through the other door followed by Sergeant Sanderford and four others I didn't know, all wearing civilian clothing.

I leapt from the booth while yanking the revolver from my purse and pointed it at the commander's face.

"Thank you, Jim," she said.

My eyes flitted over to Sergeant Wichman. He stood near the booth, exuding the coldness I associated with him when he was in the presence of the commander. The question was, was he acting his part as an undercover agent or was he selling me out?

My distraction cost me. The commander was within reaching distance before I could bring my eyes back to her. Her foot smashed the gun out of my hand, and then she slammed her fist into my barely-healed shoulder. I fell against the edge of the table with a cry of pain, clutching my shoulder. Warm blood soaked my shirt and seeped between my fingers. Linda screamed again.

"Shut her up!" The commander jabbed a long finger toward the poor waitress.

Lieutenant Justet shoved Linda into a booth and placed the muzzle of his gun on her forehead. Her fist jammed into her open mouth, but no further sound came out. The other patrons cowered in their seats. I hoped none of them would try to be a hero and get themselves killed.

"Well, well, well, Caz." The commander smiled, her tone conversational. She wasn't even breathing hard. "I never would have thought Jim Wichman could have such a good read on you."

"Yeah, he's a brilliant piece of garbage."

She leaned in close, whispering in my ear. "When he told me he'd left you alive, I nearly baked his insides with fifty thousand volts and ate his entrails for dessert." She withdrew, speaking in normal tones again. "He said you would be able to lead us to someone who could help us. Rannen has proven . . . rather disappointing."

"What'd you do with him? Where is he?"

"He's alive, but that's not what you need to be concerned about. What I need from you right now, *Caz*," she grabbed my shoulder, digging her thumb into the wound, "is to tell me where I can find your brother."

I gasped, trying to pull away. Wichman moved in on one side and Sanderford appeared on the other. They each took one of my arms, locking me into a tight box.

"Who?" I gritted my teeth against the pain.

"Don't play with me. You contacted him. There's no way you're here talking to me without a financial backer with a personal interest. So stop playing the amnesic inmate and tell me—"

A wail of police sirens erased the rest of her words. The volume increased in the seconds it took us to register them, until it was clear they were only a few streets away. The commander jerked her head at one of her men, and he left.

Pressure in my head constricted my flow of rational thought, and to my surprise laughter bubbled from my throat.

What's pathetic now? Pathetic. Pathetic.. Caz started up a mantra, and suddenly the words were no longer trapped within my head.

"You're pathetic," I snarled.

The commander's eyes popped. "What did you say?"

She gouged her thumb deeper into my bloodied shoulder. I choked back a gasp, feeling the stitches split and the bandage work into my flesh. I shoved at her. She didn't let go.

The muscles in my chest and arms contracted, and with an unexpected surge of fury I released all my pent up voltage through the gaping skin in my shoulder.

Light exploded around us. My back cracked against the table edge in a stripe of pain. The commander's hand ripped away. She stumbled, trying to keep her balance, and then smashed with a crashing rattle into the booth opposite. Acrid smoke stung my throat. Sanderford and Wichman fell away from me, coughing into their hands.

I waved away the smoke. An offhand glance at my shoulder showed a bloody, melted mess and a small flame, which I calmly batted out.

"Rethan power," I said. "Sometimes a life sentence has its perks."

The commander cradled her arm to her body. A jagged black and red burn circled her smoking hand. I expected her to be angry. Murderous, even. But her face only showed subconscious pain—and humor. Her mouth opened, making a tight O shape which she held for a moment before being able to get anything out. It was one word, "Wichman."

The cool, heavy metal of a gun ground into my temple.

"Try any more of your electric hocus-pocus, Rose, and I'll blow your brains all over this diner." Sergeant Wichman sounded angry.

I could do angry. It had been near the surface for days. Whisper behind my back and I'd want to start a fight. Look at me wrong and I'd clench my fists and force myself not to throw a punch. And heaven forbid anyone actually picked a real fight. Justet had learned the hard way.

Adrenaline and rage coursed through my body, heightening my senses, tightening my muscles, and loosening my tongue.

Words unleashed in an animalistic snarl. "Will that be before or after the cops have arrested your traitorous ass?"

I knocked the pistol away from my head and slammed my elbow into Wichman's jaw. I dropped into a crouch, putting me level with Sanderford's bad knee, and I swept both his feet out from under him. I landed on my butt and slid across the slick floor, scrabbling under the bench of a nearby booth for the weapon. I found the textured grip of the .357 and rolled onto my back, aiming.

Wichman stood above me, rubbing his jaw, his 9mm on me. The commander was behind him, her burned hand protected next to her body. Sanderford got to his feet, his pistol pointed at my chest. He was going to fire it unless someone stopped him. My finger tensed on the trigger.

A chatter of voices and movement near the café door penetrated my little bubble. I couldn't bring myself to remove my gaze from Sanderford. The commander turned her head. Then, as if in agreement, Sanderford and I both turned to look.

"Turn on those cameras and make it look good, Jonas."

Xavier Coy, dressed in an immaculate, flashy red shirt and black leather pants, stormed through the door. He was buried in an army of crew, cameras, props, and lights. Flashing red and blue lights raced into the street. The piercing sirens wailed into silence. Screeching tires, slamming doors, and shouted orders turned everything to chaos.

"And—CUT!" a beefy man shouted. He leaned against the doorframe, his chubby face glistening sweat, his voice shaking.

"Get down! Get down! Weapons down!"

Cops swarmed toward the café. Sergeant Wichman set his pistol on the table. Sanderford held his weapon another second before tucking it into his belt. Lieutenant Justet threw his 9mm onto the opposite bench. The commander tugged with one hand to straighten her shirt, her eyes locked on Xavier.

"Ah," she exhaled.

"Officers." Xavier raised his hands and flashed them one of his bleached smiles. He exited the café, turning the star power to overload. "What's this all about? We have a permit to film here today."

For a moment I forgot all about the threat to my life as the police officers lowered their weapons and started chatting up a storm with the movie star. I got to my feet and set my gun on the table next to Wichman's. My fingers shook. I rubbed my hands together to still them.

Angie pushed her way into the café, looking impeccably svelte in a butter-yellow pantsuit and white patent heels. She murmured quiet "excuse me's," while pushing past the commander, Sanderford, and Justet like they weren't volatile members of a renegade secret ops team. She helped Linda to her feet and sat her with the older couple one booth over. Her voice was quiet as she spoke to them, flashing a bright, comforting smile. She removed several fat envelopes from her purse and placed them before each person. The older gentleman partially pulled out a wad of cash before shoving it back into the envelope and reaching over his terrified wife to shake Angie's hand.

I dropped onto the edge of the bench behind me, pressing my hand to my shoulder. My eyes locked on the commander. She spoke with Wichman and Sanderford in whispers. Justet made his way up behind the commander's little grouping and gave me a thin, almost apologetic smile. It was quite sweet, from the man who'd thrown a grenade at me.

"Ma'am, we've got to go." Justet gestured toward the kitchen.

The commander turned to leave, her eyes on me. She'd just reached the kitchen's swinging door when I was possessed with sudden inspiration.

"I know where the Heart is," I said. The commander whirled around, her eyes wide. I continued, "I'll tell you where it is in exchange for Marshal Rannen."

Two police officers made their way toward the door.

"Ma'am, we have to go now." Justet pushed the kitchen door open.

"You already have the key." Blood pounded in my ears. "I think my information would at least be worth that much to you."

"I'll be in touch." The commander took one last look at the officers meeting Angie's interference and tossed a small flip phone toward me. I fumbled to catch it, and when I looked up she'd disappeared into the kitchen with her men.

I placed a hand over my eyes. Inhale, exhale.

"Are you all right, ma'am?"

I drew my hand to my mouth. A young police officer with soft brown eyes stood before me.

"Yeah, I'm . . ."

I wanted to say fine, but was I? I was tired of fighting, tired of the fear, and sick to death of Caz. But mostly I was tired of chasing answers and falling short. And when it came down to it, I'd rather hunker down in a foxhole than get caught unawares again. I stared at the swinging kitchen door, where the commander had disappeared moments ago. Yes, I was fine. I was going to bring the fight to me, and I was going to be ready this time.

Brave motives were one thing, but it didn't make my body any happier. Every muscle, bone, and sinew wanted to crumble into a heap on the floor and not move for a month.

You won't give it to her though, right? Caz asked. *You wouldn't really.*

"You're bleeding. Are you sure you're okay?" The officer asked.

"Yeah." I glanced at my blood-soaked shirt. My mouth twitched, the pain wanting to translate to my face. "It's fake movie blood and, uh, stuff."

Stuff like silvering hair and eyes. I looked past the officer out the café's front window. Where was Thurmond? I pressed my lips together. I hadn't had even a moment to consider him, but now I couldn't understand why he wasn't here. He should have come in with guns blazing the second the commander showed up. At least, that's what he said he was going to do. I searched every face of the growing masses of humanity outside the window.

"You sure you're all right, ma'am?" The officer touched my shoulder. I jerked my arm away. He pulled back, showing me a friendly hand. I took a breath and forced my lips into a calm smile. I shoved the phone the commander gave me into my pocket.

"Actually," I said, "could you tell me where I can find Mr. Coy?"

He pointed with a pen to a group of police officers outside the door. He shrugged and turned his attention to the guns on the table.

Xavier's clothes were so loud it was a wonder I hadn't seen him on my own. I made my way toward the door but paused for a moment near the booth. I rapped my knuckles lightly on the top of the bench.

"Linda? Are you okay?" I whispered to the waitress sitting by the older couple.

Her eyes were wide and frightened. I didn't really expect an answer and turned away.

"I'll be fine," she said in her scratchy voice. I looked back. Linda patted the white envelope on the table and gave me an encouraging smile. "Take care of yourself, sweetie."

I tried to return the smile but only ended up nodding, and joined Xavier outside. I interrupted his conversation with another officer.

"Xavier, have you seen Thurmond?"

"No. Boderick's over there. Why don't you ask him?" His voice was distant, impersonal.

I followed his finger and was barely able to pick out the Rethan sitting on a shadowed stoop out of everyone's way. Conversations quieted. People parted, and I traversed the cleared path right to Boderick's feet. He hugged his arms around his knees, his fearful eyes wide.

"Bodie?"

He answered before I was able to formulate the question.

"They took him." Boderick gave me a rapid nod. "J-just before the rest of the group went inside."

My stomach clenched around a blistering shard of guilt and rage. My ears rang, drowning out the crowds. I kneaded a thumb against the ache in the side of my head.

Well, Caz said, *We can't be having that now, can we?*

A scorching, high-voltage wave powered through my nervous system. Painful tremors collected in every nerve ending, turning my entire body into a giant mass of energy I couldn't contain. With a silent scream of release, electricity surged from me in a pulsing wave.

Cell phones flickered and died or burst into flames in their owner's astonished hands. Lights in the lampposts and the flashing lights of the police cars exploded in a shower of sparks. Glass burst from windows of cars and buildings, and screams filled the air as people ran for cover, shielding their heads with their arms.

The pulsing power diminished and died, aside from miniscule, blue streaks of electricity coursing across my skin.

I held my face in my hands, my mind a thousand miles away from the chaos I created.

CHAPTER 28

I tapped my cell phone against the passenger door of Xavier's stretch limousine, surrounded by the mess I'd made. Only two squad cars remained. The others had been towed away for repairs hours ago. The police had finished taking statements, and the officers were now working crowd control on the masses of fans and news teams here, respectively, to see their favorite actor and report on the disaster they dramatically entitled "The War on Technology in Monterey."

Xavier stood on the inside of the police tape, shaking spectator's hands and signing autographs.

I hated him. I hated his pretentious smile, his exotic accent, and his fake enthusiasm toward the throngs of adoring fans. I hated that he had helped to save my life not once but twice, making me indebted to him. But I especially loathed the way he was pointedly ignoring me when I'd made it very clear I needed to talk to him *now*.

I flipped my phone open and snapped it shut again. It was actually Angie's pink, bedazzled spare, which she had loaned to me for this mission. The other phone the commander had given me lay quietly in my pocket, refusing to ring.

I flipped the pink phone open and shut several more times before shoving it in my pocket and examining my shirt.

Angie was going to kill me—the shirt was completely ruined. I couldn't have destroyed it more thoroughly if I'd tried. Perhaps Thurmond's clothes had been damaged during the abduction, and I could sic Angie on him instead.

Caz broke through my thoughts, *Nice, Kris. Humor at a time like this. Real classy.*

I rubbed the ache above my ear. Out of all the phones that exploded, mine was lucky enough to stay intact. Lucky, or well protected inside the blast radius. They both needed a quick charge, easy enough thanks to my magic hands, and I had already tried calling Thurmond several times. I didn't expect an answer but was still bitterly disappointed with every unanswered ring. The voicemails I'd left were, for the most part, embarrassing tirades of concern. Then I'd called every number on the black flip phone, not that there were many, heaping violent threats toward the commander on the two people unfortunate enough to answer. All I got were quick hang-ups. I hoped my intent was at least being passed on.

I pulled the pink phone out of my pocket and flipped it open again. This time I scrolled quickly through the message information and found the one I'd already listened to over a dozen times. I put the phone to my ear. Thurmond's voice spoke from the other end.

"*Dammit*, Rose! Why aren't you picking up? Get out of there! It's Justet! I'm almost there, don't—get the hell off me!" A grunt of pain accompanied a crashing sound before the message went silent.

I snapped the phone shut again. My lips mashed into a tight line of anger. Angie strode from the café with a tall cup of coffee and click-clacked her stilettos across the road to Xavier. She whispered something in his ear. He glanced at me and gave Angie a tiny nod. Xavier offered an enthusiastic wave to the crowd and a sparkly grin. They groaned their disappointment.

I scowled at Xavier when he looked in my direction. His step faltered. He retrieved the coffee from Angie and took a sip.

"What has your panties in a bunch, Miss Rose?" Xavier smacked his lips and sipped the coffee again. "I got you out of your predicament, didn't I?"

Xavier's limo driver, a squatty man with a ridiculous hat, jumped from the driver's seat. He saw me leaning against the door and made a motion to push me out of the way. I allowed a sliver of electricity to crawl up my arms and folded them across my chest. He tripped back, treading on Angie's toe and knocking her cell phone out of her hands.

"Good grief, Alex." Angie bent over to pick up her phone.

Xavier waved the man off and put one hand in his pocket.

"What has my *panties in a bunch*, Xavier," I stabbed at him with my phone, trying not to yell, "is that you've been having lunch and signing autographs all day when Thurmond has been abducted."

"What do you want me to do about it?"

"What do I—?"

"I don't know exactly who you think I am, Miss Rose, but our interests do not necessarily go hand in hand." Xavier's eyes narrowed. "I helped you out last week for my own reasons, and today because I happened to be in the area and owed a friend a favor."

"So?"

"So this means that I have my own life, and I can't be following you around all the time cleaning up your messes because you're too stubborn—and confrontational—to try other solutions."

"But they took Thurmond!"

"Two hostages aren't much different than one."

"You're unbelievable!" I threw my hands in the air, vaguely aware of a change in pitch from the crowds. "Well, here's something that might interest you. I told them I knew where that Heart thingy is."

"You did *what*?" He grabbed my arm, his nails digging into my skin. His coffee sloshed through the narrow opening.

"Yeah." I yanked my arm away. "So now you can stop dancing away from the topic and tell me everything I need to know!"

"I already told you, I don't—"

"Don't give me that!" I bunched his shirt collar and shoved him.

The quiet from the previously noisy crowd made me look over to see a sea of accusing faces targeting me for assaulting their idol. Two police officers moved our way. I breathed in and out of my nose. The last thing I needed was to send out another electro-magnetic pulse wave and give a face to the warlord against Monterey's technology.

"Get in the car, Miss Rose." Xavier motioned for his driver to open the door.

I wrenched it open before he could move and threw myself onto the seat opposite the door. Xavier sat across from me. A large gentleman in sunglasses, who followed Xavier around, worked himself through the door and plunked down next to me. Angie's voice outside the limo rose as she fended off the cop's questions. A moment later she slid in next to Xavier and crossed her long legs. The door slammed behind her, darkening the interior.

The door opened, and Boderick poked his head in. I glowered at him and he disappeared, shutting the door quietly. The front passenger door opened, and Boderick took the seat next to the driver.

We drove in silence, the air between us thick in accusation. Xavier gave no indication that he had any desire to continue the conversation. We stopped at a red light and turned left onto Cannery Row. I broke the silence.

"Now will you tell me?"

He stared out the window. "I hardly think this is the time for—"

"It's the time and the place! That psychotic Rethan has Thurmond and thinks I have a world-ending device I'm only sort of convinced even exists!"

"This Heart of Annihilation—" Xavier turned his eyes on me.

"Aha!" I jabbed a finger at him. "I knew you knew what it was!"

"I don't—"

This final denial obliterated the last of my fragile restraint. I lunged across the tiny space between us, fingers clawed. I suppose I was aiming for his throat, although I wasn't entirely sure what I planned once I had him in my grasp.

The bodyguard caught me by my shoulders and threw me back against the seat. Pain rocked my shoulder. I gasped. Tears blurred my vision. From hurt, from frustration, from my world falling apart.

Electricity shivered across my hands. The blue shimmering glow in the dim interior cast light on everyone's expressions. The bodyguard held my arms against the seat, a twitch of his eye the only indication he was concerned over holding a live wire. Angie pulled out her phone and brushed a lazy finger across the screen.

"Now settle down, Miss Rose. If you electrocute this car, you're going to cause an accident." Xavier sighed with an exasperated roll of his eyes and waved his hand for his bodyguard to release me. I jerked my arms away. "And don't think the police department won't be able to connect it to the last temper tantrum you threw."

He pulled a glass from a compartment behind him and filled it with a small amount of amber liquid from a crystal decanter. He drained the cup in one swift swig, refilled it, and tossed that one back as well.

"Tell me where the Heart is," I said.

"I don't—"

"Tell me."

"I can't do—"

"Tell me!"

"I won't tell you anything about a device you were willing to murder two hundred and thirty-six Rethans over!"

I shivered, my teeth clacking together. I was so cold, and my head hurt. A dark cackle filled my mind.

Tell me. Tell me. Keep yelling it and you may get it through his thick skull. Like as not he'll just turn you over to the authorities. He's good at that.

"Shut up!" I yelled at Caz.

Angie looked up. The glow of her phone illuminated an unperturbed expression, as if my outburst was nothing more than weather related small talk. She reached under her seat and handed me a white hand towel. A new flow of blood was saturating the chest and sleeve of my shirt. I snatched it out of her hand and pressed it against my shoulder.

"I don't kill people," I said. "That wasn't me."

"I know, I know," Xavier said. "You're a different person now." He poured himself a third glass but only swirled his beverage around and around. He waved a hand at me. "This peachy little thing you've become, without the slightest ambition beyond your next paycheck." His leaned forward in his seat. "But that doesn't change what you did twenty years ago. People change, and I've seen you do it more than most." He sat back. His eyes shifted away. "I wouldn't take that as a compliment either."

"How do we know each other?" I narrowed my eyes, searching the familiarity of his face for evidence to help me pin down the relationship that created such mutual dislike between two nearly complete strangers.

"I was the one left to clean up your mess after you were sentenced to RAGE."

"That's not an answer."

"You cost me my Rethan life!"

"Why won't you answer the question?"

"Because I don't like the answer any more than you will!" He stabbed a finger at me.

"Were we friends? Lovers? Siblings?"

I stopped. My hand went to my mouth. I sat back against the seat, really seeing Xavier for the first time. That furrow between the eyebrows was suddenly very familiar. The way he used one side of his mouth to express emotion was also like someone else I knew, and his nose was nearly identical to the one I saw every day in the mirror.

The commander's words came to me. *Tell me where I can find your fluxing brother.*

I dropped my hand. "The commander is looking for you."

What else was I supposed to say? How do you greet a sibling you haven't seen in twenty years, especially an estranged brother you don't remember? Funny how I didn't feel any more affection for him than thirty seconds ago.

"Who?" Xavier refilled his glass.

"The commander—"

"Who is that?"

"Who do you think? The Rethan who tried to kill me and kidnapped Rannen and Thurmond. She was in the café. Didn't you see her?"

"No."

"About your age. Tall and thin, with sharp features like a hornet. Freaky scar across her eye."

Xavier slammed his glass on the seat next to him. The liquid sloshed over the sides, wetting his hand. "That's who took Rannen?"

"Yeah. And Thurmond too."

"Damn her." Xavier's hand shook on his glass.

"So you know her, huh?"

"Yes, I know her." He drained the glass again and handed it to Angie. Both his hands rubbed through his hair and down his face. He scrunched his eyes tight, whispering "damn her" several times before looking back up at me. "You know her too."

"Who is she?"

"She was . . . well, it was rumored she had something to do with your crime. You would've known her as the one who sentenced you to RAGE."

I shrugged, nonplussed.

"It doesn't matter anymore. If only I could pry open your head and find out what you did to her to make her turn on everything she valued. But now you're just an empty-headed little human who committed an atrocious crime over two decades ago."

I told myself I didn't care what he thought. I told myself to keep it together for Thurmond and Rannen. But I had to know!

"What was my, uh, crime anyway? Besides the whole murder bit."

"Murder isn't enough?"

"People need reasons to do something like that. I had to have a reason."

"You're insane! Always were. You were just waiting for something to put you over the edge, and you got it. Oh yes, you and your Heart of Annihilation. Sometimes I didn't know what was more important to you, the weapon you birthed or your actual family. Unfortunately, the question was answered when you murdered the entire DC Council. During a meeting I was supposed to attend."

A massive ache above my ear caused my vision to swim. My lips tingled. I tried to take in oxygen but my lungs felt full, as if I were drowning. I dropped my head between my knees.

A vision opened in my mind, like a movie screen unfurling in front of my eyes. A small, angular building provided the backdrop, familiar and homelike. The iron gate hung open. Lightning burst across a dark sky. I felt my feet striking the ground, my hands swinging at my sides.

My mind blistered and raged in a thousand different directions. But one thing was clear: I was there for blood.

CHAPTER 29

Caz
12 minutes pre-RAGE

Electricity crackled out of Caz's palm and ran the length of the silver, blood-encrusted blade which hung from her limp hand. Her head pounded a rhythm of pain above her left ear, and she pressed a knuckle to the spot. She knew there was no hope of escape. She just needed to see Xander one last time. To know if she'd lost him completely.

The structure before her was gaudy, even extravagant by Rethan standards. Copper covered almost every surface and shivered with occasional trails of voltage collected from the gathering electrical storm. The silver gate stood open, as though it wasn't there for the privacy of council member Vincent Paliyo and his family. Caz rested her weight against the gate, unable to do more than keep herself standing.

Vin was dead, his family in shambles. Why close the gate when their ruin was already broadcast to the world?

If it weren't for the support of the gate Caz was sure she would not be on her feet. Her eyes burned from her brief escapade to the hellish Third Dimension, and every muscle screamed in exhaustion. At least the Heart of Annihilation was safe. The marshals would show her no mercy. But her precious weapon, the ultimate creation of her superior intellect, would never be found.

Her thoughts rattled around a never-ending track of rage, revulsion, pleasure, betrayal, and pain, threatening to shred her mind. She was reminded by the dried blood tightening her skin and flaking from her clothing that this was no dream or delusion.

"Xander!" she shouted. The word rasped painfully against her sandy throat and echoed with a hollow twang against the metallic structure. "Xander! I know you're there! Get your ass out here!"

The house remained dark and silent. The wail of sirens filled the air, warning the entire dimension of excessive voltage fluctuations due to her unauthorized dimensional jump. The marshals would be here soon. They had to know she would come here in the end. Caz stumbled away from the support of the gate. She brushed at the flaking blood on her arm. There was so much . . . so much blood.

"Xander!" Caz screamed. Her voice reached a peak and screeched across the sirens. Spots of light flecked her vision. She planted her feet apart to keep from falling and raised her eyes to the roiling sky. "Xan!"

"I'm here, Caz."

Xander stood on the steps, his arms folded and his expression lost in the darkness. Lightning scorched across the sky. The handsomeness of his face was obscured behind a black expression Caz was unable to read. Thunder growled from overhead, and the sky suddenly opened. Water deluged her, drawing the collected electricity within her body to the surface and dancing her skin with sparking light. The blood, rehydrated by the rain, streamed from her arms in red, watery trails.

"Xander," Caz breathed his name. "They're dead."

"What in Gauss's law are you talking about?" His tone sounded off.

"They didn't listen, Xan." The pleading in her voice made her cringe. She had to make him understand. "They didn't realize."

Lightning flashed across his face again. Revulsion was there. Revulsion and something else. Self-righteousness? Serenity? Attikin's ass. He'd been dosed with serenity! That made him all Rethan now, the traitor. How would she ever convince him of the inevitability of the bloodshed, of the absolute necessity of her actions?

Caz lifted the blade and pointed it at Xander. "What did they tell you?"

"Tell me? I don't understand?" He didn't move. His maddening voice remained neutral.

"I can see it in your eyes. They told you. They told you about the council. They told you about Vin." Caz's hand shook. "What did they tell you?"

"Who?"

Caz wanted him to come at her, show his anger, fight and argue his point. This insane composure made her want to take the blade to his throat as well.

"The marshals! Zell, that liar! Or, excuse me, *Deputy* Veella. She told you I killed them, killed them all, slashed their throats."

"Did you?"

"Did what?" asked a small voice.

Lightning revealed a slight figure standing behind Xander. Caz's heart constricted in pain so agonizing bile rose in her throat. She dropped the knife to her side. Her shoulders slumped. How long had he been there?

Manny didn't run to her. He didn't call her name. He didn't smile his toothy smile. There were no warm hugs or light kisses. No delight in his eyes—only dread. He partially hid behind his uncle, holding two Pyk Styks in his hands. Caz retreated a step.

"What did Mother do, Uncle Xan?" Manny's stare pierced her heart.

"Go back inside, Manny." Xander pushed the boy gently back toward the house.

"I'll make it like before," Caz whispered. Rain trailed like tears down her face and spat like daggers from her lips. "Like I never left. Like Vin never left. Manny, Xander, I can fix this."

"Get out of here, Caz!" Xander took an aggressive step. Caz reveled in the hate in his eyes. Serenity could only take you so far. "You've done enough. The last thing Manny needs is—"

"I killed them, Xan. I did." Caz locked her eyes on Manny. His shoulders stooped, his hands tightening on the Pyk Styk. His small body shivered in the rain. "Killed them all. Every one of them."

Movement shuddered from the shadows in the massive yard. Lightning flashed on the silvery hair of the mass of marshals surrounding the grounds. Each held a weapon Caz recognized as one of the first her parents ever developed. Short barreled, black against the white skin of their hands, capable of striking an opponent with a raw charge of electricity to stun them into a moment of immobility. A prehistoric weapon, the likes of which hadn't been used in decades. In their passive, *serene* society, there was never a need to use them.

But now someone, fearing that Caz's cleansing river of blood would continue past the walls of the Dimensional Congressional building, had finally raided the ancient Rethan arsenal. A single shot from any of the fifty or so marshals would allow her to live but drop her in her tracks. Fifty would obliterate her.

Zell made her way out of the masses of marshals and deputies. She didn't carry a weapon herself, only stood with her hands behind her back—the very epitome of a serene Rethan official. Blood showed through the white bandages covering her left eye and half her face. With a smirk, Caz touched the thin edge of her blade, remembering the flash of silver as it sliced across Zell's eye and down her cheek.

"Cazandra Fisk." Her voice was detached and cold. "Your brother, Xander Fisk, has witnessed you admitting to the slaughter of one hundred and twenty-two members of the Dimensional Congressional Council."

Caz shot a murderous look at Xander. He flinched and had the decency to drop his eyes. Her question was answered. She'd lost him. Caz ground her teeth. Glacial rage filled her chest with ice. She glared back at Zell.

Zell raised her eyebrows in question. The bloody bandage wrinkled. Her hand shuddered toward her eye but she went on. "You are also guilty of the murders of twelve marshals in the council chamber and the one hundred and one other Rethans killed today by a device of your making planted in Attikin square. A singular death was also discovered in the portal chamber, bringing the total to two hundred and thirty-six deaths at your hands. By your own admission, your guilt is beyond contestation."

The marshals surrounded her and Zell in a tight circle. Xander and Manny stood frozen on the porch. Dark resolution locked Xander's face into a cold mask. Manny buried his face in his uncle's sleeve; his shoulders shook. Caz forced the pain behind a wall in her churning mind as Zell continued.

"Under the power given me by a committee of your peers, and as acting officiate in this unique situation, you are hereby sentenced under the laws of etiquette and serenity to the Reverse Aging Gateway to Earth, to be carried out immediately." Zell held up her hand as the marshals moved forward. They halted, and she stepped very close to Caz. She softened her voice to a whisper that was almost lost between the rain and sirens. Her words were meant only for Caz. "However, Caz, if you can tell me where you've hidden the Heart of Annihilation we can, perhaps, negotiate your sentence."

Caz's eyes roved over the thin lips, the sharp nose, and the one visible eye. Laughter bubbled up her throat. She lifted her knife out to the side and let it clatter to the ground.

"You'll never find it," Caz said. "Be prepared to spend your life wondering where it went. Enjoy your years of cringing at every siren with the expectation that at any moment the power of my Heart of Annihilation will be unleashed upon this dimension."

Zell kicked the blade out of Caz's reach and then bent to retrieve it. She held it between two fingers as though it would taint her tranquility, passed it carefully off to another marshal, and gestured toward the gate.

The soft whir of a motor whispered beneath the rolling thunder, pelting rain, and wailing sirens. The enormous, portable portal trundled up the walk in all its silvery glory. It came to a halt just behind Zell.

Zell touched her hands to the base of the portal and applied a charge. Any one of the marshals could have done it, but Zell seemed to take satisfaction in the act. Blue light zapped from her skin and the portal whirred to life. Electricity bounced from plate to plate within the perfect circle until it created a solid-looking wall. She gave Caz a curt nod and joined Xander and Manny on the steps. Their figures were distorted through the curtain of rain.

The portal cast intense blue light all round, throwing everything from the white boots of the marshals to the imperfection in the metallic ground into sharp relief.

Caz knew what was coming. She'd known from the first slice of the blade. But this was never about escaping their unfair judgment. This was about what was right. That didn't stop the terror clawing her insides.

RAGE: the most serene form of torture ever created.

She wrenched at the arms holding her, screaming and screaming. More hands grasped her, forcing her to her knees and then her stomach. Someone grabbed her right hand, splaying her fingers apart, and pressed cold, searing pain into her palm. A brand. Caz struggled to free herself. Silver cuffs clamped onto her wrists and drew out every particle of electricity within her body. She might as well be dying. The emptiness of the moment, the complete absence of a power so essential to her physical and mental state, drained her body and unraveled her mind. Her cheek was pressed into the wet ground. Caz strained to see Xander and Manny one last time. The marshals obscured her view.

Hollow, sick, senseless, Caz's screams echoed against the metal walls of her home, battering her once beloved brother and young son. She was dragged gracelessly from the ground, where she dangled limp in their grasp. Her traumatized body abandoned her will to fight—to win. The blinding light of the portal distorted her vision. A lurch, and the hands released her. The swooping sensation of falling, and her mind crumbled into darkness.

CHAPTER 30

Rose

I swallowed back the raw, animalistic noise wrenching from my throat. All my muscles were tensed into painful knots. Flexed veins stood out on my hands. I lifted tearing eyes, blinking at the stunned expressions of—*Xander*—Xavier and Angie. I pressed my hand to my mouth.

"Did you," I swallowed and cleared my throat, "Did you ever find it?"

"What?" Xavier's hand dropped from his mouth.

"The Heart of Annihilation? And the kid. Who was the kid you were protecting when I got arrested?" Manny. My son. I shuddered.

Xander's face reddened, and his mouth opened and closed several times before he was able to get any words out.

"Don't you talk about him. Don't you dare even mention him!" Xander raised himself from his seat, and I thought he might launch himself at me. At a soft touch from Angie he sat back down, his back rigid. "You're just some criminal. The DCC Slayer. It would be better for everyone if you were erased. From the past, from the present, and I definitely don't need you in my future!"

My cheeks flamed. I felt like a snarled, fiery ball of emotions that would consume everything around me. And Xavier sat in the eye of the storm.

Sitting there across from me, a glass in his hand, a distasteful curl on his lips, I loathed him and desperately wanted to kill him. I wanted to send hundreds of thousands of volts of electricity through his brain until smoke and fire exploded from his eyes and his face melted from his skull.

Pleasure coursed through me like an inferno. *Melt his face. Kill the traitor!*

My head blistered in pain. My hands tremored, and I threw a fistful of electricity at Xavier from behind my bloody hand towel.

Xavier jerked his head to the side. The white sizzling ball punched through the seat where his head was seconds before. The limo slammed to a stop, and the engine ground into silence.

I buried my face in my hands and rocked. Back and forth. The sounds of panic and confusion roared around me. Back and forth. Back and forth.

I'm Kris. I'm Kris Rose. I'm not a murderer. I'm Kris. I'm—

Pressure squeezed my brain.

No, she said. *You're me.* Oily blackness sluiced through my mind. Unbearable malevolence. A blur of fury. *We're the same. We're murderers.*

Thurmond wasn't here to draw me away from the edge this time. Dad was gone.

I had Caz.

Caz and me. Me and Caz. A single entity of evil. Lost in a world with no understanding of us. *We're the same, you and I. We're the same.*

Another voice crept across Caz's. Not so much a voice, rather, but the memory of a voice. Gentle inflections, soft whisperings, and loving words challenged the darkness.

I don't know a better person, Krissy. Dad once said. *I hope you can always be yourself. Don't ever let anyone try to change you from this person you are right now.*

The unbearable pressure lifted enough to allow me to crawl my way back to the surface. I rubbed my face and peered between my fingers to find the limo door wide open and the vehicle nearly empty. Xavier alone sat on the seat near the rear window. His legs were crossed, his black leather pants creased to perfection down the front. He draped one arm across the back of the seat, a drink clamped tight in his hand. His other hand caressed the .357 lying on the seat beside him. A smoking hole glared from where he'd been sitting before. White fire-extinguisher foam dripped from the edges onto the seat.

"I'm sorry, Xavier. I didn't mean—"

Xavier lifted his hand from the gun to stop me. "That's enough."

"You have to believe me—"

"There's only one reason you're still here right now and haven't yet been arrested or shot."

I pulled my knees to my chest and brushed a hand against my wet cheeks. Xavier continued.

"Right now my main concern is for that of Rannen. This commander of yours has had him for almost a week now, and my only connection to find them is you. I'm not a heartless person, and I understand that the fact that Mr. Thurmond is also being held causes you a great deal of distress." He leaned toward me, swirling his drink. His silver eyes gave off unwavering sparks. "But make no mistake I'm not going to help either of them for your sake."

"I wasn't worried about that."

"I happen to have a replica of the Heart of Annihilation in my penthouse." Xavier said. "I knew, when I came to this dimension, someone would eventually come to me looking for it. So I had it made specifically for an instance such as this. I only want one thing from you in return for my help."

"What's that?"

"After we have gotten your friend and Rannen back, I want you to stay the hell away from me. I don't ever want to see your face again. I don't want to answer your questions. I don't even want to remember we ever knew each other."

I nodded quickly.

"Anything you want."

"And I'm warning you—keep that temper in check. You try to assault me again and my bodyguard has orders to shoot to kill. Do you understand?"

I understood better than someone like Xavier Coy could ever comprehend. I understood the feeling of being at the point of a loaded weapon, not to mention the deep and maiming desire to avoid any more pain remotely associated with being shot. I also understood that I couldn't promise self-control when it wasn't myself that needed the control.

A cold chuckle echoed inside my head. I drew a sharp breath and gave a dishonest nod.

CHAPTER 31

The elevator door slid open with a cheerful chime, and I stepped into the entryway of Xavier's elegant penthouse. The beautiful high-rise building looked out over a private beach, although twenty-five floors up made the beach part hard to see. Three half-circle steps descended into a masculine sitting room and an accompanying stainless steel kitchen. Four dark marble pillars separated the rooms, rising twenty feet to the second story balcony and what must be the bedrooms. The sun shone through the vast wall-sized windows, cutting patterns of light across the polished, mahogany floors, zebra skins, and black leather couches. As I watched the light turned a brilliant orange, then faded as the sun sank out of sight over the bay.

I felt dirty and out of place. Xavier and Angie, on the other hand, matched the room perfectly. They tossed their jackets on the couch and moved about like lead actors in a soap opera.

Boderick appeared about as uncomfortable as I felt. He shifted from foot to foot, his eyes darting around the room. The bodyguard stationed himself near the elevator so he could watch the entire room.

I stood on the top step, running a finger across my lips and trying to sort through what needed to be done. Get the Heart replica. That shouldn't be too hard. Xavier said it was here in the penthouse. Second: contact the commander—that would be more difficult. I fingered the flip phone in my pocket. She said she would be in touch. I guess that meant waiting for her to call—I hated waiting. And third: attempt not to kill anyone in the meantime.

That one was going to be a challenge. Every thought in my head invited Caz to surface, to flout her influence and drive me to madness.

"Ang, why don't you take Boderick upstairs and show him a place to clean up?" Xavier said from somewhere deep in the kitchen. "Oh, and while you're up there, get something for Miss Rose to change into so she doesn't bleed all over the furniture."

I glowered at Xavier's back, wanting to smear blood on his disgustingly chic zebra rugs and scratch my nails across his horribly flawless couches. Angie smiled at Boderick. He cast me a frightened glance as she took his hand, whispered something in his ear while leading him up the stairs.

They disappeared into a room. Xavier beckoned to me. "Come have a seat, Miss Rose."

He indicated some high barstools next to a marble-covered island. Without waiting to see if I would comply he turned his back and pulled a large first aid kit from a cupboard above the microwave. I narrowed my eyes. So he hated me so much he wanted to tend to my shoulder? I didn't understand Rethans.

What's to understand? It wouldn't be proper etiquette *to let you suffer. And if there's one thing Rethans are good at it's—*

"Leave me alone," I said under my breath.

Xavier paused, eyeing me, and then spoke.

"Angie called Dr. Tolman, but he can't be here until later tonight. Let's patch you up the best we can, shall we?" Xavier pulled out a swath of gauze and soaked it in peroxide. "Why don't you take off that shirt so we can see the damage?"

I folded my arms. I think I would rather be shot again than strip down to my bra in front of Xavier Coy, even if he was my brother. He stared at me in expectation for a moment before releasing a gruff, aggravated sound. He turned and pulled a pair of kitchen shears from the knife block. With a tired sigh, I limped into the kitchen and took a seat on the padded, black barstool.

Xavier worked the scissors next to my skin, cutting off my butchered shirtsleeve. The cold metal of the scissors raised the hair on my arms. He dabbed at the crusted blood with peroxide and slowly worked off the fabric where the blood had glued it to my skin. Fortunately the shirt wasn't burned onto my flesh but rather the bandages, and with a bit of care he was finally able to remove it. He tossed the whole mess into the trash behind him.

I felt the pain worsen as I saw the blood oozing in a gooey, unhealthy way from the injury. The majority of the stitches split open along the four-inch horizontal gash below my clavicle. The skin around it and across my chest was red and terribly tender. Probably burned.

Xavier Coy, movie star, dabbed and cleaned the wound with brusque, efficient hands. I blinked back tears and bit my lip to stop the trembling.

"Were you a doctor on Retha?" I asked to break the silence.

"No," His response was curt, but then he continued more gently. "I started off my career on Earth playing a doctor on a soap opera. I had to spend a lot of time observing real doctors in order to make my acting more authentic. I picked up a thing or two."

He tore off a piece of surgical tape. I flinched as he stretched it across the wound to hold it closed.

"Oh. Well, thanks," I said.

"You're welcome." He almost sounded genuine.

"So, you and Angie, huh?"

He lifted his chin. The overhead light caught his eyes in a flash of silver. Then he chuckled in spite of himself.

"Is it that obvious?"

I shrugged. "Don't worry. I don't think your minions have a clue."

"Did you really call my people *minions*?" The underlying tension crept back into his voice.

"Maybe." I released a laugh and covered my mouth to stop it.

He relaxed again and reached for a bandage.

"Sure, they give me whatever I want." He placed a thick pad on top of the wound and busied himself winding a roll of gauze over my shoulder and under my armpit again and again. "That's the benefit of being rich and mysterious."

"Do they know you're a Rethan—besides Angie I mean?" I asked.

"Of course not. They, like most people in the Third Dimension, have no clue about the realities of our planet. I don't think they could handle it anyway." Xavier tied off the bandage, turned to the sink, and started scrubbing the blood from his fingers.

"So was I . . . am I . . . really your sister? This terrible Rethan person?" The words were out before I could stop them.

Xavier turned. Soap dripped from his hands. Somehow I knew whatever he said I would believe, and then any residual denial would go right out the window.

"Yes." The word was not as cold as I would have expected.

I rested my cheek on the cool countertop, so filled with discouragement I didn't think I'd be able to lift my head again. I felt like some hodgepodge person. A Frankenstein. A single body with a fragile, stitched together mind. And the stitches were unraveling.

"You know, Miss Rose, there's something about you . . . as in *you*," Xavier pointed at me, "that is very different than I expected. I see Caz in you for sure, but I see someone else as well. Then again . . ."

His cheeks sucked in, and he looked somewhere behind me. My breath made foggy circles on the counter.

"I remember my dad telling me once that the course of our lives is never set in stone," I said. "We always have the ability to change it."

Xavier's face took on an odd look. "Your dad? He never would have said something like—I mean, you hated your father."

"You mean *our* father?"

His eyebrows went up in surprise and then lowered in resignation. "Yes. Yes, of course."

"No," I said. "I mean my dad here—on Earth. He said that."

"Oh." He looked into my eyes. "Perhaps. But I think there are some things that can't be atoned for."

"Like murder?"

"Like murder," Xavier agreed.

"Would it help if I said I was sorry?"

"No." Coolness crept back into his voice. Whatever brief truce we'd had vanished.

"I'm sorry anyway," I said.

Xavier turned back to the sink. A loud cracking sound rattled the windows. Xavier jerked his head around. I rotated on the stool.

A shimmer of blue erupted around the edges of a door near the elevator. My heart leapt into my throat, choking off the word of warning I wanted to scream at the bodyguard. The door smashed inward. One hinge tore into the man's chest. He landed with a heavy flump on his back. The other hinges ripped from the doorframe. The door swung from a single screw, revealing a mass of black figures shrouded in a fogbank of smoke.

I toppled off the stool. The counter struck my hip and grated across my ribs before I hit the floor on my back.

A black boot stepped onto the glossy floor. A second followed. Electricity retreated into the commander's fingertips. Her silver eyes glowed. A self-satisfied smile lifted her lips.

I scrambled to take cover behind the island and found myself next to Xavier. His shaking hand could barely hold the .357.

"I told you I'd be in touch, Specialist Rose!" The commander's voice bounced off the high ceilings, marble pillars, and floors before settling with deep fear in my chest.

"Are you kidding me?" I shouted. I don't know why I was yelling at her. She'd saved me an agonizing wait near the phone. "This is not in touch! When you say 'in touch' it usually means a phone call!"

Xavier gripped my arm. His face was ashen, his lips tight against his teeth, his eyes popping.

"This is much more efficient. No depending on all this primeval Earth technology, not to mention the opportunity it gives me to provide you with a demonstration." Her voice crackled in a very Rethan-like way. The tang of ozone filled the room.

Boots thumped in the entry—a lot of boots. I couldn't see them from where Xavier and I cowered, but there was no doubt we were heavily outnumbered and outrageously outgunned.

"Xavier," I whispered, "Don't you have an alarm system or something? It sure would be nice if the cops came to our rescue again."

"Of course I do, but it didn't go off. She must've fried it before blasting the door off its hinges."

"What about another gun?"

"Why do you need a gun? Can't you, I don't know, volt them?"

"You've been here for a while, can't you volt too?" I said, wanting to punch him in the face.

I heard the crashing of ceramic and wood splintering. With a crunch, one of Xavier's couches knocked over a spindly side table and shattered the lamp perched on top. The couch flipped up once and came to rest against the window. Xavier and I huddled closer together. He made a noise in his throat.

"Of course I can, I just prefer not to."

"Now might be an excellent time to shove your preferences up your—"

"I want you to come out here, *Specialist Rose*," the commander shouted, "and you, Xander. I know you're in here somewhere. Come out. Come and see what I have to show the both of you."

Whispering and snickering accompanied her remark. I couldn't help myself. I needed to see what I already suspected. My glance around the corner of the counter was brief, the image everlasting.

All the furniture in the room was toppled, and anything that could be thrown or broken was. I made a rough estimate of thirteen people, all carrying either a rifle or a pistol, all wearing camouflage. The commander herself still wore her black SWAT-like uniform and a white bandage around her left hand. She ran two fingers across the scar on her face.

I recognized Sergeant Sanderford, wearing a knee brace over his uniform; and Lieutenant Justet looking rumpled, splotchy, and sour. Luginbeel slunk next to the window wall. A white bandage covered his nose. There was a large bruise on one side of his face, and his arm was in a sling. He could barely grip his rifle. His expression seemed dead, fear having left him a battered empty shell in the midst of an incomprehensible war.

More men poured from the concrete stairwell, jostling a fighting figure into the room. Thurmond's shirt was torn along the seam of one sleeve, and a ragged hole jagged across the knee of his jeans. Tendons stood out on his arms, which were tied behind his back. From the smears of dirt and dried blood on his skin and clothing, it appeared he'd given them quite a fight. They wrestled him to the center of the room.

"As you can see, Specialist Rose, I have your friend as a hostage," the commander said. "I am also aware that this is the home of a person by the name of Xavier Coy, otherwise known as Xander Fisk. Xander, why don't you come out and see what we brought *you*!"

I shot a look at Xavier. His eyes were closed and white knuckles clenched against his mouth. For a moment I wanted to join him, curl into a ball and forget who and what and where I came from. Let the debilitating fear send my mind far away from here.

"Xavier," I whispered, shocking myself into action. I bumped him with my elbow. He didn't move. His shoulders shook so badly I wasn't sure why he wasn't rattling the entire island. "Xavier! Give me your gun!"

He drew it closer to himself and his fingers tightened on the grip.

I could have wrestled him for it, but the outcome seemed sketchy at best. What else did I have? I closed my eyes. I had my Rethan-born internal weaponry. I only hoped the commander had used the majority of her energy frying the door. It wasn't like they were going to shoot me dead on the spot, anyway—they thought I knew where the Heart was.

Right. The Heart. My eyes flew open.

"Xavier. At least tell me where that Heart replica thingy is."

Xavier shook his head. His hand still covered his mouth. I was afraid he was going to hurl.

"Jerk," I said, pounding my head twice against the cupboards. I exhaled three tight breaths and pushed to my feet.

Every eye and weapon adjusted to me. Other movement ceased. I skimmed the room, taking in the dark scowls, the weapons, and Thurmond's face before finding the brightest spot. Sergeant Sanderford and three other soldiers stood near the stairwell, with Marshal Rannen towering over them like a tank next to an array of army trucks. Every visible inch of his translucent skin had taken on a bruised, purple hue. A thick gash started at his collarbone and disappeared under his filthy, bloodstained uniform. His eyelids slouched over unfocused eyes, his lips slack. His hands were behind his head, feet wide apart. I couldn't help wishing he'd take one of those ham-sized arms and start knocking the heads off his captors. He flinched a look at me.

Something in my mind recoiled as the-voice-that-was-Caz beat a hasty retreat without so much as a whisper, taking with her the empowering rage I just then realized I was depending on. I felt as weak and vulnerable as any one person would be in a room full of gun-toting hostiles.

With an effort I pulled my gaze from Rannen. I showed everyone my empty hands.

"Specialist Rose." The commander smiled, tapping a pistol against her leg.

"Where's Sergeant Wichman?" I asked.

The question of his absence was more out of curiosity than anything. I wasn't entirely sure where his loyalties lay, but at the moment all I cared about was that he wasn't here to help any more than the last four times.

"Bottom of the bay by now," the commander said with a conversational smirk. She rested her shoulder against a pillar and folded her arms. "Did you know he works for the DLA? I couldn't have one of those on my crew no matter how useful he was."

"So what now? You're going to kill me?" I kept my tone aggressive in an attempt to keep them at a respectful distance. I nodded in Luginbeel's direction. He backed up, his eyes wild at being singled out by the likes of me. "If not, you might want to take the rifle away from the private over there. 'Cause I swear if he shoots me again, you'll *never* find the Heart."

"You don't get it, do you, Specialist Rose?" the commander said. "You're not the DCC Slayer anymore, and this impotent little thing you've become is nothing." She placed her hand in her pocket. "Now. You were probably asking yourself why I bothered to take your friend here as a hostage when I already had Rannen. Well, I figured a demonstration would be in order. To show you just how serious I am."

The commander snapped her fingers, and the two soldier's flanking Thurmond forced him to his knees. One placed a pistol to his spine.

My heart took a longer pause between beats and a chill swept my body. A cackle started in my throat before erupting into a brief explosion of laughter.

Everyone jumped, including me. I fell silent again. The rest of the men followed suit.

"You're not going to shoot him," I said.

"And why is that?"

"'Cause if you do I'll force you to kill me, leaving you nowhere nearer to finding the Heart than you were twenty years ago." I rubbed the sudden ache above my ear, only slightly surprised to realize that I was completely serious. My eyes watered. "And I'll take out a hell of a lot of your troops in the process. Starting with you, *ma'am*."

Our eyes locked, the commander's wide and mine narrowed and tearing. A general shifting of feet preceded the lowering of weapons.

"That's better." The commander's face relaxed into a smile. "I knew you were in there somewhere, Caz. It's good to see you again."

"Wish I could say the same." Caz broke the surface. The words were painfully rough against my vocal cords. I pressed my knuckles to my mouth.

The commander snorted a laugh and pulled her hand out of her pocket. The chain for my dog tags was shorter than ever, with only enough chain to wrap around two fingers. The tags themselves had been discarded, and the tiny key dangled brightly on the dull chain. The small half circle, once such an essential part of me, looked like a foreign object with the addition of the other half of the key. As always, the sudden and intoxicating rage welled in my chest, accompanied by a desperate longing to slash throats and remove heads in order to retrieve it.

My breath hissed in and out of my nose. It was all I could do to stand there and not make the situation worse.

The commander stepped closer, so only the counter separated us. She held the key high, dangling it like a carrot before my nose. Her thumb rubbed across it with long, seductive strokes. I curled my hands into fists, my arms shaking with the effort of not sending a bolt of lightning between her eyes. Her voice quieted, and for the first time a hint of grief softened her features.

"What happened, Caz?" She whispered just loud enough for me to hear. "There was no reason for me to be there that day. Why did you call me there?" She touched the scar on her face. "Why would you do this to me?"

The pleading in her voice jerked my mind back through years and dimensions before settling on a single moment of time. The moment had been overlooked, even by Caz, because everything surrounding so far eclipsed it.

But now it mattered. Now it was relevant. I felt the weight of the bag pulling at my shoulder. The thump of my feet on the stairs. The white, frightened face meeting me at the top.

CHAPTER 32

Caz
5 hours and 46 minutes pre-RAGE

Zell paced outside the towering double archways that provided entrance to the council chambers. Right where Caz requested she meet her. And right on time, despite the explosion in the square just moments ago. The destruction could still be heard outside and smelled in the smoky air. Echoing fear showed in Zell's eyes.

The archways to the council chamber, usually covered by white webs of deadly voltage designed to keep everyone out, now stood dark, silent, and empty; their energy consumed by Caz's device. Why the leaders of a pacifist society felt the need for protection said volumes about what they thought of their utopia. None of it mattered now. Caz had stripped them of their unnecessary fortifications, leaving them vulnerable to the unthinkable assailant.

Caz paused at the top of the stairs, switched the heavy bag to her other shoulder, and glanced at her wrist. In another minute the council would be adjourning the plenum. Zell spotted her and rushed her way.

"Cazandra! The marshals are mustering, but I slipped away when you said . . . What happened? What's going on out there? Where's Xander?"

Caz reached into her pocket and clutched one of the many resurrected weapons from the marshal's armory that she had re-envisioned and improved. The white, snakelike stone wrapped around her hand, with the egg-sized transformer resting in her palm. The IC 4000 was perfect for today. Perfect for Zell.

Caz placed her thumb on the silver trigger and removed it from her pocket. With a tilt to her lips, she pressed the muzzle at Zell's neck.

Zell's expression went from anxiety to confusion. Caz held Zell's eyes with her own.

"What is this?" Zell tried to draw away from the weapon.

"This?" Caz made a scoffing sound. "This is me finally putting your duplicitous, scrawny ass in your place. Now walk. Or I'm going to kill you."

Fear found its way into Zell's face. She didn't appear to be able to drag her eyes from Caz's. Her chest rose and fell in ragged breath.

Caz raised her eyebrows and prodded Zell in the neck. "Go."

Zell finally moved. She took several stumbling steps backward and then managed to turn to the side, keeping Caz in sight.

When they reached the archways Zell jerked to a stop, as if the web was still there.

"Caz." Zell's voice broke. Moisture gleamed at the corners of her eyes. "You said Xander was in trouble. Where is he? What are you doing?"

Caz shook her head, her voice a quiet rattle. "You really still think this is about Xander?"

Zell's hands fluttered. She folded them together. "You can't bring a weapon into the council chambers."

"Can't I? I'm the daughter of Crav and Lissen Fisk, the greatest munitioners of our time. And we make weapons, precious. Off you go now." Caz pressed the muzzle deep into Zell's pulsing carotid artery. Zell gasped and nearly went to her knees.

"You can't bring that weapon inside," Zell repeated, unmoving. She was putting up more resistance than Caz anticipated.

"Zell, Zell," She tsked. "Don't let this weapon make you concerned for the council. This is the weapon I made only for you. Now, let's go have a little chat with the council, or you are going to find out exactly how much love I've put into this thing."

Seconds ticked by. Any moment the council would adjourn. The members would disperse into their private chambers, or discover that murder and mayhem was taking place outside their doors and flee through the room's secret escape routes. And yet she waited. Waited for Zell's feet to move. Waited for her to put herself willingly into the council chamber, into the very middle of what was soon to be the most infamous moment in Rethan history. Waited for her to incriminate herself.

Caz was counting on Zell, a child of a Rethan utopia, to lack any courage.

Zell shuddered a surrendering breath and took a step. Caz topped her a few steps inside the archways. Zell hiccupped. Caz adjusted the IC 4000 so the muzzle rested on Zell's spine and rubbed her thumb across the cold curve of the trigger.

"Please—" Zell's voice was grating.

Caz caught Zell's eye, gave her a thin smile.

"Thank you so much for being here. You don't know what it means." She squeezed the trigger.

The weapon made only the most miniscule zapping sound. With a groan, Zell collapsed onto her side. Her hair flopped across her face so only her eyes were visible; wide and unblinking.

Caz nudged her in the leg with a foot. Four thousand icy volts, sent through the weapon's transformer, created a type of voltage foreign to Rethan physiology. Sending it down an enemy's spine was painful but not deadly. It simply caused instant, but temporary, incapacitation. Paralyzed, but conscious. As far as Caz knew it lasted barely over fourteen minutes. She hadn't tested it, and was rather smug that her mathematics were thus far spot on.

Caz smiled to herself. None of the council members deep in the chamber seemed to have noticed them. She took a knee and brushed the hair away from Zell's face. The IC 4000 she pulled from her wrist and set on the floor near Zell's head.

"Zell, can hear you me?" Caz released a charge into the lock on her bag. It snapped open. She stared into the bag for a moment and then gave her full attention to Zell. "Your purpose here is not happenstance. You worked your way into the Fisk dynasty. You made yourself indispensable to my brother, my son, and *my* husband. Don't you see, Zell? You thought there was an opening for you to fill. But you were wrong. So disastrously wrong. Now," Caz smiled, "are you ready to see what I'm going to do about it?"

Caz examined her face for an expression. Horror would have been her first choice, but the weapon had done its work too well.

Caz lifted the elegant blade from her bag. She'd make her react. Make her feel. Her lips pursed. She stood over her enemy and, with a rapid flick of her wrist, slashed it across her face. The skin opened wide and pink, flayed from brow to cheek. A second later the crevasse filled with blood.

And still Zell didn't react. Blood pooled around her head. Caz glanced at her IC 4000. What a remarkable weapon. She examined her handiwork on Zell's face. Let Xander think her pretty now.

And now Zell was no longer important. No longer a part of this moment. Caz had done away with her like all the others. She was now irrelevant. Irrelevant. *Irrelevant.*

"Irrelevant, Zell. That's what you are. Irrelevant and pathetic." Caz sniffed, rubbed her nose and turned her attention back to her bag.

CHAPTER 33

Rose

Irrelevant. Irrelevant. Irrelevant, pathetic. Caz repeated the words in a sing-song voice. *Irrelevant. Irrelevant.*

My head crushed under Caz's anger. The pressure in my skull, the tension in my chest, the way electricity collected to me bespoke the deep and maiming emotions screaming to get out. I groaned and dug my nails into my hair.

My mouth opened, and words spilled out in a voice I only recognized from deep inside my head.

"What happened? It was perfect. From the second you fell to the moment I . . . But then Vin . . ." Caz quieted, strangled by a memory she couldn't express.

I slapped the counter, my breathing hoarse. An all-out territorial war blasted shrapnel across my cerebrum. I kept my eyes on the commander, afraid to look at either Rannen or Thurmond and find frightened, reproachful stares.

"What do you want, ma'am?" I asked between breaths, grateful to hear my own voice this time. The pain in my head eased.

Her eyes narrowed, and the beseeching look froze into her standard subzero expression.

"I want the Heart of Annihilation." The commander shrugged her shoulders, throwing off the past.

"Why?"

"For many reasons." A grin stretched across her face. "Do you have any idea, Caz, what the Thirteenth Dimension would be willing to pay for a weapon designed specifically to wipe them out?"

I shook my head.

"Do you know what the Rethan government would pay to keep them from getting their hands on it? What about the Liberated RAGE Movement? Or Ehtar?"

I didn't respond.

"The question simply remains, 'who will pay more?'" the commander went on. "We have a bet going if you want in on it. Who will pay more, but more importantly who would be willing to use it?"

"You're crazy!"

The commander's face turned from playful to furious in an instant. She slammed her fist on the counter.

"Not as crazy as you!"

Anger ripped through my head like a hundred bullets. I dropped my elbows to the counter, holding my head with my hands and groaning with the effort it took to keep from exploding.

Xavier stared up at me from his spot behind the counter. His eyes met mine, filled with smugness as though he had predicted not only the commander's line of questioning but my reactions as well. I gave my head a violent shake. Xavier wouldn't help. I was lost. Who could help me? I found Thurmond's face.

His eyes were angry but trusting, his head turned in such a way I could almost hear him saying, *Dammit, Rose. Get it together.* A shiver raced up my spine, forcing the pressure to retreat to a thick condensed spot above my left ear. I turned back to the commander—and found myself staring into the muzzle of her pistol.

"So where is it, Caz?"

"Close," I said.

"How close?"

"Maybe it's here in this apartment."

"It's not. I would've felt it."

I ran my tongue across my bottom lip and glanced toward Xavier again. He didn't give any indication that he was even following the conversation any more.

Suddenly Lieutenant Justet took a step forward, halted, scratched his nose, and then, as if making a decision, positioned himself in front of Thurmond.

"Ma'am, I think this has gone far enough. The deal was the cash for the portal." His voice would've grated on my nerves had I not the impression he was pleading my case. He looked at the commander. "You never said anything about murder of—of humans. You talk a good game, but no way is any money worth this."

The commander stared at Justet, her jaw working, chewing over his unbelievable disloyalty. She jerked the pistol away from my face and turned it on Justet. A cacophony of voices tumbled over each other, echoing off the high ceilings and marble columns. Justet dropped his pistol in surprise. He raised his hands, and his voice joined in the uproar. The commander turned her head toward me. With a tiny twitch of her cheek she squeezed the trigger.

In the same instant I sent a volt racing toward the gun. The sizzling, blue bolt knocked the pistol from the commander's hand as it fired. The bullet sailed away from Justet's head and shattered one of the enormous windows. Most of the glass fell outside, but shards also blasted across the room. Everyone ducked. Warm evening air flooded the room in a briny breeze. The couch leaning against the now nonexistent window tottered and then disappeared.

A bolt of blue lightning erupted from the commander's palm, sizzling across the ten or so feet separating us. I dropped on top of Xavier. The microwave over the stove exploded above our heads. A shower of sparks smattered across my back. The door banged open and swung lopsided on its hinges. Xavier shoved at me. I used his shoulder to push back to my feet. Electricity flowed into my fingers before my head cleared the counter. Another volt of lighting sizzled past my ear, forcing me to jerk my head to the side.

Afraid of giving the commander another chance to return fire I kept the circuit open, allowing the electricity to sizzle from my body in an enormous, continuous surge. A similar bolt of electricity burst from both the commander's hands. The two charges exploded into each other, connecting somewhere over the barstools. Arbitrary bits of lightning and sparks scattered in every direction.

Electricity struck the walls, cupboards, and furniture, sending deadly bits of shrapnel everywhere. Smoke burned my eyes, fogging the scrambling figures. Their cries of panic and pain were lost behind the deafening zapping coming from the conjoined bolts.

My arms screamed in fatigue. I could see nothing beyond the blinding light. I slid my hip along the counter until I felt empty air. I used my entire body, one step at a time, to push the commander's stream of electricity backward. A hollow, echoing chortle sounded in my mind. Caz's fury drove every collected ounce of power into my hands.

The voltage drained away from my body until all that remained was the last little bit from my shoulders to my fingertips. I needed to end this now, but if the commander had even a watt more energy than I, she would take my head off. I needed more power.

Like from the largest source in the room, perhaps?

My body's learning curve had been steep over the past week or so, and it only took a quiet millisecond of concentration to make it understand what to do. The nerves all over my body seemed to reach out, attracting amps in force. The scattering blue and white fragments of light throughout the room abandoned their random, primal destruction and raced toward me. Burning and jolting into my nerve endings, my skin absorbed the power, sending it straight back out through my hands. I took another step, feeling the commander's force deteriorating. Taking my advantage, I released my remaining charge into a single pulsing blast. At the same time, I dropped from the line of fire.

The illuminated body of the commander disappeared behind an overturned couch. My volt exploded into the black leather before dying out.

Echoes of light flashed across my retinas. Small fires flickered throughout the room. I touched my fingertips to the ground to stabilize myself. My breathing was ragged. I willed my eyes to adjust to the smoky darkness.

Shapes slowly sharpened. I found myself in the middle of the main room, my toes touching scorched zebra hide. Chunks of wall and ceiling fell throughout the penthouse with crashes and puffs of dust and charcoal, exposing raw framework and internal wiring.

Heads popped up from the debris. There was lots of coughing, murmured expressions of concern, and the clicking of rifles and pistols being checked. I tried to orient myself with where I'd last seen Thurmond, and found the marble column behind me pockmarked by electrical shrapnel. A pile of rubble lay next to it, mostly drywall and wood shards covered by an overturned potted palm. I recognized the shoe sticking out from under the pile of wreckage.

"Thurmond!"

I scrambled to the pile. I tossed aside the plant and tore into the debris, indifferent to the ragged materials shredding my hands. The shoe stayed stubbornly still.

"Thurmond! Where are you? T!"

The pile shifted. Drywall slithered onto the shoe, burying it from view.

"That hurts, dammit."

Thurmond wormed his way out of debris over five feet away. He kicked aside the larger pieces with a shoeless foot. His hair and skin were covered in white dust, and he coughed into his shoulder. He scooted himself backward, his hands cinched behind his back and the rest of the pile collapsed, sending up a pillar of dust. I was on my feet and to his side in a second, grabbing his arm and helping him onto his knees. Triple streaks of blood clawed across one of his cheeks.

He sat back on his haunches, his head dropping to his chest as he exhaled a breath before looking up at me. His eyes were neither accusing nor angry. His head tilted to one side, his lips slightly parted, and it took me a moment before I recognized the expression. Pity.

I picked angrily at the knotted ropes on his wrists. I didn't need pity, I needed a plan.

A hoot of laughter drew my attention.

"That was amazing, Caz." The commander came out from behind the burned couch, brushing her hands across her sleeves. She wasn't smiling, even though the breathless sound coming from her mouth mimicked laughter. "Just like the old days, eh? Let that temper take you and to hell with the consequences."

I barely managed to suppress another Caz-like response.

"You're out of charge though, right?" She walked around the couch with such a sure step that it negated the question.

"So are you," I said.

My fingers worked harder at the knots, although I kept my eyes trained on the commander. Thurmond kept shooting me looks over his shoulder. I felt the knots loosen, and Thurmond worked his hands out. He rubbed his wrists.

"Look around you. What do you see?" The commander waved her bandaged hand, drawing my attention to the soldiers once more on their feet, their weapons mostly at their sides although a few were aimed at me.

"I see a huge mess created by my own very powerful self." Half-truths were almost as good as full ones. The ache was starting up in my head again. "Not to mention how I nearly made your scrawny ass a permanently fried resident of the couch."

"That's what I want to hear." The commander laughed. "Let the Slayer come out and play, Specialist Rose. There're some things I'm dying to ask her."

The pressure built. I panted for breath. I shook my head as much as in response to her request as trying to deny Caz total access to my mind.

"Fine." The commander dropped her playful pretense and worked her way across the massacred room toward Thurmond and me in Rethanquick strides. She grabbed a pistol from Sanderford's hands. Thurmond retreated, using his shoulder to push me with him until my back hit a nearby column. The commander raised the pistol as she approached. Her aim was not at me but on Thurmond.

"Fine!" I shouted. "You're right. Fine. Fine!" I tried to step around Thurmond. He jabbed me back with his elbow. "I'll take you to your stupid Heart in—in exchange for the freedom of your prisoners." I nodded in the direction of the stairwell where I'd last seen Rannen. He was still there, on his knees now, rifles pressed into his ribs. "Me and the Heart for them. That's not such a bad deal."

"Oh no, Caz. You see, I don't trust you. *I* have the hostages. *I* have the weapons. *I* have the power. You tell me where I can find the Heart, and I *won't* kill your friend right in front of your eyes. How's that for a deal!"

"No! Take my deal. Take it. Take me! Take the damn deal!" I shoved Thurmond out of the way and put my face right in the commander's.

Her lips lifted in a tight smile. She took a step back, which I mistook for retreat. A second later she was in my face, grinding the pistol into my bandaged shoulder. She wrapped her hand around the back of my neck, holding me in place.

"You destroyed me," she whispered in my ear. I struggled, but she clamped her nails into my skin. She was so strong. "Back on Retha. You set me up to go down with you. But I'm not going to kill you. Oh no. I'm telling you right here and now Caz, that there is nothing more important to me than letting you live long enough to witness your precious Heart of Annihilation sold off to the highest bidder. Or maybe we'll set it off somewhere. Retha? Would that bother you? How about Earth? You like this slag heap, right?"

She shoved me away. I staggered, but found my feet in time to watch Thurmond's fist catch the commander on her jaw. Her head snapped to the side. Thurmond followed his first strike with a roundhouse kick to her gut that made her stumble but not fall. She righted herself in fast-forward. Her Rethan speed compensated for being caught off guard, and her pistol took Thurmond on the side of his face with a blinding crack. His head smacked against the nearest marble column and he slid to the floor. His eyes were wide but unfocused. Blood flowed from his mouth.

The commander was over to him in a single stride. She pressed the pistol against Thurmond's forehead, her mouth a thin line.

"Don't!" I gasped.

Her eyes bore into Thurmond rather than me.

"Tell me where I can find the Heart, Caz!"

"It's here. Upstairs." I couldn't breathe.

"No it isn't!" Corded muscles stood out on her arm like she was struggling *not* to pull the trigger. "I already told you. I would be able to feel an energy source of that magnitude. Where is it!"

"I-I-I . . ." The replica was a no-go and nothing else in my arsenal could save Thurmond's life—except the truth.

"Caz!" the commander shouted.

"I can't!" The realization struck me as I said the fatal words. How could I tell someone as unstable as this Rethan where to find a weapon of mass destruction, even if I did know where it was? The desire to scream clogged my throat. I lurched to her side, wanting to weep out my helplessness and screech out my rage—destroy the world myself rather than have to suffer any more loss because of my bull-headed obsession with finding the truth.

A memory scorched through my mind and drew me away from Xavier's once elegant penthouse.

The bright blue of the sky, the hot wind scented with eucalyptus. My feet brushing through dry grass and then meeting the crunch of gravel. A building rising before me, long and low with dozens of white, scalloped arches. The entrance sitting below an old, southwestern triple bell tower.

Caz had committed this moment to memory long ago. I felt the raw-ness of her throat, the cold from the portal room still deep in her core, the warmth of the Heart of Annihilation tucked under her arm. Her mind rattled around in circles and then scattered before coming back to the center.

Pain erupted in my cheek. The vision vanished. I stumbled back. The butt of the commander's pistol cracked against my jaw. I fell to the side, but was up when the pistol came swinging down again. I threw up my arm to block her. Our wrists crashed together.

We stared at each other past our touching arms. Her other hand swung around, striking toward my nose. I blocked her again, and then again. I retreated under the force of her blows. Jab to the jaw, elbow to the temple, fingertips to the throat.

I may have had a chance if I'd possessed full use of both arms. She snuck in a fist to my chin that drove my back into the counter, and fol-lowed with the pistol across my bruised cheekbone. Pain ripped across my face. My hand went to my cheek, feeling the hot and swollen skin. A warm trickle of blood oozed from a gash.

"The location, Caz!" The commander twisted the fabric of my shirt until it cut into my neck.

Hatred burned my throat. My head was a pressurized knot of tension. I pressed my lips tight to prevent any inadvertent information leakage. A particularly sharp prod to my brain, and I saw the scalloped arches and bell towers again. Towering Japanese holly hovered like a proud parent over the expansive squat building.

"Don't you see it, Caz?" The commander's voice eliminated the vision before it could fully materialize. "Can't you feel your loss; your utter aloneness on this dimension? You are nothing now—but you could be again. Tell me where I can find the Heart, and we'll find a place for it. A place where it can fulfill its full potential. Like you always wanted."

A laugh echoed from the knot in my brain. Caz wormed forward.

"We? There is no 'we.' There never was a 'we.'"

My jaw clenched so hard my teeth ached. I shook my head in a desper-ate attempt to dislodge Caz's hold. The commander gave an incredulous scoff. With a hard shove against the counter, she released my shirt. In a few quick steps she was back to Thurmond. He was on his knees now, his arms held behind his back by Sanderford and another soldier. The commander ground the pistol into Thurmond's forehead.

My head exploded in pain, and a flash of blue light shattered my vision. I saw, as though in a dream, the light from a portal pulling out the detail in the eucalyptus trees and sagebrush, making it glow even against the brightness of the sun. The sculpted arches and triple bell towers stood as the background for a simple man in simple clothing, tools in his hands, a wooden cross at his feet. I felt the sphere cradled to my stomach, its warmth and pulsing energy warping my brittle mind.

The vision vanished, leaving me disoriented and blinking at all the figures around me. I knew that place. I'd been there before. Me, Specialist Kris Rose. I'd lived there and trained there as a soldier.

The skin of Thurmond's forehead puckered around the muzzle of the pistol. His eyes squeezed shut. His jaw muscles created ripples under the skin. The moment seemed eternal. The trigger of the pistol was depressed so far I couldn't understand how it hadn't fired yet. I pictured the brass casing housing the gunpowder that would release the bullet. The spiral within the chamber to give the bullet spin and momentum. I imagined the bullet racing down the chamber, not even meeting light before bursting into Thurmond's head. His eyes would deaden, and I would never be able to tell him about Dad, or how much I cared, or how sorry I was.

"Hunter-Liggett." The words exploded from my mouth like a grenade—small enough to hold in the palm of your hand but with far-reaching consequences I couldn't begin to comprehend. "The Heart's at Fort Hunter-Liggett, here in California. I'll take you there. I'll take you right to it. Don't kill him!"

Horror settled in my stomach and overwhelmed the tenuous relief that the information was out. All I could think of was what it cost Dad, and Thurmond, and Rannen, and Wichman, and everyone else who had the misfortune to stumble across my path.

"Excellent!" The commander lifted the pistol with a jerk.

Breath went out of Thurmond. He rubbed the depression in his forehead. The commander took a step away from him, her head cocked, studying my face for deception.

I placed a hand on my mouth to hide a nonexistent tell, letting my eyes express my truthfulness. The shrill wail of distant sirens. Our little circle of drama expanded past ourselves to the soldiers, and then past the soldiers to the world around.

"Let's get moving before those cops arrive, shall we?" the commander sounded downright cheerful. She grabbed my arm. I allowed her to drag me across the room.

Soldiers muscled Thurmond to his feet. Rannen was being ushered out the stairwell door by Sanderford and Burrows. Rannen forced them to stop for a moment and looked over his shoulder at me. He seemed puzzled, his eyebrows knotted, and he opened his mouth to say something only to close it. Shaking his head, he allowed Sanderford to push him out the door.

I listened to the echoing thunder of boots descending the twenty-five flights of stairs. The commander paused at the door, pinching my arm to stop me. She leaned over me like a drill sergeant trying to hammer information into a difficult private and forced me to look into her inhuman eyes.

"If I find you've lied to me, Specialist Rose, or you have something else up your sleeve, I swear to you there will be no more restraint. No more mercy or second chances. Give me any excuse. I would like nothing more than to decorate my clothes with the blood of your friends."

CHAPTER 34

I rested against the cold wall in the back of the small U-Haul moving truck. Blackness pressed hard on my eyeballs, until I closed them to make the darkness feel more natural. I buried my hands in my hair, trying to block out everything but the sound of the freeway. The *whizz-whizz-whizz* of the tires was soothing. Such an ordinary sound, normal to billions of people the world over, to the point of being imperceptible white noise. I focused on it to the exclusion of all else. Miniscule rattles and seams in the pavement broke it up on occasion, but for the most part the steady *whizz-whizz-whizz* could go on forever.

Except the driver had a much closer destination in mind.

"Damn padlock." Out in the darkness Thurmond kicked and swore at the door, damning the commander, Retha, U-haul, the state of California, and everything in between. The venting went on for a good ten minutes, after which there was nothing but the steady sound of the road. His boots tromped unsteadily in my direction as the truck swayed.

"Rose?" His voice was now soft, cajoling.

I dug my nails deeper into my skull. I didn't want to hear anything that might connect me to reality. Reality sucked. I had sacrificed the entire world to keep Thurmond alive. And for what? He was still dead. I was dead. Rannen was dead. Just because we were all still currently breathing didn't mean we should make any long term plans.

"Rose." Thurmond's voice was more insistent this time. The truck rattled over a series of bumps. Warmth from his body leeched into my shoulder as he sat by my side.

"Dammit, Rose. Talk to me."

I grunted, it being far easier than saying, "shut up, I would prefer to spend my last moments on Earth wallowing in self-pity, if you don't mind," or even, "go away."

The realization that self-pity was exactly how far I'd fallen only succeeded in making me feel lower, if that were possible. His strong hands found mine and untangled my fingers from my hair. Thurmond pulled my hand onto his lap, intertwining our fingers.

"How's your face?"

Throbbing. Oozing. I grunted. It was less than I deserved.

Thurmond continued, "Mine's fine, by the way. Thanks for asking."

A wisp of concern worked its way past my pity party. I pictured myself reaching out and finding the spot on his face where the commander had pistol-whipped him. I would touch it softly and express heartfelt appreciation that it wasn't much, much worse.

"That was a pretty amazing show you put on back there," Thurmond said. Then, before I could think about responding his voice changed to a higher pitch. "Thanks, Devon, I've been saving the good stuff for our first real date." His voice went back to normal, "A date? Is that what you call it? I liked the car service and escort you sent. Very urbane."

An uncharacteristic giggle unfurled from my throat. I covered my mouth to stop any more inappropriate lightheartedness.

The weight of the truck shifted, and I felt as much as heard Rannen approach. The thudding of his big feet and the enormous weight of his body should have flipped the truck, but we rumbled on. He settled on the other side of me, rubbing his wrists. I'd burned through my ropes the second the commander's men had thrown us into the back of the truck, and then untied Thurmond and Rannen before sinking into despair.

No one spoke again for several minutes. Our breathing skipped in and out of sync. Then, a deep sigh and the smell of ozone.

"I hate to say this under the circumstances," Rannen said, "but it's really good to see the both of you."

"You too." Thurmond spoke over my head. "They give you a rough time?"

Rannen made a movement next to me that felt something akin to a shrug.

"Is the Heart of Annihilation really at this Hunter-Liggett place?" Rannen's voice echoed a quick, tinny repeat.

I didn't speak. My mind was galloping alongside the vision of the old mission with the triple bell towers, searching for the specific spot the destructive, soccer ball-sized sphere was hidden.

"Yes." I rubbed the sudden ache above my ear.

Rannen's large, cool hand pulled my hand away from my head and laid it on my lap. The image shattered. Caz retreated. With a little squeeze Rannen released my hand. "How do you know?"

"I saw that Caz . . . well, I remembered when I . . . when *she* hid it there."

"*You* hid it there?" Rannen's voice became deeper than normal, with a curious lilt to it.

"I guess. At least that's what I saw. It's there near the mission, somewhere. Mission San Antonio de something or another."

"What is this Heart thing anyway?" Thurmond asked. "Why does the commander want it?"

"Uh—" It's a device capable of destroying an entire dimension. Retha maybe, or how about—*dun-dun-dun*—Earth? I was saved the trouble of answering.

"Caz Fisk was developing a weapon before she was sentenced to RAGE." Rannen's voice was almost lost against the noise of the road. "There's not a lot known about it, because she destroyed her lab before she went to the DCC building that day. What is common knowledge, though, and correct me if I'm wrong, Kris—"

"How would I know if you're wrong?"

My surly interruption made Rannen pause, and when he went on there was a detachment in his voice that hadn't been there before.

"What is common knowledge to most Rethans, Devon, is that this device is capable of absorbing all the life energy from an entire dimension. She developed it initially to combat the Thirteenth Dimension. It was supposed to simply be added to the Rethan arsenal as a deterrent. But that was before the Thirteenth Dimension obliterated a dimension her husband was visiting."

It was as though he was voicing my memories, although more like the memory of a memory, piecing themselves together in my head.

"Wait, she was married? You were married?" Thurmond sounded surprised.

I tried to pull my hand away from his grip so I could cover my ears. He held me fast.

Rannen didn't answer immediately, and the silence stretched out long and awkward. He went on.

"After her husband died, she sort of went off radar. She'd show up occasionally, but then the government pulled her funding."

"Funding for what?" Thurmond asked.

"She was a brilliant munitioner. I guess on this dimension it might be called a gunsmith or a munitions expert. But with Rethan-grade weaponry, of course. I guess the government thought she was too unstable to continue her work. The Rethan you keep calling the commander, and the man she was about to marry, were the only ones Caz had any contact with those few months before she committed the crime. You know him, I believe. He calls himself Xavier Coy, now. He's Caz's brother."

No one can choose their relations. Caz's whisper came as a surprise. Like she'd been eavesdropping and couldn't pass up an opportunity to malign her brother.

"Xavier's your brother? You're kidding!" Thurmond sounded amused.

"Yeah," I said. "I wish he was kidding."

"Well it sort of explains a lot."

"You mean about why he'd rather see us all die than hand me his stupid gun?"

"What are you talking about, Kris?" Rannen asked. Shadows of anger colored his voice.

"Xavier—Xander, whatever you want to call him, was hiding behind the counter with a gun while the commander and her freak squad beat the snot out of Thurmond and me."

"He was behind the counter?"

"Bastard," Thurmond said.

"That means he knows where we're going," Rannen sounded hopeful. I didn't think he should.

"Fat lot of good that'll do us."

"Your brother has a great deal of money, Kris. He can buy an army and be there when we arrive."

"He's not going to be there. He hates me!"

"He doesn't hate you. He's just angry with you right now. And a little scared of Zell."

"Well he should be a *lot* scared of me, because I swear if I ever get my hands on him . . . !"

The taste of metal filled my mouth. A powerful surge of loathing squeezed my brain in a vice.

CHAPTER 35

Caz
5 hours 23 minutes pre-RAGE

Caz stared at the solid wooden doors behind the commandant's throne. Her fingers were slick on the handle of the blade. She switched the weapon to her left hand, wiped her hand on her pants, and then returned the weapon before wiping the other. She did this several more times before acknowledging the action would never render her hands clean.

The surface of the doors were rough and textured to emphasize the exotic nature of the material. Caz ran her fingers along the crack between the doors, leaving a streak of blood, and then touched the elaborately designed golden keyhole at eye level.

Former Commandant Ben Attikin was the first munitioner. In fact, he was the very reason munitioners became such slags of society. He'd created the weapon the Thirteenth Dimension had used for the last several centuries to routinely destroy entire dimensions.

He'd built Attikin Dome—a.k.a. the Dimensional Congressional Council building—and the munitioner's lab which was handed down to Caz's parents.

This information came as quite the surprise to Caz, and, what could she say, an unparalleled delight. It was this very information that set her entire plan in motion. It was the key.

Caz hooked her finger on the chain around her neck and drew out the jingling keys she always kept with her. A half circle silver key, forged from the promise ring Vin gave her. The tiny, magnetized bead hovered inside the curve, containing a precise amount of voltage to keep it in place.

The second key on the chain got her into the lab. It was a primeval-looking thing, all tarnished black and gold. It opened another door as well.

She inserted it into the keyhole and turned. It caught for a moment, then creaked into action. Rust-colored dust puffed from the hole. Crack, squeak, groan. A flash of light burst from the keyhole. Caz pushed at the doors, and they ground open. Cold blue light flooded across her skin.

The portal chamber was as mythical and mysterious as the dome under which it was housed. It was said that Ben Attikin knew the marshals were coming for him. His time was limited, and he'd done what any leader, jealous of his secrets, would do. He'd locked up the most important chamber in all of Retha and secreted the key away. It was over a century before it was discovered by none other than Severnz Fisk, Caz's grandfather.

At the time they only thought it got them into the munitioner's lab. A bit of inspiration and digging on Caz's part found her the truth.

Caz's breath misted before her. Retha in its entirety was a cold place. The chamber made Retha feel like the over-heated Ehtar dimension. The hairs on her arms lifted in a shivering wave.

From the outside, the dome was beyond impressive. It was a monument, comparable only to the shrines of Cadvar, or the pyramids on Earth created by some of the first Rethan settlers. From the inside it was breathtaking. Twenty-six columns of pristine white stone rose upward to create the bones of the dome, crisscrossing at the peak. Plates of metal covered at least seven of the arches, each made of a different metal. Gold for the Thirteenth Dimension. Copper for the eleventh. Silver for Retha's return archway. The others Caz was unable to name—the tenth might have been bronze, on down to the base dimensions and equally base metals such as steel, brass, and tin.

A tall stone basin stood in the center of the room, shimmering full of silver coins. Dimensional catapults.

Once Ben Attikin was exiled, the portal chamber had become unavailable to the council. They'd had to use their existing portals, clunky things with an equally clunky portal in the other dimension. Not that they hadn't wanted the power to cross dimensions without the need of a matching portal on the other side, and the dimensional catapults to bring them back.

The portal chamber remained locked. Some other protection or power kept them out beyond the simplicity of the key. And here it stood for centuries, an embarrassing monument to their impotency and empty, devoid of any Rethan contact. No one currently living had ever been inside—until today.

Steam wafted from Caz's skin. One would think that on the brink of success, moments away from destroying the Thirteenth Dimension and finally laying Vin to rest, Caz would pause, inhale, and rejoice in the moment.

She did none of these things. This wasn't a moment for reflection, this was a moment for action. Caz tucked her bloody knife in the belt at her back and retrieved the Heart of Annihilation from her bag. Its warmth seeped into her cold hands. The golden light cast shadowy claws onto the floor.

The pillars for the Thirteenth Dimension lay on the far side of the chamber, directly across from the entrance. Bright blue light eked from behind the pillars and all around, pulsing in a faintly hypnotic way. It took Caz far longer to cross the portal chamber than she thought it would. Her anticipation made the distance seem that much farther. Her steps were lonely and hollow against the sterile stone.

She'd barely reached the stone basin in the center of the room when she heard a crack in the silence. Caz stopped mid-step and spun to face the door. Her shoes squeaked, leaving a circular smear of blood. A figure stood in the doorway.

"I never thought you'd actually do it." His voice echoed around the vast chamber, bouncing off the columns and echoing into the far distant dome.

The visible carnage beyond almost detracted from the figure standing in front of it. He leaned casually against the door, one hand in his pocket. His clothes were plain, earth-toned. His hair had grown long enough to pull back, although a perfect silver curl rested across his forehead and drooped elegantly into his eye.

"Vincent." Caz's lips numbed against his name. His features were so familiar and yet older somehow. "Where in Gauss's law did you come from?"

"Ather—"

"Lost to the void."

"Well, yes."

Caz switched the Heart of Annihilation to her other hand, realizing for the first time that Vin's eyes weren't on her but on the device itself. She curled it close to her body to protect it, as a mother would a babe.

"So, you're what? A specter? A ghoul? Come to haunt me for my horrendous deeds?"

Caz wasn't sure if this was what she actually thought, or if she was simply making polite conversation with the impossibility posing as Vin. She recognized, somewhere in the anger, bewilderment, betrayal, and selfishness warring inside her, that this wasn't real. Couldn't be real. Of course, neither could the hundred and twenty-two bodies lying in individual, grotesque heaps behind Vin.

She'd killed them. It was easy. Too easy. She was a munitioner, after all. Her bag had held enough weaponry to take them all out. Some in large groups, some individually as they ran screaming for the doors. She'd mopped up the rest with the methodical slashing of her knife in an anticlimactic cascade of blood.

"No specter, Caz," Vin said. "It's me. In the flesh."

Caz nodded and then shook her head. "Fine, *Vin*. Close the door, would you? You're letting the cold out."

She rotated and gazed into the basin of catapults. She gathered several coins, squeezing them until her hand hurt. She frowned and turned back around. Vin was still there, standing away from the door. He reached out a groping claw.

"Give it to me, Caz."

"No." Caz pulled the Heart of Annihilation close.

"Caz."

She saw it now. The frustration under the surface. The irritation, admiration, aggravation, sheer conflict-ridden love/hate Vin always carried in his eyes when he looked at her. It was this, more than what her eyes and ears were telling her, that put aside the rational portion of her brain screaming that this was impossible. This was Vin. Not lost on Ather. Not part of the Thirteenth Dimension as a voiceless form of energy. It was just Vin.

She was going to kill him this time, no question.

"How are you here?" She narrowed her eyes, barely holding herself in check.

"I faked my death on Ather so I could fulfill my higher purpose."

"Being . . . ?"

"Give me the weapon, Caz."

Caz dropped her shoulders with a little laugh. She shoved one hand in her pocket and raised the Heart of Annihilation to rest on the tips of her fingers of her other. Tempting, taunting.

"Okay, Vin. Okay, yeah, sure. I made it for you after all using the sweat of my brow, the tears of our son, and the blood of hundreds of Rethans, but I did it. I did it so you can . . ." Caz licked her lips, letting her forehead pucker in overdramatized thought. "Wait, why did you need it again? Not for the council, surely." Caz waved her hand at the bloody council chamber.

Vin took a step back, looking uncertain. "Well, no."

Caz smirked.

"For the good of Retha." Vin rubbed his hands together, glanced behind him and then back at her. He took several hesitant steps in her direction. "The Liberated RAGE Movement is the future of our people."

A shiver coursed across Caz's skin. The LRM? The extremist faction that had clawed at their relationship throughout the years was the one responsible for taking him away entirely? Making her believe he was dead?

Vin went on. "We are determined to put an end to the two laws and make our people proactive again. I mean think about it." His voice grew stronger as he mounted his platform. "We don't need more *drones*." He used her word, probably to gain sympathy, and came closer. "We need a dimension who wants to be the top, the leaders. The benevolent power that the lower dimensions will bow to. We need more Rethans like you."

"More like me, huh?" Caz jerked her chin toward the door and the massacre beyond.

Vin did a half-head turn but kept his eyes on her. He was within spitting distance now.

"We're on the same side. I mean, look! As much as it pains me to say, you have helped us. You've opened the portal chamber! You've eliminated the corrupt council."

"They'll reform."

"But they can now be molded to something stronger. You may not see it, but we have the same agenda."

"You don't know what I want. What I want to do with this device." Caz was suddenly not so sure of this herself. What do you do when the very reason for act upon extreme act of violence has been negated?

"Send it gift-wrapped to the Thirteenth Dimension?" Vin wheedled.

"That was the plan. Sure. The plan. It was the plan until—"

"Give me the weapon, Caz."

"Do you even have any idea what it does?"

Vin didn't respond.

"I didn't think so. Now," Caz huffed, straightening, "if there's nothing else, I need to get on with my revenge for your murder."

Her feet streaked through a tiny puddle of blood that had collected under the knife. She hadn't gone two steps toward the golden pillars when she felt a touch to her earlobe. Vin's chilly fingers and thumb caressed the softness of the skin, sending chills down her back. She rotated slowly. A coil of white stone wrapped Vin's hand. Her discarded IC 4000, the one she'd left by Zell, was aimed at her face.

"That thing doesn't kill, you know," she said.

Vin adjusted his thumb on the trigger. "I don't need to kill you to get what I need."

"What about Manny?" She hadn't meant to bring him into this, but there he stood between them, an ethereal monument to their failure.

"What about him? Isn't he buried somewhere in your trail of bodies?"

"How could you even think . . . You left him first!" Her guts wound tight.

"I left him with you!" Vin jabbed the weapon at her. "Who'd you leave him with?"

"Don't stand there in all your self-righteous glory and pretend you deserve—"

"Enough!" Vin actually stamped his foot. "I'm not playing anymore, Caz."

She saw the truth in the lines around his eyes, the pucker of his lips, his thumb against the trigger.

She saw who he truly was, a mere husk of the Vin she'd fallen for as a child. The one who grew up with her, married her, and gave her a son. This wasn't the determined Rethan, so unlike any other dead-eyed male, who locked her into an obsession ending here in a trail of blood. This one was annoying and childish, one who abandoned her for the sake of politics. He'd stolen Vin's face, his soul, his love for her, and shoved it into an extremist she could no longer look at.

Caz reached behind her back. "I was never playing."

Vin opened his mouth to rebound the argument.

The blade came out of Caz's belt in a smooth arch and slashed across Vin's throat in a hissing whistle. A velvet ribbon of blood appeared under his chin.

The IC 4000 fell to the floor. His hand went to his throat. Blood flowed from between his fingers.

Vin dropped to his knees, gagging on the blood pouring from his mouth, disbelief and horror on his face. Caz retched, gagged with him, and retched again. Vin collapsed onto his face.

Emotions scorched through her mind, electrifying, terrifying—completely devoid of satisfaction. She tasted the food she'd eaten that morning, and bile.

A wail wrenched from her throat. Her cheeks felt wet. She screamed. Vin's body, his head centered in the growing pool of blood. Everything blurred.

Caz ran. She didn't know where. It didn't matter. Nothing mattered any more. Her shoulder struck something hard. A soft, earthy light penetrated the blur. She felt the power of the voltage surrounding her, drawing her far, far away.

CHAPTER 36

Rose

My body shook in a violent uncontrollable rattle against cold metal.

"Devon, she's seizing! Help me hold her!"

"Dammit, Rose!"

My tumultuous mind heard the voices but could not place them. I felt the chaotic lack of control in my body, but it was as though it belonged to someone else.

Slowly my body quieted. Silence. Maybe seconds. Maybe years. Coherency gradually filled my world. Fingers touched my neck.

"I think she's okay." A hollow voice echoed somewhere nearby.

"What happened? One minute she's fine and the next—"

My body ached. I couldn't speak or move.

"It's not the first time, or something like it anyway." Thurmond. "The worst was at the portal after the soldiers left. Her heart stopped for a few minutes. I think she's having memories from Retha. I guess if what everyone says about her is true, those memories have got to be damn near unbearable."

"She seems like such a pleasant little thing when she's not being tormented by Rethans." Rannen sounded sad. "Sometimes I can hardly believe she's the same person."

"Are you sure she's—?"

"Yes. I knew her on Retha. She looks like she did then. A little younger, but it's her." Quiet for a moment then, "But she doesn't act like Caz. I see Caz in her for sure, but Caz wouldn't have traded anything for the Heart of Annihilation. Especially not the life of a human."

"What was she like?"

Rannen sighed. "It really depended on who you were. She could be funny and charming, or intense and determined, or downright disturbing. She scared the pants off most Rethans. Mostly through her reputation, not only as a munitioner but as someone who couldn't maintain the two laws."

"Which are?"

"Etiquette and serenity. The standard we live by to keep our society at peace."

"Sounds like pacifist bullshit to me."

"Perhaps, but it keeps violence and crime to an almost nonexistent level. Not that there aren't problems with it. There's a universal sameness to Rethans." A scoffing sound. "Caz called them drones. There wasn't anything worse in her book."

"I just can't for the life of me believe Rose was this homicidal maniac." Thurmond sounded somewhat defensive. "Granted, I've seen some things in the last week or so that I never could have imagined of her. She was really going to nuke a whole dimension, huh?"

Rannen exhaled a noisy assent.

"I mean," Thurmond went on, "if she weren't so damned determined to find this Heart thing. To find answers." Thurmond was quiet for a moment. "Not that I blame her. I'd do the same thing in her boots. But still. How hard to find do you think this Heart is going to be?"

"I don't know," Rannen said. "It's been missing for over twenty years, so—"

"I shouldn't criticize," Thurmond said. "But she should've just let the commander kill me." His statement was one of supreme logic, devoid of the intense, emotional state I'd been in when I'd made the decision. "We're talking about putting a nuclear device in the hands of a sociopath. How could our lives possibly be worth that?"

"It was worth it to her because she loves you, Devon," Rannen stated. "Are you telling me you wouldn't have done the same?"

Thurmond was silent for an uncomfortable moment. "I'd like to think I wouldn't—"

"She saved you. She saved me. And that means a lot coming from her, although it's not very helpful in the grand scheme of things," Rannen trailed off, and when he went on his voice sounded small and frightened. "What are we going to do?"

I knew exactly what to do. If I were to be honest with myself, I'd known for quite some time. I'd kept shuffling it off in hopes of a better option. However, something in the vision of Vin and Caz and learning exactly what she . . . what I was capable of, made me grasp the certainty of what needed to happen.

I took a deep breath, feeling life enter my limbs. Warmth coursed through my torso, drawing electricity from the world around me.

I rolled my head. Hands ran across my scalp.

"Rose?"

"Wh-appened?"

"Bad dream or somethin'," Thurmond said. "You okay?"

I felt moisture on my face and wiped drool from the corner of my mouth, thankful that we were being transported in pitch darkness.

"Yeah, I'm . . ." I turned onto my shoulder. All my muscles were achy and tight. I was helped into a sitting position. "We're not there yet, are we?"

As if in answer, the truck rattled. I could picture the endless rows of vegetables and elegant rakes of vineyards as we drove through the salad bowl of the world. The Gilroy Garlic festival would be in full swing this time of year, and the wineries would be busy with drunken taste testers. That world slept as we drove past, quietly rolling toward our deaths and possibly that of billions.

I suppose it could be worse. I wasn't wielding a bloody knife and slicing people's throats.

I shuddered. No, actually I wasn't sure what was worse.

"Rose, we were talking while you were . . . Anyway, you can't give it to her. The Heart. You can't let the commander get her hands on it."

"I know," I said quietly.

"Stall for time," Rannen said, his voice high and hopeful. "Xavier will come."

I wished I had anything near the confidence in Xavier that he was exuding.

"Sure, Rannen. Stall for time," I said bitterly. "You really don't think the commander's not going to put a bullet in your heads if I tried that? Sorry guys, but I sort of used up your ninth lives with my last pointless stunt."

"Of course, Rose, if you'd rather knock the commander's head out of the park with one of those electrical things you do, feel free." Thurmond chuckled darkly at his tasteless joke.

The violence of the image pressed against my mind. It hurt. I locked my hands back into my braid and rocked back and forth, trying to banish the pleasure Caz was feeling for Thurmond's idea.

"Okay, not funny. Sorry." Thurmond pulled me into a secure embrace and breathed into my hair.

The truck slowed. My heart hammered against my rib cage. I clutched Thurmond's shirt, terrified to let go. Rannen leaned closer on my other side. The engine continued to idle, then we turned right and accelerated again.

My stomach plummeted. That was most likely the turn from US-101 onto Jolon Road, which gave us less than fifteen minutes before we arrived on the base.

"Xander will come," Rannen said, his voice stubborn. "I know he'll come."

"Why? He hates me." If there was one thing I'd learned from Caz and her visions, it was that I couldn't trust Xander to help me.

"But he doesn't hate me. I guarantee he'll be there."

"Who are you to him, Rannen?" I whispered against Thurmond's shirt. Rannen didn't answer, and I was beginning to see a pattern when the questions got too personal.

Thurmond started to say something, but Rannen's voice cut over the top. "He's my uncle, Kris. He raised me. My uncle Xan."

The words hung in the air, heavy with implication. The last few pieces of the puzzle fell into place.

Xander, my brother. His nephew, Rannen. Rannen—Manny. My son.

I broke out of Thurmond's grip and stumbled to my feet. The truck swayed, threatening to knock me down. My head pounded in unbearable anguish.

I felt the Rethan rain on my skin, the intermingled rage and terror tearing me apart. I saw through Caz's eyes as she caught sight of Manny hiding behind Xander.

The little face staring back, eyes so filled with despair she thought she would drown. Her laughter dying to quiet whimpers.

Shackles clacking onto her wrists, drawing all voltage from her body in an exhausting flood of numbness. Something scorching her palm. Acrid smoke pouring from her hand, searing her nose in the scent of burning flesh. Caz tearing her arms away from the marshals before they could send her through the RAGE portal. Falling to her knees, her hands reaching for her son.

"Rannen!" She was screaming his given name, making him hear her. "Rannen!"

My head blistered as the vision vanished. I rolled my neck. What had I done? Despair, corroded and pungent, dragged me down to the murkiest recesses of my mind. Caz waited, a predatory creature wanting nothing more than to annihilate her captor—kill the warden—vanquish Kris Rose.

"Rose!"

The sound of my name pulled me away from the demonic clutches. Like a drowning woman breaking the surface of a lake, my mind gulped in Thurmond's voice.

My heart. My soul. It hurt so much. I'd found out who I was, the person I'd overcome. I'd become someone different . . . better. And yet none of it mattered, except what I did right now.

I opened my eyes in the darkness. My cheeks burned. Thurmond touched my arm. I threw it off.

Where was the door? I felt along the wall until I found the latch. Thurmond had already tried to get it open. It was padlocked from the outside to keep us from escaping. But electricity caused heat, which could cause . . .

I gripped the inside handle and sent a hot electrical charge against the latch, different from any other current I'd wielded before. The latch burned red, scorching the flesh of my branded hand. Destroying that connection to a life I'd never wanted.

With a lurch the lock gave, and I flung the door upward with a thundering rattle. Cool moonlight and rushing wind flooded into the back. Trees flowed past, nestled against low canyon walls. The curvy road wound under the tires of the truck, not too fast, but faster than I liked. I held my burned hand to my body, inhaling the cool night air and rocking with the movement of the truck.

Dad once said, *You can make every right decision in the book, and things can still go wrong. You can only hope the peace you get from doing what's right will carry you past the dark times.*

Dad was right. He was always right. And the right decision couldn't be about the temporary welfare of my small circle of comrades when an entire dimension was at stake. The trouble was, I'd already proven that sacrificing Thurmond was impossible, and Rannen . . . I scrubbed a hand down my face. The answer was so simple.

I needed to eliminate the threat to Earth. And the threat in this case wasn't deadly weapons, the commander, or even Caz. The threat was my willingness to sacrifice the whole world to spare Thurmond and Rannen.

"Dammit, Rose, why didn't you open it before?" Thurmond stood at my shoulder, staring down at the road.

Rannen weighted the truck on the other side of me.

"Hey, Rannen." I rested my hand on his arm and looked up into his silvery eyes. "I remember my dad telling me to always do my best and let the chips fall as they may. I'm sorry that Caz . . . I mean, that *I* didn't do my best on Retha. You know, as your mother. I'm so sorry."

Rannen's face relaxed, and he chuckled. He touched my shoulder. "Someday I'd very much like to meet your father, Kris. Anyone who can turn someone like Caz into a person like you is worth getting to know."

I forced a smile and said, "Roll when you hit the ground."

Rannen swayed, his eyes locked on the road, and then launched himself out. The weight of the truck shifted alarmingly, throwing me into Thurmond's arms so that I didn't see Rannen land.

Thurmond held me tight. I swallowed. His intoxicating closeness, his musky scent combined with soap, wasn't making this any easier.

"After you," I said, pulling away.

"You just said goodbye to Rannen," Thurmond said, his arm still tight around my shoulders. I sensed him trying to catch my eye. Why did he have to be so observant?

"Go." I jerked my chin toward the road. "There's not much time."

"You first," he said with a stubborn tilt of his head.

"T, could you just . . ."

Thurmond's answer was to hug me close. I wrenched myself out of his arms but he grabbed my wrist and held tight. The burn on my hand throbbed and my shoulder ached from the strain.

"Get off the truck, T," I said, through clenched teeth.

"We'll jump together."

"Devon . . ."

His eyebrows drew over his eyes. "Don't think I don't know what you're doing."

What are you doing? Caz hissed into my mind. My head pounded.

"Get off the truck or I'll make you get off the truck!" I shouted.

"No way in hell, Rose."

His fingers dug into my wrist. He was much stronger than me and he knew it, but there was one thing he hadn't taken into account. The truck jolted around a bend, throwing us off balance.

I directed a small charge of electricity into my free hand and sent my fist smashing into his jaw.

CHAPTER 37

I clung to a rope dangling from the door, swaying with the movement of the truck in an attempt to stay on my feet. The road rolled under the tires, the moonlight speckling through the trees. All was quiet except the rumbling of the motor and the wind rushing past.

Loose strands of my hair, a pure Rethan silver, flicked around my face. Sweat beaded my forehead from the fight with Thurmond. I'd been able to push him out when the truck slowed around a bend, unconscious but still alive. He'd rolled a few times and come to rest on the shoulder of the road. I'd watched him until he was out of sight, hating what I'd done, hating the necessity of it. Hating myself.

Very clever, Kris, Caz whispered. *Eliminate Zell's leverage. The Heart of Annihilation is as good as ours.*

Aside from the whole friggin' brigade the commander was sure to put in our friggin' way. Yeah, I was a friggin' genius.

The canyon opened into a flat plain covered by dry, yellow grass and scattered trees. Eucalyptus, if I were to guess. I recognized where we were now. My heart crowded my lungs. Fort Hunter-Liggett rose to the left, a collection of lights and simple, blocky buildings. Power poles lined the road, the scalloped wires surging with electricity. I flexed my fingers. It felt good to have the voltage building again.

A cluster of men and military vehicles blocked the road. For one hopeful moment I thought it was the soldiers of the base, come to stand in the way of the commander.

The commander's bright silver head of hair shone in the moonlight. She was buried among her troops, there to greet me and keep me compliant. My eyes narrowed. We'd just see about that.

The truck slammed to a halt. I gripped the rope to keep myself from pitching head first out the back. I set my face into the cold mask which I envisioned on Caz. Time to sell this.

The first soldiers to round the truck faltered in surprise at the sight of me standing in the open back, one hand holding the rope, a smile plastered on my face.

The warm California air carried the scent of eucalyptus to me. I inhaled deeply, aware of the pounding ache above my ear. Caz pressed cold memory fingers against my brain.

I made eye contact with the nearest soldier and then casually examined a trickle of electricity striking between my fingers. I threw in a hint of dramatization for affect. He stumbled backward, lifting the rifle. I followed him with my eyes. Sergeant Sanderford pushed him out of the way and limped to the base of the truck.

"Get your ass down here, Rose. Time to lead us to that weapon." Good ol' Sanderford. He stared at my hands. I rubbed them together, making the voltage crackle and pop in a bright blue light.

Sanderford tossed his head and the soldiers stepped back, leaving room for me to jump out of the truck. I held the grin tight on my face, my eyes locked on Sanderford. I finally released the rope and sat quickly on the edge of the truck bed before my legs could give way.

Sanderford glared when I didn't make another move and then craned his neck to look around me.

"Where's Thurmond?"

"Thurmond?" I lifted my eyebrows, feigning genuine curiosity. "Oh yeah, him. Rannen too, right?" I shrugged. "Dumped their corpses on the road a ways back."

I glanced around at the other soldiers, a smirk on my face, and swung my legs childlike.

"You killed Thurmond?" Sanderford's mouth hung open in disbelief.

I was suddenly worried that I'd underplayed my hand. I widened my grin, letting the electricity crawl up my arms. He clenched his jaw, his face set in uncertainty.

"Ma'am?" Sanderford hollered over his shoulder. When the commander didn't immediately appear, Sanderford grabbed the arm of the nearest soldier. "They can't be dead. Go find 'em and bring 'em back here."

I stopped swinging my legs. The tall staff sergeant, who looked like he'd rather cross Al-Qaida than butcherous little ol' me, took a hesitant step away. I read his name from his uniform and let it slide off my tongue as if we were old army buddies.

"Sergeant Jacks, I wouldn't do that if I were you." He jolted to a stop. I went on. "You wouldn't believe the fight they put up when they realized exactly who they were riding with. I had to fill them full of enough voltage to drop a mammoth. Which means there's enough residual energy running through their bodies to take down you and any other vigilante who gets too close."

Sergeant Jacks didn't move, indecision all over his face. I lowered myself out of the back of the truck, not trusting my leg to take any jumping. Sergeants Sanderford and Jacks, along with the rest of the soldiers, widened the circle. The rattling of weapons sounded as they were all lifted to aim at me.

"Rose, stay there," Sanderford hissed, his voice tight in fear. "I don't want to see or feel nothin' electric."

"Don't worry, Sarge." I winked. "I promise you won't feel a thing."

"Don't shoot!" The commander shouted from the back of the crowd.

I saw her bright silver head working through the pack. It was time to lead her far, far away from the Heart of Annihilation and let the chips fall as they may. I strode toward the road without any hesitation. They parted to let me through.

"Rose, stop right there! Don't move!" Sergeant Sanderford demanded. Several other voices joined in.

"Don't shoot! Don't shoot!" the commander shouted.

I turned my back on them and stepped onto Mission Road. My toes touched the thick yellow line down the center and I stopped, suddenly wary. The glimmering lights of the base stood off to one side. My fingers trembled. Something felt wrong.

Fort Hunter-Liggett was a small base with less than three hundred permanent residents. Even when different trainees were cycled in the count never came to more than four thousand, but on any given night Mission Road was always alive with joggers, while the noise from the officer's club and rec center echoed throughout the valley.

Now, nothing. Only quiet and emptiness. An alien feeling that wasn't right.

I sensed a source of power so potent I tasted the metal of it on my tongue. I stared past the soldiers, down the road toward the base and the historic Mission San Antonio de Padua.

My head pounded for attention. I squeezed my eyes shut. My mind spun down the track of Caz's memories until I felt the space between dimensions compressing her lungs. The desperate pain of a portal jump.

The wild, pungent scents only found in the Earth. The warmth of the Heart of Annihilation cradled in her arms. Her hands glistening with the still wet blood of her husband, Vin. Stumbling across the coarse ground. Her feet hitting something more solid, almost like a road.

I rubbed my arms, trying to remove the feeling of the outlandish fabric covering my skin, the bloody hands clamped around the silver, glowing object. My hands curled together as though still holding it, feeling its warmth and incredible power.

I stood on the same road Caz had all those years ago. The electricity within my body magnified. The Heart called to me from less than a mile away.

The Heart of Annihilation! Caz shouted, so close to the surface.

I groaned, squeezing my head between my hands. I couldn't allow her control over my body. There was one chance to save the Earth from Caz's . . . from our precious Heart. I needed to destroy the source of the information. Run as far from the Heart of Annihilation as possible.

And then I had to make them kill me.

Kill you? Kill me? With the Heart so near? No way, Kris.

I whirled around to face the commander's soldiers. Sanderford stood in the foreground, his weapon up, his mouth open wide as he barked orders at me in his best drill sergeant voice.

"Don't shoot! Don't shoot her!" the commander continued to yell, shoving her frightened troops left and right in her attempt to get to me before the unthinkable happened.

I drew voltage into my hands and opened my palms to release the pent up energy in Sanderford's rifle.

"Kill me!" I shouted. "Someone just kill me!"

Pressure crushed my head in unbearable agony. My mind jumbled and a dark malevolent force surged past my defenses. A scream tore from my throat.

CHAPTER 38

My heart skipped, and then resumed beating in a completely different rhythm. My breathing paused, and then came an inhale I didn't control, tongue flickering out to touch my lips in an obsessive gesture. My eyes blinked open of their own accord and stared down the road, past Fort Hunter-Liggett, zeroing in on a barely visible building.

I tried to scream again, but nothing came from my mouth. I knew the worst had happened. Something I should have anticipated. Caz had taken over, leaving me nothing but an observer in my own body.

She didn't look back at the soldiers. I wasn't even sure she remembered they were there.

One foot in front of the other, Caz followed the road as she had over twenty years ago after her blind jump through the portal. I witnessed her memories as she recalled the heat of the sun on her skin and the dust clogging her throat. The stickiness of Vin's blood clinging to her skin.

But none of that mattered now. For over twenty years she had been trapped as I was now, and during all that time she only had one desire.

Step, step, step. I couldn't stop my feet. Caz's mind rattled through memory after bloody memory. Xander, Manny, Zell, Vin. Engineering the Heart of Annihilation. Murdering the council. Vin's ultimate betrayal. We lost track of the present as we circled the past, leading us to the one thing we wanted more than anything.

My feet stopped their mindless tread, and Caz looked up from the ground. A building stood before us, long and squat with arches trailing to the left into the darkness of the night. The entrance had three larger archways topped by a matching number of bell towers. A cross was mounted above the center bell, another one behind on the higher roof.

Caz breathed in deep, remembering the man with ancient, wrinkled skin standing before her, dirt smudging his hands and face. A large wooden beam had laid at his feet near a small pile of tools.

He'd been kind and compassionate, sensing Caz's need if not her violent state of mind. He'd helped her hide the Heart of Annihilation so that she could one day return to claim it.

"Is it dangerous?" he'd asked. And Caz had lied about the horrific potential of the unremarkable silver sphere. Lied so he would save it for her in this moment in time. Lied so she could finally claim the object that had consumed her life.

My knees hit the ground in front of an old wooden cross. Gravel bit into my flesh and pain jarred through my body. I felt Caz recoil from the pain, weakening her hold even as she reached for the cross.

With every ounce of willpower I possessed I surged forward, squeezing my hand around the pain like an anchor connecting me to my body. I could have cried in relief as my fingers obeyed my commands, closing into a fist. I dug my nails into the scorched flesh, sending pain racing through my hand and up my arm. With a nauseating wrench and agonizing pressure in my brain Caz cried out, freeing me from her control.

I gasped, my eyes tightly shut, my hand still clenched in a painful fist. Slowly I relaxed my hand and opened my eyes. Soldiers pressed all around me, their eyes on something in front of me.

Only then did I realize where Caz had led us.

CHAPTER 39

A primordial and animalistic cry of the deepest pain echoed through my head and wrenched from my mouth.

I stared at the cross, trying to put Caz's memories into the context of why I was kneeling here. The building behind it came into focus. Delicate white arches extended for several hundred feet, accentuated by the scalloped roofing and the triple bell towers of the Mission San Antonio de Padua.

My hands went to my head. What had I done?

I hadn't managed to get myself killed, that's what I'd done. I'd been so focused on saving Thurmond and Rannen, and concentrating on the commander and her men, that I hadn't factored in Caz's will to live.

That was your plan? Caz snarled. She was so strong. *You were going to kill us? You stupid little girl!*

"What have you done, Caz?" I whispered, my breath shuddering in and out. "What have you done?"

"Live to fight another day," Caz replied, using my mouth.

Motors rumbled around, accompanied by the tread of boots on gravel. The commander's troops massed in the dried grass around the mission's circular drive.

"Boderick!" the commander's voice rang out.

I jerked my head up. The commander stood next to me, her mouth pulled into a pucker of excitement. She breathed an exhilarated snort through her nose. Her eyes were on the concrete base of the wooden cross.

"Boderick!" the commander called again. I finally registered the name. Boderick? Bodie. The Rethan tech guy. The one who knew everything about portals.

"Set up the portal." The commander smiled. "We have the Heart!"

The sphere lay for over two decades, sunk into a foot-by-foot slab of concrete and then buried by more concrete designed to stabilize the cross. The only visible portion of the Heart of Annihilation was a circle the size of a cookie showing a weathered imprint of the symbol: a half circle and dot where the center should be. Like the brand on my hand. Like my pendant. I reached for it.

The commander pushed me aside and crouched next to the base of the cross. She laid a trembling hand on what was visible of the Heart. She breathed in, her eyes lifting to the stars. I rose to my feet.

"So that's it, huh?" I couldn't decide whom I hated more right now, her or myself.

The commander caressed the Heart one more time before getting to her feet. She yelled across the chattering of her troops, "Sanderford! Get over here and find a way to get the Heart out from under this cross!"

Sergeant Sanderford limped past. The commander turned back to me. "Caz, look at this! Just look—look at it! You want it, don't you? I can tell."

"I don't," I said in an unconvincing sputter.

Of course I wanted it. No. Caz Fisk wanted it! Not me! Caz—*Kris*—Caz! Dad would never forgive me if I grew up to be the DCC Slayer.

I buried my face in my hands. My head ached so badly. And I was afraid. I grated my fingernails against my scalp as my mind sorted through Caz's sinister database of two hundred thirty-six ways to murder a massive congregation of people.

The vehicles assembled themselves in the dry grass around the mission's circular drive. A Deuce and a Half rumbled up, making a wide turn. The soldiers gave it room to back up to the mission steps. The brakes squealed. Men climbed in the back before the motor had even shut off and started unloading large silver crates. I recognized them from the Rethan camp in Arizona. The crates were opened, and the silver plates belonging to the portal were pulled out.

"Stay close, Specialist Rose. You're not going to want to miss this."

As soon as the commander called me by that name, I knew I no longer had her attention. Caz Fisk was the person she wanted to share this with. Specialist Rose was just an irritation.

"You can set it up on the main archway!" she shouted, her boots crunching on the gravel.

Camo-clad figures washed around me, the single stationary buoy in a piranha-filled lake. No one paid me any attention, although they were careful to give me a wide berth. Just people—humans—about to start a war with a dimension they understood nothing about.

Boderick scuttled by, flanked by two soldiers. His shoulders were raised to his ears, his chin on his chest, and his hands opened and closed at his side. My breath escaped in a short, angry burst. Light erupted from my fingers and plowed into the soldier on his right.

The bolt struck him square in his torso. He spasmed onto his knees, clutching his stomach before falling onto his side. The next volt took the other man high on the shoulder. His rifle clattered across the blacktop.

We covered the twenty feet or so in seconds and wrapped our fingers around Boderick's throat. Our nails dug into his skin. A distant upheaval marked us as a target but Caz only had eyes for the ratty little face. His mouth opened and closed, gawping like a fish drowning in air. Hands scrabbled across my arm.

"Ricks, you traitorous little rat! I'll kill you for this!"

"Cazandra." His eyes rolled. His lips turned blue. "Caz, p-please don't. Xander he's . . . help!"

Caz lost her control of my body. The pain in my head receded. Xander what? I released Boderick's neck, raised my hands, and dipped my head in preparation for the assault.

A body struck me from the side. My hip hit the ground first, followed by my bare arm. The graveled road skinned my shoulder in a bloody, searing skid. It was all I could do not to scream. I kicked at the man on top of me. Sergeant Sanderford wrestled me up. The second I was on my feet Sanderford forced me back to my knees, beckoning for assistance. Blood warmed my stinging shoulder. My upper arms were grabbed from behind. I groaned. Sergeant Jacks held one arm. I blew silver strands of hair out of my eyes and glared at the owner of the other clammy set of hands. Luginbeel's mouth hung slack, his eyes locked in terror on my face. He only held onto my arm with two fingers and a thumb, as if that would keep him from getting electrocuted.

Sergeant Sanderford brushed at his pants. He raised a fist. I flinched, waiting for the strike. Sanderford gave a self-satisfied grunt and pointed a finger at my nose.

"If the commander hadn't told us she still needs you for something, you'd have a bullet in your head right now."

"Go to hell," I whispered. The darkness all around fed Caz, increasing her mental girth, starving me out.

"Keep her contained until she's called for." Sergeant Sanderford did a military back-step and limped off toward the mission.

"Hands up, Rose," Luginbeel blustered the order, his voice nasal. I clenched my teeth.

"That's *Specialist* Rose to you, you little dipstick," I said. "I still outrank you."

The muzzle of a rifle poked into my back, and I reluctantly lifted my hands. Gravel bit into my shins and legs. Blood trickled from my skinned shoulder, saturating the shredded bandages Xavier had put on only hours before.

With a cracking sound the wooden cross toppled, crashing into the weeds. Jagged shards of wood spiked from the splintered bottom. I couldn't help but be struck by the sacrilege of destroying a religious symbol of peace and love in order to retrieve an object of unimaginable destruction.

The concrete crumbled away from the sphere, as if the Heart had waited all these years to be freed. The commander knelt next to it and brushed away the debris. The sphere pulsed with a pale yellow glow. Its intense power leeched to me across the distance. Caz eased forward, reaching for it.

The commander blew at the remaining dust and worked her fingers into the half circle and dot symbol.

A commotion drew my attention. I blinked to clear the spots of yellow light from my vision. A head of silver worked its way through the crowds. The soldiers fell away to reveal a team of familiar faces. I'd hoped for him, even said a few prayers, but honestly I hadn't really expected him to show up.

Xavier wore the same red shirt and black leather pants but exuded a distinct aura of unkemptness. Angie followed a step behind him and carried a large designer bag that looked unusually heavy.

They passed within several feet of me. Xavier gave me a cursory glance that revealed nothing. I looked in the direction he'd come, hoping he hadn't found Thurmond and Rannen to bring along with him.

The men closed back in. I breathed a small sigh of relief. The commander lowered the Heart, amusement in her face.

"Xander Fisk." She drew out the name, tasting it on her tongue. She held the Heart in one hand and put the other in her pocket.

"I heard you were looking for me." Xavier's voice was smooth. His eyes showed no emotion.

"I don't need you anymore." She hefted the Heart of Annihilation. "I found what I was looking for."

"I didn't come here to talk to you about the Heart."

"I don't know why you'd want to talk about anything? There was a time when you wouldn't even acknowledge my existence."

"Don't patronize me, Zell. Things were going south well before this whole thing started." Xavier sounded tired, like he'd explained this a thousand times before. "I only came here to watch Caz's expression when you do away with that fluxing thing."

I deflated. Xavier wasn't here to help?

"You mean when I set it off in the Thirteenth Dimension? Are you sure that's the dimension I'm after?"

Xavier stiffened. "The Thirteenth Dimension killed Vin. Who else would deserve the kind of attention you've put into this operation?"

"Xander, Xander." The commander waved her head, a smile on her lips. "Destroying the Thirteenth Dimension was Caz's passion. I'm hardly one to go about fulfilling the greatest desire of the one who destroyed my life."

"Then what dimension are you after?" Xavier pressed.

"Retha."

There was a sickly blanch to Xavier's face. "Because?"

"Retha failed me in every way. Etiquette and serenity? Please!" The commander's lips trembled. "I had nothing to do with what Caz did! I was a victim as much as anyone, and yet it wasn't enough to sentence Caz. She had to have had a partner! Right? It had to be the one who found Vin! The one with a known relationship with that—" the commander jabbed a finger at me, "that—"

"They failed me too, Zell," Xavier said. The commander dropped her arm.

"That's hardly a line I would have expected to hear from a member of the Dimensional Congressional Council." She didn't move, but it looked like it was costing her a great effort. As to whether she wanted to run toward Xavier or away, I couldn't tell.

Angie shifted behind Xavier. She fingered the latch on her bag. The commander shrugged and walked off toward the mission. Xavier hesitated, cast me a look, and then hurried to catch up with her.

"The DCC is dead. I've moved on from their delusional spouting." Xavier did double time to keep up. Angie followed. "They banished me as efficiently as they did Caz. As they did to you when they sent out that warrant for your arrest. The two laws have turned the new council into a power-mongering—"

The commander whirled on her heel. Xavier almost ran into her.

"Is that right?" She leaned toward him with a leering smile. "So after all these years of stringent standards and brotherly loathing toward that slag of a sister you, what, finally decide to make genocide a family affair?"

"This isn't about Caz!" He spoke a little too fast. "She took everything from me! My work. My home—"

"Your fiancé?"

Xavier stared at his hands, his face in shadow.

"But you got something in return. Didn't you?"

He jerked his head up, his eyes wide, warning her off. A grin stretched across the commander's waspish face.

"Poor abandoned thing needed his uncle Xan to play daddy *and* mommy. No room for an evil stepmother in little Manny's life."

Manny! Tears pricked my eyes at the anguished cry. My head blistered in pain.

I struggled to pull my arms free. Sergeant Jacks's fingers slid through the blood covering my shoulder.

Xavier and the commander stopped before the main entrance to the mission, observing the nearly completed assembly of the portal. The Heart pulsed under the commander's arm as the two Rethans stood shoulder to shoulder in a familiar and almost friendly way. I wanted to kill the both of them. Make them suffer, destroy them for what they'd done to Manny, to me, for even touching my Heart of Annihilation.

I rolled my head to alleviate the pain in my head. When I opened my eyes I found I was staring at Angie. Her fingers flew over the screen of her phone. She caught my gaze and opened her bag wide. She placed her phone inside next to a dull, silver, soccer ball-sized sphere. Hooking the strap of her bag on her arm, she gave me a prompting nod. I stared at her for a few seconds, perplexed. Then her thumbs and forefingers came together, making the shape of a heart.

Of course! The Heart replica! A plan blossomed in my head. Angie left her bag open. She dropped her eyes and moved closer to Xavier. I needed to provide a distraction so she could switch the hearts.

My brief count of the men came to just over sixty, with only about three quarters of them visibly armed. Flexing my fingers, I tried to judge how much electricity I had absorbed. Not enough to take them all out, but it would be sufficient to give Angie what she needed.

A bright light flared from the mission entrance. Like the portal back at the Rethan camp, it sent hundreds of thousands of tiny blue charges skipping from plate to plate, creating a solid-looking wall of color. Through the color, however, I could see a landscape beyond filled with elegant infrastructure, much more highly advanced, technology-wise, and the active bustling of a populated city.

Retha. But not Retha as before. Retha's population. Their people. The commander wanted to set off the Heart of Annihilation there and destroy the entire dimension? My two hundred and thirty-six kills suddenly seemed like a pittance.

I inhaled deeply of Earth's rich scents. The dirt, the wind, the vegetation. Despite my Rethan heritage, this was home. I loved this dimension and the wonderfully flawed people that populated it. I concentrated on all the souls who didn't know they were counting on me for their survival, in Earth and in Retha. My mind cleared.

The distraction Angie requested would most likely get me killed. I knew that. I'd made peace with my demise. I'd taken so many lives out of this world, my own life was a small price to pay to try to make things right. I only wished that I'd been able to part with Thurmond on better terms.

A ripple of laughter rose from the commander and Xavier. Their heads tilted together, their lips smiling. Anger flared in me again but this time without the unbearable pain. It was more like righteous anger, something that seemed downright pure compared to the devilish malevolence that embodied Caz Fisk.

A quick glance showed Luginbeel and Sergeant Jacks's gaze riveted on the portal, their weapons aimed idly at my back. A deep breath of preparation. I pushed myself to my feet.

"Holy crap!" I pointed off in another direction, making my voice crackle in panic. "The aliens are coming!"

Luginbeel knocked into Jacks, who almost dropped his weapon. Jacks swore and shoved at Luginbeel, who was swinging his rifle wildly off in the direction I was pointing. I slammed my elbow back into Luginbeel's shattered nose. He squealed in pain, dropped his rifle, and grabbed his face as blood drenched the bandages. I ducked as Jacks raised the rifle to his shoulder. My volt hit him on his hand. The rifle zipped a burning round past my cheek. His second round flew wide over my shoulder. My next volt took him square in the chest. He flew off his feet, his body arching before slamming onto his back. The rifle clattered from his hands. His head lolled to the side. Blood leaked from his nose.

I took off at a sprint toward the commander. Bullets whizzed past my head. Pointless shouts echoed all around like a furious wind. The two Rethans turned in surprise as I closed the remaining distance. I smashed into the commander, shoving with all my might at the sphere cradled under her arm.

The Heart went flying away and bounced up the shallow steps of the mission. It rolled past the feet of Boderick, who was standing near the portal, before I lost track of it. The commander and I crashed into Xavier, and we all tumbled onto the mission steps in a painful heap.

Hands swarmed across my body. I was yanked off the commander and thrown onto my stomach. Rifle muzzles pressed into my head. A weight knelt on my spine.

"Don't you move!"

"Don't move!"

"Don't you dare move!"

The commands tripped over each other. I was baffled that I was still alive and had no intention of disobeying.

Boderick clutched the touch screen Officiate Lafe had used to program the portal. His mouth gaped, and he stared back at me. I sure hoped I had read him right. He could ruin everything.

Xavier and the commander disentangled themselves. Xavier swore. The commander looked panicked as she struggled to her feet. Her eyes roved wildly searching for the Heart. Angie pulled Xavier to his feet. She snapped the latch on her empty bag.

The commander made a triumphant exclamation and scrambled to retrieve the dull sphere resting next to the steps a foot away. I noticed the absence of the yellow glow from the device in her hands but it appeared she hadn't—yet. Where was the real Heart?

"Brilliant, Caz." The commander tucked the Heart replica under her arm without looking at it closely. "Did you really think that was going to work?"

"My options were limited." I spoke against the ground. "And it's Rose, by the way. My name is Rose."

"Rose? Really?" the commander said. "Well I have news for you, *Rose*. I have absolutely no reason to keep you around anymore." The commander turned her face to the portal, waving a flippant hand over her shoulder. "Kill her."

I gulped.

"No, wait." The commander whirled back toward me. She crouched next to my head. I scowled back. "Do you remember how this device powers up? Of course you don't—*Rose*. Caz would."

I squinted past the commander to the blue portal light.

"The Heart of Annihilation is powered by a simple negative current. It was designed so that when used on Retha, the negative currents in the air are enough to power it once the code is entered. However, since we have to launch from Earth we will need a greater source of power."

I considered letting her good friend Caz Fisk out to tell her where she could shove her Heart of Annihilation operating manual. She continued:

"Once I insert the key and punch in the code to activate it, I will allow *you* to place your overzealous little hand on the Heart so it may absorb your negative currents." She smiled and licked her lips. "Have you ever been unbalanced? Electrically speaking, I mean?" She paused and rose to her feet. Looking down at me with scorn, she laughed. "It's not very comfortable. I was willing to make the sacrifice myself, but why deny you the opportunity?"

I kept my face as neutral as possible in order to hide the feeling of momentary triumph. The Heart *replica* wasn't capable of absorbing anybody's negative currents. I exhaled into the gravel and tried to shift my shoulder to alleviate the pain.

Angie's phone beeped. She drew it out of her limp bag. The screen brightened her face for a moment, then she grabbed Xavier's arm. They backed away. The commander tracked them with her eyes.

"Where are you going, Xander? This is the moment you've been waiting for." Her shoulders dropped. Her lips pulled tight against her teeth.

Xavier and Angie dropped all pretenses of sneakiness and ran as fast as they could, hand in hand, toward the base.

The commander lifted the pistol and whispered so softly I barely made it out.

"Outrun this, Xan."

Her finger tightened against the trigger, but instead of the efficient, emotionless murder of which she was so proficient, a furious wail escaped her throat. She dropped the muzzle a millimeter before firing.

An explosion of dust kicked up at Xavier's heels. Xavier and Angie stooped, hands up, but continued running.

Rumbling motors thundered down Mission Road. Headlights flashed across the vast walls of the mission. Every soldier's face was illuminated in a brief bath of light as they turned to look at the dozen black Humvees fanning out in a wide circle around the mission. The shadows of several battalions' worth of soldiers followed close behind.

"This is the DLA," a magnified voice boomed from the closest Humvee. "Put your weapons on the ground!"

CHAPTER 40

A blinding spotlight swept my face. My breath went out of me in a whoosh. I rested my cheek on the gravel. The men holding me down released my arms. The knee in my spine lifted as Sanderford stood. I pushed onto my knees and then shakily to my feet.

"Place your weapons on the ground and lay down," the magnified voice thundered from the leading vehicle. "Weapons down and no one will get hurt!"

The rifles lifted, one by one, their owners aiming at the vehicles. Heads swung to look from the commander, to the Hummers, and back to the commander.

My head pounded and a chuckle burst from my lips. "I would guess this moment makes you just about as irrelevant as they come, Zell."

With one Rethan step, the commander was at my side. She grabbed a fistful of my hair and dragged me in front of her. Her knuckles dug into my head. I grabbed her hand with both of mine.

Cool breath brushed next to my ear, and she whispered, "You think so, do you, Caz. You think this is the end?"

I felt the sphere rub against my back, and her grip on my hair loosened. Then a cry of rage.

"What is this? This isn't . . ." The commander yanked at my hair, her mouth next to my ear again. "You! What happened to it? Where's the real one?"

"That is the real one," I lied.

"No, it isn't. There's no keyhole. It's a fake!" The Heart replica dropped next to my feet with a dead clunk.

Sanderford stepped into my line of sight. His cheek was pressed against the rifle's stock. His thin sandy hair glowed white in the light of the portal.

"Your orders, ma'am?"

"Stand down!" the DLA voice intoned. "Release the inmate and put your weapons on the ground!"

I wanted to scream at the stupid magnified voice to put down the stupid megaphone and get down here and make sure we were in the clear. I pictured the glowing sphere sitting all alone near the mission, a wild card waiting to be discovered.

None of the commander's soldiers moved, least of all the commander. Whatever else they were—traitors, mercenaries—they were at least one hundred percent committed to their commander.

I twisted against the commander's grip, willing to lose my entire scalp if it meant I could get away from her. She kneed me in the side. I gasped at the explosion of pain in my ribs. My knees sagged.

"Ma'am?" Sanderford questioned again.

"Fire."

The commander's voice wasn't loud, but Sanderford immediately echoed her order with his thundering drill sergeant voice. He fired a three round burst at the closest Humvee.

The might of the Dimensional Liaison Agency and masses of supporting troops behind them returned fire on the commander's exposed army.

A fifty-cal round took Sanderford full in the chest. He was thrown from his feet, blood bursting from his upper body. Gunpowder scorched the air. Screams of pain filled in where the chatter of weapons didn't. Pings of misaimed bullets hit the mission's bells, and an eerie tolling accented the sounds of war.

The commander yanked on my hair. I stumbled as she dragged me up the mission steps, using me as a shield. Bullets plowed into the ground, sending up little puffs of dirt. They were wide, and I hoped it was because they were afraid of hitting me. I clawed at her hands, sending volt after volt into her skin. Her hand jerked, but she only gripped tighter. The barrel of a pistol ground into the back of my neck.

"Don't tempt me!" The commander's tone left no doubt in my mind that my life could be counted by seconds should I attempt any more resistance. We backed up the last step, past the light of the portal, and through the secondary archway.

I knew what was coming, so I wasn't surprised to hear the commander's grunt of satisfaction. She threw me against the wall. My cheek cracked on the stone and she held me there, taunting the DLA sharp-shooters. The pistol dug into my side as she bent to retrieve the real Heart of Annihilation.

Chunks of rock exploded from the steps and worked their way toward us. I closed my eyes, every muscle, nerve, and skin cell braced for hot, searing pain.

Power surged through my torso. With a cry, I released all the built up energy through every pore of my body, as I had near the café in Monterey. I opened my eyes to see the EMP rippling outward, its expansion appar-ent as headlights, spotlights, and even streetlights on the distant base exploded in a shower of sparks. A familiar hum sounded from behind me and the blue light from the portal vanished. Oozing blackness saturated the battlefield.

The shouting of the soldiers and the firing of weapons paused for only a second and then resumed. The flashes of fire created staccato bursts of light across the field.

With a scream of fury, the commander yanked me backward by my hair. "You've ruined everything!"

"It's over, ma'am! No portal, no plan! They're not going to let you walk out of here."

"You think you've won because I can't send the Heart of Annihilation to Retha?"

I didn't like where this was going.

"You won't win again, Caz. Take the portal. Take Vin. You can even take your brother! Have it all, right up until the point I rip it out from under you!"

Again? Caz wasn't laughing this time. She bled fury into my system. Her words rose to my mouth. "So you confess your little tête-à-tête with Vin?"

The commander's guilty silence was confirmation enough.

I tried to pull away from the commander's death grip but she dragged me to the large wooden double doors of the mission. She shoved me at the doors.

My hands and chest thrust them open so they banged into the walls. I fell on my stomach. My chin cracked on the stone floor, making my teeth crash together. I rolled onto my back. Moonlight glimmered through lofty, oval windows, highlighting the delicate wooden panels on the cof-fered ceiling. The doors slammed shut, muting the battle outside.

The commander—*Zell*—leaned against the door. Her bony chest rose and fell. Her silver eyes caught the filtering moonlight in a metallic glint.

Her expression was unhinged, but the hand pointing the gun was steady. Caz squeezed my head in a vice. I couldn't draw breath.

"I never slept with your husband, Caz."

Zell advanced on me, her finger tight against the trigger. I crawled away from her. As we reached the back pews she flipped a small table stacked with lit candles. Wax splattered the floor and pews. The candles went out, taking all the warmth from the room—except for the golden glow coming from under her arm. "*He* thought our relationship was something more. I didn't. I simply *worked* with him."

"*Worked*?" I alternately slid back on my butt and crab-walked while keeping the argument slow. "Worked with him on what?"

"On getting the Heart of Annihilation away from you, for our people in the Liberated RAGE Movement. With that kind of leverage we could have turned our dimension into something great. But you," she jabbed the gun at me, "you, a lone psychotic Rethan, had to ruin everything!"

My head blistered, and it was suddenly Caz shouting back.

"I would have given it to him! Had he just treated me like his wife. His partner."

Caz's fury rippled into my nerves, but I managed to regain control. My back hit something solid. I glanced up at the alter adorning the front of the chapel. The white linen cloth bunched above my shoulders. To my left a large arched doorway showed an exit into the mission's courtyard. The green grass, the Japanese holly, and the peaceful quiet of the religious structure stood in stark contrast to violence surrounding it.

Wooden pews slanted away from Zell on either side, and she perched the Heart upon the tips of her fingers.

"No you wouldn't, and you know it. I gave everything I had to Vin, and you know what I got for it?" She slammed the glowing sphere onto the ground. I recoiled. She crouched to my eye level. "No Xander, no Heart, no assistance from the LRM, and the gratitude of a dead man."

My head pounded in anguish. I couldn't fight off the memory of the slash of blood across Vin's neck.

"And don't think I don't know it was all thanks to you," Zell continued.

She knelt, and her fingers felt along the half-circle symbol. The Heart of Annihilation emitted a tinny beeping sound. The pistol didn't waver in her grip, but she was no longer looking at me. She withdrew the key from her pocket. The little pendant, always such a tender reminder of the love of my father, became the crucial element that would destroy the world. I only caught a glimpse of it between her white fingers as she inserted it into an invisible slot. She twisted it with finality and pressed a few more buttons to finish the activation sequence. The familiarity of the code repeated in my mind. Backward. Forward. Backward. Forward. A numerical anagram. I remembered programing it myself.

Hold it together. Get the Heart. Don't let her activate it.

A whirring sound emitted from the innocent looking sphere. The pulsing light brightened, shimmering across Zell's silver hair.

"How is destroying Earth going to help you?" I whispered.

"You're on Earth."

"So are you."

"Vin's gone. I'll never get near a portal again. So as pathetic as it sounds, all I have left is watching you lose everything you hold dear—like you did to me."

"That's completely moronic."

She shrugged. "Charge it."

"No."

"Place your hand on it. The Heart will do the rest."

"Forget it."

With a deafening pop, pain ripped through my left thigh. The gun smoked in Zell's hand. I screamed and fell onto my side. I gripped my pant leg, horrified at the amount of blood flowing between my fingers.

"I'm not asking you, Caz! This is an order!"

She didn't wait for me to comply. Her fingers dug into my hair again, and she forced my face downward into the whirring light.

I resisted, hovering over the Heart of Annihilation, fighting against helplessness and despair. With a heavy shove, my cheek touched. The Heart was warm and soft, but any sensation of it was swept away as I felt the currents in my body separate. With a rush of stinging, crackling pain all the negative currents condensed, exiting through my cheek and into the Heart of Annihilation.

Laughter—exhilaration—pain.

The remaining positive currents scattered throughout my being. Like a magnet, more currents flocked to me, attempting to restore the balance. Energy condensed into my chest in an agonizing ball of voltage.

A loud thud forced my eyes open. Zell stood over me, pointing the gun at my head. She wasn't looking at me. Her mouth opened and closed, but I couldn't seem to connect a voice to it. With a whoosh, sounds began to reconnect and the world became clear. Too clear. Painfully clear.

"Kill me and the weapon will activate! I dare you!" Zell shouted.

My head lay on the cold stone. I rolled to the side to find familiar faces highlighted in the intensifying golden light of the Heart. Thurmond and Rannen stood clumped in between the pews. They both held rifles aiming at the commander. She knelt next to the Heart. Shards of white lightning leapt from her grazing fingers.

Thurmond's eyes spoke his uncertainty. Was she bluffing? Could he stop it all by just shooting her? He stared at the commander and then his gaze flicked to me. His finger adjusted on the trigger. He didn't set the rifle down, nor did he fire it.

Idiot, Caz said. *Always check the voltage amount in the host before committing to activation on an alternate dimension.*

Detailed information of the Heart of Annihilation's crowded my brain. The EMP had decimated my reserve of voltage, not leaving enough to activate the Heart entirely. Zell, it appeared, was willing to make up the difference—whatever it took.

She released the electricity slowly through her fingers. A pained grin twisted her face.

"Poor Caz. Finally at the end, losing to me of all people." She was barely able to get the words out.

I groaned in agony and frustration. My life snarled together in a tangled ball. Retha, Earth, Caz, Kris. We were all the same. Hopelessly entwined together—forever in a matted mass of madness.

"Please," I begged.

The crackling shards of electricity leaping from Zell's fingers brightened.

"Please what, Caz?"

"Please don't do this."

"You want to stop me? You can stop me. I'll even tell you how." She purred in victory. "Let loose with those positive currents. Don't hold them in anymore. They'll destroy me as well as the Heart. Of course they'll also obliterate everything within a hundred miles or so."

Laughter curdled from my throat. Piercing guffaws of insanity. I pushed myself into a sitting position and laughed and laughed, exchanging the pain for madness. Thurmond's face contorted in alarm. Rannen's mouth drooped as his worst fears were realized.

My laughter scattered throughout the chapel, bouncing off the floors and shattering against the pews and walls. I couldn't help it. I was going to kill them. And why shouldn't I? The DCC Slayer, the worst criminal ever known to Retha, would willingly give her life to save this dimension as long as it meant Zell would lose everything.

Power—currents—voltage. They built upon the hard knot in my chest. It was already more than I could stand. I needed to release it. The thought filled me with such satisfaction that a tiny protesting voice inside of me became only a whisper in the crackling song of hate.

"Rose!"

The word brought to mind soft petals and a sweet aroma. Beauty and sunlight. Laughter and hope. Hope. Dad's voice spoke into my mind.

If there's one thing I hope for in this life, my daughter, it's that you learn of your value and harness it to do good in the world.

Don't sacrifice what you believe to be right. There's always another solution.

Electricity leaked from my pores. My skin burned, and my hair crackled around my head. I needed to release it. The overwhelming energy was going to force me to free it in a blind torrent of destruction.

You can never be forced to do anything! You always have a choice!

I had a choice.

"I have a choice!" My voice bounced off the walls and ceiling, rebounding around the room.

There was another choice. Another way.

I forced my limp, bloody hand into my pocket. I was barely able to draw out the M-16 tracer round I had taken from Justet's office not so many days ago and yet two lifetimes. I gripped it between two fingers and lifted it eye level—aiming.

I looked into the commander's eyes barely three feet away.

What are you waiting for? Caz asked.

"I don't want to become you."

How does letting a dimension die in agony make you better? Kill one, save a billion.

I jabbed my thumb on the end of the round, powering a small amount of electricity into the primer, igniting the gunpowder.

The bullet released from the brass casing, throwing my hand backward. My eyes followed the rapid arc of light as it sped into the commander's chest.

She collapsed onto her side. Her lips parted in dismay. A gurgling cough rose out of her throat. The shine of fresh blood spread across her chest more rapidly than I thought possible. The bullet casing clinked to the stone floor with a soft tinkle.

"Oh." Her voice was quiet, almost sad.

For a moment I felt a wave of pity and regret. For the pretty young marshal who had cared for Manny when his own mother couldn't. For her sadness at losing Xander. For her life wasted in chasing a psychopath like me.

Zell's eyes found mine. "I knew you'd . . . never change." She coughed, spattering the tiles with blood. "Killer . . . that's what you are."

"No!" The word sparked with the last of my energy. "My dad told me a person can resort to violence in order to protect their lives, family, or freedom. I'm a protector, not a murderer."

"Then protect them from this!"

Zell rested her hand on the Heart of Annihilation and released an enormous charge of white, sparking electricity into it. A smile warped her face. Her eyes turned opaque. Her head dropped to the floor.

In the same second, the Heart's light amplified a thousand fold, becoming a brilliant whirring sphere.

I instantly felt the drain of my natural energy. My legs numbed. Thurmond's face was washed out by the blinding brightness. His arm hung across the back of a pew. Rannen sat on the floor, shielding his eyes.

Rannen would die. Thurmond would die. I would die—as well as all the rest of the inhabitants of Earth. Entire cities of people collapsing where they stood, too tired to move or think, watching their loved ones shrivel before their eyes. Trees, grass, flowers, animals. All withered. All dead. Societies built on centuries of toil, love, war, and sacrifice, becoming nothing but ash.

I lay my head on the floor, too tired to hold it up anymore.

Listen to my voice, Kris.

A sequence of numbers rattled across my mind—*two, three, six, three, six, three, two*—and then again, and again.

The code! With impossible effort, I lifted my head and dragged my heavy body toward the spinning light. I was mere inches away but it could have been miles. Electricity seeped from my skin. The stone floor cracked under my hands.

My body became only a husk of currents. The light was so blinding I couldn't see the actual object any more. My hands swam through the light before finding the solid mass I was seeking. My fingers slid over the hot surface until they found the grooves making up the half circle and dot—the Rethan symbol for annihilation.

Thirteen numbers coded in the sequence to deactivate it—turn the key, apply the remaining positive currents.

My numb fingers stumbled across the numbers, pressing them far too slowly. Energy surged past me into the Heart of Annihilation. I pulled the sphere into my stomach, curling my body around it to protect my dimension from the deadly vacuum.

I could save them. I could make it right. Like it was before.

I pressed the last six, three, and two, fumbled for the key, and folded it into my palm.

With a cry of pain and release I forced the positive currents out of every pore touching the Heart's surface. My legs, torso, and arms deadened. My heart fluttered, stopped, resumed beating, and then released its energy into another Heart. The light from the Heart of Annihilation diminished and then exploded next to my stomach.

An echoing boom, and then silence.

The light and images around me darkened. My fading mind searched to feel something one last time. I caught a glimpse of Thurmond rushing toward me, his lips mouthing my name. Rannen's eyes.

CHAPTER 41

Bright light. Noise. Sounds. Fading. Blackness.

More light. Unidentifiable sounds. A voice. A name. Nothing.

This time the light dimmed. Murky images emerged. Sounds assaulted my consciousness. I cringed. At least I thought I did. I couldn't feel my body.

The images and sounds clarified, but I was having trouble making my mind work. I couldn't think of who or what I might be. Bright flashes of light drew sludge from my brain.

A hint of memory—something about a young boy with silver hair. The sound around me formed syllables to a language I couldn't understand. I blinked, trying to wash the fog from my eyes.

The lack of feeling vanished and was replaced by throbbing agony. A spasm of pain jerked through my leg, through my shoulder, through my heart. Voices again. Clearer now, speaking softly in golden whispers. I wanted to scream.

The torturous spasms abated, a dull-pulsing taking their place. My vision cleared. An intense golden light surrounded a figure and a face leaned in close. Golden eyebrows contracted for a moment over golden eyes devoid of pupils, and a word was uttered in a breath of sweetness. *Kris.*

"Kris!"

The golden light vanished. Only darkness and pain. Lips covered my mouth. Warm breath inflated my lungs. Rhythmic pressure was applied to my chest.

"Kris! Come on! Don't quit on me!"

The firm, desperate mouth around mine again, and the warm inflation of my lungs.

"Kris!"

Kris.

I gasped. My back arched. Terror at not being able to breathe drew out a panicked fit of coughing. I dragged in ragged draughts of air. My eyes fluttered open. A bulb of white light blinded me. I couldn't see any faces, only vague shadows behind it. My head was cradled in an enormous lap and I heard, of all things, cheers and laughing.

"Kris!" Thurmond's voice died away with a tremor of emotion.

I raised a shaking hand, wanting to rub the bleariness from my eyes. Thurmond's hand caught mine, gripping too tight. I felt the brush of his lips.

"Where the hell is that stretcher?" That sounded like Sergeant Wichman. But he was at the bottom of the bay. Wasn't he? A blurry figure moved away from the crowd.

"Don't move, sweetheart. We're getting help. Just keep breathing, okay?"

I wanted to explain to Thurmond why I'd hit him and thrown him out of a truck, but I couldn't get my mouth to work.

"Don't try to talk," Thurmond said. "And don't apologize, either. I understand why you did it."

A spasm jerked through my leg. I gritted my teeth. The pain wasn't as bad as I thought it should be, and a good sight better than feeling nothing at all. Someone was putting pressure against my leg. The light shifted, and Justet's red hair and splotchy face came into view. His eyebrows were high, his dirty face gawking at me in horrified fascination while he pressed a bloody bundle of fabric against my leg. I squeezed Thurmond's hand.

The familiar smell of ozone brushed my face. I rolled my head in Rannen's enormous hands. His lips lifted in a smile, showing me his bright white teeth.

"Of all the women on this planet, I had to get the most selfish *and* the most selfless one to be my mother."

"Rannen." I tried to remember why I felt the need to apologize to him. I tried to sit up.

"What're you doing? You can't get up right now." Thurmond pushed me back.

"I can't lie here anymore."

"Rose, your heart was stopped for almost five minutes, and you have a bullet in your leg. Don't you think you could at least wait for the medic?" Irritation crept into Thurmond's voice.

"Rannen, can you help me sit up?"

Rannen shook his head. Why couldn't they understand how important it was for me to see what happened to the Heart and the commander? I looked past Rannen's large forearm.

The steel gray of early morning light kissed the mission courtyard. The grass and trees were brown and dead, their energy absorbed by the Heart. My eyes followed the path of light to find the spot where the Heart had been. A charred black hole, not much larger than a soccer ball, was all that remained. The body of the commander was not far from the hole. Someone had covered her face with a jacket, but the gun was still clamped in her dead hand.

Glacial rivers of hate and echoes of terror coursed through me. I shivered and shivered as though being doused with buckets of icy water. I couldn't tear my eyes away from the body and the burned-out hole.

"Rose? Hey, Kris!" Fingers snapped in front of my face. I continued to quiver, mesmerized—horrified. "Someone get a blanket or something! Where the hell is that damn medic?"

Warm arms wrapped around me. A hand caressed my hair. My name was called over and over. Still I couldn't look away from that dead hand with the gun.

ᚳHAPTᚱᚱ 42

Earth

3 minutes post-RAGE

Anger. Fury. Hatred. Fear. Where there once was power, now there was only overpowering weakness.

A cry leapt from Caz's throat. Her limbs flailed helplessly about, refusing to respond to the commands she was trying to give them. A bright light pierced through her eyelids. She squeezed them tight. Movement caused her to scream again, not in pain but in frustration at her weakened state.

Caz unleashed her fury into another wail as her body was jostled roughly into a large pair of hands. She blinked her eyes open and stared into the warm, hazel eyes. Her memories scattered like fugitives seeking someplace to hide.

A gentle bouncing movement quieted her rage. She whimpered, trying to remember why she was so mad. Whispered voices bounded across her consciousness, making little sense to her fragile mind.

"She'll be angry for a while. It takes some time for all the memories to fade."

"She's calming down already."

"Are you sure you want to do this, Agent Rose? We've never had a worse criminal incarcerated here. They say her mind is broken. Even RAGE may not be able to fix that."

"Shhh. She's falling asleep."

The bouncing, combined with the man's soothing voice, made her eyelids droop. She'd forgotten that somewhere on this complicated planet was contentment and peace.

"What're you going to call her? She can't keep her same name."

"I had a sister named Kris."

The name sounded nice. Like a person who didn't have to be angry and vengeful. Nothing seemed as important as succumbing to the peaceful voice and calming movement.

Kris. I liked the sound of that.

CHAPTER 43

Rose

A familiar beeping returned me to consciousness. I blinked my eyes open to see white walls adorned with a blasé watercolor painting, an IV pole, and a heart monitor making the regular beeping sound. Apparently I was lucky enough to get a real hospital room this time.

Late afternoon sunlight streamed across my lap. A wide expanse of blue sky, with a light ruffling of clouds and a sea of buildings, created a picturesque scene outside the window.

I let my eyes wander the room while trying to sort through the jumble of recent memories, feelings, and thoughts. The whole week or so seemed like a monster of a nightmare, and I shrunk away from delving too deep.

Past the ugly curtains and closed door, my eyes finally landed on a sleeping figure. Thurmond slouched in an uncomfortable chair, his arms folded across his chest, his legs stretched out and crossed at the ankles. I was struck with a moment of déjà vu as I remembered him sitting this way outside the RV after the battle at the Rethan camp. This time his head rested on his chest, and he breathed with deep peacefulness.

I smiled at the way his chin wrinkled against his chest and the characteristic way his brows furrowed angrily, even in sleep. He was wearing the same clothes I last remembered him in, although the shirt now had a tear in the sleeve and the jeans sported a large reddish-brown smear across one leg. A cut swelled on his lip where the commander had pistol-whipped him, and three deep scratches on his cheek. There was also a thick blue and red electrical burn on his jaw, and the old, ropey scar from the bullet grazing his head. Other than that he seemed fine. I snorted at the relative qualifications of the term.

I wanted to talk to him. But not enough to wake him up. His breathing deepened, and his head lolled.

A glimmer of light on my shoulder caught my attention. I fingered a strand of hair. I would have liked it to be brown. I was expecting silver. I rolled it between my fingers. The multifaceted shades shimmered a brilliant, metallic gold in the sunlight.

"It's been like that since you destroyed the Heart." Thurmond's voice made me jump. He sat up and ran a hand down his face. "Same with your eyes."

"Hey, T, how're you doing?" I smiled. He dragged his chair closer.

"Been better." He rubbed his jaw where I'd socked him and smiled. "That's quite the hook you've developed."

"Sorry."

He shrugged. "Don't be. It was a smart move. Sometimes I forget you're a Special Forces trained soldier with brains *and* brawn."

"I mean, it worked, right?"

"Yep. Saved Rannen and me from the evil clutches of Sergeant Sanderford." His smile was brief. His eyes flitted away from my face as he remembered. He picked up my hand and rubbed his thumb across the back.

"How are they, by the way? The guys from our unit?"

"Justet is fine. So is Wichman."

"Wichman?" My throat constricted. "Yeah, I thought I heard him back at the mission."

"Yep." Thurmond grinned. "To hear him tell it, that old bastard is damn near immortal." Thurmond sighed and the grin wilted. "I guess I don't have to tell you Sanderford's dead. He never had a chance. He was so shot up they had to identify him by his tags. Lewis is also dead, as well as about another thirty of the commander's troops."

Thurmond shrugged and didn't continue. He stared at my blankets, absently rubbing the back of my hand with his thumb.

I frowned. Those guys put me through a lot, and I really didn't have any love for them toward the end. But we had at one point been friends and comrades. Why, then, did I feel so doggone neutral toward the fact that they had died a violent death in a large part thanks to (*Caz*) me?

"Luginbeel's okay, though," Thurmond said. "His nose is pretty bashed up, but I have a feeling you know that already."

I couldn't help the twitch at the corner of my mouth and didn't meet Thurmond's eyes. I heard a small chuckle and cut him a glance. The smirk on his face was all it took. I released a snicker that quickly turned into an all-out, gut-busting laugh. He let me go on for a minute but didn't seem to be able to join in with much enthusiasm. My laughter petered out, and I cleared my throat.

"Aren't you going to ask about yourself?" His expression was curious.

"What, you mean besides the gold hair and weird eyes?"

"Yeah, besides that." He nodded toward my legs hidden under the hospital blankets. "Take a look."

I flipped back the blanket, exposing the faded, blue hospital gown and my bare legs. My left leg should have been wrapped up tight in a thousand layers of bandages. I stared in stunned silence.

I could see where the bullet entered, a little higher than midway up my thigh, but instead of a raw open wound only a large, ugly scar remained. The hole appeared as though it had been healing for several months, not several hours. I ran a finger across the purplish divot. It was painful to the touch but nowhere near what it should have been.

"Has it really been that long?"

"No. That happened last night."

"Then . . . what . . . ?"

"You got me. The DLA doctors don't know either. They think it might have something to do with you destroying the Heart of Annihilation, but they're just lowly earthlings. A Rethan might be able to tell you different. Same with the hole in your shoulder. It looks like it's been healing for months, though the millions of other smaller injuries you sustained are as bad as they were last night." He brushed his hand against my cheek and shrugged.

"Is the bullet still in there?"

"Maybe. There's no exit wound. They're going to do an X-ray later to find out." Thurmond pressed his lips together. I could tell there was something else on his mind, but he just shook his head. He stood and placed his hands on either side of my face. "Kris, you are the most remarkable soldier—the most remarkable *woman* I've ever met."

He rested his forehead against mine, his eyes closed.

I gripped his arm. The IV tugged at my hand. I couldn't decide whether to thank him for sticking by me through everything, or apologize for getting him involved in the first place. Somehow I knew whatever I said would have me coming off as an unbelievable sap.

He pulled away and sat next to me on the bed.

"The doctors want to try to re-inject you with that camouflage serum stuff."

"Try?"

"They don't know if it will work because of the whole gold hair and eyes thing. It's chemically engineered for Rethan physiology, so they're not sure," his voice trailed off.

I ran my hand lightly across the thick scar above his ear and then rubbed my thumb on his bottom lip. He leaned his face into my hand, his eyes closed. The shadow of a beard scraped lightly across my palm and my fingers tingled. I retracted my hand quickly in sudden fear of volting him again.

"Oh, knock it off." He grabbed my hand.

Our lips met. I lost myself in the moment, far beyond the hurt of dimensions, commanders, and bullets. The exhilarating taste of his mouth, his breath against my tongue, the soft, tender movement of his lips. All too soon he pulled away. One side of his mouth lifted in a grin. I touched my fingers to my lips and smiled back. Thurmond cleared his throat.

"Been wanting to do that for months." Thurmond tapped my lips with another brief kiss and then sat back.

"There are a lot of people who need to talk to you. You up for visitors?"

"Like who?"

"Well, Xavier for starters."

I made a face. The warmth from the kiss fizzled, leaving me cold and irritated. My head ached. The last thing I wanted was Xavier coming in and reminding me again how I'd murdered two hundred and thirty-six Rethans, including my husband, and abandoned my only son.

My son. Rannen.

"Rannen's here, too," Thurmond said, reading my mind. He looked to the door and scratched his nose before turning back to me. "Justet also mentioned he wanted to apologize. I took the opportunity to tell him to go to hell for you."

"Well, he did sort of try to help back at the penthouse," I admitted grudgingly.

"I don't care. I said I'd pass on his apology. That should be enough for him."

I didn't say anything. On one hand, if I saw his face again, I might be inclined to get some more practice with my right hook. On the other, as much as I would love to savor my grudge against Justet, I thought it would be rather hypocritical of me.

"We should give him a chance. I got a second chance."

Thurmond rubbed his hands across his scalp.

"I didn't mean it that way, Rose," he finally said. "I just . . . it's just . . . you know what? Never mind. I'll send him in a little later if you want me to." He rolled his eyes. "I still think he has a thing for you, though, so don't be surprised if I have to deck him."

"Get in line." I grinned.

Thurmond barked a laugh. "Wichman needs to talk to you too."

That was quite an appointment calendar. I felt exhausted thinking about it. All I really wanted to do was hang out with Thurmond and talk about light and irrelevant topics to make me forget all about Retha, the commander, and even what to do about Rannen. I massaged the scar on my leg, wondering if it would hold up if I jumped out the window. Thurmond got to his feet.

I fumbled for the button that would raise the bed higher. "Aren't you going to stay?"

"No, sorry. I've got to talk to Wichman before he comes in." Thurmond shook his head, stepping away from the bed. "You should probably speak to Xavier and Rannen alone, anyway."

"Fine, leave me to the vultures." I dropped my head on against my pillow, dreading Xavier's stupid, tanned face and bleached teeth.

Thurmond paused, one foot out the door. He was about to say something but then he shook his head and disappeared without another word.

Before the door could latch it was yanked open again. Rannen filled the doorway. He was still wearing his dirty Rethan uniform, but at least the cuts on his face and chest had been tended to. He ducked to enter the king-sized hospital door, and his smile lit up the room.

"You're looking better, Kris." He was across the room in two steps and dropped into the chair Thurmond had vacated. The chair groaned, making me fear for its life. Rannen folded my hand into his enormous paw.

"Thanks, Manny . . . Rannen. Or Marshal Rannen?"

"Rannen's fine. Your new hair color though," he paused, brows furrowed. "Frightening, yes?"

I shrugged. Frightening? Not really. Weird for sure, but frightening?

Rannen's expression was bemused, but then he sat back with a pleasant sigh. His happy contentment seemed so genuine that I felt my tension and fear regarding him slide away. I even considered talking about the more pressing topics but chickened out, grasping at the opening he'd given me.

"Yeah, about my 'frightening' hair. You don't happen to know why it's not Rethan silver anymore, do you?"

He opened his mouth to respond, but the clearing of a throat redirected our attention to Xavier, who was leaning against the doorframe. Sometime over the last few hours he'd found time to dye his hair black, shave, shower, and change his clothes. His new clothes were immaculate as always, but more ordinary than I was used to. Jeans and a button-down plaid shirt made him look like an immigrant worker rather than one of the most prominent celebrities in the country.

"You look like an inhabitant of the Thirteenth Dimension." His expression was conflicted. I figured he still wanted to hate me but perhaps he didn't feel as justified as before. He frowned. "You're going to scare the hell out of a lot of Rethans, looking like that."

"The Thirteenth Dimension? How?"

Xavier only narrowed his eyes. I mimicked his expression, and he looked away. Whatever he knew, he wasn't telling. And I certainly wasn't about to beg it out of him. He made no motion to move farther into the room or to say anything more, so I bit back the hundreds of insults and accusations and turned expectantly to Rannen.

"Rannen?"

Rannen shook his head, his eyes on the floor. I backed off. I was alive and relatively well. So my hair had changed color. Who cared? I could shrug off the whys for now.

"Listen, Rannen." I paused and waited until he looked at me. "About what I did back in Retha, you know, before—"

Rannen heaved out a sigh and held up a hand. He smiled briefly, glancing at Xavier and then back to me. "Don't bother with an apology, Kris. I'm happy to know that the person I was always led to believe you were doesn't exist anymore."

If only that were true, Caz whispered.

I gulped, and tears came to my eyes. I blinked them back, feeling silly. "You're going to forgive her?" Xavier broke in. "Just like that?"

I thought I had grown on him as Kris Rose, but apparently grudges die hard. Especially now that I knew the personal nature of the offense.

"She's different now," Rannen rumbled.

"That doesn't change what she did before! What she was!" His face flushed, and he looked from Rannen to me. He seemed to catch Rannen's frame of mind, and his eyes widened. "You're really going to forgive her?"

"Why shouldn't I?" Rannen lumbered to his feet. The chair screeched like it was dying. "Kris has proven herself to be one of the most self-sacrificing people I've ever met."

"That's not Kris! That's Caz! The mother who abandoned you over twenty years ago!" Xavier gestured at me. His words struck me through my heart. "Not to mention that she . . . she murdered your father, Manny!"

My stomach clenched in sickening pain. That's right. Vin. Rannen's father.

Slashed his throat.

I rubbed my left temple. Rannen frowned at the floor. He didn't seem surprised or even angry, rather sad that Xavier had pulled such a stunning trump card. When he looked up it wasn't at Xavier but at me, his expression resolute.

"I never really knew that other person, and just because I was raised to hate my mother doesn't give you the right to try to make me hate her now."

"One moment of selflessness doesn't erase everything she did in the past!"

"Uncle Xander," Rannen said softly. He stepped close to my bed and tucked a strand of hair behind my ear. He then turned on Xavier. "I will always appreciate the love and care you've given me over the years. However, it's time for me to make my own decisions regarding my mother, and for now, it seems, we are going to disagree."

Xavier stood perfectly still, his mouth moving as he tried to throw out a brilliant retort. Finally, he shook his head and opened the door before turning back to me.

"Remember our deal, Miss Rose." He shoved his thousand dollar sunglasses on his face and disappeared. The door closed with a hiss and a clack.

I was a little disconcerted by Rannen's implausible affection, not to mention a little worried as to how to be his mom. How do you mother a child who has outgrown you in every way?

"What deal did you make with him?" Rannen asked, sitting again.

It took me a moment to remember what Xavier was talking about. "Something about him helping me find you and Thurmond, as long as once we did I'd stay away from him."

"Sounds like a win for everyone then." Rannen grinned.

I grinned back, enjoying the smell of ozone like a warm summer rain within the room. Thurmond poked his head in.

"Hey, Rose." He looked apologetic, but went on. "Wichman says he needs to speak with you right now. He has to leave on another assignment but wanted to say goodbye."

"That's fine, Devon," Rannen said. "We're done here for now anyway. I've got to go help Uncle Xander find something nice for Angie. Apparently she didn't know about his relationship with Zell before last night." Rannen smiled and touched my head. "We'll talk again soon."

"Okay. Looking forward to it." I snickered to myself over Xavier's dilemma.

Rannen shook Thurmond's hand before ducking out.

"You patch things up with Xavier?" Thurmond asked, holding the door open.

"Nope." I leaned my head against my pillow. "If he wants to continue being a big fat jerk, that's his choice."

Thurmond had a strange look on his face, and I noticed him tapping a cell phone against his leg. I was about to ask him what was wrong when Wichman entered. He was wearing a dark business suit with a blue tie, looking every inch the secret government agent that he was. His mustache twitched. I raised my eyebrows.

"You wouldn't really have pulled that trigger in the diner, would you?" I said. I was having a hard time erasing the betrayal I'd felt at the time, despite what I knew now.

"Don't be stupid, Rose." He smiled, and I felt the grudge slide. Everything *had* worked out, after all. He tapped his knuckles against the rail of my bed, one hand in his pocket. "I'm sorry how everything went down. Anyway, I wanted to stop in really quick and say thank you for what you did last night. There's not really words to describe the incredible sacrifice you were willing to make. On behalf of the United States—actually, the entire Third Dimension—thank you. You're a real hero."

My cheeks grew hot.

"Yeah, sure. No problem." It was actually a *huge* problem. But whatever.

Sergeant Wichman chuckled. Then his face grew serious.

"I also wanted to say I'm sorry about your father." My stomach gave a painful jerk, and a thousand questions flooded my mind. Thurmond looked at me in surprise. I dropped my eyes to my blankets. Wichman continued. "He was a great man. Great agent."

"Yeah." My heart fluttered.

"I worked with him for twenty years in the DLA." He smoothed down his mustache and cleared his throat. "You didn't know that before, did you?"

"No. Well, not until we talked in the café."

"He was tired of the RAGE inmates coming through the portal and being thrown right into whatever-the-hell foster family was willing to take in a psychotic child. He firmly believed that with the proper amount of love and the teachings of a value system, even the most horrifically inclined person could become an asset to society."

I jerked my head up to look at him. "He knew who I was?"

Wichman nodded. "At first it was a social experiment of sorts. Take— forgive me—the worst, most crazed criminal of the bunch, and try to make you into a normal person." He grinned. "It didn't take him long, though, before he fell in love with being your dad. Within a few of years, he retired from the DLA and took a job as a part-time police officer in your hometown in order to spend more time with you."

I tried to picture my dad as someone other than I had always known him and failed. To me he was just my dad: the guy who went to every soccer game and dance recital. He was the one who baked terrible birthday cakes and interviewed my dates before we could walk out the door.

Realizing now that he'd known who I was, the atrocious person I was on Retha, didn't dampen my love for him. He'd looked into my eyes and believed the best of me.

"Anyway, Rose, I thought you might like to know. There's been a development in your father's case and I have to leave to follow up on a lead. It's not a great one, but something. I'll let you know what we find out. Call me anytime." Wichman lifted a hand in farewell. He shook Thurmond's hand and stepped out the door.

I rubbed my fingers in my hair. The bed sank on one side, and I looked over at Thurmond.

"Why didn't you say anything?" He frowned. "I've been trying to get your dad on the phone for hours."

I shrugged. "It was a long time ago. Before I'd even gone to basic training. He called for backup on a stop over a stolen vehicle. Dispatch received the call a little past midnight. Backup arrived six minutes later only to be blown to hell, and Dad was just gone."

"Gone as in . . . ?"

"Gone as in missing. The other officers were dead and could be iden-tified, but there was nothing left of Dad—just gone, with one of those RETHA coin-catapult things in his place."

"So he's in Retha, then?"

I shrugged and traced a pattern on my blanket. I didn't want to remem-ber. I wanted to block out the memory of the night I'd gotten the call as I'd done for the past five years. I had his voice in my head, and his arms wrapped around my heart.

Thurmond took my hand. I blew out a breath.

"The thing is, we'd been in the middle of an argument. I wanted to join the army. He wanted me to look at other options, said he was worried about me being around too much violence. Go figure." I coughed a laugh. "I remember him telling me, a few days before he disappeared, how much he believed in me. How he knew I'd make the right choice about this. In typical Dad fashion he told me he believed that whatever I chose would allow me to save the world in my own way."

"And look how you saved the world . . . by saving the world." Thur-mond squeezed my hand. "I'm actually glad I could be here to see it."

"Seriously?"

"You bet."

"Oh, well in that case I'll forgive myself for dragging you into my messes, over and over—"

"You do that. Hey, I got you something." Thurmond pulled out a silver chain from his pocket. Dangling in sparkling innocence from the end of it was a small, silver, half-circle pendant about the size of my thumb. "I found it in your hand and thought you might like it. It was from your dad, and without the other part it's not exactly a key anymore . . ." he trailed off in uncertainty.

I hesitated and then reached out to rub my thumb across the pendant.

The last time I'd seen it, it was being held between thin, white fingers and inserted into a glowing sphere. I recoiled.

Thurmond slowly lowered the chain onto my blanket.

"Do you want to talk about what happened?" Thurmond stared into my face with an intensity I'd never seen from him.

"Like what? A lot happened." I rested my head against the pillow, dropping my eyes to the silver loop of chain. I wished we could glaze over the whole shooting the commander bit.

"Like how you saved the world with that damn stunt of yours?"

"No. Actually, I don't want to talk about that."

Thurmond made a sound in his throat, not yet ready to give up. I looked out the window. A cold weight pressed against my mind.

I could feel the round between my fingers and the smell of gunpowder as the bullet left the casing, speeding toward her heart. I saw again the arc of light and heard the echoing repeat. I closed my eyes with a shudder and rubbed my hands across my face, only to watch her blood spill again and again.

"Okay, okay. You know what? You're right." Thurmond's voice held a hint of panic. "Let's not talk about that right now. Okay?"

"Come on, T." I pushed the heels of my hands against my eyes, trying to press away the tension as though ironing out a stubborn wrinkle. The pressure only deepened into a blistering ache above my left ear. "Why the hell would I want to talk about that? Another notch on my already imposing belt impresses you? A little rehash of the all-around blackening of my soul seems like a good post trauma debriefing? Hoo-freakin'-rah!"

"I didn't mean—"

I jabbed a finger into his shoulder and then slammed my fist into his chest. He grabbed my wrists, his face set. I struggled to free myself.

"You can't tell me that watching me kill that horrible Rethan isn't seared into your mind forever!" Anger oozed from me like hot tar. I thrust my hands down to break his grip.

"Rose—"

"If you don't want to hang out with a murderer, go ahead and leave!" I shoved him away. He stepped back, his hands up, on the defensive now. I rubbed a knuckle above my ear. "I don't need your damn help, Corporal! Never did—"

"Kris!"

You didn't think I would just go away, did you? Caz laughed.

I tapped my forehead with my fist, allowing the ache in my head to fade completely before I was able to look up at Thurmond.

"I know you didn't mean it," he said.

"I'm sorry. I shouldn't have hit you. I should have—"

"Don't worry about it." He ran a finger down my cheek. "I can only imagine what's going through that head of yours. But dammit, Kris, I'd like to think you understand me well enough by now to know I'm not going to take off just because you cussed at me."

"Thanks." I pressed his hand to my lips. "I'll try to keep the swearing down to a minimum . . . or get Caz to, rather."

"Caz?"

"Yes, Caz. The DCC Slayer."

With a sour laugh, I plucked the silver chain from the bed.

ACKNOWLEDGMENTS

They say it takes a village to raise a child. The same could be said about a novel. *Heart of Annihilation* would never have made it past the dark, creative recesses of my mind without the host of very fine people in my life encouraging me onward and upward.

My parents, who filled my mind with knowledge and imagination from the day I was born. They gave me unlimited time and love and books. Let's not forget the books.

My husband and children, who have been the best cheerleading squad a girl could ask for. They've packed my life with adventure and joy while patiently allowing me to hide behind my laptop as I pursued my dream of publication.

And who could survive the storms of the publishing industry without the support of a very special group of friends and fellow writers. Thank you, Angie, Kate, Callie, Terra and Meghan for endless reading, editing and discussions that helped grow this book. For patting my sad, little head every time my writing world crashed down around me and for celebrating with me when the sun returned.

Thank you to WiDo Publishing for providing my precious manuscript with the very best chance in the big bad world. And my editor, Amie McCracken, for taking my humble novel past ordinary to extraordinary.

Lastly I'd like to acknowledge my friends and former comrades in the U.S. military, and all the service men and women who have fought and continue to fight for our freedom. You are my heroes.

ABOUT THE AUTHOR

C. R. Asay joined the Utah National Guard at the age of seventeen. After spending time in the 625th Military Police Corp she transferred to the 19th Special Forces group as a counterintelligence agent. She retired from the military after marrying her best friend and graduating from college so that she could embark on the most exciting adventure of all; being a mom.

The short story version of her first novel, *Heart of Annihilation*, earned an honorable mention from the L. Ron Hubbard Writers of the Future contest. C. R. Asay currently resides in West Jordan, Utah, with her husband, four children, and a dog. There is always a dog.